SOUTH CAROLINA 1781

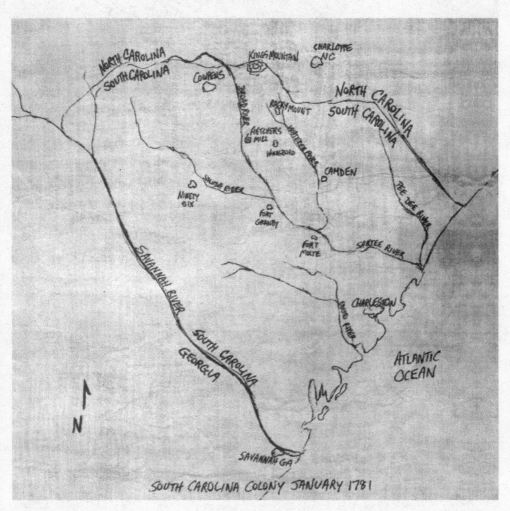

SOUTH CAROLINA COLONY JANUARY 1781

DECISION AT
FLETCHER'S MILL
A Novel of the American Revolution

David Caringer

ELM HILL

A Division of
HarperCollins Christian Publishing

www.elmhillbooks.com

Decision at Fletcher's Mill
A Novel of the American Revolution

Published in Nashville, Tennessee, by Elm Hill, an imprint of Thomas Nelson. Elm Hill and Thomas Nelson are registered trademarks of HarperCollins Christian Publishing, Inc.

Elm Hill titles may be purchased in bulk for educational, business, fund-raising, or sales promotional use. For information, please e-mail SpecialMarkets@ ThomasNelson.com.

Library of Congress Cataloging-in-Publication Data

Pre-launch ISBN: 978-1-595558008

Library of Congress Control Number: 2018949422

ISBN 978-1-595557896 (Paperback)
ISBN 978-1-595558183 (Hardbound)
ISBN 978-1-595557940 (eBook)

"For what is a man profited, if he shall gain the whole world, and lose his own soul?"
JESUS CHRIST

TABLE OF CONTENTS

PROLOGUE

It was 1781. The war for American freedom from the British Crown had been slogging on since before the colonies declared their independence in 1776. The English people and their rebellious colonies were exhausted with war. A bloody stalemate existed now in the northern colonies. The French had entered the war on the side of the rebels. George Washington and his Continental Army had endured many years of hardship. The rebel forces won some surprising victories at places like Saratoga, Trenton, Princeton, and Charleston. But they also suffered many tragic defeats at the hands of the most powerful army on earth.

The continentals survived brutal winters outside Boston and at places like Valley Forge and Morristown. During the worst of these struggles for survival, the Continental Army slowly changed from an undisciplined mass of militias to a defined fighting force under the leadership of Washington and the tutelage of Friedrich Von Steuben. They had lost many battles, but the Continental Army still stood. They were now able to face the British wherever called upon.

The French were a growing presence in the American conflict. The war had spread globally. It could have been considered a world war in scope and destruction. The British were now entrenched in New York. They needed to find another way to crush the rebellion before the cause to retain the colonies for their king was lost. They were repulsed once at Charleston. They would try again. This time, they divided their sizeable force and sent the stronger part south to open another front. Invading the Carolina colonies, they would push northward through Virginia to create a huge envelopment around Washington's forces from both east and south.

Institutionalized slavery was a fundamental part of the planta-tion-oriented economies of the southern colonies. This absurd feature in everyday life had existed for generations. It would continue. Individual humans and whole families were bought and sold, abused, and destroyed for the sake of cheap agricultural labor. Slavery was seen by many clergy-men in the south as an evil necessity. Some even thought it was Biblically sanctioned through their own sad misunderstanding of Scripture.

The second British invasion attempt at Charleston was initially successful. They enjoyed early victories as they had in the north at the beginning of the war. This began to change slowly when the Royal Army failed to understand the effectiveness of rebel partisan militia. These irregular forces conducted guerilla warfare under the outstanding lead-ership of men like the "Swamp Fox" Francis Marion, James Johnston, and others. British conventional methods had to be cruelly adapted to be effective. The south was soon plunged into terror and chaos as the desper-ate struggle settled on the land like a violent plague. With time, the chaos even found its way to a once-peaceful place in western South Carolina known as Fletcher's Mill.

CHAPTER 1

A sudden gust of cold damp wind swept through the scattered trees and scrub. This brought tears to the eyes of twenty-year-old Private Billy Morgan as he strained to see traces of movement at the far end of the sloping meadow. The gray light of dawn didn't help much. Billy was a twisted mixture of conflicting emotions. The fear and excitement he felt in this moment was overshadowed by his humiliation and the contempt of those men around him who now saw through his lie. He crouched close to his only real friend, Silas Whitaker. He felt small comfort in the fact that they were part of the thin line of militia riflemen far out in front of the more substantial lines of continental troops. Billy would have once felt honored to be hand-picked for this job in recognition of his astounding accuracy with the rifle. He couldn't shake off the taunts and jeers he brought on himself from the men that he so wanted to accept him.

Billy and Silas left their homes in western Virginia and walked more than one hundred miles to join the militia in North Carolina. Over a thousand American rebels, both continental regulars and militiamen, searched the distant tree line now for the approaching enemy. It was very cold for South Carolina on this January morning. Billy and many of the men around him shivered uncontrollably. The rain stopped, but the sky remained steel gray even as the daylight increased. The continental regulars and the militiamen from Georgia and the Carolinas had camped in the meadow overnight and were prepared for the fight they knew was coming.

The commander of this combined American force was none other than the "Old Wagoner" himself, Brigadier General Daniel Morgan. They were detached from the main southern Continental Army of General Nathaniel Greene. They had marched from North Carolina into the western "backcountry" of South Carolina to harass the British loyalists and to strengthen the exploits of the "Overmountain Men" and other rebel forces responsible for the decisive victory in October at the battle of Kings Mountain. The British had split their southern forces as well and sent a rather large battle-hardened contingent in pursuit of Morgan's small army. General Morgan retreated northward through the driving rain and soon decided to make a stand here with his back to the swollen Broad River.

Silas punched Billy and pointed slightly to the right, saying, "There!" in a whispered gasp. Billy also noticed the movement as he shifted his gaze. Two distant horsemen in the hated green uniforms of the British "legion" moved slowly into the bottom of the meadow and stopped. One of them put a glass to his eye and slowly surveyed the line of militiamen drawn across the upper part of the meadow.

One of the horsemen was Lieutenant Colonel Banastre Tarleton. Tarleton was in command of this combined force of British cavalry and light infantry. His scouts watched the rebel militia for almost half an hour before reporting the enemy presence to him. He received the news while he was back with the infantry commander trying to cajole more speed out of his exhausted troops. Tarleton was elated as he hurried forward to verify that he had finally caught up with the rebel force they were chasing.

Tarleton knew the value of lightning-quick strikes against frightened militia. He wore a well-earned reputation among the rebels, and his own troops, as a callous "butcher" of the militia he so deeply despised. He understood the landscape in this area from the available maps and the descriptions given by the loyalist militia guides under his command. Tarleton knew this large sloping meadow was called the "Cowpens" because it had been used for many years as an area to collect the local herds. He also knew that his enemy was trapped with their backs to an impassable river that was swollen by the recent torrential rains.

Colonel Tarleton scoffed as he concluded that "General" Morgan had blundered into this trap in such a predictably amateur way. Turning around, he galloped back into the trees and began shouting the orders necessary to bring his superior force into the correct formation for attack. He planned to send his cavalry dragoons forward first. They would be followed by the lines of advancing infantry. There were two small "grasshopper" canons at his disposal also, but he didn't intend to wait for them to be brought up. Tarleton's force consisted primarily of the best available cavalry and the finest British light infantry. He believed that this ragtag rebel mob would flee in terror as they witnessed the inexorable advance of His Majesty's Finest. It had happened so many times before. Why should this battle be any different?

Colonel Tarleton was filled with nationalist pride and contempt for the rebellious scoundrels he faced on the field this day. He could easily imagine the panic and the sight of men dropping everything to run away in terror. He could almost hear the frightened cries for quarter. His men would give quarter to these scum, "Tarleton's Quarter." Yes, he knew the meaning of the phrase. It was used by his enemies and critics as an insult. His men had executed a great many of these wretches after they rose in rebellion against the king. They usually surrendered quickly enough at the first sight of the king's army righteously advancing with their leveled bayonets.

Tarleton wasn't intentionally cruel to honorable men, but these weren't honorable men. They dared to rebel against the king. They dared to pretend that they could stand against the Royal Army. They dared attempt to stand on this or any battlefield and resist him, Banastre Tarleton. He now reveled in the accusations and the reputation they brought him. After all, his men were simply using their sabers and bayonets to extinguish these miserable curs while they whined and plead with their hands in the air.

Billy was still stinging from the insults and catcalls he endured when his comrades learned of his earlier lie. He and Silas joined the militia because they wanted to be part of the cause of freedom as the colonies struggled to throw off the tyranny of the British Crown. Silas thought he knew Billy's family well. They had been friends since Billy was a small boy constantly tagging along with Silas and his comrades. Silas was like an older brother to Billy. When the boy's father died, it was Silas who taught Billy to hunt, fish, and survive in the wilderness. Silas was surprised when he first learned of Billy's outlandish claims. He knew Billy's father moved his family south to the back country of Virginia from the Pennsylvania Colony when Billy was just a babe in arms.

Silas and his brothers helped the elder William Morgan clear his land and build a stout home for his wife and children. Silas fell deeply in love with Billy's older sister, Rachel, and he believed she shared his feelings. William was a quiet man who never spoke about his reasons for leaving Pennsylvania. Silas thought he knew the family well, but now he realized that he didn't. When he first heard the whispered talk among the other men, he didn't know what to think. He remained loyal to his young friend regardless of what was said. He agreed to travel down with Billy out of the mountains into the southern piedmont for more than just the cause of freedom. He intended to marry Rachel and he couldn't refuse her when she asked him to watch over the young man until he got this foolishness out of his system.

Billy made a stupid mistake when they finally did join up. Like most young men thrust into the company of older men, he wanted to be accepted and respected. Rather than earning that respect through hard work and demonstrated integrity, he tried to gain it through a stupid lie. He bragged to the other men in his company that Colonel Daniel Morgan was his uncle, even though he didn't know of any real relationship with the heroic Virginia rifleman. Billy overheard his parent's quiet arguments about their estranged relatives in the north when he was a child. He knew they weren't the only Morgan family to move south into western Virginia.

Everyone knew most of the legends surrounding Daniel Morgan. He was rumored to be a great grandson of the pirate Henry Morgan. He was thought to be Daniel Boone's cousin. He was known to be one of the survivors of the ill-fated Braddock campaign during the French and Indian War. He was one of a very small number of men who ever survived 499 lashes from an English whip. Morgan was working for the British army as a civilian teamster during the war when he ran afoul of an overbearing British officer. The disagreement became violent and ended with Morgan striking the officer. He was immediately arrested and subjected to the justice of a British military court.

The sentence of 499 lashes was considered a form of capital punishment because it usually resulted in the horrific death of the person being flogged. Its purpose was, in fact, to strike terror into the English soldiers forced to witness it, so that they would not repeat the crime that brought about the punishment. Morgan miraculously survived the flogging with an undiminished certainty regarding his own innocence. He came away from the ordeal with a seething hatred for the British that never diminished, along with chronic back problems that lasted the rest of his life. Daniel Morgan was also known to be one of the true heroes of the victory at Saratoga, along with the now-hated Benedict Arnold.

Billy simply made use of the fact that no one but Silas knew him in his new militia unit and that he and the great hero shared the last name, Morgan. In fact, the whole thing started when he signed his name to the enlistment roll. The sergeant quipped, "Any kin to Daniel Morgan?" Billy responded, "What if he's my uncle?" The lie took on a life of its own after that. For a while, he was actually treated with deference by his captain and some of the others. This began to wane when he continued to embellish the "legend." Billy was struck with terror when his company learned that Daniel Morgan had been promoted to brigadier general and placed in command of their part of the southern army by General Nathaniel Greene.

The inevitable embarrassing moment occurred two days ago during the forced march across the South Carolina countryside. At a brief halt, the general and his small entourage of aids rode back past Billy's company and left the trail for a small hill about thirty yards away. His colonel used the moment to impress the general by dragging Billy, "his nephew," over for an impromptu family reunion. When Billy resisted, the colonel became furious and wanted to know why. Billy tried to quietly confess the lie to the colonel just as the general started back toward the trail. The general heard part of what was said and stopped his horse a few feet away. Billy felt the sky darken as Daniel Morgan shook his head slowly and spat tobacco juice onto the ground at Billy's feet. The general then laughed deeply without saying anything and rode on up the trail.

Billy returned to the rest of the unit covered with sullen shame. The story soon spread. He found himself to be the butt of every cruel joke his comrades could invent. The only man who didn't participate in the cruelty was Silas. The two would always be fast friends in spite of Billy's failure. Silas seemed to see a youthful version of himself in this young Virginian. The two men shared a common love of the land. They shared a common love of Billy's sister. They were both excellent woodsmen, and they were both astoundingly accurate shots with their long colonial rifles. Regardless of his immaturity and his dramatic failure with the "Uncle Dan" story, as it was now laughingly known, Billy was probably the best marksman in the small militia company. He and Silas had obtained meat for their suppers on several occasions when other hunters and foragers came in empty-handed. Silas only narrowly avoided a few fistfights when the truth about "Uncle Dan" came out, but it passed.

General Morgan moved through the camp the previous night, visiting the units on the hillside and along the banks of Thickety Creek. He gave hearty talks of encouragement to the frightened militiamen, along with detailed instructions to each of his unit commanders. The speeches he made that night would become legendary as he used humor, threats, pleas, and promises in his unique "Old Wagoner" way to build the spirits and the tactical understanding of his men.

Billy and Silas listened intently to him among a large number of men around their campfire. They heard him say, "Men, I know you're scared. We're all scared. I'm scared. None of us would be normal if we wasn't. But let me tell you what scares me most. It ain't the British. It ain't their swords, or them bayonets. It sure ain't old Benny Tarleton! No. I ain't scared of any of that! What scares me is lettin' you good fellas down by not seeing how yer brains work in battle and failin' to use you right. I know rifles. I know riflemen. I know some of you could pick one of them fleas off old Benny's moustache at three hundred paces…." He paused to let the laughter die. "That's part of what I wanted to talk to you about. We're gonna line the best shots among you up as a picket screen about a hundred paces out front of the rest of you.

"The regular continentals will be lined up about 150 paces behind your main body near the top of the hill. Colonel Washington and his cavalry are gonna be around back of the hill out of sight. As Benny gets here, he's gonna see you boys out in the open and come chargin' in here thinkin' he's got us whipped. I want you pickets to give special attention to their officers. Anybody hangin' back from the line on horseback is a fair and special target for ya. They'll probably see what's happenin' and charge you with some of them dragoon cavalry fellas. It's OK to shoot them too. The thing is, I know how long it takes to load a rifle. Just shoot, reload, shoot again, and run." This brought a muffled chorus of protest from around the fire.

The general paused a few seconds and then went on, "Now wait a minute! Just shut up and listen. When you knock down some of their officers and empty some of those dragoon saddles, they're gonna be good and mad. When you skedaddle, they're gonna think they got you whipped again, and they'll come on like a herd of drunk mules with their tails on fire. You boys in the second line are just gonna shoot three rounds each, and then I want you to run too. They'll turn into a chargin' mob as soon as they see that. I want you to run around the hill on our left side. As you disappear, Benny's boys will run headlong into our continentals near the top of the hill, and they'll be flanked by our cavalry comin' past you in the other direction. The only thing they'll be able to do is die or give up." He paused again, and this time the wisdom of what he was saying began to dawn on some of the men even though there were still muffled complaints about being expected to deliberately run away.

This morning, Billy and Silas were among the hand-picked riflemen positioned in the line of about 150 skirmishers far in front of Colonel Andrew Pickens's main body of militia. They watched as the British dragoons rode out of the trees at the far end of the meadow and formed a line. When the cavalry began to move slowly forward, Billy forgot his fear and jumbled thoughts. He selected a target near the center of the line of horsemen. The cavalry began to trot. The seconds seemed to slow perceptibly as a bugle blast sent the horses into a gallop.

Billy felt a momentary twinge of anxious dread as he realized that he could now distinctly see his target's face under the bouncing dragoon helmet. He had never before aimed his rifle at another man. Pushing this aside, he took a sharp breath and exhaled slowly as he calmed his aim and squeezed the trigger. Almost all of the skirmishers fired at the same time. The smoke billowed and blew quickly away as Billy saw his target collapse and fall from the saddle. Many of the saddles were empty now.

The cavalry charge continued, but some of the horsemen began to shy away as a few more rifle shots took deadly effect. Some of the galloping dragoons were sporadically returning fire with their short carbines. Billy was frantically reloading as he watched a huge dragoon still charging toward him. Silas suddenly screamed and swung his unloaded rifle, butt first, at the nose of the charging horse, causing it to lurch to a halt and throw the dragoon forward. The cavalryman began to swing his saber before he was thrown. Silas couldn't avoid the blade and the weight of the man as the horse now stumbled and rolled onto both of them. Billy momentarily froze in horror as his brain struggled to accept that his friend could not have survived the impact of both the rider and the horse. The area around him was filled with smoke, screams, shots, and galloping horses.

The dragoon's horse regained its footing and darted away. The dragoon began to rise. Billy stared in stricken shock at the crushed body of his friend. Silas seemed to be impaled with the cavalry saber, which was broken off about a foot from the hilt. The shock turned to rage as Billy ran forward and began beating the dragoon with his rifle butt until the man again collapsed. The rest of the charging cavalry went around, over, or through the militia pickets to continue their attack against the next line further up the hill. They were met with two ragged volleys that emptied more saddles and brought the charge to a confused halt.

The sound of drums grew closer as the British infantry came up the slope following the now broken cavalry charge. Some of the riflemen managed to reload and began to shoot at the mounted officers directing the advance from behind the lines of infantry. The officers weren't difficult to distinguish even if they hadn't been mounted. Several of them fell. Billy was screaming and continued beating the now inert dragoon until someone grabbed his sleeve and started dragging him away toward the left flank. He tried to struggle free until he recognized the kindly face of Sergeant Duncan. The sergeant was saying something as he pulled Billy along. They were beginning their withdrawal as ordered by the general the night before.

Billy still hadn't reloaded. This was difficult even under ideal circumstances. Loading these long rifles involved pouring the measured powder into the muzzle, then wrapping the oversized lead ball in a thin scrap of leather soaked with grease, and forcing it down the barrel with the ramrod. The rod was returned to its holder loops along the barrel to avoid losing it. The lock was moved to the half-cock position, and the pan was opened. A measured amount of fine grained powder was poured in to prime the weapon and the pan was closed. These rifles took a long time to load even with an expert rifleman handling them.

British infantry with their Brown Bess muskets were trained to fire and reload as many as four times per minute. A good rifleman could fire and reload about once per minute. The rifle's advantage was that it could accurately hit targets from over two hundred yards, while muskets were only effective within seventy-five yards. Conventional infantry warfare at this time involved large numbers of massed muskets facing each other across small open fields. The side that could reload and fire more rapidly usually won the battle. The musketry would be followed with bayonet charges to secure the defeated enemy.

Billy now began running along with the other surviving men from his group of forward skirmishers. They quickly merged with the now retreating members of the second militia line. Billy was still filled with rage and grief. Silas was his only true friend in the entire unit. He couldn't believe he just left him out there alone. Shaking his head and dragging his sleeve across his blood and tearstained face, he continued the laborious process of reloading as he ran to keep up with his comrades.

CHAPTER 2

Ira Fletcher was the wealthiest man in the county. His ancestors were fletchers charged with constructing arrows used by the bowmen of the British Royal Army. The family changed their occupation from fletchers to millwrights when the military use of gunpowder made arrows irrelevant. The family name remained Fletcher. Ira's father, Benjamin, decided to move to the New World with wife and children in 1726. He inherited considerable wealth from his own father, but the New World beckoned with a promise of greater opportunity. Ira was twelve years old when his family set sail from England. Ira's mother and older siblings were taken with fever and perished during the passage.

Benjamin and Ira found the vastness of South Carolina quite intimidating as they stood together on the Charleston dock at the journey's end. They prayed for courage and protection before pushing further inland. Father and son spent months searching for a new home and the elusive "greater opportunity." They eventually found a steep hill in a forested glen along a creek feeding into the Broad River. Benjamin knew this was the perfect place for a mill. It offered a swift waterfall with a natural cave cut deep into the rock behind the water course. The surrounding land was perfect. The forest held plenty of timber and stone for construction.

Benjamin purchased two hundred acres on both sides of the creek. He was a devout Methodist who abhorred slavery but desperately needed manpower. He bought four stout slaves and granted them immediate freedom on the condition that they stay with him seven years as paid laborers. This was unusual behavior in the South Carolina of 1727. Benjamin, Ira, and these now free laborers spent those seven years effectively. They cleared the land, built a home, diverted part of the creek to an upper mill pond, and constructed a two-story stone mill house with grinding stations on both the upper and lower floors.

The massive mill wheel was fed and turned by water from the mill pond. The wheel turned an axle that was carefully hewn from the trunk of a single giant oak tree. The axle turned the upper "load-stone" grinding wheel directly. It also turned the lower grinding wheel through a hand-made set of gears and axles. The upper grinding wheel was considered permanent and weighed nearly a ton. The lower grinding wheel was much smaller and could be replaced with a saw blade when needed. The mill house was constructed on the side of a very steep hill over a natural cave. Both floors could be accessed from outside via an external stone stairway. The mill house was a marvel of modern ingenuity and work-manship when it was complete.

Ezekiel, one of the former slaves, stayed on at the mill when it was finished. Benjamin trained him well, and he slowly took responsibility for day-to-day management of the complex mill operations. Ezekiel, or "Zeke" as Benjamin called him, seemed to become a living part of the mill with the passage of time. This eventually earned him a last name. This was something that was almost unheard of for a black man in the southern colonies. Ezekiel, the miller, slowly became Ezekiel Miller. Ezekiel was a shining example of industry, integrity, and hope to Benjamin Fletcher and his friends. The rural colonial slave owners who learned about this odd phenomenon at Fletcher's Mill didn't share these unorthodox ideas though.

Ezekiel's strange position of authority at the mill soon seemed like a threat to the slave-owning planters' fortunes and way of life. Benjamin became very rich and influential as time passed. Ezekiel became quite influential in his own right. Petty jealousies and grudges began to form which would someday fester into open conflict when the conditions were right. The mill drew customers from all over the county and beyond. Benjamin's investment bore fruit. He made more land purchases and gradually amassed a great fortune in real property and hard cash. More people moved near the mill, and a village slowly developed.

The village and Ira grew at roughly the same pace. The boy was educated by his father, and by Zeke. Benjamin longed to send Ira to the best schools in far off Charleston. He never remarried after the death of his wife, but he was determined to find a wife for his son among the Charleston gentry. Benjamin was in this mindset when he purchased a grand old house in the city. He and Ira left the mill operation in the capable hands of Zeke and moved to Charleston in the spring of 1735.

Benjamin continued to purchase land in the area near Fletcher's Mill. He soon owned several very productive farms. Agricultural labor on large farms in the southern colonies was almost exclusively the burden of slaves. Benjamin abhorred the very idea. He continued to confound his neighbors by purchasing slaves and granting them freedom in return for working his farms as paid laborers. When this became impractical, he changed the arrangement so that the farm laborers took a personal interest in farm output.

Benjamin became a pioneer in what would eventually be known as "share-cropping." He gave employment to anyone who was willing to work regardless of their skin color. His personal fortune continued to grow. Other large planters continued to seethe with resentment over the unorthodox outlook Benjamin had regarding their dependence on slavery. They knew their high profits wouldn't continue if they were forced to pay for labor. Money was a blinding influence. Greed ruled these planters' souls. They found it easy to hate anyone who showed empathy for the suffering of mere slaves.

Tensions nearly reached a boiling point when several of these area planters decided to boycott Fletcher's Mill. They began to transport their crops farther away to other mills for processing. Benjamin had a reputation for reasonable milling prices, but many of these men felt they could no longer tolerate the way he did business. Benjamin reacted by giving his larger farms to several of his share-croppers. These families were already working some of his largest landholdings. He obtained written guarantees in return for these deeds. These farms would always use Fletcher's Mill to process their harvests.

When the boycotting planters realized they now faced higher prices at more distant mills, along with greater shipping costs, they were furious. The stubbornness of these men brought several to financial ruin. Some found themselves forced to sell large land parcels to raise capital needed to satisfy creditors. Benjamin was one of the few men in the western part of the colony with enough money to buy rather than sell, and he ended up owning even more land.

Complaints were made to colonial authorities. Benjamin enjoyed growing influence with the royal governor and members of the royal court. They knew him to be a man of impeccable character and great financial means, even if he had strange social views. The planters' complaints fell on deaf ears, and Benjamin continued to prosper. This seemed to Benjamin as though it was confirmation of God's blessing. The villagers at Fletcher's Mill shared this opinion, and they also continued to prosper.

Ira was too old for primary school training, and not formally educated enough to succeed in college at this time. Tutors were hired and the young man was soon immersed in study involving everything from mathematics to philosophy and classic Greek. Benjamin was a wealthy man with growing influence. He associated with other wealthy men and soon became involved in colonial politics himself. Ira was ever more deeply immersed in the mysterious world of upper society as he neared adulthood. The young man's prospects seemed boundless. He quickly caught the eye of many young ladies and their parents as a wealthy youth with a bright future.

Ira eventually fell in love with a beautiful, sweet-natured belle of Charleston society who returned his affection wholeheartedly. Mary Simpson was well educated and displayed a refined grace that seemed misplaced in one so young. She was quick to laugh but not foolish. She was generous and soft-spoken without seeming weak. Mary was a devout

Christian with impeccable character who enjoyed a good joke and the pleasure of long walks in the garden with Ira. She agreed to marry him as soon as he asked her. Benjamin quickly came to love Mary as deeply as he loved his son. She had that effect on everyone around her. The couple settled into a life together that seemed too good to be true.

Tragically, smallpox took Benjamin right after Ira's twenty-first birthday. Ira was devastated. Mary desperately tried to help, but anything she did to ease his pain seemed to push him away from her. Small disagreements soon blew up into loud arguments and increasingly raw emotions. Ira seemed to lose his moral compass with Benjamin's death. He inherited all of his father's material wealth but little of his noble character.

Benjamin's estate contained large accounts in some of the Charleston banks. This money now belonged to Ira. He also inherited Fletcher's Mill, the property around the mill, a large house overlooking the mill village, over one thousand acres of prime farmland, and the mansion house in Charleston. Money was not a problem in the conventional way, but its abundance soon caused other difficulties as Ira progressed from grief at the loss of his father to arrogant self-indulgence.

Ira felt totally adrift. He contemplated what he saw as a boringly predictable future for himself and his new wife. Outwardly he did his best to settle down and establish himself as a productive member of society, but at home Ira became increasingly violent and unpredictable. Mary spent many long lonely nights crying out to God for Ira to come through this and once again be the man she loved so dearly. Ira seemed to grow worse as each day passed.

Alcohol became a problem for Ira that was difficult to keep secret. On one stormy night, Ira found himself locked up by the Charleston constabulary after a particularly raucous party resulted in a fire that destroyed most of a fine old house near the docks. The magistrate was a friend of Ira's late father. He agreed to set Ira free the next day with a written pledge to sell the Charleston house, pay for the damages, and move back to Fletcher's Mill. The Charleston mansion sold easily, and the damages were quickly settled to the satisfaction of the Charleston authorities.

The couple said goodbye to all their friends and family in the city. Mary was blessed with a longed-for peace as life became more stable for them at Fletchers Mill. They were welcomed as landed gentry by most people in the growing village. Mary was pregnant within a few months with their only child. The entire village celebrated the birth of their son, Isaiah, with them. Ira learned to control his drinking and his fiery temper. Isaiah grew to be a fine young man. With Zeke managing the mill and Ira managing everything else, the family and the village continued to prosper.

Ira eventually turned away from the bottle and the irresponsible ways of his youth. Mary's saintly influence drew him to the Bible. He finally came to the end of himself one day and surrendered his life to Christ at the small village church. The circuit parson baptized him in the mill pond on the same afternoon. Ira spent the next few years reading and absorbing scriptures. He used every opportunity he could find to share the Gospel with anyone who would listen. Ira and Mary continued to mature into the roles God and society blessed them with. He developed into a fiery preacher of the Gospel who traveled throughout the colony spreading the Word with all the intent that he had used in his earlier less noble pursuits.

Years passed. Isaiah was married to a beautiful young woman from a wealthy Camden family in the summer of 1763. Ira presided over the wedding with Mary beaming in the wings. The ceremony was a beautiful affair done outside under a flower-woven trellis arch with two hundred witnesses present. Most of the guests were landed gentry just like Ira and Mary. They represented both sides of the tense political environment. The assembly managed to lay aside their differences for the day in order to celebrate the promise of a bright future for these two young people. The future seemed promising indeed for the new couple. Natalie quickly became more than just a daughter-in-law to Ira and Mary. In the autumn of that same year, they were delighted to learn that they were going to be grandparents. On a bright spring morning in 1764, they welcomed their new granddaughter, Elizabeth Mary Fletcher, into the world.

Ira was away from Fletcher's Mill preaching near the coast when the jealousy and contempt of his family's enemies finally exploded into conflict. The resultant tragedy changed everything. Some men who hated him as much as they had hated his father used his absence as an opportunity to raid the village. The raiders apparently intended to hang Ezekiel, but they couldn't find him. Instead they killed Ira's son, Isaiah, on his own front porch. Ira's daughter-in-law fled to Ira's house with the baby. The fiends set fire to Ira's home and tried to destroy the mill before the villagers rose to fight back and put the last of the fires out.

Ezekiel managed to break into the house, pull the baby from her dying mother's arms, and carry her outside to safety before the roof collapsed and took Mary and her daughter-in-law to join Isaiah in heaven. Ezekiel refused to give up the baby even when some of the local ladies tried to pry her from his shaking arms. He was severely burned in several places and finally passed out from shock. One of the ladies, Mona Partridge, carefully pulled the baby free and cared for her until her grandfather returned.

Some of the villagers said they recognized the scoundrels. Two of the raiders were caught and held until Ira returned from his trip to learn of the disaster with a grief and fury that bordered on madness. After questioning the two prisoners, Ira had them beaten until they lost consciousness. He waited patiently for them to wake up, and then had them hung by the neck from a tree in the village square. Ira's grief was vented in violence as he led a group of mounted villagers to the next county. They found each of the culprits and exacted the most excruciating vengeance Ira could imagine. He was not the same man when he returned home several days later. Years passed slowly after that as Ira, Ezekiel, and Mona struggled to rebuild.

The "troubles," as they were known at the time, started quietly and far away. Rumors of colonial subjects voicing and acting on their discontent with the British crown and the sometimes onerous Acts of Parliament reached Fletcher's Mill very slowly. Year passed into year and the "troubles" came ever closer to home. Ira tried to maintain his reputation as a loyal subject of the crown, while he couldn't help nursing a growing appreciation for the resentments of the colonial leaders. This was especially true with the new "Stamp Act." News of open armed conflict in far off Lexington, Concord, and Boston was alarming in 1775, but the clash was expected.

Ira was a close friend of Dr. William Bull II, who was the acting royal governor in the absence of Lord Charles Montagu who held the actual royal appointment. Dr. Bull was replaced as governor in June of 1775 by Lord William Campbell, who held the position for less than four months before fleeing Charleston to save his own life in September of the same year. The South Carolina Committee of Public Safety seized control of the colony under the leadership of Mr. Henry Laurens who would later become the president of the Continental Congress.

Laurens was a very wealthy man who was deeply involved in the slave trade as coowner of Austin and Laurens, the largest slave trading company in North America at the time. Ira and Henry Laurens were in complete disagreement regarding slavery. This made them natural political enemies. Henry Laurens' son, John, also disagreed with his father. Henry's animosity intensified when his son sided with Ira. Most of the wealthiest landowners in the colony tended to dislike Ira for the same reason. He was naturally thought to be a loyalist by both the British authorities and the leaders of the growing rebellion.

The initial colonial defense of Charleston from British invasion in June of 1776 was greeted with celebration on the part of local people who agreed with the rebellion. Many people in the Carolinas chose to remain loyal to the mother country, while their neighbors, friends, and family members vehemently chose to rebel. It wasn't long before simple disagreements became openly violent acts that threatened to tear the fragile society apart. Ira and other civic leaders did what they could to maintain the peace to no avail. Old grudges and animosities were now increasingly settled with acts of cruelty that would earlier have seemed like sheer madness. Houses and barns were burned. Crops were destroyed. Enemies were named. Sides were drawn. People were both angry and terrified.

The British again besieged Charleston at the end of March 1780. The rebel Continental Army held out until May 12 when their commander, Benjamin Lincoln, finally surrendered his 4,650 troops to British General Sir Henry Clinton. Clinton left control of the southern British campaign in the hands of Lord Charles Cornwallis and sailed back to New York after Charleston was captured. Cornwallis led a ruthless campaign to bring all of South Carolina under submission to the Crown as his army moved north. The continentals suffered another humiliating defeat about 50 miles east of Fletcher's Mill at the Battle of Camden on August 16 of the same year under the abysmal leadership of General Horatio Gates. Both armies did extensive foraging along their routes of march, but Fletcher's Mill was far enough away from these routes to be left mostly alone by both sides. Or so it seemed to Ira.

George Washington replaced Horatio Gates with General Nathaniel Greene as commander of the southern Continental Army following the disaster at Camden. Continental resistance in the Carolinas almost completely disintegrated except for dispersed small bands of irregular militia by the end of September 1780. These partisan forces began a guerilla war that wrought havoc on British supply lines and any Tory groups they could identify. On October 7, about 900 continental militia fighters known as "Overmountain Men" led by James Johnston, John Sevier, and William Campbell almost annihilated a larger British and Loyalist force of 1,200 men led by British Major Patrick Ferguson at the Battle of Kings Mountain. This ferocious hour-long battle resulted in 290 British killed, 163 wounded, and 668 captured. Conflict between loyalist and rebel colonials became almost indescribably brutal.

CHAPTER 3

Colonel Tarleton sensed his anticipated rout of the rebels when he saw the retreat begin. He demanded that the infantry commanders press their attack forward at higher speed. They lost effective control of some of the smaller units with the deaths of their junior officers. The lines began to lose cohesion until the senior sergeants took over the duties of their missing commanders.

Billy and the other retreating militiamen were moving swiftly around the colonial left flank toward the rear when they were passed by Colonel William Washington and his continental cavalry moving in the opposite direction toward the battle. Billy managed to get his rifle reloaded somehow. He could feel the raw emotion and anger of the men around him. They could still hear the drums and gunfire behind them.

The British infantry continued to move steadily up the hill and finally came in contact with the massed lines of continental regulars. A large contingent of Maryland troops was already engaged at close range by the vaunted 71st Black Watch regiment of Scottish Highlanders. The rhythmic music of the bagpipes and drums provided an eerie background to the measured tramping approach of this feared regiment in their dark green kilts. A confused message caused the Maryland Continentals to begin a slow fighting withdrawal back up the hillside until the orders were clarified and they stopped to face the oncoming enemy. They were now

standing their ground and firing volley after volley in disciplined precision into the advancing ranks of Highlanders.

Rage and grief took over Billy's senses. He was crying and shouting
at the same time as he moved out ahead of the running militiamen. They
continued to the rear slope of the hill before pausing briefly for their
stragglers to catch up. Colonel Pickens was shouting something that
slowly began to make sense to Billy. He intended to keep them moving all
the way around the hill and reenter the fight on the British left flank. That
was all Billy needed to hear. The colonel moved his horse out of the way
so the men could pass on around the hill.

Billy shouted his own encouragement to the older men behind him
and ran toward the roaring sound of massed musket fire. The others hesitated at first, but when the colonel didn't do anything to hinder this young
fool, they followed him in their own mad, screaming, glorious attack with
nearly complete abandon. What some of them would later call the "fighting furies" gripped all of them. Billy wildly continued to charge toward
the growing roar. He felt no fatigue, just an increasing rage that seemed
to grip him deep in his chest and propel him onward. The thundering
footfalls and fighting howls of the other men striving to follow him added
greater impetus to Billy's relentless charge.

General Morgan was watching the battle from near the top of the hill
with his staff as he communicated with his commanders through several
breathless couriers. He saw Colonel Washington's cavalry smash into the
British infantry on their right flank. Then he heard a strange screeching
noise over the gunfire coming from the lower side of the hill to his right.
Glancing in that direction, he saw Billy leading a mass of charging militiamen as they rounded the hillside and crashed into the British on their left.

The smoke was thick and the noise was almost unbearable. Many
British bodies lay strewn on the battlefield, but they continued to close
ranks, reload swiftly, and fire into the line of continentals fifty yards away.
These were tried professionals. They knew they could outfight any standing army in the world. They would surely force these ragged colonials
from the field. Many of them had fought the rebels into shameful retreat

on numerous battlefields from New York to Philadelphia and Charleston since the beginning of this long war.

The rebels weren't showing any sign of retreat this time, however. The British regulars encountered the shocking force of a massed continental cavalry attack as they tried to follow the fleeing militiamen and turn the rebel left flank. They found that the Maryland troops were reinforced by more continental regular units when they shifted focus back to the center of the rebel line. The British left flank was then hit with the shrieking charge of the now returning militia.

Billy hadn't reached the British line in his headlong rush when he saw a Highlander sergeant trying to pull his soldiers into a square to face the charge. Billy hauled the long rifle to his shoulder, while still running, and shot the man from thirty yards away. These screaming militiamen appeared to have gained the strength of wild animals as their unformed but powerfully compact mass slammed into the stalled British regulars. The British line reeled back as it absorbed this unexpected shock. Billy's rifle was empty again, but he didn't care. He was completely caught up in the madness of this moment. These people had killed his friend. He continued to attack any British soldier he saw before him. The madness seemed as if it would never let go. He moved back and forth trough the enemy line using his rifle butt as a club with a speed and agility that shocked those militiamen who were still with him. They strove to follow his example with little conscious thought.

Billy parried bayonet thrusts and sword blows until his arms were numb. He kicked and screamed as he beat the terrified enemy soldiers to the ground. The resulting fear in the British troops caused them to pull away from this seemingly unstoppable maniac and the wild men behind him. The left flank of the British line slowly began to falter and then totally collapsed. The melee seemed to last hours, but it was over in a few terrifyingly violent minutes. Without warning or command, the British simply stopped fighting and began to drop their weapons. They were flanked on both sides. They now faced a disciplined advancing infantry force to their front. The militia charge gradually lost energy as the militiamen realized that the fight was gone from their enemy.

A sharp fight continued between the remaining British dragoons and Colonel Washington's cavalry. The continental horsemen held a contempt for their British counterparts that wasn't just the result of rumors they heard about "Tarleton's Quarter." They were taken with the same mad fury displayed by the militiamen on the opposite rebel flank. Colonel Washington saw the two grasshopper canons in the enemy rear and led his men to attempt the capture of this valuable artillery. He found himself personally engaged in the battle as the British fought to stop this from happening. A few of the enemy cavalrymen wore the green uniforms of the legion.

Colonel William Washington was a distant cousin of General George Washington. He was a master horseman and a valiant soldier. He held a solid reputation as a leader and commander in his own right, apart from being related to the commander in chief. Washington suddenly realized he was facing Tarleton himself in this desperate part of the battle. He narrowly escaped death from a British saber slash when his own manservant drew a pistol and shot the enemy soldier at point-blank range. The British managed to rescue the canon and flee with them into the woods at the lower end of the meadow. Most of the feared members of Tarleton's Legion never entered the battle. He was holding them in reserve to "clean up" the battlefield after the rebel army tried to surrender. When the incredible defeat became obvious, they simply fled. The whole affair lasted less than one hour.

The battlefield became eerily quiet before cheering started among the continental ranks. Billy found himself doubled over in near exhaustion, strangely close to where he was when the battle started. Orders were being shouted as continental soldiers were detailed to take charge of over eight hundred British prisoners and collect all of their now discarded weapons. The smoke slowly cleared as the cold winter breeze continued to blow. The area where he and Silas began their day looked barely familiar to Billy. It was now strewn with the dead and wounded bodies of both men and horses. The debris of this awful modern warfare was everywhere. The cheering died away, and the cries of the wounded replaced it. The stench of open wounds and burnt powder was almost overwhelming even with the breeze.

Billy was nearly blinded by tears as he searched the battlefield for the body of his friend. Some militiamen began to slap him on the back and gleefully congratulate this ferocious young madman. They had followed him into a headlong charge that would be thought suicidal when considered by anyone not directly involved. All the shame of his earlier lie was now totally forgotten. These men were looking at him now as if he was some kind of hero.

Billy no longer cared what they thought. He was looking for Silas. He was desperate to find his friend. Silas didn't abandon him earlier when he found himself at the lowest point in his life since his father died. He knew that Silas saved his life in the opening moments of the battle here today. The charging dragoon would surely have killed him this morning if Silas hadn't heroically charged the horse with the butt of his rifle. Billy felt tremendous shame that he had survived when Silas had not. He suddenly found himself standing over Silas' body. His knees lost their strength and he collapsed at his friend's side in overwhelming grief. The sobs began to ebb, and Billy reached out to roll Silas over. He was again shocked to find that the broken cavalry saber only penetrated Silas' coat under his arm and pinned the folds of the garment to the ground. Silas was bloody and unconscious, but he was still breathing.

CHAPTER 4

Old Ezekiel Miller slowly shook his head as he looked further into the parlor of the house. He turned toward the girl and said, "Now Miss Elizabeth, you know your grandpa isn't gonna like this! He's gonna blame me for this mess, and I'll have to spend the rest of my day cleaning up while he carries on like the world done ended!"

Seventeen-year-old Elizabeth Fletcher laughed, "Oh shush, Zeke, I know what I'm doing, and I know Grandpa will love it." She continued to sort the small cloth patches into various piles of different colors.

Elizabeth was on a mission to sew the most beautiful quilt she could for her hope chest out of this seemingly worthless collection of old garments and cloth scraps. She had been cutting and sorting all morning when Zeke came in from the mill and saw what she was about. Mona Partridge was teaching her to sew. Elizabeth was determined to make something of it. Zeke and Grandpa would have to recognize that she was just as intent on growing up as they were in keeping her a little girl.

Grandpa Ira was away on another preaching circuit. Elizabeth was the woman of the house. She was going to make this quilt or bust before he got back. She said, "Now Zeke, you just go back to the mill and leave me alone. I love you, but you're in my way now."

Ezekiel began to argue, "But, Miss Elizabeth...."

She laid down the cloth and shears she was holding and gently pushed him back outside, saying, "Shush now. It's all right. Go on back to work."

She closed the door and he was left standing, bewildered, on the front porch.

Ezekiel didn't have time for this foolishness. There was over a ton of grain to process and bag before tomorrow morning. There was work to do on the lower wheel, and he was expecting "special visitors" later tonight. Zeke was having trouble with the Johansen boy, and he considered letting the boy go. He just couldn't do it, though. Zeke possessed a God-given love for the people around him. He genuinely cared for the two young men who worked with him at the mill. Tobias Griffin was clearly the more intelligent of the two, but Zeke also saw a promising future for Peter Johansen if he could just get over his selfishness and pride.

Ezekiel believed he understood Peter better than Peter understood himself. Tobias' family lived in the village, but Peter had no one. The boy seemed to be lonely most of the time. Peter built up such a shell around himself, though. He was very difficult to reach. Zeke regularly prayed for both boys just as he prayed for Ira through the years. He shook his head again with the detached grace of his seventy-five years and started up the road toward the mill.

Ezekiel neared the massive stone structure and noticed a small group of men on horseback at the front of the building. Three large empty wagons with surly and impatient-looking teamsters were lined up along the lane leading to the front door. The men on horseback wore the distinctive uniforms of British dragoon cavalry. One of them was holding the reins of a beautiful horse whose saddle was empty. Zeke slowed his pace but continued to approach the doorway. He lifted his hat and nodded a smile in greeting when the men noticed him. They said nothing but edged their mounts away to let him pass. Zeke noticed that the door was ajar. He pushed it open and stepped into the shadows of the large entry foyer which also served as the business office and one of many storage areas for the mill. Zeke hung his hat on the peg near the door and turned to face a large impeccably uniformed Royal Army captain.

Ezekiel's apprentice miller, young Tobias, was standing almost at attention in front of the captain while the officer leafed through the mill's open business ledger. Peter Johansen was sitting on a stack of fine flour bags near the shuttered window on the other side of the room. Zeke smiled at the captain as he told Peter to get up and get to work cleaning the lower mill station. Peter brushed past him with a sullen look on his face but said nothing. Tobias looked greatly relieved at Zeke's arrival and followed Peter out of the room.

Ezekiel said, "May I be of service, sir?"

The captain looked inquisitive and responded, "I need to speak with your master. Please tell me where I might find him."

Zeke said, "I'm a free man, sir. I'm also the chief millwright here. The owner of the mill is Reverend Ira Fletcher."

The captain shrugged and said, "Then where can I find Mr. Fletcher?"

Zeke explained that Ira was away on his preaching circuit and again said, "Can I help you, sir?"

The captain abruptly closed the ledger and looked sternly at Ezekiel as he said, "I heard rumors about this place, but I scarcely believed them."

Zeke replied, "Yes, sir. Can I help you, sir?"

The captain seemed to swell slightly as he said, "My name is Captain Reginald Crispin. I'm the deputy quartermaster on the staff of His Majesty's army serving under General Lord Cornwallis. My men and I are here to requisition provisions. We had been told of the wealth in this building. Now that I see it with my own eyes, I am astounded. I had no idea that three wagons would not suffice to carry these provisions back to the army. Where can I requisition more wagons?"

Ezekiel stared openmouthed at the man for a moment before he managed to say, "Sir, do you intend to take everything from the mill?"

The captain shouted, "Of course I do! Your precious Mr. Fletcher will be paid well for everything!" Captain Crispin stomped past Ezekiel and out the door as he shouted for the teamsters to bring the wagons forward.

Zeke followed him out the door pleading, "Sir, most of the materials in the mill belong to the mill customers, to the area farmers and their families."

The captain spun on Zeke and stepped very close, almost spitting in his face as he shouted, "Then your precious Mr. Fletcher will have to show where his real loyalties lie by using his own legendary fortune to reimburse his customers until he is paid by the Crown!" The captain turned his back to Zeke and again shouted orders to his men and the teamsters.

The noise of angry shouting had been growing from the direction of the village for several seconds and it continued to get louder. The horses began to shy and stir. The dragoon sergeant holding the captain's horse moved closer and held the reins out to his officer. Zeke said, "But sir...." and he reached forward to grasp the captain's arm. He remembered later that he never actually felt the blow as the sergeant struck him on the side of the head with the flat of his heavy saber. Everything went black, and he was spared witnessing what happened next.

The source of the shouting voices became clear as a crowd of about thirty villagers, old, young, male, and female moved into sight around the bend in the lane. The people were led by Tobias and a huge older man, Tobias' father, Robert Griffin. Mr. Griffin was the village blacksmith. He was one of the strongest men in the county, and he was carrying his best two-pound ball-peen hammer. Several of the villagers were armed with clubs, pitchforks, and even a few old fowling pieces.

The villagers' shouts turned to rage when they saw Ezekiel on the ground. They began to surge forward. The sergeant shouted an order bringing the dragoons into line and spreading them out in front of the mill entrance and the wagons. The crowd slowed to a stop when they saw the brandished sabers and the still holstered carbines. Captain Crispin was holding a fully cocked pistol in his free hand.

The blacksmith shouted, "What is going on here? What have you done to old Mr. Zeke?"

The crowd milled several yards down the road. They continued to shout in anger at the alarmed British soldiers. More villagers joined them as people rushed to see what was happening. Fear began to spark greater emotion on both sides in this momentary impasse. Someone in the crowd noticed the teamsters and their wagons and correctly deduced the reason for the army presence. A few young men began to move around the mounted soldiers toward the wagons in the distance. A sharp yell from Robert Griffin brought them back.

The blacksmith realized that the situation was growing hopelessly out of control and could end badly for everyone involved. These soldiers were foraging for food and supplies. There was nothing he or any of his neighbors could do to stop them. Griffin turned to his neighbors and tried to reason with them for calm before turning back to the mounted officer and asking again what had happened. The terrified captain shouted at him to be silent and raised the pistol as if to enforce the point. The effect on the crowd was opposite what was intended. They became louder and started again to move slowly forward.

CHAPTER 5

The battle of Cowpens lasted less than one hour. It was ferocious and stunningly decisive. It was an astounding victory for the Continental Army. The British defeat at Cowpens was both a shock and a humiliation to His Majesty's forces in the Carolinas. Banastre Tarleton barely escaped the field with two hundred of his men. He entered the battle with almost fourteen hundred. Those killed, wounded, or captured were from some of the best units in the Royal Army.

Cowpens would be recognized as a tactical masterpiece on the part of Daniel Morgan. It was arguably one of the most successful double envelopments in modern military history. It was also seen as an example of prideful foolishness on the part of Lieutenant Colonel Banastre Tarleton. The continental losses included 12 killed and 60 wounded. The British lost 99 killed, over 200 wounded, and 829 captured. Thirty-nine of the British killed in action were valuable, tactically proficient junior officers. Tarleton somehow managed to save the two grasshopper canons, but the continentals captured a huge amount of powder, ammunition, weapons, and other crucial military supplies.

Billy Morgan gave little thought to any of this. This was a horrendous ordeal for him. It involved stark terror, almost insane fury, and shocked disbelief at discovering that Silas Whitaker somehow survived when he thought him dead. Billy managed to gently roll Silas onto a makeshift stretcher with the help of Sergeant Duncan and Private Plunket. They moved him to a clearer spot and laid him back down long enough for the sergeant to go search the hillside looking for medical help. Plunket backed away slightly as Billy bent over Silas trying to clear the blood and dirt from his friend's face.

Silas bled profusely from his head wound, and the right side of his face was swollen terribly. Billy doused his oily rifle cleaning rag with drinking water from his own bottle and began to swab Silas' face as carefully as possible. Silas' left eye twitched and slowly came open. He brought Billy's face into focus with difficulty, then began to cough. This caused immediate searing pain in his chest and lower abdomen. He managed to rasp, "What … what happened?" A coughing spell started again, and he quietly croaked, "I think my ribs are busted."

Billy said, "Just stay still, Silas. I'm gonna take care of you."

A shadow moved over Billy and Silas. They heard the deep voice of General Daniel Morgan just above a whisper as he said, "He looks like he's hurt bad, son." Billy looked up to see genuine concern in the older man's face. The general said, "I'll have my surgeon look at him, son." To Private Plunket, he said, "Stay with this man til the surgeon gets over here." The general reached out and gently grasped Billy's upper arm, pulling him to his feet as he whispered, "We need to talk."

Billy stepped a few yards away, trailing the giant strides of the legendary general. He expected to be chewed out now that the battle was over. The embarrassment over his lie hardly seemed to matter anymore. To his surprise, General Morgan stepped away from him a few paces, then turned around to stare at him with a giant grin on his face. A few seconds of uncomfortable silence ensued before the general slapped himself on the thigh and let out a startling peal of laughter followed with the words, "Let me shake your hand, young man!"

The general covered the few paces that separated them with his own right hand outstretched and his face split into a jovial grin. Billy didn't know what else to do, so he timidly offered his hand. The general grabbed it and slapped Billy several times on the back as he continued to laugh. He shouted, "That was the most amazing thing I ever did see!" Billy felt himself almost lifted off the ground as the older man spun him around so that the gathering crowd could stare at the two of them. The general roared, "That was the most astoundin' bit of soldierin' I've seen in years! Wait, I know you young fella! Seems to me we're related somehow...." He looked sidelong at Billy and winked. He continued, "Yeah, that's right ... ain't you my cousin's boy?" Before Billy had time to react, he was shocked to listen as General Daniel Morgan described him as a distant cousin of some kind. The general bewildered Billy even further by referring to him as "Lieutenant" Morgan.

Billy stammered, "But ... sir ... I'm just a militia private...."

General Morgan leaned close and whispered, "Shut your mouth, boy! Don't ever argue with me again!" He stepped back and laughed, "Congratulations, Lieutenant. I've got lots of business to tend to right now, but I'll want to talk quiet with you later today. Get your friend seen to with my surgeon like I said. Then find me again. I've got a job that needs done, and you're the one to handle it." He stepped over to where his horse was being held by an orderly and swung painfully up into the saddle. Without another word, the general pulled the horse's head around and started back up the hill followed by his retinue of aids and messengers.

Billy looked on in disbelief. The nearby group of men suddenly converged on him and began to loudly congratulate him and pat him on the shoulders and back. It slowly occurred to Billy that the shame he felt from his earlier lie wasn't really gone. It was altered slightly with the realization that General Morgan had publicly claimed him as a relative. That brought feelings that were difficult to understand. His emotions were so jumbled that he felt overwhelmed, bewildered, elated, and euphoric all at the same time. Billy was exhausted and felt like laughing and crying at the same time. He knew one certain thing now. Billy would gladly march into the jaws of death for Daniel Morgan if asked. He had no idea what the new task might be, and he didn't care. The fact that Billy would be trusted with any kind of mission was enough to guarantee his complete devotion to the cause, whatever that meant.

A small elderly man in a once fine suit of clothes slowly worked his way through the crowd and approached the place where Silas was lying. He identified himself, in a thick Polish/German accent, as General Morgan's personal surgeon. Dr. Mikhael Bolt leaned quickly over Silas and began a process of searching and probing which would have brought painful protest to even an uninjured man. Looking around quickly, he sent Private Plunket to collect a bundle of twenty straight sticks about four hand-breadths in length and the diameter of his little finger. His accent and the strangeness of the instructions made him repeat them twice before Plunket understood. This brought a slightly annoyed look to the doctor's face which was instantly replaced by the stoic expression he seemed to wear most of the time. Dr. Bolt returned immediately to his patient, identified the worst of the injuries, and deftly treated them with an undeniable skill that left Billy feeling greatly relieved. It was now clear to him that Silas would get the best possible care.

Doctor Bolt gave Silas a strong dose of some brown liquid from a stoppered vial he removed from his huge leather satchel. He continued to clean and bandage the wounds as Silas gradually became quieter, apparently under the influence of the strange liquid. Plunket hurried back with the bundle of sticks. The doctor nodded a curt thanks and began sorting the sticks into a row on the ground. He then stood up and enlisted the help of Billy and Plunket as he straightened the now bandaged and sleeping form of Silas Whitaker on his back. Gently opening Silas' coat and shirt, he probed and examined his abdomen with mumbled comments and nods. Dr. Bolt carefully closed the shirt and coat. He again requested help from the two other men as he carefully eased a sheet that had been folded into a long narrow rectangle under the injured man's abdomen and chest. Working slowly, he arranged the sticks vertically along Silas' ribcage using his coat for padding as he wrapped the sheet snuggly around his patient's body. He secured the end of the sheet to itself by sewing it swiftly in place with a dexterity that surprised the two observers.

Doctor Bolt took another quick look at and around Silas and then stood to face Billy. He looked up into the young man's face with care and concern that again surprised Billy. "This man … he is your comrade...your friend?" Billy was afraid of what might be said next, so he simply nodded. The doctor nodded also and said, "He will live I think!" Brushing his hands on the front of his coat, he continued, "There are at least three broken ribs. His left shoulder, it is dislocated. His skull, it could be cracked, but I am not certain." He looked back down at Silas briefly and then back up at Billy. "I have immobilized his ribcage as best I can here. The bleeding has stopped, and I have sedated him. I need to reset his shoulder, but I can't risk doing that here and now." Billy nodded as if he understood all that he was told. The doctor continued, "He is severely concussed even if his skull is not cracked. I have taken a great risk giving him so much laudanum, but I feel we must keep him from going into shock. We must get him inside a building somewhere soon." Billy nodded again, but felt completely helpless. He was staring down at Silas' now motionless body.

Billy watched and listened a while longer as Dr. Bolt continued to make arrangements for transporting Silas to a place more suitable for proper medical care. He bent over his unconscious friend and gently grasped his uninjured shoulder momentarily as if to reassure himself that Silas really had survived. Standing up, he turned again to the doctor and thanked him profusely for all that he had done and all that he would do to care for Silas. Dr. Bolt nodded quietly with no real emotion on his face. He then turned back to Private Plunket and began barking instructions.

A few men who had witnessed these events moved quietly near Billy. One of the men, Private Howard from Billy's company, cleared his throat and said, "Excuse us, sir, we was wonderin' if we could help you with...." Billy looked sharply at Howard. The older man seemed to flinch away. Howard had been one of the loudest of his tormenters over the last few days. "Help me with what?" Howard removed his worn slouch hat and held it before himself in both hands. The barrel of his long musket was propped inside his right elbow with the butt of the weapon resting on his right foot. The man had his head lowered and his face was covered with a look of almost comic humility. Billy didn't know the other two men, but he had seen them in the ranks of the other company. These two had the same low expression as their spokesman. Howard tried again, "Well you see, sir, we followed you into that last part of the fight, and we agree with the general, I mean … your … your 'uncle' sir. Fact is, we ain't never seen nothing like that either…." Billy didn't know what to say, so he remained silent. Howard went on, "We heard the gen…. I mean your uncle … promote you to be an officer and all, and we was lookin' at your clothes, and we was thinkin…."

Billy looked down at himself and suddenly realized what Howard was trying to say. He looked back up and said, "What would you suggest?"

The older man brightened as he lifted his head. "Well, you see, lieutenant…." He nodded toward the thin scarecrow of a man at his right. "Jimmy here, he was goin" through the baggage those English fellas dropped down by the tree line before they came chargin' up the hill. One of them must have been a Hessian officer or somethin,' cause his sack looked different than the others, and it had a pretty clean dark blue coat tied to the outside of it. Inside, he also found a pair of good quality trousers, stockins, and two good white wool shirts. We found a useable officer sword too with a fine leather belt and scabbard and all the trim…. This stuff looks to us like it'd fit you just fine. Jimmy here wanted to keep it all, but he showed it to me and we talked about it, and then we heard the gen … I mean your uncle shoutin' … and we thought of a better use for it like…."

Billy couldn't help smiling now as he realized the tremendous respect and generosity he was being shown by these hardened men. Howard went on, "Thomas here also 'found' two pairs of good calf-skin boots on a couple of those dead lobster officers. We don't know if either of them would fit you, but you could try both on." Billy again looked down at his torn and filthy clothing. He was so covered with mud and blood that it was difficult to see the threadbare knees of his trousers. His shoes were ready to disintegrate. His coat was just as filthy, and the left shoulder was torn beyond repair. The only thing he was wearing that was still in fair condition was the belt and shoulder sash holding the weight of his canteen, cartridge pouch, and powder horn. He still had one pretty good shirt and the remains of a knit sweater in his rucksack back by the creek, but he couldn't deny that these offered treasures would be very valuable to him indeed.

Billy looked up at Howard in subdued gratitude and said, "Thank you very much for thinking so kindly about what I need. I will gladly accept the sword, trousers, shirts, and coat, but I just can't bear the thought of wearing a dead man's boots...."

Howard leaned in close and said in a kindly voice just above a whisper, "Now, none of that, young man. You done us all real proud today, and we would follow a fella like you anywhere.... We want you to have this stuff, and we want you to have our service too. Besides, those dead lobster officers ain't goin' to miss em, and it ain't like we can return this stuff to their grievin kin. Nobody in their right mind would bury good boots on them bodies anyway. It's just as well you have em as somebody less deservin'...."

Billy reached out and grasped Howard's hand as he smiled and said, "Then I heartily accept your kindness, men!" They all slapped him on the back and led him down the hillside toward the tree line where their booty was now hidden.

Newly promoted Lieutenant William (Billy) Morgan, now better attired, walked up the hill later in the direction taken by General Morgan. The boots he had selected fitted him perfectly. This path took him past a large group of filthy and exhausted men. They didn't look familiar to him at first, but when he got close, he realized that these were all members of his militia battalion. He finally saw his captain and Sergeant Duncan standing and talking with the colonel. Billy remembered now that Sergeant Duncan hadn't returned when he walked off earlier looking for medical care. He needed to explain what had happened after Duncan walked away, but he didn't even know where to start. He knew he had to tell someone about the conversation with General Morgan, and he felt very conspicuous in his newly acquired clothing.

Walking up to the three older men, Billy stopped and stood waiting to be noticed and expecting a rebuke for his impertinence. The conversation continued in low tones until the colonel's horse started slightly and Sergeant Duncan turned to soothe it with a pat on the neck. Noticing Billy, Duncan said, "Here he is now, sir."

Billy stammered, "I b ... beg your pardon ... I...."

The colonel interrupted him, "That is perfectly all right, Lieutenant. We were just discussing your amazing display of military prowess today...."

Billy looked down not knowing what to say. They clearly already knew about the amazing development regarding his new rank.

The colonel said, "I'm very sorry to lose you, son, but it seems that your 'uncle' has a much more important task planned for you." He smiled broadly as he reached out to shake Billy's hand. The others did the same.

The captain said, "Lieutenant, I believe you should go and report to General Morgan as soon as possible. He doesn't appear to be a man accustomed to waiting on junior officers ... even if they're kin.... I believe he's set up headquarters over on the north side of the hill in the wood-line."

Billy experienced a moment of apprehensive uneasiness. He looked down again briefly and then raised his head while clearing his throat. The colonel asked, "Is there something more I can do for you, Lieutenant?"

Billy stiffened his spine and looked the man directly in the eyes as he said, "Yes, sir. There is. I would like to request that you transfer Privates Seth Plunket, James Rice, Thomas Rhodes, and Richard Howard to my service. They have already proven very useful to me and I think I might need steady help with whatever the general has up his sleeve."

The colonel seemed to consider briefly and then smiled as he said, "Consider those men yours, Lieutenant Morgan."

Billy hadn't cleaned his rifle and wasn't sure where the rest of his kit was. He and Silas had left their rucksacks and bedrolls where they spent the night up by Thickety Creek. Sergeant Duncan saw the uncomfortable look on his face. It was as if he was reading Billy's mind as he said, "Now Lieutenant, you don't worry about your gear. I've already sent your kit over to headquarters because I knew you'd be heading there eventually after what General Morgan said, and yes, I sent Whitaker's stuff too. I'll fetch the four men you requested and have them waiting for you when you get finished with the general."

The colonel said, "Now go on, son. The quicker you report to the general, the sooner you'll get started with whatever he has planned."

Billy nodded and straightened himself up to what seemed like 'attention.' He touched his forehead in what would have to pass for a salute and said, "Then, with your permission, sir...."

The colonel saluted briefly and said, "Godspeed to you, young man. I hope to hear even more noteworthy news of your future exploits!"

With that, he turned and continued speaking with the captain. Billy knew he had been dismissed. He turned away and began the slow walk up and over the hill to find out what new insanity awaited him.

CHAPTER 6

The angry crowd moved closer. Captain Crispin pushed his horse between two of the dragoons and leveled his pistol at Mr. Griffin the blacksmith. In a voice that betrayed both annoyance and fear, he shouted, "This man has assaulted a king's officer! Free or not, he will face the king's justice!" A large stone flew from the back of the crowd and struck the dragoon sergeant on his left cheek with a sickening thud. The sergeant was knocked back in his saddle, while his feet remained caught in the stirrups. The sergeant's horse reared and lurched sideways toward the terrified captain.

Crispin was not an infantry officer. He was not a professional soldier in the truest sense. He lacked the disciplined will and iron nerve of many Royal Army captains. Crispin was a quartermaster, a supply officer, who had purchased the captain's commission he held. His startled reaction to the stone hitting his sergeant, followed by the violent action of the horse, was unintentional. The damage it caused was very real. The pistol discharged as the captain and his mount flinched away from the sergeant's horse. The weapon was pointing at Robert Griffin's left leg just above the knee as it fired.

The one-ounce lead ball left the muzzle of the weapon so close to the head of the captain's horse that it took part of the animal's ear with it as it entered the blacksmith's leg, knocking him to the ground in stunned agony. The other dragoons surged forward without orders or warning.

They covered the distance between themselves and the small crowd in moments. Most of the villagers drew back and started to run. Tobias fell to the ground trying to aid his father. A massed rifle volley struck the mounted dragoons in that moment from the brush lining the rail fence at the corner of the mill house.

None of the people involved in the confrontation noticed the concealed approach of the small militia company. These were some of the feared Overmountain Men. The militiamen didn't intend to get this close to the mill until well after dark. They had heard the sound of shouting at the mill several minutes earlier. Their captain was speaking quietly with a well-dressed elderly stranger who was leading a beautiful horse as the company walked along the trail toward the village. The man had joined them a mile back down the trail. They first took him for a well-dressed country parson.

The stranger's countenance changed instantly when he heard the commotion near the mill. The old man's face became a mask of indignant rage as he moved quickly toward the sound. He looked as if he would stomp right out onto the road to confront the trouble directly. He only stopped when the militia captain grabbed his coat and pulled him toward the bushes at the side of the mill house. The militia company witnessed the events on the open road in front of them. Every man knew what was coming when the rock was thrown and the pistol discharged. They all knew the British dragoons would show no mercy to any of the civilians. No instructions were given. None were needed. Half of the twenty riflemen raised their weapons and fired simultaneously. All of these men were expert marksmen. The range was very short.

The saddles were suddenly empty, as the horses shied from the noise and billowing smoke to gallop away from the awful scene in terror. The stone broke the sergeant's cheekbone and knocked him from his rearing horse. He was now lying unconscious near the still prostrate form of Ezekiel. The teamsters whipped their draft animals into frenzied motion when the first shot was fired. Now they frantically drove away in clouds of panic and spraying mud.

Captain Crispin's horse reacted in fright and pain by darting away from the scene. Its course took it between two old pine trees across the road from the mill. The captain lost control of the reins and one stirrup. He tried in vain to hold onto the saddle pommel until he was knocked from the back of the animal by a low hanging limb and fell ignominiously to the ground. Tobias shrieked in rage and snatched his father's hammer from the roadbed. Running the short distance to the now disarmed and humiliated captain, he was about to use the hammer in a manner different from its designer's intentions. A sudden shout from a familiar booming voice brought him to a stop just before he began to swing at the captain's head. Out of the still billowing smoke stepped the tall imperious form of Reverend Ira Fletcher.

Elizabeth heard the commotion from the house and hurried up the road just in time to see the final events take place. She cried out as she saw Ezekiel lying in a shallow puddle of mud and blood on the ground. She ran to the old man at once. Finding that Zeke was alive, she knelt in the icy water and rolled him onto his back. Pulling his head onto her lap, she began to brush the blood and mud from his face and shirt front.

Several of the villagers returned to Mr. Griffin and tried to hold him still. One of the older women tore part of her apron hem loose and used it as a tourniquet to stop the flow of blood from the shattered limb. Ira shouted orders to some of the men about collecting the scattered cavalry horses and removing the fallen dragoons from the middle of the roadway. He strode to where Tobias was standing over the fallen captain. Ira quietly but firmly told the young man to give him the heavy hammer.

Tobias was sobbing and shaking almost uncontrollably as he stood over the captain with obvious intended malice. He couldn't speak. He was barely aware of Ira's presence as the older man reached gently out and took away the weapon. The captain was cowering in panic and pain. He was still unsure of what occurred moments earlier. It had all happened so quickly. He was in control, at one point, performing his duty as he understood it. The situation changed in blurred seconds. Looking around, he could see that all of his men were either dead or dying. The civilian teamsters had deserted him. Now he found himself looking up into the stern piercing gaze of a most unusual man.

Ira Fletcher was tall and straight. He appeared quite vigorous for his advanced age. His long white hair was swept back and tied into the fashionable queue where it fell from beneath his tricorn hat. He wore a now soiled dark gray suit of impeccable quality. His stockings were the finest imported silk. The buckles of his shoes were solid silver. He now held the hammer in his left hand and his silver tipped cane in his right. Crispin wasn't sure what it was about Ira that commanded respect. He was obviously wealthy, but that wasn't it. He carried himself with an almost regal demeanor. His eyes were a penetrating steel gray. His features were sharp, but neither harsh nor apparently cruel. He looked more frustrated than angry in this moment.

Ira quietly said, "It would appear, sir, that you are now a prisoner of the Provisional Militia of the sovereign State of South Carolina." Captain Crispin's misplaced bravado began to return.

He said, "And you, sir, appear to lead these rebel scum that murdered my men!"

Ira physically restrained Tobias following this absurd statement. He shook his head and replied, "No. I'm not their leader. I met them just outside the village as I was returning home. We heard the commotion in front of my mill and came to see you and your men accosting my millwright and threatening my friends. These fine young men simply took it on themselves to stop your armed men from a massacre of innocent civilians."

Captain Crispin picked himself up from the ground and now stood with his head lowered and his hands balled in fists just under his chin. He turned slightly and glanced from Ira to one of the militiamen who was moving toward them. "You will all hang in any event," said Crispin.

Ira stared at him silently, then turned away to address the approaching militia leader. "Captain, you can lock this officer and his sergeant up in one of our storage rooms until you and your men leave this place. I will expect you to take them with you." The wounded dragoons apparently wouldn't survive the night no matter what medical treatment they were offered.

Captain Luther Robertson replied, "Aye, sir, although I don't know what we will do with them. We travel light and we don't usually have the pleasure of such august company...." He smiled at Captain Crispin with a malicious leer that conveyed anything but friendly charm.

The British officer tried to straighten himself into a stance that might have resembled a position of attention with his chin jutting forward and his chest thrown out in cartoonish pride. He raised his voice slightly as he said, "I'm a king's officer, and I expect to be treated as such! You filthy vermin must turn me over to some kind of formal military authority as soon as possible! The rules of civilized warfare demand it!"

Captain Robertson raised the muzzle of his still loaded rifle and placed it squarely under Crispin's nose. He exerted just enough force to make Crispin rethink his assumed posture. "Mister, it'll be a miracle if my men don't take your scalp while I'm asleep. You better get real humble really quick. My boys and hundreds like us don't have much use for your King George or charlatan toy soldiers like you. I can't speak for what's happened up north, but down here we've whipped you fellas every time we found you. I'll do my best to keep you alive long enough to hand you over to those 'formal authorities' you mentioned, but you would do well to keep your mouth shut and your head down until that happens, if it does happen."

Crispin looked like he was about to say something else until he looked past the militia officer and saw a momentarily unveiled flicker of seething rage pass over the otherwise placid face of Ira Fletcher. He somehow grasped that his only real hope of survival was submission to this militiaman. Whatever he had heard about Fletcher, it seemed clear that this man of the cloth could become a remorseless enemy. Crispin lowered his arms and head now in humiliated surrender. A short time later, he and his sergeant were locked in a dark storeroom on the lower floor of the mill.

CHAPTER 7

Lieutenant Billy Morgan found the headquarters tent beyond the hill in the northern tree line. A cold drizzle was falling again. Men were coming and going from the tent in great haste. Four sentries guarded the outside. What appeared to be the rest of the guard detail cared for their personal equipment around a fire in another clearing about thirty yards away. Several horses were tethered near the back of the tent. A small group of officers huddled by the horses engaged in a heated but whispered discussion. Billy recognized a small pile of gear belonging to Silas and himself near the front of the tent. No one seemed to notice him as he stood still on the path feeling great trepidation at the thought of entering Daniel Morgan's tent.

Billy heard the booming voice of the great man coming from inside the tent and it startled him back into motion. The general was clearly less than pleased with some unfortunate soul. He was creatively letting the poor man know of his displeasure. The shouting stopped abruptly. A small, nattily dressed Continental Army major came out a few seconds later. The ugly little man looked like he was about to start sobbing before he saw Billy.

The blue of Billy's newly acquired uniform coat with its once-bright yellow facings seemed to startle the major. It was the shade of blue and the yellow that was striking. This had been part of a Hessian uniform. Hessian blue had been a source of fear and loathing for continental soldiers on many battlefields for the past five years. Billy's men had helped him "Americanize" the coat as much as possible. He now wore his leather belt and accoutrements on the outside of the garment in a fashion that wouldn't have been acceptable to its former owner. He couldn't do anything about the color of the coat, however, and it was this that brought the startled major to a spluttering halt in front of him.

Billy said, "Morning, sir!" in a courteous but straightforward manner.

The major quickly realized that he was confronted by a young man of inferior rank. He seemed to swell slightly with the realization. He asked, "What's so good about it? Who are you?"

Billy responded with eye-to-eye frankness, "Lieutenant William Morgan, at your service sir."

The major momentarily toyed with the idea of berating this unfortunate young man in the oddly familiar coat. He had just received one of the most scathing, if humorously worded, reprimands of his military career from General Morgan.

The major's sense of self-preservation started gnawing at him when the lieutenant's last name registered on him. Billy stood patiently in front of him, awkwardly blocking the path with his long rifle balanced on his shoulder, and a friendly smile on his face. The major finally shrugged and pushed his way around Billy on the narrow path. Billy shook his head in bewilderment at the enigmatic nature of New Englanders. The guard outside the tent asked him to identify himself and then opened the flap to announce him and allow him to enter.

Billy was greeted by the booming voice of his supposed uncle, General Morgan. "Well, get on in here, boy, we got work to do!"

Billy noticed that there were two other men in the tent with the general as his eyes adjusted to the dim light. He was shocked to realize that one of these people was none other than the diminutive Dr. Bolt. The other man was a ramrod straight Continental Army sergeant. This man wore the slightly soiled uniform of one of the Maryland infantry regiments. The doctor was sitting on a chest at the side of the tent as he wrote in a journal with the stub of a pencil. The pencil itself was a surprisingly modern device to see in this place. The doctor's large satchel was sitting open at his feet and several dubious-looking bottles were visible inside. The sergeant was clearly at respectful attention, but the glaring scowl on his face made it obvious he was not pleased with the nature of the current discussion. Billy took all of this in as he lowered the butt of his rifle to the ground and waited for the general to continue.

General Morgan turned back to the sergeant and said, "This is him, Strickland. I don't rightly care what you think. You're gonna do what I tell you or I'm gonna have your hide removed to use as a saddle blanket!"

The sergeant painfully allowed himself to turn and gaze at Billy with a scowl of subdued distaste. "Yes, sir, but how...?"

That was all he managed to say before the general exploded into a thunderous roar, "Shut your mouth, Sergeant! You are going to escort this fine young officer on this mission and you are going to ASSIST him in the accomplishment of the mission! I said I don't want to hear any more debate about it! I meant that! You might as well know this is your last chance with me. If you make a shambles of this, I'll shoot you myself and hold the general court later!"

Silence prevailed thickly for a few seconds before Sergeant Strickland lowered his gaze slightly and said, "Yes, sir. I understand, sir."

A messenger came into the tent behind Billy and walked up to where the general was now sitting behind a field table. Bending over, the messenger whispered something to the general and waited for a response. The general gave the messenger detailed instructions that were clearly intended to be conveyed to someone else. He made the messenger repeat the instructions back to him before allowing the man to leave. Billy didn't know these instructions would affect his future. He managed to hear something about gathering troops and wagons and having them stationed at the other side of the hill near the trail heading south.

General Morgan turned to him and said, "William, I'm still so proud of what I saw in you today that I can't hardly believe we're kin." Billy was shocked at the use of his first name, but he remained silent. The general went on, "I've no doubt that you are pretty curious by now regardin' what it is I'm wantin' you to do."

Billy said, "Well, yes sir I am … a bit."

The general stepped around the field table. Billy couldn't help noticing a hand-drawn map on the table. The map appeared to be very detailed. The general looked first back at the sergeant, and then at Billy. He said, "You see, we have a little problem that has come up as a result of our shockin' success this morning with old Benny's troops. It seems we done captured an amazin' amount of enemy weapons, ammunition, and other supplies." Billy understood.

The general continued, "Lieutenant, the job we was given by General Greene when we came down here was to apply pressure to the British and draw some of them away from him. Then we was to provide aid and assistance to the Overmountain Men and others like Francis Marion and his boys. We've definitely applied pressure to the lobsters by whippin' em here today and takin' so many of them as prisoners. We now have an ideal opportunity to follow through on the second part of our instructions by sendin' some of the 'valuables' we've captured to our friends further south."

General Morgan sniffed loudly as if he just remembered something and said, "That Yankee major that left just before you came in here is Major Throckmorton. Throckmorton is supposedly in charge of the supply train for this army. Personally I think he's a liar and a thief, but General Greene inherited him from Gates when he left and Greene seems to trust him for some reason." The general paused again for a moment before continuing with, "Throckmorton just tried to tell me that all of those captured supplies now belong to the United States and that I've got no right to just be givin' them away to anybody else…. I shoulda throttled the little weasel before I let him get out of this tent. No tellin' what trouble he'll cause for some other unfortunate souls today. Anyhow, you'll have to deal with him and get a good inventory written down listing all the items you're taking with you. I'll give you written orders about that so he can't give you any trouble."

Understanding began to dawn on Billy. General Morgan again continued, "I can't send all of this stuff south. We need a lot of it for our own boys, but I plan to send three wagons loaded with as many muskets and as much powder and shot as we can pile onto 'em to our militia friends as soon as the wagons are loaded. You and Sergeant Strickland here are going to escort this stuff all the way to its destination and see it's delivered to those that need it most. After that, I want you to work your way back to the main body of General Greene's army up across the river. I'd say come back to me, but I ain't sure where we'll be. I'll give you written orders layin' all this out along with a letter from me givin' you authority to do anything you feel best to make this happen. Strickland here is a good sergeant, and he knows how to fight just like you. Problem is, he sometimes gets into the spirit store and forgets who it is he's supposed to be fightin'...." Billy couldn't help glancing at the sergeant, who was amazingly still standing at attention.

General Morgan looked over at Dr. Bolt and said, "I've also decided to send the good doctor here with you. He ain't helpin' me much with my back trouble, and you're goin' to take some of our worst wounded fellas with you in one extra wagon.... I expect one of them men will be your friend, Whitaker." Billy was again shocked at the general's detailed knowledge of names. "Doctor Bolt will watch over the wounded fellas til you can get them somewhere for better care than we can give them out here. Once you get them someplace like that, you will leave them with the doctor and go on with the rest of your mission."

Billy finally responded in the only way he knew how, "Yes, sir. I understand, sir."

The general turned back toward him and quietly said, "I doubt that very much, young fella, but I seen you fight today. You're gonna cover some very difficult ground with wounded men and valuable stores over about a forty-mile stretch. It's gonna take days even if you don't run into trouble with Tories or regular British patrols. We have good reason to believe the enemy is still out there watchin' us. That's what cavalry does normally. Benny's got his tail singed today. I know he ran off with some of his men, but I think he will leave some of them back here to find out what we are doin' with all these prisoners and with all this stuff."

The hair began to stand up on the back of Billy's neck as he realized the importance of what the general was telling him. It occurred to him that this important job was being given to him personally, and he didn't feel at all up to the task. It was like the general read his mind again as he gazed steadily into Billy's bewildered eyes. "You'll do fine. son. Besides, I'm sending Strickland along with you to make sure you stay out of trouble. He'll help you with the troops. A few of them are these bone-headed Yankees. The rest of them are militia."

Billy nodded, and the general turned back to the map on the table. Tracing his finger across from where it showed their current location at the Cowpens, he ended up pointing to a small dot much further south near a creek and a small village. "You'll take the weapons and military stores here where you'll meet up with the local militia." Billy leaned further to read the handwritten place-name under the dot. He had never heard of the place, but the name was Fletcher's Mill.

CHAPTER 8

Ira sat in the warm candle-lit parlor near the fire. The militia captain sat in the other chair smoking a pipe and staring into the fire. The two men spoke in low tones for over an hour. Ira was learning things that he wouldn't have imagined regarding the activities of his friend and mentor, Ezekiel. He was angry at first, and quite confused. Ezekiel was still unconscious. He had been moved to an upstairs bedroom in this spacious house and was now being looked after by Elizabeth and Mona. Ira wondered why pieces of different colored cloth were lying all over the parlor sofa and the grand table in the dining room. Elizabeth offered no explanation when they carried Ezekiel in from the road.

Ira turned back to the captain and asked, "Just how long has this 'arrangement' been in existence?"

Captain Robertson exhaled a great cloud of smoke toward the roaring fire and smiled wanly. "Well, Reverend Fletcher, we've been using your mill as a cache for weapons, powder, shot, and food provisions since before Christmas."

Ira sat back in shock. "Are you serious? Why wasn't I informed?"

Robertson said, "Now, you'll have to take that up with Mr. Zeke, sir … if he recovers.…"

Ira was completely taken aback. He said nothing for a few moments as he too stared into the fire. Another question struck him. "But how was this 'material' brought in and out of the mill without my knowledge or the cooperation of any other local people? Do you realize, sir, that you have endangered my granddaughter and all my assets without my permission or foreknowledge?"

Robertson nodded solemnly. "Yes, sir. We do understand, and as a matter of fact, we did have the cooperation of several villagers. We never intended to endanger Miss Elizabeth or you. I think that was why Mr. Zeke insisted that you be kept out of it."

Ira stood abruptly and began to pace. He grew angrier with each passing second. He understood why his friends kept these activities secret. However, he could not abide being thrust blindly into the conflict like this. The thought of the added danger to Elizabeth in this already very dangerous world made him furious. He could barely control the emotion welling up inside. He fought to keep his voice low as he turned back to the seated militia officer. "You and your compatriots have placed me in a very difficult position, young man! I can't believe you would endanger me, my family, and this community by bringing your unwanted conflict here!" Robertson removed the pipe from his mouth but said nothing. Ira blurted, "At least one of those teamsters will reach the authorities at Winnsborough or Ft. Granby by tomorrow night or the next morning at the latest!" The import of this realization seeped into his own consciousness slowly and robbed him of the energy supplied by his earlier anger. Real fear started to grow like a cold stone in his chest. He slumped back into the chair and buried his face in his hands as he struggled to discern some way out of this mess.

The room remained silent for nearly a minute as both men stared into the fire searching for words. Captain Robertson sat back slowly and said, "Sir, even if the lobster-backs get news from those frightened men, they won't know the details of what happened. Besides, they have plenty of other concerns along their main supply routes. Colonel Marion and his boys have been giving them fits. They don't dare send a small patrol this way to check on this incident, and they can't afford to send a large body of troops quickly. Cornwallis is all the way up in North Carolina."

Ira stared at him and asked, "Then what do you suggest we do here?

What about the area Tories? Evil men have inflicted great pain here in the past!" The memory of his personal loss washed over him with those words and he felt the return of an almost uncontrollable fury. He was on his feet pacing again.

Captain Robertson stood. Facing Ira, he said, "My men and I will be operating in this area. We will do everything within our power to protect you and this village. We only ask that we be allowed to continue using the mill as a cache for military stores."

Ira almost shouted, "I don't want your protection! I don't want to be in this situation in the first place! I don't want to choose sides in this evil conflict!"

Robertson stared at the floor for a moment, then raised his head with tears streaming down his face. He took a half step forward and snarled, "Reverend Fletcher, how can you possibly remain uncommitted to liberty.... How could your wealth be so important that it blinds you to the tyranny of the Crown and anyone loyal to it?"

Ira was standing still now. Competing thoughts raced through his mind. He was a very wealthy man with substantial real estate and other assets. He was powerfully connected in colonial politics. He enjoyed significant material blessings throughout his life. He did not want to be displaced and poor. He loved Elizabeth and was almost fanatically committed to her enjoying a bright and stable future. He knew many of the area Tories. Many of them were the same men who hated him for his rejection of slavery. These were the kind of men who had already taken so much from him. He couldn't deny a growing animosity toward a Crown defended by these loyalist toadies.

Part of him wanted to stomp out of the house and rouse the villagers to join him as he dragged Captain Crispin and his sergeant from their makeshift prison. He would have them flogged without mercy, venting his raw seething rage on their writhing backs. He would have them executed using a rope thrown over a limb of that same old oak tree in the village square. This would serve justice by bringing retribution on these two fools for the broken and unconscious body of Ezekiel upstairs. That vengeance might also satisfy the raging fire of hatred he still carried for the men who murdered his wife, his son, and his daughter-in-law. This irrational thirst for revenge hardly let him consider that he had already found and destroyed those men. He toyed with the idea that he could legally and logically dispense justice this way. Wasn't he the sole arbiter of right and wrong here? He was the sole political authority in the village. He could avenge this evil. He could....

Ira realized that he had been lost in thought as he stood in front of the still staring Robertson. With this came the realization that he was straying into the same madness he so quickly judged in other men. He wasn't the sole authority here. God was. Reason reasserted itself. He couldn't kill these men. Ira took that path years ago, and it didn't solve anything. Vengeance belonged to God. He was not God. Vengeance did not belong to him. Finally, all the strength seemed to drain from him. He felt the weariness come over him again. Ira remained standing in the same spot staring at the floor with his shoulders slumped and his hands clasped behind his back.

Captain Robertson was staring at him with great concern. He was not aware of the inner turmoil roiling through Ira's mind, and he didn't understand that Ira was not reacting to his own angry outburst. Ira finally glanced up and noticed the captain's silent stare. He then straightened himself up, cleared his throat, and slowly resumed pacing. Robertson quietly said, "I'm terribly sorry, sir. I don't know what comes over me sometimes. I hope you will forgive me for that outburst. You and the people of this village have been quite generous to me and my men. We will do anything in our power to protect you, your property, and your friends whatever you decide regarding our supply needs."

Elizabeth was busy in one of the upstairs bedrooms working carefully with Mona to treat Ezekiel's wounds and make him as comfortable as possible. The blacksmith, Mr. Griffin, had been taken to the village animal apothecary for any treatment he might offer the poor man's shattered leg. The same was suggested for Ezekiel, but Elizabeth and Mona wouldn't have it. They were now bent over the old man trying to clean the rest of the blood from his face and head. Mona displayed great nursing skill as she cleaned the open gash and then used five stitches to close it. She boiled the needle and thread for several minutes before using them, not because she understood anything about germs or infection, but because she just couldn't abide doing it any other way.

Mona Partridge was absolutely devoted to the Fletchers. Her family moved to this village to be close to the new mill those many years ago, and she grew up here. Mona, although a few years younger, became a close friend to Mary Fletcher when Mary and Ira moved back from Charleston after the death of Ira's father. Mona had never married. She was a very pretty girl in her youth. She enjoyed the attention of several young men in the village but her parents were poor, and no one ever asked for her hand. Mona thought her youthful beauty faded with the passage of time. She didn't realize that her physical appearance had kept pace with the sweetness of her personality. Mona matured into a beauty who was far deeper than her outward looks. The reason for her spinsterhood was a matter of availability. She grew less interested in pursuing a family and children of her own as the years passed.

Mona eventually moved into the role of aunt with the birth of the Fletchers' son, Isaiah, through her close friendship with Mary. Mona adopted the place of great aunt automatically when Elizabeth was born years later. She bonded with the baby almost instantly. The tragic death of Mary and the baby's parents thrust her into the role of surrogate grandmother to this precious child. Most, if not all, of the "ladylike" things Elizabeth learned came from Mona. Ira welcomed her into this position wholeheartedly because he knew Elizabeth needed her. More years passed as the child grew, and slowly, ever so slowly, Mona began to feel something growing inside her that she thought was gone forever. Her devotion to Elizabeth, Ira, and Zeke slowly changed to allow an ever growing love for her best friend's widowed husband to secretly take root.

Elizabeth sat down in the overstuffed chair near the bed and reached out to light another candle on the side table so that they could see more clearly. She said in a quiet plaintive voice, "Aunt Mona, please tell me you think he will mend. I don't know what we'll do…. We just can't lose Zeke! God wouldn't take him from us yet, would he?"

Mona continued to work quietly as she replied, "Keep praying for him, dear, and trust the good Lord to help us. He knows more about what we need than we ever will!"

Elizabeth said in a voice that was almost a whimper, "But I love him so…. He's the only one besides you that understands how I feel about … things…."

Mona looked over at the girl and spoke almost too sharply, "Now hush that kind of talk. Your grandpa loves you, dear, and Zeke should be fine with time."

Elizabeth straightened at this rebuke, but she couldn't be argumentative with Mona. She said, "Aunt Mona, I didn't mean anything against Grandpa…. It's just that he can't see I'm no longer a little girl! Why, I'm fully grown and I'll be ready for a family of my own someday soon." Mona sat on the edge of the bed and reached over to grasp Elizabeth's hands in her own.

"Elizabeth, your grandpa is just afraid. He loves you."

Elizabeth felt her eyes begin to tear as she asked, "Afraid of what? Afraid of me leaving? I won't go! Afraid of my love for him dying? That will never happen!"

Mona let go of the girl's hands and lowered her head as she whispered, "He's afraid of change…."

The two sat quietly for several seconds until both of them noticed that Ezekiel was beginning to stir.

The conversation between the two men in the parlor was interrupted by Mona's voice softly calling Ira from the top of the stairs. Ira remembered Ezekiel's broken form on the roadbed as he replied, "What is it?" with deep concern.

He was already headed up the stairs when he heard Mona say, "Zeke is awake, Ira, and he's asking for you."

Ira entered the room to find Elizabeth leaning over Ezekiel as he lay near the edge of the large ornate bed. Zeke's elderly frame looked small and quite frail in his present condition. A white bloodstained bandage was wrapped around his head so low that Ira could barely see his open eyes blinking in the dim light of the candle.

Mona said, "He's awake, but he's not himself. He barely knows us and he doesn't remember anything that happened today. He feels cold at his feet and hot at his head. We think he's starting to fever. I've stitched the cut on his head to stop the bleeding. We've cleaned him up as best we can, and I don't know what else to do...."

Ira gently squeezed his granddaughter's shoulder as he leaned over to look into Zeke's face. Ezekiel stared up at him and seemed to focus. He spoke with a deep rasp in his throat, "Reverend, we been workin' on that large load o' wheat. I still got near a ton to grind an' ah...." His voice trailed off to an imperceptible whisper as his eyes slowly went shut.

Ira said, "What we can do best for him right now is pray. God can do anything, even when we are powerless." He then added, "I've sent young Peter Johansen off to fetch Dr. Scott from over by Winnsborough. The boy should be back with him by tomorrow." Ira wrapped his arm around Elizabeth as he grasped Ezekiel's bony old hand.

Mona stood and watched with overwhelming love for this little family as Ira offered what she thought was a beautiful prayer for his injured friend.

The prayer was more inflated and churchlike than Ira wanted it to be. His recent struggle with intended malevolence seemed to block his will to speak openly with the Loving Father that he knew God to be. The prayer trailed off to a quiet, "In the Mighty Name of Jesus, amen...." He and Elizabeth sat together this way for several minutes. She was softly sobbing. Ira was desperately searching for something he could say or do to help Zeke and ease Elizabeth's fear. Ezekiel was asleep again. Ira leaned over and gently kissed his granddaughter on the cheek before rising. He said, "Stay with him, Beth. I've still got business to tend to with our militia friends. Let me know if there is any change at all." With that, he turned and went back downstairs after exchanging a concerned look with Mona.

Captain Robertson was still seated before the fireplace. Ira joined him, and they continued to stare into the fire as if the light would somehow displace the darkness both men felt. Ira eventually asked, "Do you swear that you can protect this village and my granddaughter, young man?"

Robertson didn't flinch as he responded, "You know I can't do that. I will swear to do my best to make the enemy pay dearly for any attempt on this place and these people!"

Ira didn't look away from the fire as he shrugged with resignation. "I will, in any event, allow you to continue to use my mill and its environs for your military needs, Captain…."

Robertson straightened with restrained surprise. He said, "I wish to reassure you, sir. The main body of the British army has moved into North Carolina. We know that General Greene was sent down by General Washington to rebuild our regulars after that disaster at Camden. We also know that General Greene has dispatched Daniel Morgan south to help us with over a thousand trained men. It seems that Cornwallis knows that. We've heard that he has sent Benny Tarleton to chase Morgan with about the same amount of force. We still don't know how that turned out…."

Ira interrupted the young captain by turning away from the fire and staring at him again. Ira said, "Even if you did swear to protect us, we both know we are in grave danger here. It would seem, sir, that the only real source of safety for any of us is Almighty God Himself."

CHAPTER 9

The meeting with General Morgan went on for another hour. The plan was worked out in detail that overwhelmed Billy. He and Sergeant Strickland eventually found themselves walking back up the muddy path followed by Dr. Bolt and his assistant who was now burdened with a surprisingly vast amount of medical supplies. The weight was obviously staggering for the thin young man. The assistant spoke exclusively with the doctor and then he used very few words in a foreign language.

Strickland was walking silently beside Billy in what seemed like rigid march step. Billy couldn't help changing his stride randomly so that they would be out of step with each other. This clearly annoyed the sergeant who repeatedly skipped a half pace while trying to stay in step without saying anything to this frustrating young upstart. Billy forced himself not to laugh when he realized what was happening. The strange parade continued around the hill to where Sergeant Duncan was waiting with the collected wagons. He was surrounded by an odd assortment of twenty men wearing uniforms, homespun, and rawhide hunting clothes. Privates Howard, Plunkett, Rice, and Rhodes were standing separate from the others.

Sergeant Duncan called the men into a military formation as the new lieutenant walked up with his small entourage. The men were assembled in three ranks. There were only two sergeants. Billy instinctively realized that he would have to choose between these two. He would appoint one of them as the tactical leader of the men. He would appoint the other to oversee all of the administrative and supply issues. He didn't know how he understood this. Billy lacked any military training other than what he learned in the brief time he belonged to the militia. In fact, he didn't have much formal schooling at all. Almost all of the "book learning" he possessed came from his mother and his older sister. The "life learning" mostly came from Silas and brief experience.

Billy had endured a whirlwind of battle and strange events all day. He started the morning as a private in the North Carolina militia. Now, less than five hours later, he was a new lieutenant with responsibility for an important mission assigned by General Morgan. That was another thing. Last night he was being laughed at by everyone around him because he invented that stupid lie about Daniel Morgan. Now everyone around him was treating him like a hero. The general himself was claiming him as long-lost kin. It was enough to make his head swim. He was terribly hungry, and he hadn't really slept for quite some time. All of this felt like a strange dream. The battle itself seemed like it couldn't possibly have happened the way he now remembered it, yet here he was on part of that very battlefield facing all these men.

Billy still needed to decide between the two sergeants. He knew Sergeant Duncan well. He knew very little about Strickland. The way the man acted since they met with the general made him seem like some kind of marionette. What had the general said though…? "Strickland here is a good sergeant and he knows how to fight just like you." Billy couldn't remember much of the rest except that it was something about Strickland's weakness for spirits. He considered this important choice now while absently watching the doctor and his assistant carefully load their equipment into one of the large wagons. The two odd men were engaged in a quiet technical debate in their strange foreign language.

Billy eventually decided what to do and stepped over to speak with both sergeants in a low voice. He started by introducing the two men to each other. He then leaned close and said, "Look here now. I have great respect for both of you. Sergeant Duncan well knows that until a short time ago, I was a private in the ranks." Duncan smiled and nodded. Billy continued, "I've come to know that Sergeant Duncan is very diligent in overseeing the things we've needed in the field. He has always been fair when it came to dividing food, water, and ammunition. I know him as a man of character who can be trusted in any situation." Duncan smiled again and mumbled a subdued thanks. Billy went on, "General Morgan said some good things about Sergeant Strickland and his fighting ability. I know I can trust the general's judgement even though I lack experience in these things."

Billy deliberately chose not to say anything about Strickland's alleged history of problems with alcohol. Sergeant Strickland looked him directly in the eyes. There was the faintest show of gratitude in the man's almost unblinking gaze, but Billy caught it all the same. It meant a great deal to Billy in that moment. "I've decided that I'm going to ask Sergeant Strickland for advice and counsel in all tactical matters. Sergeant Strickland, you will act as my second with the men. If something happens to me, you will take command. You understand the mission as well as I do. You're one of few professional soldiers we will have with us." He paused for a second and then turned to the other man. "Sergeant Duncan, you have a way with the men and a way with their supplies. I want you to handle all of our administrative needs. I'll defer to you for advice and counsel in all matters regarding the men's equipment, weapons, ammunition, and rations. This will be no easy task.

"We're going to escort these wagons filled with seriously wounded men and a large amount of critical supplies. We have to cover a considerable distance over rough ground. The Tories and Lobsters are scattered all over the place out here. We've been ordered to get these wounded men to some safe place where the surgeon can give them better attention. The general also told me to get these supply wagons to our militia friends at a place called Fletcher's Mill as quickly as possible. We're to move north to rejoin the main army under General Greene after we make these deliveries."

Sergeant Strickland glanced at the formation of men. Duncan seemed to realize what he was thinking even though Billy missed it. Duncan turned around and shouted for the men to fall out and continue to ready their personal equipment. Billy realized that this interaction between the two men was a very good sign. He didn't see that the men had been standing there for several minutes waiting for him to tell them what to do. Both sergeants noticed it, though, and they communicated without speaking. The appropriate sergeant took immediate action, and Billy was served without any lecture or embarrassment at his failure.

General Morgan had given him a carefully drawn map. It showed their intended route and all known information about possible friends and enemies along the way. The distance was approximately forty miles as the crow flies. Their route would take them over broken terrain using any available concealment. The countryside would be covered with pockets of Tory sympathy and British patrols. These would have to be avoided. The small convoy would cross the Broad River and several rain-swollen creeks. The direction was roughly southeast.

General Morgan made it clear that their highest priority, if attacked, was to protect the military stores. The wounded men were important, but their value paled in comparison to the priceless weapons, powder, shot, and assorted military supplies. Billy produced the map and spread it out in the back of one of the wagons. He roughly understood how to carry out the mission, but he lacked confidence and wasn't sure what to expect from the men with him. They spent the next half hour discussing the situation until Billy fully grasped what needed to happen.

A great deal of preparation was accomplished over the next few hours. Billy and the two sergeants organized their small company into three squads. He didn't know if he had the authority to do it, but he promoted privates Howard, Rice, and Plunkett to temporary corporal rank. The corporals were each put in charge of one of the three squads. This seemed to fit right in with everything else. The newly promoted corporals worked well together and managed to get all of the supplies loaded into the wagons. The loads were covered with canvas tarpaulins to keep the powder dry and the loose equipment from falling out on the rough terrain.

Sergeant Duncan and several privates worked with the doctor and his assistant to carefully load the wounded men. They stacked the men into the wagon by laying three of them on the bed of the box cushioned with blankets. The others were arranged across the top of the box on stretchers. The doctor insisted that the men on stretchers were tied down to keep them from rolling off. Two wounded men died before the expedition even started. The surgeon was forced to amputate limbs from both of these men earlier. They later died of shock. It looked like the rest of them might survive. This would be the last wagon in the train. The assistant would drive. The doctor would walk alongside or ride in the back with the wounded men.

Billy talked with the doctor at length in regard to the critical medical needs. They studied the map together looking for any place that might offer the security and protection from the elements that the patients needed. Both realized that the best thing they could do for the men was to transport them all the way to Fletcher's Mill as quickly as possible. There didn't seem to be anywhere else along the route that would meet the doctor's needs without surrendering the men to the unreliable mercy of their enemies. A makeshift tent of sorts was built over the top of the wagon bed to retain some needed warmth and to keep the men dry.

Billy thought it would be a miracle if any of the wounded survived this journey. He again started to fret for Silas. Billy made it a point to spend a few minutes with his friend before he was loaded onto the wagon. Silas was conscious and in terrific pain. Billy tried to cheer him a little by telling him what transpired with General Morgan and his promotion. Silas was pleased that Billy had survived the battle and earned a reputation for courage and leadership in the middle of it all. Talking made him cough, though, and coughing brought him agony. Billy finally wished him well and nodded for the waiting soldiers to load his friend along with the others.

Sergeant Duncan took control and politely stopped Billy several times from personally getting involved in the labor. Sergeant Strickland mysteriously wandered off somewhere. Billy began to suspect that he may have found the "spirit stores" as suggested earlier by General Morgan. Billy's frustration with Strickland led him to get ever more involved in the work at hand. Duncan finally pulled him aside for what sounded like a fatherly chat. He explained that he understood how any new lieutenant must feel when there was work to do and he wanted it done a certain way. He explained that this was "sergeant's work." Young officers were to tell the sergeants what they wanted, then leave it to the sergeants to get it done. In other words, Billy was to stay out of the way while older and wiser men saw to the needed work.

Billy sat down on a fallen log at the side of the trail after this conversation. He began to meticulously clean his rifle while preparations went on around him. He was doing this when Strickland marched up with an unexpected companion. The other man was not a regular continental soldier. His long hair protruded from beneath a weather-beaten slouch hat. He wore buckskin trousers and shirt with no jacket. A length of heavy fur was rolled and draped crosswise from his left shoulder to his right hip and fastened to his leather belt at that point. The belt held many of the same items Billy carried, only more of them. These included a tomahawk and two long cavalry horse-pistols. The man carried his long rifle with a deft familiarity that told Billy a great deal without words being spoken. His face was deeply worn so that it looked almost like the tanned leather of his shirt and trousers. He wore high moccasins on his feet and walked with an animallike sure-footed gait. The two men stopped in front of Billy and stared at him without speaking until he stood up.

Billy finally couldn't take it any longer. "Sergeant Strickland, who is this and where have you been?" Strickland hesitated. Billy blurted, "Stand easy, Sergeant!" Strickland visibly relaxed, but it was as if he had been given the command "Parade rest." Billy said, "Look, Strickland, stop acting like this! I can't stand it anymore! Look at me when I'm talking to you!"

The sergeant turned his head and stared directly into Billy's eyes while he replied, "Yes, sir!" The strange-looking man next to the sergeant edged slowly away as if he expected a physical fight to ensue.

Billy took a deep breath and let it out slowly in a manner oddly similar to what he did as he was aiming his rifle. Staring into Strickland's eyes without flinching, he felt like he was engaged in some type of contest with the man.

Billy quietly asked, "What is it, Strickland? What's bothering you about me?"

Strickland seemed surprised, either by the question or the way it was asked. He hesitated. Then, as if he changed his mind about something, he replied, "It's your blasted uncle ... sir."

Billy couldn't conceal his surprise as he straightened up and said, "What...? My uncle? You mean General Morgan?"

Strickland looked straight ahead again as he said, "Yes, sir. The general, sir."

Billy didn't want to discuss the relative strength of the Morgan family relationship. "What about the general?"

The wild-looking man and Sergeant Strickland were clearly friends or at least closely acquainted. Billy would learn that the man's name was John Red. Strickland gave Red a brief sideways glance now as if to gain resolve. He hesitated, then asked, "Do I have your permission to speak freely, sir?" Billy nodded. A deliberate calm slowly asserted itself over the sergeant. He relaxed his posture with effort and turned to fully face the young lieutenant. "You see, sir, it's like this. The colonel ... I mean ... the general, when he was just a colonel, used to pick me out for a volunteer for all the jobs nobody else would take.... He said it was 'cause I was the most likely Yankee he could ever find and he just hates Yankees.... He's done stuck me on some of the lowest worst jobs anyone could imagine all the way from before that awful winter at Valley Forge. In every fight, he keeps pushing me into the worst of it. Finally I thought I was free of him when I came south with the Maryland boys. Then he up and shows again, and now he's a general and all."

Strickland paused to catch his breath. Billy didn't speak. He didn't know what to say. The sergeant lowered his voice a little and seemed to lean forward as he continued. "That was when he stuck me on another impossible detail ... I had to 'escort' a wagonload of rum kegs we had 'liberated' from a Tory warehouse up by Charlotte. We was supposed to take it to Wilmington and trade it for canvas and cordage to use for tents and such. On the way, we was bushwhacked by one of them Tory bands fightin' with that treasonous Benedict Arnold.

"There was ten of us on that run. Me and John Red here was the only two that made it back alive and I was hurt bad." He nodded toward Red who was now seated on the log formerly occupied by Billy. "When we come in, the general wouldn't listen to anything we said about what happened. I don't know what made him madder—that we had lost the rum, had failed to bring back the tentage, or that all of those good men had been killed. He threatened to have me tried and whipped. He never accused me of bein' a coward, but everybody knew he wondered why me and Red lived when everybody else was killed. The fact is we was both left for dead ... me because I looked dead. John Red was just good at playin' possum. Most scouts are good at tricks like that. Why, Red tells me it's kept him alive more than once. Anyhow, the general, he wasn't listenin' to anything we had to say, and I reckon he made a decision then to get shut of us one way or another when the situation allowed."

Billy was finally beginning to understand what must have happened, when the sergeant became even more animated and confirmed his speculation. "This morning, after survivin' that wild fight along with the boys from Maryland, I got pulled out and sent to see the general one more time.... He had decided that I needed to redeem myself and overcome my failure with the rum ... by babysittin' you!"

CHAPTER 10

Peter Johansen endured all the humiliation he was prepared to accept. He was sick and tired of playing servant to an old black man and a preacher. He'd been pushed around by that fool Tobias who pretended to be somebody special. Peter knew he had more brains than the whole bunch of them. He did most of the work anyway. He saw no future for himself here. Besides, he knew things. He knew secrets that the king's men would like to know. There would be big trouble here. These people were all traitors. He'd seen things they didn't want anyone to see. He'd watched on those dark nights when strangers came and went with no lights shown in wagons carefully kept quiet. He knew the secret about the old cave at the back of the mill. He knew most of it anyway. They kept him out of many things. He knew they didn't trust him. He knew no one liked him. He was attracted to Elizabeth from the first time he saw her, but she never noticed any of the things he did for her. She wouldn't care if the earth opened up and swallowed him. She wouldn't even notice he was gone.

Peter made up his mind today when he saw the militia massacre those poor British soldiers in such a cowardly way from the bushes at the side of the road. He saw them coming across the field behind the mill and considered crying out to the Royal Army captain ... what was his name—Cristus, Cristal, Crispin...? Yes, that was it, Crispin. He could have warned the soldiers. He should have warned them. He was terrified,

66

though. He knew it in his soul. He was a coward today. The shame of letting those poor men die without warning bore down on him like a physical weight. He must do something to redeem himself. It was his personal duty to report what he knew about this place, wasn't it? It was his duty to help Captain Crispin somehow. But how? He would help him escape! That's right. He would help the captain and the wounded sergeant escape from these people. He would tell Crispin everything he knew about this place. He would serve his king in the only way he knew how. This would make things right!

Peter befriended the militiamen who were guarding the outside of the storeroom and makeshift prison. The night turned cold and both men were hungry. It was easy to convince them that he would stand their watch while they went to eat and fetch warmer coats. He assured them that Tobias, the assistant millwright, would be here soon. The two boys would have no trouble securing the mill. After all, this was their home. They laughed together when Peter reminded the two guards about Tobias threatening to brain the British captain with a hammer on the road earlier. He was soon alone in the front room of the mill, but he wasn't sure how long this solitude would last.

Ira had ordered Peter to take two of the best horses and go fetch the doctor from Winnsborough. The two horses were saddled now. He wondered if anyone would notice the absence of a third horse from the stable. Probably not, with all of the confusion. He quietly saddled another horse and led all three of them out to the side of the road near where the disastrous events occurred earlier. Damp blood was mixed with the mud on the road here. The horses flinched away from it as he tied them to the fence rail. He returned to the mill and lit a candle before going to the side storeroom where the prisoners were being held. Peter wasn't worried about anyone seeing him. They were all down at the village and at the Fletcher house. The militiamen were camped down in the woods along the old Camden trail. No one was here right now but him and these poor prisoners. He could help them. He knew he could. He didn't care if old Ezekiel died. They would all hang for treason anyway.

A thought startled Peter and made him pause halfway down the corridor to the storeroom. What about Elizabeth? Would she hang too? He didn't want that to happen. She had treated him with such contempt. But what if he could save her somehow? She would be grateful to him. She would finally notice what he did for her, wouldn't she? No. It was hopeless. She would die of grief if they hung her precious grandpa, even if they pardoned her for being a fool in this nest of traitors. She would have to face justice with the rest of these scum. Lifting his head in self-righteous bravado, he moved down the hall to the storeroom door and fished the keys from his pocket. He didn't know what would happen to him after this. He hoped to be welcomed into the loyalist militia to fight for the king. He would no longer be welcome here, and he didn't care.

Peter heard a low groan from inside as he pushed the door open. He used the candle to cut through the musty darkness and peer into the room. Captain Crispin was asleep on a stack of grain bags. The sergeant was curled into a fetal position on the floor in the opposite corner. A small pool of dried blood was under the side of the sergeant's head. It seemed to have dripped from the edge of a crude bandage covering the man's scalp and frightfully swollen cheek. The sergeant's breath was labored. He groaned quietly as Peter leaned over and gently shook him. There was no other response.

Peter straightened up and looked over at Crispin. It seemed odd that the captain was sound asleep in the most comfortable place the room could provide while this wounded man lay in his own blood on the floor. Peter momentarily hesitated at the realization. But this was the way things were between people of quality and their social inferiors. It was the way things should be. He quietly stepped over to the sleeping captain and reached down to shake him by the shoulder. Crispin stretched slowly, then sat abruptly upright. In a strangled voice, he nearly shouted, "Who … what is going on?"

Peter whispered, "Captain, I'm Peter Johansen. I work here at this mill. I'm a loyal subject of the king. I want to help you."

Peter didn't know why he was whispering. He didn't believe a voice could be heard from outside the mill, and no one else was anywhere near right now. Time was short. The captain swung his legs off the pile of grain sacks and stood up.

"You want to help me ... how?"

Peter spoke more openly. "I want to help you escape, sir!"

Captain Crispin glanced over at the sergeant's prostrate form. "What about good Sergeant Smythe here?"

Peter said, "I have three horses tethered outside at the road, sir."

Crispin looked closely at him and said, "Three horses?"

Peter responded, "Yes, sir. I hoped you would take me with you." The captain said nothing.

Peter said, "Sir, I know things about this place and what has been going on here. I need to report these things to the authorities."

Crispin looked curious. "Things ... what kind of things, boy?"

Peter felt as if he'd been slapped with the use of the term "boy." He stood silent for a few moments. The captain stared at him in the candle-light. The sergeant moaned and slowly turned himself onto his back. He was awake now and looked around the strange candle-lit room with the frightened eye of an injured animal.

Peter could hesitate no longer. He had entered the room in good faith. The door was still standing open. He knew that the captain could overpower him if he tried to leave again without helping the men escape. He began to realize, deep inside, that this was all wrong. These men were not his friends. The people he was going to betray had never harmed him. They were really very kind. He was acting like a "boy" to come here like this. What would a "man" do? It was too late for any of that now. He must do his duty. Loyalty to the king was more important than any sentimental feelings for his "friends." The captain was still staring at him. The sergeant was sitting up now. Peter placed the candle on one of the wall shelves. He saw no friendship or kindness in either of these men's faces. The sergeant's cheek and head were so swollen that it was difficult to see any expression at all. The captain's visage only showed glaring expectant distaste.

Peter lowered his voice again and told these two British soldiers almost all he knew about the events he'd seen at Fletcher's Mill. He didn't tell them everything. For some reason, he only gave vague information about the old cave at the back of the mill and the barrels of powder he knew were stored there. He started to share the rumors about hidden treasure, but suddenly thought better of it. He changed what he was about to say into a derogatory comment about the undeserved Fletcher family wealth and the status of old Ezekiel Miller.

Peter couldn't explain why he hesitated to share the rumors about treasure Benjamin Fletcher left to his son Ira. Local legend held that old Ben kept most of his astounding wealth in the form of gold and silver coins. These were supposedly locked in wooden boxes and buried in a little known shaft far deeper than the expanded portion of the cave behind the mill. Peter hadn't seen any treasure. He hadn't seen any sign of deeper tunnels or caverns under the cave behind the mill. He was in the deepest known part of the cave only once, and that was a long time ago. He believed the legend, though. The Fletchers were so rich. They owned everything for miles around.

Peter didn't understand that material wealth could be held in many forms other than gold or silver. None of that was important right now anyway. These men were only interested in the powder, shot, and military stores. He would stick to that and leave the other secrets alone for now. He told them about the mysterious visits late at night and the strange armed men who came and went while Ira Fletcher wasn't here. He told about old Ezekiel making him and Tobias drive loaded wagons down to the east ford on the Camden Pike and leave them there. They would be sent back the next day to retrieve wagons that were now empty or loaded with different contents. He told them about muffled discussions between groups of strange men coming from inside these very store rooms late at night. He even told them about seeing the militia company approach the mill from across the field today while the British soldiers confronted the angry crowd on the road in front of the building.

Peter finished the rest of the story with the innocence of the young fool that he was. The two men listened without interruption to all of it.

They now glanced at each other before turning their attention back to him. Fear grew in Peter's chest. They were looking at him with a growing malevolence. He shrank back and gasped, "Sir, will you take me with you?" Crispin strode over to him and shoved him against the wall.

Peter was uncontrollably terrified now as the captain snarled, "Why would I take a miserable little rodent like you with me? You clearly knew about this treason for some time yet you haven't bothered to report it before now? What about my men? Why didn't you give warning to them before they were murdered today? Did I hear you right? You knew of the rebel approach and you did nothing to help us?"

The captain grabbed the front of Peter's shirt and held him against the wall with surprising strength. He began to slap Peter on the side of the face as he asked these questions in quick succession. Peter tried to pull his forearms up to protect his face. He whimpered, "Please, sir … please … please … don't!" Crispin perceived the uplifted arms to be some kind of assault against his person. He reacted by punching Peter in the face. The boy's body went limp. Crispin threw him to the floor and stomped his booted foot against the boy's larynx to stifle any cry the contemptible young whelp might make. Peter died quickly without realizing how much trouble his disloyalty would cause.

Captain Crispin ordered Sergeant Smythe to his feet. He didn't bother to help the injured man. He stepped on Peter's chest as he stretched to blow out the candle before hurrying out of the room. They were mounted on the horses and fleeing northward within minutes. Crispin was determined to reach the remnants of the Royal Army garrisoned in the little village of Rocky Mount. He and the teamsters obtained their dragoon escort at Rocky Mount while passing through the place days earlier. The two escapees were miles from Fletcher's Mill before anyone found Peter Johansen's body in the storeroom.

CHAPTER 11

Lieutenant Billy Morgan reeled from Sergeant Strickland's words. He then looked into Strickland's eyes and understood that no personal insult or animosity was intended. A stillness prevailed as they both considered their circumstances. Billy broke the silence. "Well, Sergeant, I promise not to be a burden to you in any way. I'm just as surprised to be leading this job as you are to have been saddled with it. I can only imagine what you've been through up till now. I make you a solemn promise. I'll do nothing to cause you more grief. I'll listen to your advice and follow your lead with the men whenever possible, and we'll do this together. Besides, you won't have to return to General Morgan's service when we're through with this."

Billy paused a moment. "You know that we're ordered to rejoin General Greene up north when we're finished delivering this material. You have a clean slate with me. I trust your judgement as a soldier. You can't have survived this long without knowing what you're about. I assure you that I don't share the general's ways or manner ... even if my last name is Morgan." He held out his hand offering to shake on the bargain.

Sergeant Strickland hesitated as he looked deeply into Billy's eyes. He finally relaxed and grasped the offered hand. "It's a bargain, sir. And, by the way, I watched you fight this mornin' from over in the middle of the Maryland line. We saw you charge into that bunch of Scotsmen like some kind of wounded lion ... oh, that was somethin'...! I think you and

I might just be able to do 'things,' Lieutenant!" The smile was real. The moment passed quickly, but both men would remember it.

Major Theodore Throckmorton picked this very instant to show up and demand Billy's attention. Strickland saw him first. He was riding on an old haggard-looking horse. The major's nose was elevated. He looked left and right with distaste at all of the still visible scars on the battle-strewn landscape. Throckmorton was accompanied by two plainly dressed men as odd and out of place as himself. One of them was enormously fat and sat astride what appeared to be a draft horse. The other man was trim, well-dressed, and riding an ornately saddled mule. None of the militiamen in the area stood to attention at the major's approach, but many of them did pause in their other activities to stare. This contributed to the petulant look on Throckmorton's face. Sergeant Strickland cleared his throat and nodded toward the visitors. Billy took the hint and turned in time to see the major dismount the poor old horse and hand the reins to one of his minions.

Billy stepped forward to meet the senior officer with a show of tired but undaunted respect. The major paused to look around at the wagons and all of the men now standing expectantly. It was a rare moment in which he was actually the center of attention, and it immediately went to his head. Focusing his attention on Billy, Throckmorton changed his peevish expression to one of self-endowed superiority. He sniffed loudly and stared for another moment. He then used his high-pitched and annoyingly nasal voice to demand, "These wagons will be unloaded immediately, Lieutenant!"

Billy was not sure he understood the order at first, but the words were quite clear. He replied, "I'm sorry, sir. Did you just say that we were to unload these wagons? Why on earth would we do that?"

Throckmorton seemed to swell again like he did earlier in front of the headquarters tent. He raised his voice even higher and shouted, "I demand that these wagons be unloaded immediately! They were not properly requisitioned in the first place, and they have obviously been loaded with contraband!"

Billy couldn't help arguing, "Are you calling these wounded men 'contraband,' Major?" He was wearing a wry smile with this question. His expression launched the unpleasant major into an even deeper foul mood.

"Of course I'm not referring to the men, you young upstart! I'm talking about the confiscated war material in the other three wagons! You had no right to take this property in the first place, and I demand that it be returned to my keeping immediately!"

Billy was growing angry. Sergeant Duncan noticed this and decided to intervene.

Duncan stepped up next to his new lieutenant and interjected, "May I be of service, sir?"

The major looked sharply at him and snapped, "Who are you? I'm speaking with this young upstart thief at present! I'll deal with one scoundrel at a time, thank you!"

Billy felt a flash of heat in his face and a surge of adrenaline in his body. He closed the distance between himself and the major before his mind fully comprehended the implications. He felt himself slapping the man in the face so hard that his hand stung.

Throckmorton took a half step backward and tripped on his own heels. He sprawled ignominiously to the ground with a yelp. The surrounding militiamen looked on in silent shock until someone started to laugh. The two quartermaster helpers stepped threateningly forward, but froze in place when they noticed the rifles now aimed at them. John Red held his tomahawk in his right hand and one of his huge horse pistols in his left. The smile on his face was anything but humorous.

The major rolled over and struggled to a standing position. Billy shouted, "How dare you call me a thief, sir?"

Sergeant Duncan was restraining him, and Strickland stepped forward to block any advance the major might make. Billy shouted again before the major could say anything else. "I demand that you retract your vile words and apologize to my men and me!"

The major's nose was bleeding. He wiped it with the back of his hand. "You'll hang for that, boy! There were many witnesses to what just happened!"

Strickland responded before Billy could speak. "What witnesses, sir? What are you talking about major?"

Throckmorton looked furtively around with the searching eyes of a hungry ferret. "All these men saw what happened, Sergeant!"

Strickland smiled as he too looked around at the other men. The weapons were lowered now. The complacent faces in the surrounding group showed no sign of surprise or recognition that something out of the ordinary had taken place. Red's pistol was back in his belt, and he was now using the tomahawk blade to scrape flakes of mud from the side of his moccasin leggings.

Major Throckmorton drew strength from his two minions standing close by. He hadn't noticed their timid recalculation of the circumstances seconds earlier. The fat one was now brushing debris from the side and back of his master's coat. The major took out a ridiculous laced handkerchief and wiped his nose clean as he said, "I see that you are involved in this piracy also, Strickland. It doesn't surprise me. I will have satisfaction, though. And proper authority will prevail here."

Billy heard this although the major was attempting to speak quietly now. He shouted as he shrugged Duncan away and again surged forward. "You will have 'satisfaction'? It is I who demand satisfaction, sir!" His newly acquired sword was in his hand. The major involuntarily stepped back a pace and tripped over the smaller of his two assistants, nearly falling again. This brought quiet laughter from some of the men, and muted growls from others. Several trigger locks clicked to the fully cocked position. Everyone within fifty yards of the event was now staring in openmouthed expectancy.

Strickland and Duncan changed roles without any obvious communication between them. Duncan stepped up to the major, while Strickland grasped Billy's arm and drew him away to the other side of the wagon. Duncan realized that no good would come of this confrontation. He was determined to bring it to a close as quickly as possible. With the most conciliatory voice he could muster, he entreated the major to ignore the egregious behavior of his hot-headed young officer and allow a more experienced sergeant to be of assistance.

Throckmorton sensed that he might have his way, in this oddly lop-sided situation. He again demanded that the wagons be unloaded. He further insisted that Billy was under arrest and demanded that he receive an armed escort to General Morgan's headquarters with the prisoner disarmed and restrained to prevent any further egregious assault.

Sergeant Duncan asked, "To what purpose, sir?"

Anger flashed in the major's eyes again as he repeated his ridiculous claim that the military supplies were stolen property. Four of the nearby men quietly moved forward to disarm the three visitors after watching their lieutenant strike the senior officer. They were now standing immediately behind the major's party with their own weapons held at the ready.

Duncan became very calm as he excused himself and walked around to Billy and Sergeant Strickland on the other side of the wagon. "Lieutenant Morgan, did the general give you any written orders or instructions?"

Billy said, "Yes," and produced the orders from inside his coat.

Duncan read the orders and the separate letter from General Morgan granting Billy full authority and access pertaining to the delivery of these four wagons and their contents to their intended destination. He looked up at Billy and very quietly said, "Sir, please let me handle this with the major. I don't want to see such a promising young officer's career cut short by either a dueling pistol or a hangman's noose."

Billy nodded. He was exhausted, and still far too angry in this moment.

Sergeant Duncan stepped back around the wagon to where Major Throckmorton still waited in quiet but animated conversation with his two companions. The talk ceased as the sergeant approached. The helpers moved back as Duncan began to speak.

"Major, I deeply regret the unfortunate events that happened here, but I'm afraid you misunderstood the circumstances."

Throckmorton gasped, "Whatever are you talking about, Sergeant? You saw that man strike me in front of these witnesses!"

Sergeant Duncan retained his calm demeanor. "Sir, do you insist on that version of events even though none of these men will agree with you?"

The major stamped his foot at that and shouted, "Yes I do! You will carry out my orders immediately!"

Duncan shrugged his shoulders in apparent resignation and said, "Then I will escort you both to General Morgan, fully armed. We will take your men with us. The escorting soldiers will be taken from among these present 'witnesses' as you call them. When we get to the general, I will report that you came here in direct disobedience to his oral and written orders and attempted to provoke mutiny among these chosen men. I will further report that you insulted his nephew, Lieutenant Morgan, in a cowardly fashion and attempted to 'arrest' him with the help of these two civilians as he executed his oral and written orders." He gestured toward the two men who now wore looks of genuine fright. The major didn't say anything, but his mouth kept opening and closing and his face was bright red.

Duncan continued, "Major, I know you haven't spent much time with General Morgan. You were General Gates' quartermaster, right?" Throckmorton was unable to speak. Duncan said, "You see, sir, General Morgan has his own history with officers like you provoking their juniors to the point of striking them, and then arresting them for their troubles. You probably haven't heard the story of the 499 lashes, and how the general says the British still owe him the last of the 500 they had sentenced him to. The odd thing is the way history seems to repeat itself. That event happened when the general was so young, not much older than his nephew is now, and it also happened in an argument over wagons...."

Major Throckmorton knew the legend. He had been around General Morgan long enough to believe the stories were probably true. He suddenly felt a change of heart. To save what little face he still possessed, he asked, "What written orders are you referring to, Sergeant?"

Duncan unfolded the orders given to Billy by General Morgan. He allowed the major to read the document, then took it back before producing the separate authorization letter. This paper, signed by General Morgan, gave the lieutenant almost absolute authority regarding these wagons, their contents, and any continental or militia troops involved in their safety and transport. Major Throckmorton shook slightly as he handed the letter back. He then spun on his heel and stomped away to retrieve his old horse. His helpers stared at Duncan momentarily before they too went back to their peculiar-looking mounts. The three men rode quietly away without another word.

Sergeant Duncan explained to Billy and Strickland what happened in the quiet conversation. He assured Billy that he didn't believe anything further would be heard from Major Throckmorton. Billy wasn't so certain. There was a lot of work to do yet, and they needed to get started on their trek toward Fletcher's Mill as soon as possible. The men around him continued to treat him with a deference that he felt was undeserved. He didn't realize that new legends were forming about the hot-headed fighting antics of another man with the last name Morgan.

CHAPTER 12

Morning came slowly for the tense frightened villagers of Fletcher's Mill. Sleep had eluded most of them. The apothecary decided the only way to save Robert Griffin was to amputate his leg. This was done in the early hours before dawn without the use of any kind of sedative other than locally distilled corn liquor. The patient mercifully passed out before the operation was completed, and the stump was cleaned as much as possible using the same corn liquor. The apothecary managed to sew a long flap of skin over the end of the stump in what looked to him to be a fairly neat piece of work. The leg was now bandaged as well as could be managed. No one believed Griffin had any real chance of survival unless God intervened. The apothecary and his wife were with Mrs. Griffin and young Tobias now. They were all deeply engaged in prayer to this end.

The body of Peter Johansen was found inside the mill storage room by the militiamen when they returned to their duty. The alarm was immediate. Fear spread quickly and seemed to be well founded. It didn't take anyone long to realize that everyone in the village was now in even deeper and more immediate danger. They all knew that Crispin would most likely flee to the nearest British army unit, probably at Camden, Winnsborough, or Ft. Granby. He didn't even need to travel that far to alert their enemies regarding the recent happenings in this otherwise out-of-the-way village.

Captain Robertson immediately dispatched four of his men on borrowed horses to track the escapees and try to apprehend them before they could reach the help of any area loyalists or the Royal Army. The Johansen boy was buried in a field near the village next to the dragoons killed the day before. It was thought wise not to inter these men in the small village cemetery near the edge of town. A brief ceremony was conducted by Ira Fletcher over the graves. As soon as this was done, Captain Robertson drew Ira off for a quiet, but intense, conversation regarding the immediate future of Fletcher's Mill and the people of the village.

Both men were more troubled now than they had been the night before, and for very good reason. Their earlier concern was that the teamsters who escaped the scene of the confrontation at the mill would go to the British forces with a wild tale about an incident at the mill. These men fled before the worst of the events had taken place, though. It seemed likely that the official military reaction would be slow and measured in this case. Now two soldiers would be making the report. One of them was an officer. The other was a wounded sergeant.

These men would report that several heavily armed dragoons were killed by a sizeable militia force immediately in front of Fletcher's Mill while they were reacting to the uprising of local villagers. Any responsible military authority would immediately decide that there was no alternative to decisive military action. The tenuous hold the Crown held over the loyalists in the area demanded it. Political considerations aside, Captain Crispin was a Royal Army quartermaster. He had seen a wealth of food supplies in the mill that could not be ignored by an army forced to forage for everything.

Captain Robertson discussed all of this and more with Ira that morning. Ira's only question remained: what could they do? His personal fortune, thousands of acres, his home, the mill, all of it would now be forfeit to the Crown. There was nothing he could do about that. Crispin seemed like the type of man who would say or do anything to further his own ends. The man was frightened and humiliated yesterday in the road. He had seen and spoken directly with Ira at the scene of the small, startling, pitched battle.

Ira also reflected on the way the Johansen boy died. His larynx was crushed and his neck was broken. There were marks on the sides of the boy's face that indicated he was beaten before he was thrown to the floor. A closer look at the boy's neck showed that the final blow was delivered with a booted foot. Ira didn't doubt that this was the work of Captain Crispin. The sergeant was severely injured with a broken cheek bone. His face was so swollen that he would only have been able to see with one eye. What kind of man would kill a young boy like this? Rumors abounded lately about British cavalry killing captured militia soldiers in cruel and inhumane ways ... something called "Tarleton's Quarter."

Both Ira and Robertson understood that Peter had helped the two prisoners escape. Why would they kill him, though? Ira decided that it was simply a case of wanton cruelty. Robertson reflected that the boy must have told Crispin everything he knew about the rebel activities in and around Fletcher's Mill. The British would have multiple reasons to send a large force here as soon as possible to destroy this place and seize any useful materials they found. Ira knew he still had many enemies in the area who would be more than happy to see his demise and the destruction or seizure of his local properties. He thought of Elizabeth and her safety. He considered Ezekiel who was upstairs being cared for by Mona Partridge. He also couldn't help thinking about Mona's welfare. She had been a close family friend for many years. He considered her as a sister when she became so close to Mary. Since Mary's death, Mona slowly began to take a different place in his thoughts.

Captain Robertson recommended that all of the villagers be evacuated. Ira agreed, but there was no logical place for them to go in the middle of winter. Several families had relatives in the countryside. Many of the women and children could go to those homes. There was a danger from Tory militias taking advantage of the displaced villagers. They could cause havoc if they learned about what happened here. Ira gathered the village elders to let them decide what to do with their families and their personal property. Frantic preparation for flight began immediately after this meeting. Furniture and other belongings were loaded onto wagons and other conveyances. Women and children were burdened with clothing and small items as well. Most of the oldest men departed with the women and children to find temporary shelter for their families as far away from Fletcher's Mill as they could practically travel. The young men decided to stay behind and work together to protect their homes from whatever threat they faced.

Captain Robertson organized these young men into his militia company, pairing them with more experienced militiamen. Most of the villagers possessed weapons of one sort or another. Only a fool would live on the frontier without a useable firearm. Some of the men even had militia training from earlier conflicts. When Robertson paraded all of them on the green in the village square, he found that he now had fifty-two armed men at his disposal. He assigned his sergeants and experienced privates to do what they could to organize the men as effectively as possible in the short time available. He and Ira then spent several hours studying the lay of the land and the possibility of actually defending this place against a concerted military assault.

The mill itself was the highest building in or around the village. It was built into the face of the bluff overlooking the creek valley at a place where the creek turned sharply and dropped precipitously over thirty feet. The bluff turned with the changing course of the creek. It actually formed the upper creek bank, and seemed to get taller by staying at roughly the same level while the creek fell away across its front. This odd geologic development undoubtedly contributed to Benjamin Fletcher's decision to build the mill where it now stood. The creek was diverted to an artificial mill pond dug on the small flat plain above the bluff. Ira remembered the endless hours of digging and hauling dirt and rock in a barrow so many years ago when his father and Zeke were young men and he was just a teen. They used powder charges to blast great rocks into smaller ones, but these still had to be removed one at a time.

They also used explosives to enlarge the small cave in the face of the bluff. The mill structure had been built over this natural stone fortress. The creek was channeled to where it spilled into and down a new route where it would fill the mill wheel and cause the wheel to turn with great strength through the weight of the water. The amount of water involved could be controlled by opening or closing small gates erected at the edge of the mill pond. Water was always moving here, but the millwright could control whether or not the wheel turned by opening or closing these gates to send water to the wheel or to send it around where it would cascade down a narrow gorge in the side of the bluff much as it had done for untold centuries.

Captain Robertson now concluded that the most defensible place in the area was the mill itself. It would be difficult, but not impossible, to assault from the direction of the village even if proper fortifications were added. The bluff provided natural protection on each flank. The area above the bluff was guarded by the deep mill pond and the dense woods surrounding it. Robertson looked closer at the top of the building on the pond side. The Fletchers built this side with a high stout stone and earth levy to protect the mill from potential flooding caused by torrential rains. The building would be even easier to defend from this direction because of these natural and manmade features. This led him to believe that the most likely avenue of enemy attack would be from the direction of the village. Yes. That made perfect sense. They would attack and sack the village first. They would use the village and probably the Fletcher house as a base from which to launch their final attack on the mill. Ira agreed.

Robertson devised a plan to dig trenches and build other fortifications at key locations in and around the village. The trenches were dug along the high ground just below the mill and the Fletcher house. Fascines were constructed across the road and open areas using rows of sharpened stakes driven into the ground at angles with the points elevated to slow a mounted attack. Several men were put to work cutting and assembling traps of three stout sticks each about two feet long. The sticks were pointed and very sharp on both ends. They were tied together in the middle and splayed out to resemble three dimensional crosses. Hundreds of these were scattered in the deep grass and underbrush in the woods surrounding the mill pond.

These and many other preparations were made by the men who

decided to stay and defend this place. Captain Robertson watched the activity alongside Ira Fletcher who looked on with a stoic calm that belied the turmoil inside him. Ira silently prayed for these men along with the mill, the village, his home, and his family. He desperately hoped this young militia captain was correct. Surely there was a realistic hope for victory here. His mind returned to the night his wife and son were killed. The burning aftermath of that attack was horrible. He shuddered involuntarily. That incident involved only a small group of mounted attackers. What would happen if a large military force attacked this place?

Mona and Elizabeth refused to leave earlier in the company of the other village women and children. Ira wondered if he could force them to leave even now. Robertson slowly turned to him at that moment and looked directly into his eyes. "Sir, I believe you and I must now consider one of the most important features of our defense."

The captain had his full attention. Ira looked at him quizzically. "What would that be, young man?"

Robertson leaned a little closer and said with a quiet steady voice, "We need to identify a covered avenue of escape for the survivors should our defenses fail."

CHAPTER 13

Captain Crispin and Sergeant Smythe moved swiftly all night. They pushed their stolen horses harder than they dared as they fought their way through the forest and undergrowth. They tried to stay close to the Broad River, and often found themselves riding through the mud, muck, and brush near the bank. They were headed back to Rocky Mount. Crispin knew nothing of the fortifications at Winnsborough. Sergeant Smythe and the now dead dragoon escort were part of the cavalry detachment at Rocky Mount. Crispin passed through there on his way to investigate available provisions at Fletcher's Mill with his small foraging party. Only token acknowledgement was given to the major commanding these troops when he demanded the escort that day. He had been anxious to learn what was true about Fletcher's Mill. There was no time for military courtesy.

Crispin suspected they were being followed. He knew they would receive no mercy from the rebels if they were caught. He really hadn't meant to kill that boy in the mill. His temper just got the best of him. All of the men of his borrowed escort were now dead except the sergeant here. He looked sidelong at Smythe. The man could barely stay in the saddle. What would Lord Cornwallis say when he learned that Crispin had been overpowered by these rag-clad animals on a simple foraging mission? He had lost six good men and their horses. He was returning empty-handed with his tail between his legs as it were. The humiliation

85

was only overpowered by the stark terror he still felt considering that he might have been killed with his escort. Were the rebels pursuing them?

Crispin started to say something to Smythe but changed his mind. The horses were now struggling up the riverbank headed for an open meadow. He intended to stay in the tree line and skirt the meadow still heading roughly north. Crispin's pocket still held a borrowed compass. He was surprised at that. The rebels hadn't stolen any of his personal belongings other than his pistols and sword.

They broke through the brush above the riverbank and found a road on the other side next to the meadow. It seemed to head roughly north and south. Crispin was almost sure this was the main road connecting Fletcher's Mill to Rocky Mount. He was fairly certain that he recognized the area now, having traveled this same road headed south. He turned to confer with Sergeant Smythe just in time to watch the other man slowly roll out of his saddle. The sergeant fell to the ground hard, with one foot still in the stirrup. The horse moved forward, dragging Smythe several yards before coming to a stop in a lather of foaming sweat. Crispin prodded his own exhausted animal over to tower above the fallen sergeant.

Captain Crispin looked anxiously around, then shouted for the sergeant to get a grip on himself and remount or get left behind. Smythe didn't respond. Crispin couldn't tell if the man was even breathing. He had no intention of exerting the effort needed to find out. He finally used a stick found nearby to prod the man in the ribs and then pry his twisted foot out of the saddle stirrup. This was all done without dismounting. With little more than a frustrated smirk, Crispin grabbed the reins of the other horse and turned to kick both animals into cantering motion up the road headed north. No further thought was given to the severely wounded but still very much alive Sergeant Rufus Smythe.

Crispin continued to spur and whip the poor animals until he finally, and quite literally, rode the first horse to death. That was the only point where he actually paused for more than an hour in his headlong flight to avoid recapture. His horse suddenly collapsed in much the same way Smythe had. The animal was cantering along on the road near the river.

The next moment, its legs just folded up underneath it. He was thrown over the animal's worthless head to land on his face, and lay there gasping in fright and exhaustion.

The horse Sergeant Smythe had been riding was better rested because it hadn't been carrying as much weight since the sergeant was left behind. Crispin still held the reins of both horses in his hands as he struggled to his feet. He kicked the animal he had been riding in the side of the head in a childish fit of rage. He imagined a look of pitiful contempt in the animal's dying eye as it slumped over and breathed its last. Even in his panic-driven state, he realized that he must care for the remaining animal or end up walking.

Crispin abandoned the dead horse without bothering to remove the saddle or bridle. He dragged the other horse back to the river where both he and it drank deeply. He allowed it to eat from the tall grass along the bank before he pulled and prodded it into a deep thicket part way up the side of a large hill along his intended route. Crispin tied the horse to a branch with enough loose reins to allow it access to more grass. Then he crawled up under the cover of the low hanging thorny branches and passed out.

Captain Crispin didn't know how long he slept. It was quite dark when he awoke. His body was shaking spasmodically and uncontrollably. He was soaking wet and terribly cold. He tried to stand, unaware of his surroundings. One of the thorn branches tore a gash into his neck before catching in the collar of his shirt. He struggled to free himself and ended up ripping part of the shoulder from his uniform coat. Crouching lower now, he used his handkerchief to slow the bleeding from the gash on his neck and then tied the cloth in place with no real hope of making the blood flow stop. It took several minutes to get his bearings and work his way out of the thicket to the place where the miserable horse was still tied. Staying in this place was out of the question. He was desperate to make his escape, and movement was the only thing that seemed to offer any hope of warmth. He decided to press on and led the animal back out toward the road by moving away from the sound of the flowing river.

The carcass of the dead horse caused the living one to rebel as they neared the roadbed. Crispin dragged it along by the reins until they were several yards further along the road before he attempted to mount. The horse shied away from him and kicked him in the right thigh. His leg folded in terrific pain and he stumbled to the ground still clutching the reins. A scream came involuntarily from his lungs and further frightened the horse which continued to kick and fight him for its freedom. He yanked himself upright using the reins for support and dragging the horse's head downward in the process. The animal turned and tried to kick him again before twisting its head around and biting him on the arm. He finally let go of the reins this time, and the horse used one more tremendous effort to kick him with its rear hooves before darting off in the darkness, never to be seen by him again. Crispin collapsed to his knees and then fell into a fetal position in the pitch-dark center of the lonely mud road in this horrible foreign wilderness. He lay there weeping for what seemed like hours.

Crispin slowly began to realize that he would die right here if he allowed himself to give up completely. That he would not do. There was a score to settle with the rebels at Fletcher's Mill. He remembered the rumors heard about the wealth of the place in food stores and useable supplies. He also remembered the other rumor of gold stored there. He had seen just enough of the inside of the mill to verify the existence of food and other valuable property. That fool boy in the mill verified at least part of the other tale. There was indeed a cave under or behind the mill itself. The weeping stopped, but he was still shaking uncontrollably as he struggled to his feet.

The dim gray light of dawn started to make the roadbed visible. He looked back toward the dead horse. The animal was still saddled and looked ridiculous lying there. He stumbled back down the road to it and struggled for several minutes before he was able to work the sodden blanket from under the saddle. Wrapping the blanket around his shoulders, he turned and started hobbling northward along the road with the sound of the river to his left side to verify that he was headed in the right direction.

Crispin stumbled along this way without stopping and without seeing anyone along the road, either friend or enemy. Hours passed as he continued to drive himself northward toward Rocky Mount and the safety he knew awaited him there. He would find help. He would return to that place! He would have revenge for the loss of those soldiers and his dignity. He would search out any hidden treasure in or under that miserable mill. He would laugh as it and the whole village were burned to the ground. He would then force those despicable villagers to watch as their precious Reverend Fletcher was shackled and whipped before being escorted back along this same road to face the king's justice.

It took another three days to reach Rocky Mount. By the time he arrived, Reginald Crispin was hardly recognizable as the well-dressed Royal Army quartermaster officer who was here less than a week before. Making contact with one of the picket guards at the edge of town was a close run thing. At first he was mistaken for one of the rebels and was nearly shot before the picket recognized the ragged remains of a captain's uniform coat in the dim evening light. He did not know the correct response to the challenge. In fact, he was almost incoherent as he pleaded with the sergeant of the guard to be taken to see the commander immediately.

Major Sir Thomas Willoughby was a career officer who rose through the ranks of the Royal Army through hard work, courage, and an uncompromised reputation for impeccable character. He commanded the cavalry regiment at Rocky Mount. He was the most senior officer present when Captain Crispin was brought in. Willoughby showed genuine concern when he saw Crispin's condition, and imagined that he had been the victim of an ambush on the part of Frances Marion or others like him. Captain Crispin was cared for by the regimental surgeon. He was fed and given clean clothing by the major's own servant.

Crispin slept like one in a coma for over fourteen hours before finally rousing himself to again demand the attention of the commander. Major Willoughby began to suspect Crispin's personal honor a few short minutes into the interview. Five minutes later, he was convinced that Crispin was a charlatan and a coward. The captain gave an animated and embellished account of what happened at Fletcher's Mill. He then attempted to talk the major into dispatching a large contingent of cavalry to go back there with him and exact revenge on the rebels he insisted were using the place as a fortress.

The major had met Reverend Ira Fletcher on more than one occasion. He knew that the reverend was a close friend of Dr. William Bull who was the acting royal governor of this colony in the absence of Lord Montagu before he was replaced by that fool Lord Campbell who only lasted a few months. Campbell had turned coward and escaped to save his own skin. Dr. Bull was now considered by many in the British military establishment to still be the rightful governor since the post was abandoned by Campbell. His association with Dr. Bull made Reverend Fletcher's reputation unquestionable in the minds of many senior Royal Army leaders

Major Willoughby was a professional officer. He recognized Crispin's type. He had served with and beneath officers like this many times in his long career. Willoughby knew Sergeant Smythe. They had served together for years. The major had spoken with Smythe briefly before detailing him to escort Captain Crispin days earlier. Smythe was also a professional soldier and a wise judge of character. He hadn't said anything negative about the young captain. There was something about the sergeant's demeanor that made Willoughby believe Smythe felt little reason to respect this young man.

Major Willoughby now thought he understood what really happened at Fletcher's Mill. The realization was revolting. His dislike for the captain was almost as palpable as it was immediate. He pragmatically realized that Crispin was not a professional officer and therefore couldn't be expected to behave professionally. However, this lying fool had somehow managed to lose Sergeant Smythe, several fine cavalry troopers, and all of their valuable mounts in such a short time with nothing to show for the investment. He understood that he would probably never know everything about the incident. Willoughby was certain that Crispin was lying to him, though. He would never dispatch more valuable troops on some fool errand with this man who had already shown his incompetence and probable cowardice in the face of the enemy.

Major Willoughby stood up and stared at Captain Crispin. "I will send you from here, Captain, with an appropriate escort…" Crispin bristled momentarily at the term "appropriate escort." Willoughby continued, "… north to Charlotte where you will report to General Lord Cornwallis. I will give you written orders to this effect, Captain." He said this last part in reaction to the look on Crispin's face. He continued, "Captain Crispin, you should know that Reverend Ira Fletcher is a close and loyal personal friend of the royal governor of this colony. Your attempted infringement on this man's property will not be looked on with favor. Had I known this was what you were about when you passed through here in such a brazen manner a week ago, I would have stopped you then. I have no doubt that you have encountered rebel forces in your misguided endeavors, but please don't try to besmirch the character and reputation of the honorable Mr. Fletcher to protect your own reputation."

Crispin was astounded. He couldn't speak. His face was brick-red and his jaw hung slack. This appeared to be a sign of embarrassment to the major and it reinforced his already low impression of the captain. Major Willoughby held up his hand and demanded silence when Crispin finally regained the ability to speak. "Captain Crispin, from this moment, you may consider yourself under arrest. You will compose a written report which will be duplicated by my adjutant. One copy will stay here with me. The other copy will be sealed along with my personal report to General Cornwallis regarding your recent behavior and questionable military usefulness.

"You will remain here under close arrest until we have occasion to send a sizeable detachment to the headquarters in Charlotte. You will be secured in one of our storerooms. You would do well not to attempt an escape from this one, Captain. We don't have a stockade here, and I will not put an officer, even one like you, in the public jail. The sealed packet will be carried by one of my junior lieutenants who will escort you with this future detachment to the careful attention of the general and his staff.

I have no doubt that you will probably survive a court martial. Men like you often do somehow. You will have your written report ready for my adjutant within the hour. You will remain a prisoner of my lieutenant until you reach the headquarters in Charlotte. I will give him my personal direct order to shoot you if you attempt to escape.

"I would further add that I do not like you, Captain, but that would not be completely accurate. The fact is that I don't really know you. But I don't like officers like you. You do not display the honorable qualities of a king's officer and you are, in fact, not a soldier at all. The good men who died this week due to your incompetence deserved a far better fate. You will be kept out of my sight until you leave this place. If you do somehow survive court martial, please avoid any future social contact with me as you make me physically sick. You are dismissed, sir."

Crispin stood at attention and stared at the major openmouthed. He didn't know what to say. There was nothing he could say in any event. This real soldier had seen through him like he was looking at a detailed painting through a glass. He felt like raging and crying at the same time. When he actually began to tremble with tears running down his face, Willoughby shouted for someone to come in and remove him from the makeshift office. A young lieutenant, who identified himself as the regimental adjutant, stepped into the room and pulled at Crispin's sleeve until he was turned around facing the door. The lieutenant said, "This way, sir," and half-dragged him out of the room.

CHAPTER 14

Ira was taken aback by Captain Robertson's statement. His fear turned quickly to frustration and then to outright anger. He snapped, "What are you saying, sir? I thought you were confident that this place could be defended!"

Robertson didn't expect this reaction, but he was learning that Ira's fiery reputation was well deserved. He stepped back a pace and replied, "I do believe we can mount an effective defense here, but we have no real idea what size force might attack. Only a fool would try to defend a fixed position against a determined enemy with no hope of help or relief and no means of escape if the worst were to happen."

The anger subsided as quickly as it had flared. Ira shook his head. "Of course you are correct, Captain. I humbly apologize for my reaction."

Robertson smiled and said, "No apology is necessary, Reverend Fletcher. We are all under great stress here. I didn't intend to erode your confidence in our efforts. I'm thinking mainly of the two ladies, sir."

Ira said, "So was I, Captain … so was I." They were in this together now.

Ira felt confidence in this young militiaman that he couldn't fully explain. He knew very little about the man. It was clear that all the militia company trusted him completely and would gladly obey any command he gave at a moment's notice. That wasn't it, though. There was something else. Robertson exuded an air of dependability. Maybe it was the fact that he never seemed to lose his composure whatever the situation. Or maybe

93

it was the way he insisted on making eye contact when he spoke with you. Ira liked this young man whatever it was. He would like to think that Isaiah would have behaved the same way had he lived. That thought brought a renewed agony. He pushed it away and turned to walk slowly toward the mill.

Robertson went with him. They soon reached the area where the road passed in front of the main mill house. The mill entrance was accessed from the road via a large stone slab or step. You could hear the water from the creek running under the slab when you stood still here. It flowed out from the catch pool under the wheel and was redirected to run downhill in the deep manmade channel along this side of the road. The water traveled this way a hundred yards to where it passed back under the little stone bridge and rejoined the original creek bed to flow on into the valley.

Robertson asked, "Why did the water have to be diverted to the pond on top of the precipice here, sir? Wouldn't the force of the water flowing down the original falls have been strong enough to turn the wheel from the bottom?"

Ira was surprised at the question, but it distracted him from the dark mood he found himself falling into. He thought for a moment and then explained, "A long time ago, mill wheels were turned that way, but someone finally discovered a more efficient use of the water's weight."

This launched Ira into a detailed tour and explanation of the mill and its mechanical genius. He pointed out the way the water was diverted in the first place and showed Robertson the ingenious design of the various channels, gates, and stone water ducts that were used to harness the power of the swiftly moving little creek. He finished with, "You see, sir, the water is directed to the top of the wheel to push downward by filling the collection troughs which are open at the top when they are at this position in the wheel rotation. The very weight of the water provides all of the thrust to turn the wheel. The full trough empties as it reaches the bottom of the rotation so that the back of the wheel is lightened and the wheel continues to turn. This will happen until the flow of water is interrupted by closing the gate at the top and opening the gate on the side to vent the excess water from the pond."

Robertson thought a moment. "What if both gates remain closed? Does the water simply spill over the top and flood the mill?"

Ira smiled and said, "Yes, it does spill out of the pond, but it doesn't flood the mill." He walked up the external stairs to the top of the bluff and pointed to the high levy that protected the top and back of the building. He then pointed to four points at the edge of the mill pond where there seemed to be a low spot or notch in the embankment. Robertson hadn't noticed these before. Ira explained, "We would never intentionally close both of the sluice gates at the same time, but we do have to contend with flooding during times of very heavy rain. In fact, this very thing happened only a few days ago. The water can only rise to the point where it empties via those permanent vents. Should so much water deluge this place, the levy protects the building from flooding." It was clear that Ira took great pride in this place.

Captain Robertson took it all in with a sweeping gaze. With a sudden look of alarm, he turned to Ira. "What if someone managed to block the new channel above the mill and redirect the water to its original course while these upper control gates were open?"

Ira fought down a flash of annoyance and responded, "We would see the road flooded and close the upper gates to prevent the loss of water to the pond before going to repair the damage caused by the vandals!"

Robertson said, "But what if you couldn't reach the gates or the point of redirection because both places were under fire?"

Ira suddenly realized what he was implying. "The pond would drain, and it would cease to be an obstacle for anyone attempting to approach the mill from that direction!"

The captain stepped over to look across the pond with renewed interest. "You helped dig this pond, this 'basin' all those years ago? What is the bottom like?"

Ira thought for a moment and replied, "It isn't consistent or level, but we dug and blasted down to solid rock. It took weeks to dig out most of the dirt and clay. It was actually made somewhat easier by the original shape of the ground right here. Water tended to collect here on very rainy days even before this work was done. This was one of the features, along with the shape of the lower bluff, that my father was attracted to when we found this place."

The captain excused himself to go and get one of his sergeants from a working party below. Ira realized that this was one of Robertson's many strengths. He seemed to possess the ability to visualize a problem before it presented itself and then explain a remedy to someone else in fewer words than seemed possible. The idea of the mill pond acting like some kind of protective moat was abandoned. Men were soon very busy fortifying this side of the mill while others continued with the work below.

Ira and the captain continued to tour the mill and its environs until the discussion returned to the possible need for an avenue of escape. They finally arrived at the conclusion that the only viable route, should the worst happen, would be uphill in the creek bed above the mill pond itself. The natural shape of the hillside deepened here into a fairly long draw or shallow gorge that would allow people on foot to pass more quickly because they wouldn't be hindered by the thick undergrowth and trees on the hillside itself. Horses would be useless here. The creek became a series of small cascades over a multitude of large rocks and small boulders. This continued up the hillside several hundred yards. A person could easily climb out of the creek from there and escape through sparser trees farther along the side of this series of rolling hills. Robertson was confident that a large group could elude capture in this area by splitting up into smaller parties and scattering through the woods and hills beyond.

Ira was revolted at having come to this point in his life. The realization that he was losing everything he and his father worked so hard to establish returned to him now with a vengeance. The anger and frustration over this debacle began to rage inside him again. He was certain that all of his landholdings would be forfeit to the Crown. No matter what friends he had in court, there was no way he could explain his presence at the scene of a battle that took the lives of six Royal Army cavalrymen.

Ira started back down the hill toward his house. He walked away from Captain Robertson without explanation. It occurred to him that he would have to beg the man's pardon later. He had no intention of climbing back up the hill to do it now. His age was no excuse for rudeness, but he was just too exhausted to retrace his route. He climbed the steps of his front porch and noticed that Mona was sitting in one of the two large maple rocking chairs. She was covered with a blanket. Her latest knitting project was in her lap. She was sound asleep with a serene look on her face that seemed totally out of place under the circumstances.

Ira tried to walk quietly past the pristine sleeping figure without disturbing her, but one of the porch boards creaked. This betrayed his presence. Mona sat up and stretched before calling his name softly. The day was far gone, and the shadows were growing longer although the clouds had finally begun to dissipate in the cold winter sky. Ira said, "Excuse me, Miss Partridge, I didn't mean to wake you."

Mona said, "Oh, no matter, I wasn't sleeping deeply anyway. It has turned colder since I came out here, and I believe it is nearly time for me to relieve Elizabeth with Zeke."

She was standing now. Ira offered his arm before opening the front door for her. He noticed there was no fire burning on the grate as they entered. There were still small scraps of cloth strewn all over the room, and he finally thought to inquire openly about them. Mona explained, "Elizabeth has taken a notion to make a quilt for her hope chest, Ira. She isn't a little girl anymore. She is growing into a beautiful young lady."

Ira looked sidelong at her as he replied softly, "It would seem that I'm learning a great many new things today, although not all of them are pleasant." He stepped forward to rekindle a fire in the fireplace as Mona sat her blanket and knitting down and began picking up the cloth scraps.

Ira and Mona were seated in front of a roaring fire before long. It was almost dark outside. They sat in thoughtful silence for several minutes until Ira finally steeled himself to turn and look at Mona. She sensed his gaze and turned to face him with the weary hint of a warm smile. Ira took a breath and dove quietly into a subject of conversation that he instinctively resisted, and yet at the same time somehow needed. "Miss Partridge?"

"Yes?" she replied.

He took another quick breath before continuing with, "Would you mind terribly ... if I called you Mona?"

Mona turned her head away as she replied, "No. I wouldn't mind that, Ira," while her smile deepened significantly.

CHAPTER 15

Lieutenant Colonel Banastre Tarleton was still seething. He knew the disaster had happened. He was there. He just couldn't bring himself to grasp the details of the tragedy. How could he? How could he possibly have been beaten by that ragtag mob? There was a chance to snatch victory at the last moment, but his own troops, his 'legion,' failed him. He tried to imagine what Cornwallis would say about this debacle. Over eight hundred men were lost! He believed his career was over. How could those cowardly fools have simply surrendered like that? His own men fled the scene, though, and he ran with them.

Several members of the legion were now gone. Some of his men chose to fight rather than skulk in the trees waiting for the regulars to do the dirty work. All of his officers had survived. He ordered one legion troop to act as rear guard and fight off the still pursuing Yankee cavalry. He and the rest of the survivors withdrew far enough to turn and make a stand two miles away from the battlefield. He ordered these same men to go back to Cowpens and keep watch on the rebels to see what they did next after the pursuit was abandoned. It was the only way to maintain contact with the enemy now.

Minutes crawled slowly into hours. The night passed fitfully. He continued to receive courier reports about rebel activities. It didn't seem like Morgan was in a hurry to leave the place. Maybe he really was incompetent and the battle outcome was some kind of freakish accident. The rebels did have a huge number of prisoners and great deal of captured military equipment to deal with now. He was such a fool. Tarleton felt an agony deep in his soul that couldn't be set aside. He truly believed his subordinate commanders had failed him. However, he was the one who sent them into the battle as they became available. That was his fault alone. He should have waited for all of them to attack at once. He should have…. He could have…. He hadn't…. It was the most humiliating day of his life. He failed Cornwallis. He failed the king. He knew his own stubborn pride was the real source of this defeat.

Tarleton didn't sleep at all during the night. He was seated on a fallen log with his horse's reins in his hand and his face buried in his palms. He heard the courier march up and stand at rigid attention three paces away, but didn't look up. The man had the insufferable effrontery to say, "Excuse me, sir. I have an urgent message for you from Lieutenant Cloyde."

Tarleton finally raised his head. "What is it now…?"

The courier straightened his shoulders slightly and looked into the middle distance as he recited the message carefully from his officer. "Lieutenant Cloyde's respects, sir. The rebels are massing at the north end of the battlefield and forming the captives into columns guarded on both flanks. Their tents have been struck, and they look like they are preparing to move further west along the southern bank of the river. They are pushing what appears to be a substantial cavalry screen in our direction, but the main body seems prepared to move the other way. Lieutenant Cloyde wishes to know whether he should follow them as they leave."

The courier stopped speaking for a moment, then continued as though he had forgotten this last part until now. "Lieutenant Cloyde also wishes to inform the colonel that the rebels appear to be collecting a small caravan of four wagons at the south end of the meadow. They are loading them with equipment and wounded men. It appears that they are organizing a small escort of about twenty dismounted infantry along with these wagons. The only horses present are those hitched to the wagons. He believes these men may be part of the larger baggage train, but he doesn't understand why they are separate from the other wagons and pack animals."

Colonel Tarleton was on his feet now. He asked the courier what kind of equipment was loaded onto the wagons. The man said, "My officer didn't say, sir…, but I saw what it was with my own eyes sir."

The man stood there speechless until Tarleton said, "Well? What did you see, man?"

The courier seemed to realize the deficiency in his lieutenant's message and showed a great deal of loyalty as he again hesitated before saying, "It was weapons, powder, cartridge boxes, tentage, common military stores, sir."

Tarleton called a reliable sergeant to his side while he used his saddle as a makeshift writing table to draft a quick but detailed set of instructions to young Lieutenant Cloyde. The note read, "Lt. Cloyde, you are to disregard the larger body of rebel troops for the time being. Trail the small convoy in whatever direction it takes. Continue to communicate with me as well as you can via courier. I will be moving generally north toward Charlotte after we get what is left of our force across the river. I want to know what direction they take as soon as possible, especially if they break away from the larger force. If they do separate from the larger enemy group, you will seek any opportunity to attack and seize these wagons if at all practically possible. If that fails, you will maintain contact with them and report to me. You will seek any opportunity to ally your troop with any friendly forces you encounter. Any officer reading these instructions should understand that recovery of these wagons and military supplies is of paramount importance. You will provide all available support and assistance to the bearer of these instructions. I am writing these orders under the expressed authority of General Lord Cornwallis. Tarleton, LTC."

He folded the paper as he considered the last line. He was taking a great risk using Cornwallis' name this way, but he was already in great professional peril having lost the battle in the first place. Recovery of the equipment in those wagons would help him maintain his personal dignity, if not his reputation as a professional soldier. In any event, his duty to recover this material was quite clear. He handed the note to the sergeant and ordered him to go with the courier to ensure that the instructions were delivered properly.

Tarleton swung himself into the saddle and moved up the trail toward the main body of survivors. His staff kept pace with him as he passed along the column of defeated and downcast troopers. They had camped on the sodden hillside waiting for daylight before moving on to the river crossing. Only a few of the men showed obvious wounds. This seemed to be further evidence of their humiliation. Wounds would have been welcome. The visibly wounded men did, in fact, seem to ride higher in their saddles.

Lieutenant Robert Cloyde of Tarleton's British Legion received the new orders from Colonel Tarleton with a mixture of excitement and trepidation. He knew the ramifications of the horrendous defeat at Cowpens. It would adversely affect the careers of every surviving officer. He also remembered the relief he felt when he realized that he was actually one of those survivors. He saw many other junior officers fall that day. This was made easy from his protected vantage point in the tree line. He couldn't help feeling shamed by that sense of relief, but he was glad to be alive all the same. His current excitement came from the realization that he was going to be operating independently for the first time. He would lead his small cavalry troop without interference in this clearly important endeavor. He wasn't physically afraid now. He knew his thirty troopers could easily overpower the smaller group of rebel infantrymen escorting these wagons wherever they went. That wasn't it at all. No. He was afraid that he might fail in some other way and expose his earlier cowardice. He was afraid of his commander, Colonel Tarleton.

He folded the orders and placed them carefully inside his leather saddlebag. The sergeant was sent back to the colonel with a verbal message that the orders were received and understood. Cloyde left his horse at the base of the small hill with the other mounts and strode up to where his men were fanned out watching the rebel preparations in the distance. The first thing he noticed when he arrived was that the cavalry screen had withdrawn and the main enemy force was moving away toward the west.

The small group of wagons was also moving, but they were headed south. He knew what he needed to do. Cloyde was well trained by the very demanding Tarleton. He ordered his men to mount and prepare to move. They would head south also. They were up that road just yesterday morning. He had a pretty good idea of the perfect site for an effective ambush. Lieutenant Cloyde couldn't help smiling as he considered how easy it was to erase a mistake with quick success. Colonel Tarleton wouldn't have to wait long for the recovery of these precious supplies after all.

CHAPTER 16

They were finally moving. One of the three squads fanned out ahead and to the front flanks. One surrounded the wagons. The third squad brought up the rear. The last wagon contained the wounded men. Only the teamsters, the doctor's assistant, and the wounded were allowed to ride. Billy visited briefly with Silas before trotting to catch up with the quickly striding Sergeant Strickland. Sergeant Duncan stayed back with the trailing squad to react or provide assistance if any unforeseen problems arose during the march.

The convoy entered the trees and started down the southern trail. Sergeant Strickland glanced at Billy as he neared. "Somethin's botherin' me, sir."

"What would that be, Sergeant?" asked Billy.

Strickland looked genuinely worried. "Like I said earlier, Tarleton's men will be watchin' us leave in the other direction from the rest of our fellas...." They walked silently for several seconds before Strickland stopped and looked over at Billy with even deeper concern. "I think we need to take a 'round about' route to the mill, sir."

Billy agreed, but he didn't know the area, and he didn't like the idea of getting lost or taking unnecessary delay getting the wounded to their destination. "What do you suggest we do about it? If we were watched, they will expect us to stay on the road and they will ambush us up ahead somewhere. I imagine they would love to get these supplies back...."

Strickland said, "Red and me have been talkin' with some of these militiamen. There's a couple of them from this part of the colony. One of them was born and raised only a few miles from here. Seems there are some other trails and side lanes the farm folks use that ain't on any maps. He claims to know all of 'em."

It didn't take long for Billy and the two sergeants to question the local man, Private Samuel Spate. He assured them that they could leave the main trail without difficulty. The man told them emphatically that he knew a route which would avoid villages and larger farms. It would bring them to the mill sooner than taking the well-known roads and trails. He explained that he was at Fletcher's Mill on business more than once with his older brother. Billy suspected that the "business" probably involved questionable endeavors which would have made discretion as important as speed. People were driven to great lengths trying to avoid the excessive taxation of the British Crown. Most of the common folk understood this to be a practical necessity and applauded those who the authorities despised and labeled as scoundrels.

Sergeant Strickland instructed John Red to accompany Private Spate to ensure that the man didn't somehow lead them into trouble. He didn't know Spate, but he trusted Red with his life. Spate was ordered to direct the convoy along the most discreet route of march. Red would scout ahead to provide early warning of potential ambush or other enemy activity. The distance was considerable, but they should be able to make good time if this shrewd little militiaman, Spate, showed them the way. The animallike senses and instincts of John Red would protect them from surprise.

Billy and Sergeant Strickland agreed at once. Sergeant Duncan didn't like it, but he acquiesced to Billy's authority and Strickland's experience. The troops and wagons started out again headed south. They moved only a short distance before they turned off the main trail at the edge of a natural meadow. Private Spate led them more west than south for about a mile through broken forest and scrub that was just passable for the wagons. Red disappeared into the trees and scrub ahead of them. Billy was becoming concerned with their decision to leave the road, when they came out onto a small partially overgrown lane heading more directly south. The trail was indicated by deep ruts caused by the passage of wagons over countless years. Red was waiting there and reported that he had already checked the trail for several hundred yards ahead. It was clear of danger.

Two miles away, Lieutenant Cloyde of Tarleton's British Legion brought the heated argument with his senior sergeant to a close with a sharp demand for silence. He was fully sick and tired of the argument. The sergeant was vehemently insisting that they carefully follow the four rebel wagons and their walking escorts as ordered by Colonel Tarleton. He further insisted they could swoop in and seize the prize as soon as they were confident they were not followed by rebel cavalry. Cloyde would have none of this. He too feared enemy cavalry. This fact galled him but was unshakeable. He was convinced that the best way to fulfill the spirit of the colonel's instructions was to use his greater speed and mobility to move around in front of the convoy's route of march to an ambush position. He would wait for the enemy to come to him.

Lieutenant Cloyde shouted for the troop to mount and prepare to move out. The sergeant remained standing in front of him for a moment too long. Several of the privates seemed to be waiting for the argument to be settled before obeying the command to mount. Fury welled up inside Cloyde and he released it with a snarled, "What is wrong with you, Sergeant? Are you deaf?" He withdrew a pistol from the saddle holster and cocked the hammer back with his left palm as he asked this open question.

The sergeant looked wide-eyed at the pistol and said in a conciliatory tone, "No, I'm not deaf, sir. I will obey your command. I'm simply doing my duty in advising you of other considerations here." Cloyde slowly moved the pistol hammer back to the uncocked position and lowered it to his side before saying, "I am directly responsible to the colonel for my decisions and their results, Sergeant. You will obey me immediately. Mount your horse and prepare the men to move south to the position I showed you on the map. The rebels are too stupid to know we are here. They will continue to be stupid as they blunder down that road into our arms where we will surprise them and recover the equipment and supplies without a shot fired."

The sergeant nodded in salute and said, "Yes, sir. Right away, sir." He then spun around and mounted his horse before shouting the necessary orders bringing the small troop into a column of twos.

Cloyde holstered the pistol and swung himself up into his own saddle. He was certain his plan would result in the successful capture and recovery of the rebel wagons and the lost supplies. The fact that it was a deviation from Tarleton's orders would hardly matter when success was achieved. He was in command here. He would do this his way. It again came to his mind that doing it his way would take them away from the rebel cavalry he suspected was lurking just beyond his sight to the west. He couldn't bring himself to believe this small convoy wasn't some elaborate scheme or trap on the part of the rebels to subdue and destroy British patrols they knew to be watching from this area.

Lieutenant Cloyde let himself believe that his decision was tactically correct whether the sergeant or anyone else agreed with him. They would capture their quarry. They would do it his way. Somehow, as he rode to the head of the column and gave the order to advance, he had a horrible gnawing impression that his motives were flawed and this was all wrong. It was too late now. Trotting his horse down the hillside with his troop following dutifully behind, he shrugged off the second thoughts and resolved to carry through with his decision. Besides, he would look like a fool if he changed his mind now.

The small rebel convoy passed quietly unnoticed as the guide led them steadily south via one farm lane after another. The day progressed uneventfully. They rarely saw anyone. They neared a secluded farm at the edge of the woods many miles from any neighbors late in the afternoon. Private Spate assured Billy that he knew and trusted the farmer, John Phillips, and his family. The wagons and their escort remained concealed in the woods. Billy and Spate approached the farmhouse and barn alone from across a narrow field that still showed the stubble remains of the late season's crop.

They heard the farmer working at an anvil in the barn. Mrs. Phillips saw them approaching across the field and came out of the back of the house trailed by a scrawny little girl with long braided pigtails protruding from her overlarge mobcap. The woman was huge. She reached the barn before them, and took up a position blocking access to the door. Her expression was resolved and unwelcoming. Billy tipped his hat to the woman and little girl. The woman's arms were folded across her breast. He hadn't noticed until that moment that she was holding a formidable-looking iron frying pan in her right hand.

Private Spate said, "Hello, Sadie! I hear John at work inside. We need to talk with him."

She drew air in abruptly and expelled it with a loud and forceful, "Huh! I just bet you do…. You're no longer welcome here, Samuel! After you ran off with what was rightfully ours last time…. Why, I lowed I'd settle with you … you … you pirate! You thief! John swears the deal you done was honest, and I don't wonder he believes it, but I don't!"

The militiaman removed his hat and stood with his head lowered in as contrite a display as he could muster. He said, "Now Sadie, you know I wouldn't take unfair advantage. That cow was rightfully mine!"

Mrs. Phillips took a half step forward. It looked like she was about to put the pan into service when Billy stepped between them. "Excuse me, ma'am, we don't want trouble. We just want to talk with you and your husband for a moment. Anything that has happened between your family and Private Spate can be put to rights."

She stepped back and refolded her arms while asking, "Who is 'we,' and who are you, young fella?"

Billy doffed his hat again. "Lieutenant William Morgan of the North Carolina Militia ma'am, at your service."

The woman started to reply when the barn door opened and bumped her substantial girth from behind. A wizened little man peered around the edge of the door and asked apologetically, "What is it, Sadie? Who are you talking to, and why are you blockin' the door?"

Billy was amazed at the uncanny resemblance between Mr. Phillips and his new militia guide, Private Spate. It was as if they had been formed by the same mold.

Phillips stepped around his wife with a smile of sudden recognition. "Ho Sam! Is that really you?" He covered the distance quickly with his hand outstretched.

Spate grasped the offered hand in hearty greeting. Mrs. Phillips withdrew another pace and shook her head slowly in what appeared to be disgusted resignation. Spate said, "John, I've joined up with the militia from across the river, and this here's my lieutenant." He nodded toward Billy.

Phillips offered the same outstretched hand. "Pleased to meet you, young sir."

Billy shook his hand and said, "Can we go inside to talk sir?"

Mr. Phillips turned toward his wife and seemed to swell slightly as he ordered her to go back in the house and fetch some of the "good cider." He and his friends would be inside the barn "in conference." Mrs. Phillips stamped her foot but said nothing while disappointed resolve crept over her face. She then spun on her heel abruptly and stomped back across the barnyard toward the house with the little girl in tow. Farmer Phillips said, "This way please, gentlemen...," and led them into the barn through the still open door.

The wagons were brought up to the barnyard from the woods before nightfall. The wounded men were carried into the house by the doctor and his assistant. Mrs. Phillips underwent a dramatic change in temperament when she saw the condition of these poor men. She spent the next two hours doing everything in her power to follow the doctor's instructions and make the men as comfortable as possible. She also managed to cook up an extraordinary amount of thick stew that included venison, potatoes, carrots, and onions. The smell of cooking stew had a dramatically positive effect on the men.

Billy and Sergeant Duncan organized a watch bill to ensure that the farm was guarded from every possible avenue of approach. The draft horses were cared for by the teamsters and farmer Phillips. The wagon tarps were checked again for security. The wagon holding the barrels of powder was moved out further from the house and barn. Mr. Phillips let it be known that they were welcome to stay as long as they thought necessary. The men not on watch were allowed to sleep in the barn. Billy and the two sergeants spent several hours on the front porch talking through their concerns and plans for the immediate future.

Twelve miles away on the main southern road, Lieutenant Cloyde welcomed the coming night in growing terror. This was a horrible mistake. He sent out mounted patrols to search for the wagons along the roadway and along likely side trails when they failed to reach his position in the afternoon as expected. The last of these patrols returned without finding the rebels. They saw no rebel cavalry either. They saw no one at all. It was as if the wagons and their escort simply vanished. He knew his sergeant was correct earlier. He dared not show this now. This was his first independent opportunity to command. It was a miserable failure. The humiliation was overwhelming. The night was spent sleeplessly. Would he find his quarry tomorrow? He had to. The convoy couldn't be that far away. They were moving at walk speed with four loaded wagons and numerous wounded men. He didn't hear laughter, but he knew his men held him in disgusted contempt. That was nothing, though. What on earth would Colonel Tarleton say...?

Lieutenant Cloyde knew he couldn't give up this easily. He couldn't go back to Colonel Tarleton and report this failure. His career wouldn't survive that. It didn't matter if Tarleton himself was now in disgrace from the loss of the battle and all those men. He was probably in even greater danger from Tarleton now because of the loss at Cowpens. He knew Colonel Tarleton to be prideful and petulant. A junior lieutenant would make a handy scapegoat to absorb the wounded venting of that petulant pride. He must do something else, but he couldn't just blindly chase over the countryside looking for the lost convoy. He needed help. It occurred to him that his only reasonable choice was to head for the cavalry garrison at Rocky Mount. There he could access any available information and reinforcements for his small troop of dragoons.

CHAPTER 17

The night was far spent when Ira lit a candle and went down the hall to check on Ezekiel. He quietly opened the bedroom door and peered inside to find Elizabeth sound asleep in the chair at the side of the old man's bed. The candle on the nightstand was gutted. Only embers glowed in the fireplace grate. Elizabeth held Ezekiel's hand as she slept. Entering the room with the brightly burning candle allowed Ira to see that Ezekiel was wide awake and staring back at him from beneath the bandages covering his head.

Mona was escorted late in the night to her own home after promising to return before dawn. Captain Robertson left the house and returned to the mill where he now had a headquarters of sorts. The quiet of the large house was only interrupted by the gentle breathing of the sleeping girl. The floor creaked as Ira walked closer to the side of the bed to offer a whispered inquiry about how Zeke was feeling.

The old man responded in a croaking whisper. "I'm feeling some better now, but I been lyin' here tryin' to remember what happened, and I just can't make it out somehow...."

Ira whispered, "You were knocked down by one of those British soldiers on the morning of the seventeenth. It's been days since then, but don't concern yourself with that right now."

Zeke looked over at Elizabeth with a smile and said, "This poor girl sat up with me most of the night. I need to move, but just can't stand the thought of disturbin' her right now."

Ira said, "Well, she needs to go on to her own bed and get some real rest. There is still a lot of mischief afoot. I'm afraid we are all going to wish we had slept over the next few days."

Zeke pulled his hand away from Elizabeth's with some effort. She began to stir. Ira reached down and gently shook her shoulder so that she came fully awake with a muted cry of alarm. Ira said, "Easy now, Beth, everything is all right. You just fell asleep in the chair. I want you to go on to bed." She attempted to offer protest, but he silenced her. "No, girl. Go on to bed. Zeke and I need to talk privately."

She gave him a disappointed frown as she rose from the chair. The frown was replaced with a sweet smile as she leaned over to kiss Zeke's bandaged head. She stood back up to hug and kiss her grandfather with a muted, "I love you, Grandpa, and you too, Zeke. Goodnight."

Ira lit another candle from the one he was holding and handed it to his granddaughter as he said, "It's already early morning, Beth, but I want you to go get some good sleep anyway. I'll stay with this old scoundrel until Mona gets back." Elizabeth nodded and quietly went out.

The two men listened to her footfalls disappearing down the hall-way. Ira turned the now vacant chair to face his old friend directly and sat down. He carefully placed the fresh candle on the nightstand. Zeke stretched and tried to sit up straighter in the bed. Ira began to speak, but Zeke interrupted him. "Ira, we do need to talk. I'm startin' to remember that young British captain in the mill office. He was goin' through the books when I found him there. Horse soldiers were outside, and wag-ons.... Why.... He told me he was gonna take all of the food out of the mill.... I ... I tried to explain.... He wouldn't listen.... I tried to get him to listen.... Everything just went black...."

Ira patted the old man on the shoulder and helped him lean back on the pillow again before sitting up in the chair. He took a deep breath and plunged into a quiet explanation of all he knew about the events at Fletcher's Mill during the past few days. He was mildly surprised that

Ezekiel didn't express any significant shock or alarm when he heard what happened on the road after he was knocked out. Zeke mournfully shook his head in deep regret when he heard of Peter's death and the way it apparently happened. He said, "What an awful shame, Ira....I so wanted to help that boy. He just wouldn't let me get close to him. It's hard to believe that he helped those men escape, though." The look on Zeke's face let Ira know that he really wasn't surprised at all by the apparent moral failure of this lonely and miserable young man.

Zeke shook his head again and looked briefly away from Ira before speaking in a remarkably stronger voice. "Ira, I need to tell you some things...."

Ira leaned forward and stared intently at his old mentor. "Yes, Zeke, I imagine you do. What on earth has been happening here in my absence?"

Ezekiel looked back at him as defiantly as his injured elderly form would allow. "Now, don't take that tone with me, sir. I haven't done anything but what was right!"

Ira snapped back, "Is that so? Then please explain what I've been hearing from members of the 'provisional militia' about military supplies and contraband being stored in and shipped to and from the mill. What on earth were you thinking?"

Zeke held his hand up as if to quiet Ira's anger. He intentionally waited until Ira settled back into the chair again before he began to speak. "Ira, we've been doing what was right by these young men who are fighting for our freedom. I can't believe that you, of all people, would choose to stay out of the events that are happening all around us."

Ira remained silent. Zeke continued, "This land will be free, Ira. If not now, then eventually. The Crown can't keep these distant colonies in bondage against the will of the people here indefinitely. You need to choose what side you're on in this conflict, just as I have. I couldn't help believing you would choose the same side as me."

Ira lowered his head into his hands in deep frustration. He couldn't remain angry with this wise and gentle old man. Looking back up, he said, "What about your own people, Zeke? They're enslaved by these same colonists all around us! What about their freedom? Why do you care about this war and what happens in it? The British have promised liberty to any slaves who leave their masters and come over to the English side. We have almost managed to safely stay here in peace while this madness goes on elsewhere in the colony. Wasn't it enough that we lost Mary, Isaiah, and Natalie to those butchers...." Tears streamed down his face with the memory of that awful night.

Zeke instinctively remained silent long enough for Ira to regain his composure. "There ain't no separate peace here, son. Don't think I don't care about the slavery of 'my people' either! I can't do anything about that and neither can you. Don't forget, I was sold to your daddy in a marketplace auction."

Ira didn't want to talk about his father right now. He knew his father would have had all the answers. He would have known what to do now that the world seemed to be falling apart. Ira believed his father would have remained loyal to the Crown no matter what grievances he held with the government. He believed his father would expect him to maintain the same loyalty. Ira couldn't get past the insolent, pride-filled, meanness of the elitists in the British aristocracy though. It was this same idea of superiority that somehow allowed most of his fellow colonists to believe slavery was morally acceptable. He knew his father never accepted or agreed with that awful premise. Maybe Zeke was right. It was obviously the time to choose sides whether he wanted to or not. He knew he could never side with the Tories, but the choice was vastly more complicated than that.

Could Ira resist the fiercely loyalist Tory party and remain a Whig without turning against his king? The governor was his personal friend. He owned vast landholdings throughout this part of the colony. He had thought about his liability here at length during the afternoon. He believed he might defend himself against charges of treason should that overzealous Captain Crispin manage to report the incident at the mill. That would not be the case if the authorities came here with force and a battle ensued as expected by the militia.

A British victory in this war would mean a Tory victory here in South Carolina. That would bring ruin to him eventually because of his refusal to comply with the institutionalized slavery practiced here. Wouldn't a rebel victory mean the same thing? The governor wouldn't be able to protect him from forfeiture of all of his landholdings if he resisted the Royal Army in this time of crisis. A large part of his personal fortune was tied up in land, but thankfully, that wasn't all of his wealth. He owned the mill. More importantly, he had the silver and gold concealed in an iron-bound oak chest. The chest was hidden in a small side cavern that he and Zeke discovered years earlier when they were enlarging the cave at the back of the mill. All of the cash he inherited from his father and removed from the banks in Charleston had been converted to silver and gold. This treasure was secured in the chest. Much of the profits since his father's death were used to expand the business and acquire more land. The rest of this money was exchanged for silver and added to the contents of the chest.

No one knew about the chest or its location except Ira, Zeke, Isaiah, and Mary. Isaiah and Mary were gone. Only Ira and Zeke knew about it now. Both of them intended to use this money to ensure they could always rebuild no matter what happened in the world around them. They also intended it to buy a bright and secure future for Elizabeth after they were gone. They discussed this on many occasions. All of it was in Ira's will. Both men knew there were many rumors regarding vast sums of money hidden in or below Fletcher's Mill. They were still confident in the secrecy of the true location and actual scope of the treasure. Zeke loved Ira and his family. There was never any question in Zeke's mind that the treasure belonged to Ira. Ira loved and trusted Zeke completely. He held unquenchable respect for Zeke's loyalty and impeccable character. These two old men were more like family to each other than the majority of blood relatives.

Ezekiel leaned over to speak more quietly. "You need to tell Beth about the gold and silver under the mill."

Ira sat back as if slapped. "I will not! Why? She has no need to know about that now!"

Zeke stared at him quietly before continuing. "She needs to know about it so that she can use it if something happens to you and me."

Ira didn't want to have this discussion now. The landholdings would be lost and he knew it. The money in that chest was the only thing between them and poverty. He wouldn't trust it to Elizabeth. Not yet. No. He wouldn't do it, and he resented Zeke's suggestion.

Ira didn't try to examine the way the idea made him feel threatened. He couldn't recognize the extent of his dependence on the contents of that chest. He believed himself to be a generous Godly man. He didn't recognize the pride growing in him over the years the way someone else might. He took his wealth and the power it gave him for granted. He truly believed the people around him were better off as long as he was in authority. He didn't view this as arrogance. He couldn't see the awful truth of this mindset any clearer than other British gentry could see it in themselves throughout the empire.

Ezekiel leaned back again and sighed deeply. "Ira, you know that I love you. You know I've always wanted what was best for you and the family."

Ira looked up at him with a questioning, "Yes?"

Zeke seemed to steel himself before continuing. "Son, it occurs to me that you need some personal soul searchin'. That money ain't your source. God is. You was put on this earth for a purpose same as the rest of us. You need to remember what the Good Lord said about real treasure. You 'can't serve both God and money.' Ira, you've always held the mistaken belief that you are made up of what you have rather than Who has you. I think it's time to let go of all the world's goods and concentrate on real treasure."

Ira was on his feet now. He hadn't interrupted Zeke because he didn't know what to say. He felt somehow betrayed by his dearest friend and insulted beyond description. He stood staring down at the bed for a breathless moment, but no adequate response formed itself in his mind. Leaving the candle where it was, he eventually turned without speaking and stomped out of the room, slamming the bedroom door as he left. He never noticed the tears on Zeke's face or the old man's shaking head. He didn't hear the gentle sobs of his exhausted granddaughter as he stormed down the stairs and through the parlor. He didn't even notice Mona's shocked gaze as he brushed past her on his way down the front steps. He felt threatened, betrayed, and very angry.

CHAPTER 18

Sergeant Strickland took little time trying to explain to Billy why he wanted to leave the farm before first light. He had a feeling. He couldn't fully explain it. Something was wrong. Fear didn't really describe it right. Mr. and Mrs. Phillips readily shared everything they had with this small group of desperate men. The house and barn were sound sturdy structures and there was plenty of food and fresh water. The situation at the farm was so appealing. The doctor decided to keep the wounded men here where he had everything he needed for their treatment and recovery. Mrs. Phillips took a liking to the mysterious old physician, and she was working closely with him to treat the worst of the men's injuries. This seemed to annoy the doctor's young male helper, but it had a strangely positive effect on Mr. Phillips.

Strickland's ill feeling about the place started during a conversation with farmer Phillips while they were moving the wounded men into the house. The sergeant noted the obvious distance between the Phillips' farm and their nearest neighbors. He was used to neighboring farms being closer together. It seemed odd that this many strangers could move in and around the farm without drawing attention from curious onlookers of some sort. Mr. Phillips tried to reassure Strickland by telling him that he had no real friends in the area. All of his near neighbors were avid Tories. Any friendly relationships from before "the troubles" had been dead for some time now.

Phillips described recent threats he received from some of his neighbors when he announced he wouldn't sign the Royal Army's loyalty oath. The confrontation happened during a chance meeting several days ago with a small group of neighbors down at Monarch Mill. He had also let his feelings be known about the stupidity of parliament and the unwise advice someone must be giving the king. The men became so fiercely angry with Phillips that he found it necessary to beat a hasty retreat. Strickland concluded that this strange little man and his large outspoken wife probably managed to make themselves into social outcasts long before "the troubles."

The Tory neighbors probably believed they had ample justification for anything they might do here. This was clearly a wealthy farm by current standards. Why hadn't it been plundered? The Royal Army left it alone only because they didn't know the farm existed. Strickland felt a storm coming soon. He didn't want to be here when it arrived. He didn't think the doctor should stay here with the wounded either, no matter what conveniences the place offered. The doctor wouldn't listen. Lieutenant Morgan was more receptive, but he couldn't do anything to persuade the doctor to leave either.

The young lieutenant and his two sergeants concluded plans for the next day quickly. They would rise very early to prepare for a hasty departure. The doctor and his assistant would be left behind with the wounded. Billy decided to give one of the wagons to Mr. Phillips, along with the draft animals, in exchange for the use of his home as a makeshift hospital. He and his small force would proceed to Fletcher's Mill with the remaining wagons carrying the captured weapons and ammunition. He intended to return to the farm as soon as possible after delivering the military supplies. They would reunite with the doctor and his patients on the way back north to find the rest of the army.

Billy spent a few minutes with Silas before leaving. He was terribly worried about his friend, but he knew Doctor Bolt would give him the best possible care. He agreed with Strickland that this place wasn't safe from attack. It also seemed that it would be better not to move these poor injured men any further in this cold, damp weather. Silas was not aware of his presence anyway. He had been unconscious for many hours now. The doctor seemed to be optimistic about his chances, but Billy wasn't so sure.

The convoy left the farmyard with one less wagon. Private Spate guided them out through the fields into the woods to the southeast where he once again found the small hidden track they used the day before. Spate displayed a confidence that was reassuring to Billy and the two sergeants. The terrain was hilly, and there were large patches of deep woods interrupted by natural meadows. They traveled less than a mile when the sun climbed above the horizon to reveal a mostly clear but still cold day.

Billy was talking quietly with Sergeant Duncan as they walked along the trail well behind the last wagon. Sergeant Strickland was far out front with John Red and the lead squad ensuring that the small convoy would be alerted to any potential threats ahead of them. The other two squads were spread out along the trail behind the wagons near Billy and Duncan. Billy's thought was that they would be close at hand to react quickly if anything should happen along the route of march.

Suddenly, the silence of the morning was interrupted by the dull report of distant gunshots coming from far behind them. Billy and Sergeant Duncan simultaneously spun around to gaze through the trees at the horizon to the rear. They saw nothing at first. The convoy continued to move slowly forward. Duncan called out to one of the nearby privates and sent him running ahead to tell the teamsters to stop where they were and bring Sergeant Strickland back to the rear. Billy quickly turned the trailing squads to face the perceived threat brought by the continuing distant gunfire. He then noticed a small plume of gray smoke climbing above the trees in the direction of the Phillips farm. His heart was beating like a drum, and he was filled with anguish for Silas and the others at the farm. He knew better than to charge toward the sounds without waiting for Strickland and the rest of his small force. Billy now carried the reputation of a hothead. He was thankful that he could sometimes manage to stop and think rationally about what to do.

Sergeant Strickland ran up several minutes later. There were six men with him. He had left four men to guard the wagons along with the three teamsters. They were to pull the wagons as deeply into the nearby woods as they could while still having access to the trail. Billy appreciated the wisdom and nodded his agreement. He quickly told Strickland why he called the halt. Several more muffled gunshots rang out as Billy finished speaking, almost as if they were meant to reinforce what he said.

Billy didn't wait for the opinions of the two sergeants. He heard himself rattling off instructions to his subordinates as if he were listening to someone else speak. Within seconds, a plan was formed and implemented. They were moving swiftly back toward the Phillips farm in less than two minutes. Every man knew what he was supposed to do. They were tense and focused. These men were excited, but not foolish. They ran toward the sounds of battle with determined will. Someone was attacking their friends. Someone was going to pay a steep price for what they were doing at the Phillips farm. The farmer and his wife were odd, but they had been very kind.

The shots were heard only occasionally now. Billy's men cleared the distant tree line and spread out to move low and fast across the intervening field toward the farm buildings. The barn was being totally consumed in a roaring fire. One of the draft horses lay dead in the middle of the barn lot. The other animal and the wagon were gone. Billy halted on a low rise overlooking the scene to assess the situation and think frantically about what to do. The others stopped when he did, and went to ground waiting for him. Sergeant Strickland ran over from the left end of the line and pointed to the wood pile and rail fence near the road approaching the house from the north.

Several figures were spread out there. A puff of smoke billowed out from one of these prostrate figures followed momentarily by a dull report. The shot was answered from a window of the house a half second later. Billy looked further along the fence line toward the back of the house and saw an even larger number of men moving slowly in that direction. They were partially screened from the house by the fence and thick forest trees on that side. He noted that a few of these men were carrying lit torches. They clearly intended to set fire to the house if they could get close enough.

Billy saw one of these men with torches fall suddenly, and heard another dull thud from the back side of the house. So, the farmer, the doctor, or whoever was alive in the house could still offer a defense in more than one direction. Billy started to ask Strickland for advice in a moment of doubt, but changed his mind. He felt the not unfamiliar excitement welling up inside him. Rather than forming a question, he began shouting orders to the sergeants. Moments later, Sergeant Strickland, John Red and three other men moved swiftly to the left in a low running circle. This brought them up behind the Tories at the woodpile and along the fence at the side of the house.

Most of Billy's small force was still close to him. He waited until Strickland made it to the spot he pointed out a moment earlier and flopped down there. Billy waved his own men forward then at a slow steady trot while pushing them into a wider line as they approached the barnyard and the front of the house. No one outside the farm buildings had noticed them yet apparently. That was good.

None of the enemy attackers he could see were wearing uniforms. That told him a great deal. These were Tory raiders. They were probably some of farmer Phillips' own neighbors. He noticed that a few of them were face down and motionless out in the mud of the barnyard. Billy and his group of breathless men made it to the rail fence surrounding the pigsty now. The smoke from the heap of charred ruins that had been the barn was blowing low across the lot in front of them driven by the cold winter breeze. All of his men stopped at the fence and were staring at him waiting for the next move.

Sergeant Strickland saw Billy reach the sty fence and began counting as he had been ordered. When he reached twenty, he rose to a knee with a shout and fired his musket at the men behind the woodpile. The other four waited several seconds and fired as well. Billy heard Strickland's shot and vaulted over the fence into the sty, frightening the old sow inside and nearly falling headlong into the mud and slime. He regained his balance and ran to the other side where he was up and over that fence in moments. His men followed him as quickly as possible. They were now crossing the barn lot through the smoke at a dead run.

Tories at the side and back of the house turned in panic to fire at Strickland and his men. Billy's party split apart with half going around the house to the right and half around to the left. A ragged volley was fired by the largest group of raiders, apparently in the direction of the new threat posed by Sergeant Strickland. Billy chose that moment to let out a loud bellowing yell that was taken up by his men now emerging from the smoke at both ends of the farmhouse. They fired on the run into the now panicked Tories. They covered the distance in moments and vaulted over the rear fence in headlong pursuit of the fleeing enemy.

Strickland and his men reloaded quickly and moved forward. The rest of the fierce little battle was over in seconds. Three more raiders were lying lifeless on the ground. Seven more were now huddled in a disarmed and terrified group under the trees behind the house. Ten of Billy's men surrounded these with leveled muskets under the supervision of Sergeant Duncan. Billy, Strickland, and the others continued to pursue the remaining Tory raiders as they fled through the woods with the empty captured wagon and the surviving draft horse. Exhaustion and Billy's instinctive unwillingness to be drawn any further from the rest of his men brought them to a halt without any further contact.

CHAPTER 19

Major Throckmorton was still furious. He couldn't believe the treatment he suffered at the hands of that insolent little pup. He would have his comeuppance. Throckmorton was not a man to be trifled with. The anger seethed in and through everything he now did. He knew the course he chose was probably unwise, maybe even a little foolish. He would not be denied, though. Shortly after the main rebel force departed from Cowpens with General Morgan, Throckmorton decided to follow Lieutenant Morgan and his group of militia pirates. He and his helpers left the larger force at the first opportunity and doubled back down the now heavily trampled road. It was fairly simple to find the southern road once they got back to Cowpens.

Throckmorton might have blundered into the ambush set by Lieutenant Cloyde if he hadn't chanced upon evidence showing where the four wagons left the main road further north. These wagons left a distinctive trail that was easy enough even for him and his companions to follow. Nightfall and cowardice brought his pursuit to a halt several miles behind his quarry.

Throckmorton and his minions rose early the next morning and once again headed south. He was certain the small convoy had come this way. The wagon tracks were quite clear and there were a great many different footprints mixed closely with those tracks. These prints appeared to be as fresh as the wagon ruts. They didn't need to be cavalry scouts to follow this trail. He realized that they should easily catch up with the wagons today, and this brought the major a new frustration.

Throckmorton didn't exactly know what to do when he did catch up with the wagons and their escort. He didn't have any more real authority now than he did yesterday. That young fool lieutenant would rightly resist him again. He would just have to wait and see what happened. This was dangerous territory, and any number of things might occur to change the situation in his favor. He would avoid another confrontation unless the circumstances changed. Meanwhile, he intended to stay as close as he could to the cargo in those wagons. It was very valuable and he didn't intend to lose the opportunity he saw here.

Major Throckmorton was mulling through these thoughts a few minutes later when he imagined he heard the faint sound of gunfire far ahead to the south. He brought his small party to a halt. He had no intention of getting caught up in any kind of battle. The very thought of the horrible carnage he saw in the aftermath of real battle at Cowpens terrified him. It was only with great cunning and tremendous good fortune that he managed to stay out of that melee two days ago. The major decided to move closer to the sound of the guns now with great trepidation. No courage was involved in this choice. It occurred to him that the battle he was hearing probably involved those supply wagons and the fools guarding them.

Pragmatic greed drove Throckmorton forward. Maybe this was the sound of opportunity finally presenting itself. His two companions glanced at each other briefly, then spurred their mounts into motion behind him. The sound of gunfire became intermittent as it grew louder with their approach. There was a momentary increase in the noise and then sudden silence. He was now torn between fear at the sound of the guns and a new anxiety with regard to the silence. The distant fight was apparently decided one way or another. He desperately hoped he was not too late to take advantage in the aftermath.

Throckmorton and his helpers were moving up and over a hill with a sharp turn in the trail ahead. Suddenly, they were confronted by a strange spectacle rounding the turn to their immediate front. It was a wagon pulled by a sweat frothed draft horse that was being beaten with a whip by an obviously frantic driver. The trace harness looked somehow distorted to the major until he realized that there should have been two animals in the traces rather than this one horse. The harness and leather yoke for the missing horse were partially cut away and trailing along under the front of the wagon.

There were other men in the wagon with the driver. All of them faced back the way they had come. These men were in civilian garb, and heavily armed. Throckmorton thought they must be members of the militia party he was trailing at first. He realized his error when the wagon's driver saw him and yelled at his companions. Three of the men spun around. One of them fired immediately in Throckmorton's direction without aim. A second shot, better aimed, struck the larger of Throckmorton's helpers squarely in the chest. The other assistant abandoned his mule and disappeared into the brush at the side of the trail with a speed that seemed incredible aside from the terror that precipitated it. Throckmorton froze in fear. He wanted to turn and flee, but momentum brought the two parties face to face before his brain signaled his hands to pull the reins around for that purpose.

The wagon driver was standing as he hauled in on the distressed draft horse, bringing it to a splashing spluttering halt. Major Throckmorton's helpers were wearing civilian clothing. He, unfortunately, was not. The six Tory occupants of the wagon were suddenly shocked and delighted. They had managed to run away from the surprise attack they encountered back at the Phillips farm, only to have a fully uniformed Continental Army major ride right into their laps. The capture was complete within seconds with no further shots fired.

The strange captive was soon trussed and thrown into the back of the wagon. The driver quickly managed to tie the damaged side of the trace harness together well enough to incorporate the added strength of one more captured horse to pull the wagon. The other two captured animals were now ridden by Tories. The rest of the men remained in the wagon with their prisoner as they frantically continued northward away from perceived pursuit.

The wagon was halted a short while later at the top of a hill from which the men could see a considerable distance back down the trail to the south. The leader of the group was a tall well-dressed young man with a livid scar under his left eye. His frightened expression quickly gave way to the ferretlike curiosity and cruel demeanor of a rich young bully. He climbed down from the wagon seat and walked back to stare at Major Throckmorton for a moment. The man suddenly lunged forward, grabbed the terrified major by the lapels, and yanked him unceremoniously out onto the muddy ground. The major began to whimper pleas for mercy. This ended abruptly when the young man kicked him in the stomach and yelled, "Stop yer blubberin' you filthy rebel scum!"

The Tories were all standing nearby now. They formed a curious circle around the groaning and gasping Continental officer. Some of them stared down the southern trail in fright. The rest were overcome with curiosity about their captive. The Tory leader reached down and pulled Throckmorton to a seated position by the sparse hair at the nape of his neck. Leaning over to stare into the major's face, he asked, "Just who are you, mister?" Throckmorton didn't immediately reply. This was rewarded with a swift slap in the face that knocked him back down into the mud. He frantically searched the faces of the other men for any sign of compassion. He saw nothing but hate. The major's helpers were gone. He was alone with these fiends, and he was terrified.

Major Throckmorton couldn't believe this was happening. He thought himself to be a well-to-do gentleman. His wealth largely came from shady business dealings and the misfortune of others, but this did nothing to dampen pride in his possessions. He enjoyed feeling superior among people of lesser social standing. He desperately wished now that he hadn't decided to chase after that fool lieutenant and those wagons. He should have stayed with the army and returned to North Carolina. He could have taken any number of actions from there to recover the value of the material in those wagons. It was too late for all of that. He felt himself being yanked upright again and cringed for the expected blow. It came in the form of a boot to the center of his back followed by a punch in the face. He feared this may have broken his nose, but there was no time to think about it. The pain was excruciating. He heard himself crying out, "Stop, please stop! I have information for you! Please stop!"

The Tory leader shouted, "What are you saying? What information could something like you have for us?" Throckmorton somehow squirmed onto his knees. His wrists were bound tightly behind him. He felt blood flowing freely down his face and neck and he was afraid that he may have lost two of his upper front teeth. He was dizzy and in terrible pain. He knew he wouldn't survive much more of this. His instinct for self-preservation brought him to a quick and unceremonious decision. He told this group of evil young men everything he knew about the wagon loads of military supplies, the number of men guarding the wagons, how they were armed, and their intended destination.

The beating stopped. A muffled conversation was held a few yards away between two of the Tories and their outspoken leader. The discussion ended abruptly. Throckmorton found himself once again thrown into the back of the wagon. They were moving again very quickly. The men in the wagon talked freely between themselves. Throckmorton knew his actions were treacherous. There was still a fading part of him that actually cared. This small inner voice was easily shouted down as he bounced along in the back of the wagon. His face was horribly battered, his back and stomach were on fire, and his hands went to sleep from the cold tight lashings around his wrists. The suffering allowed him to rationalize his actions to his own satisfaction. He even began to see the possibility of personal gain in this. He soon learned from the conversation between his captors that they were on their way to the British garrison at Rocky Mount.

CHAPTER 20

Ira stomped through the early morning blackness in his dark fury with no real destination in mind. He didn't feel the cold. He had been betrayed by Zeke's words, and he didn't understand why. Was his pride so powerful that he couldn't listen to advice from his oldest friend? Was he really so dependent on wealth that he wasn't able to imagine life without it? He recoiled from these thoughts as he paced. Several minutes passed before he realized that he was now standing in the frigid darkness right outside the lower mill entrance. Why had he come here? Why was his life blowing apart like wheat husks in the wind? His troubled mind critically realized that only a miller would naturally think of winnowing wheat in the middle of seemingly impossible difficulties.

Ira opened the door and entered the inklike darkness of the front office storeroom without thinking further about the process. His movements seemed mechanical even to him. He knew this place so well that he really didn't need a light. He used flint and steel to light a candle anyway as he stepped up to the makeshift desk at the back of the room. This was the same spot where Ezekiel confronted Captain Crispin a few days ago. Was that only a few days? It seemed like a month. So much occurred in this lower level of the mill during that time. He felt his empty stomach churn as he considered that the Johansen boy was brutally murdered in the storeroom down the corridor less than twenty feet from here. The anger flared again. He forced back the feeling that he should have let

Tobias beat that miserable coward Crispin to death with his father's hammer that day.

The militiamen were occupying the upper floor of the mill now. Captain Robertson said something earlier about wanting to be high enough to have easy access to the roof and a clear view of the area surrounding this fortresslike building. Ira could hear muffled laughter and a quiet conversation from the floor above his head. He stepped over to the stairs and shot the bolt to lock the door from his side so that the men couldn't interrupt his activities or thoughts. He then stepped back to the entry and bolted that door as well.

A sudden gust of wind rattled the glass pane in the front window. A latent draft made it through the crack at the base of the door, causing the candle flame to flutter. Ira still didn't feel cold, but he started briefly at the unexpected movement of his own shadow. There were too many people here now. Too many strangers occupied this most familiar of all places. He felt himself inexorably drawn to the secret place. He was threatened. Elizabeth and Zeke were in danger. His home was threatened. Mona was in danger. Ira didn't think it odd to consider Mona in that way here and now. He removed an oil lantern from the top of the back storage cabinet, opened the glass, and trimmed the wick. He lit the lantern from the candle flame and blew the candle out before putting it in his front coat pocket.

Ira sat the lantern on the countertop and stepped away from it to look furtively around. He was convinced that he was alone here before he picked up the lantern and moved out of the room. He walked quickly up the back hallway past the storeroom that was used as a prison for Crispin and his wounded sergeant. A few more strides brought him to a door separating the front office from the lower milling station. He appreciated the organized display of tools, equipment, and materials in this room along with the smaller but still massive lower mill wheel. The room and its contents gave silent testimony to Ezekiel's work ethic.

Ira passed through the room to a large oak door that was heavily bolted and padlocked at the rear. He sat the lantern down to remove the keys from his inner coat pocket and open the locks. He carefully scanned the mill room before opening the heavy door. The dark smell of earth greeted him in the velvet blackness of the greatly enlarged natural cave. The lantern light only penetrated a short way into the cavern. He could barely see the huge stacks of bags, barrels, and casks along the far wall. An afterthought caused him to step back into the milling room. He took down a small fine flour sack from a peg on the main support pillar next to the wheel and put it into his coat pocket.

Ira removed the padlocks from the door bolt on the mill side and picked up the lantern before stepping through the doorway into the cavern. He put the lantern down on this side and pulled the door shut behind him. Closing the bolt on this side of the door, he hung the padlocks in the eyelets without engaging them. He was now certain that no one could enter the cavern behind him. There was one other way to get into the cave through a narrow winding tunnel that exited through a small natural vent in the side of the hill nearly a quarter of a mile away. This vent was very well hidden. Only he and Zeke knew about it. They discovered it accidentally long ago. Part way down this small tunnel they had found the narrow vertical crevice concealing the entrance to the room now holding the chest. He and his son Isaiah worked with Ezekiel in diligent secrecy for months to make the existence of this tunnel and the secret room impossible to find again in some future accident of discovery.

Ira moved quietly to the right side of the cave as he stepped away from the entry. Three rows of tall wooden storage shelves were lined up in parallel on huge flagstones less than ten feet from the door. The rest of the cavern floor was raw stone and dirt. The flag stones appeared to have been set in place to provide a level foundation for the shelving. All of the shelves were full of heavy crates, casks, and bags of grain. Ira stopped between the second and third shelf and placed the lantern on the stone slab floor. He then reached into what appeared to be a natural knot hole at the end of an upper shelf timber and grasped a wire loop. Pulling this loop, he withdrew a long iron bar.

Ira placed the end of the bar in a socket at the other end of the shelf and leaned over the bar so that his body weight forced it slowly down-ward with a quiet creaking sound. The timbers at the lower edge of the bottom shelf drew upward less than an inch so that a hidden set of eight iron wheels were fully supporting the weight of the shelving and its con-tents. Ira reached over to the end of the shelf and inserted the short blunt rod at the end of the brass padlock key into a small hole next to the socket holding the larger iron rod. He then released his weight from the lever and it stayed in place.

Ira moved to the far end of the shelving again and pushed. The entire shelf moved easily forward about three feet. He reached down and grasped a now exposed iron ring to pull a surprisingly light and thin piece of flagstone into an upright position revealing a dark hole with an iron ladder that disappeared into the cavern floor. Ira picked up the lantern and climbed down the ladder to a small chamber below. A strongbox with a heavy lock was on the floor near the foot of the ladder. This box contained enough silver coin to captivate the attention of anyone who somehow discovered it. Ira ignored it. He stepped over to the far end where a small stone seemed to be protruding from the floor at the base of a much larger stone forming the wall. Reaching down, he grasped the small stone and yanked it upward. The stone came free and he sat it aside. Still holding the lantern, he put his shoulder to the side of the larger stone and pushed. It rotated away revealing a narrow tunnel that disappeared into the darkness.

Ira followed this tunnel through a series of turns until he came to a spot where it bent more sharply to the left and continued into the distance. He stepped past this turn and looked back to where a narrow vertical crevice naturally cut the tunnel wall from top to bottom. The feature remained screened from view unless you knew where to look for it. Even then, it didn't look wide enough to walk through, but this was an illusion. He stepped through this opening and entered the small secret hiding place for the heavy chest that contained most of his earthly treasure.

Ira stood in the small cavern and stared at the top of the chest for sev-eral seconds. His mind was racing. He was no longer angry. The physical effort required to reach this secret place helped him focus on something other than the shame he felt regarding his own selfish pride. He knew Ezekiel was right. He knew his security did not consist of this old oak chest and its contents. Or did he? He believed in God. His father had believed in God. Ezekiel certainly believed the gospel and spent every waking moment living out his faith with a love that was unmistakable for the people around him. Ira had made a public commitment to follow Christ. He preached the gospel mixed with his own fiery rhetoric all over the colony for many years. He believed that he was blessed by God and that his wealth was clear evidence of that blessing.

Ira mechanically kneeled to open the lock on the chest and slowly lifted the heavy lid. The chest was nearly full of stacked silver and gold coins. It also contained a few small bags holding several rare costly gems. The light of the lantern glinted from the precious metal coins as he gazed absently inside. His mind barely acknowledged the wealth in the box. The flicker of lamplight on the gold brought the horrible memory of flames rushing back into his mind. His precious wife Mary, his only son Isaiah, and his daughter-in-law Natalie had died in those flames. Why did God allow that to happen? What possible good could come from the horror of that night? Ira blinked to try and clear his thoughts as he reached into the chest and removed a substantial stack of gold coins. He pulled out the flour bag as his mind began to wonder again. He sobbed quietly as he placed the coins inside the bag and tied it shut before returning it to his pocket where it settled with a heavy clink.

The flames were back. With them were the remembered screams of those men that he destroyed in the aftermath of the attack. He was overwhelmed with an avalanche of guilt and loss that threatened to crush the life from his chest. He wept uncontrollably as he fought to understand why his family had been taken, and to reconcile his cruel retribution on those men. He knew that in killing them, he had become like them. How could God forgive him? He relished the sense of control that he felt most of his adult life whether he understood it or not. Now he knew he had little control over anything.

The conversation with Ezekiel reminded him of his own terrible weakness. His pride had been pricked. Much of his grief was indeed caused by the loss of his beloved wife and son. However, he was also trapped in the prison of vendetta that was conceived on that terrible night. He could not forgive those men. He believed they were now in hell where they belonged. There was a vicious hateful side of him that relished the thought of their agony. These thoughts conflicted with Ira's own desperate desire to be forgiven for the wrong he himself had done. He didn't know how God could pardon him if he continued to hold on to the awful hate that was tearing him apart.

The sobbing finally stopped. Ira found himself all alone on his knees with his face buried in the open top of the coin-filled chest. The cold stone of the cavern and the smell of raw earth made the place seem like a tomb. He slowly began to collect himself as he closed the chest and locked it before standing up. He lifted another quiet prayer for mercy to God even while he continued to doubt that he really knew God at all. As he brushed the dust from his coat and picked up the lantern again, a different thought asserted itself. He knew what he must do. He would regain control of the events around him. His resolve strengthened as his pride once again took precedence over his values without any conscious consideration. He would see to it that Elizabeth, Zeke, and Mona survived this. He would look after his granddaughter and his friends. He was a very rich man. He would use his money to buy security for himself and those he loved. Life had always worked out this way in the past. Why would money fail him now?

The ridiculous nature of this conclusion struck Ira like a cold slap in the face. He felt God take control of his thoughts and pull him back toward sanity. He remembered the story of Judas and the thirty pieces of silver he was paid to betray Christ. Thirty pieces of silver was a pittance even then. It was the price paid for a common slave. The priests undoubtedly meant it as an insult in their twisted scheming way. Judas accepted it, though. That was amazing. Ira's thoughts wandered in this peculiar direction now and he couldn't clear his mind from considering the wasted life of Judas Iscariot. His own confused values paled in comparison to the bizarre failure of Judas.

Ira stared uncomprehending at the stone of the chamber wall as his mind was pulled deep into antiquity to the hot windswept Judean countryside. The images were so clear. They were surely brought by God Himself. It was as if he were presented with a crystal-clear view of the life and times of this most notorious of all traitors. What drove Judas? Ira knew that the man was one of the twelve original apostles chosen by Christ. Judas was there during all those miracles. He saw Jesus feed thousands with only a couple of fish and few cakes of bread. He watched while Jesus made the deaf hear, the blind see, and the lame walk. He had seen Jesus call the dead back to life. Judas saw the Master cast evil spirits out of people. He saw Jesus walk on water. He watched Jesus calm storms at sea with just a few words of command. Judas himself was given authority to heal the sick and cast out evil spirits along with the other apostles. He had used that authority.

Judas was there for the Sermon on the Mount. He witnessed the confrontations with the religious authorities. He was there during those quiet nights on lonely hillsides while Jesus, the Creator, patiently taught His friends the truth of the gospel. The Bible said that Judas was a thief though. He carried the money bag of the King and His disciples. He "helped himself" to what was in that bag. He was clearly driven by greed, by the lust for money. Judas betrayed The King of Glory for thirty pieces of silver. Jesus knew it was going to happen. He knew the real Judas all along. Judas was probably present when Jesus asked the rhetorical question, "What does it profit a man if he gains the whole world and loses his soul?" Was Judas even listening? Was money that powerful? No. It wasn't. Not then, and not now.

Ira suddenly found himself on his knees again. The weeping was different now. He cried out his shame and grief to the only One Who could give him relief. What seemed like hours passed as he poured out all of the hatred and pain. He found himself fully forgiving those men who took everyone he loved from him. He pleaded for mercy from his King and

Creator through Jesus who gave His Own Perfect Life to redeem Ira from his awful corruption. The money was no longer important. He could lose it all without caring. Ira finally felt real peace. He released all the hatred that kept him bound to the villains who destroyed his family. He was forgiven, and he knew it. He was finally, completely free.

CHAPTER 21

Billy and his men were exhausted as they trudged back down the road to the farm. The fierce fight and the terror that came with it would have a powerful effect on anyone. Billy thought the walk back to the farm seemed considerably farther than the distance they must have covered chasing the Tories who escaped with the wagon. They arrived to find the seven captured men still under guard, but now engaged in digging graves for their fallen friends at the back of the house.

Sergeant Duncan noticed their approach and stepped forward to report to his young lieutenant. Billy was surprised to learn that none of his men were injured in any way during this encounter. Duncan explained that the Tories attacked the farm at first light. The doctor, his assistant, and the farmer fought them off by firing through the windows of the stone and log house during several halfhearted Tory attempts to capture the building. They couldn't keep the scoundrels from burning the barn. The farmer lamented that he accidently shot one of the horses when he tried to dissuade his enemies from stealing the wagon Billy had given him.

None of the wounded patients were harmed. Two of them were actually able to help reload muskets for the doctor and the farmer as they gamely defended the house. The farmer's wife and daughter had hidden in the root cellar through the entire ordeal. Mrs. Phillips was now crying hysterically as she moved through and around her house bemoaning the bullet holes, her shattered milk churn, and the smoking ruins of the barn.

The milk cow was standing near the side of the road placidly staring at the strange human activities in and around the house. The old sow found freedom for herself and her piglets when the wall of the barn forming one side of her sty collapsed. She sagely decided to use this rare opportunity to disappear into the woods.

Billy and the two sergeants held a brief but intense council with the doctor and the farmer while a messenger ran to fetch the three other wagons and their escorts. Billy was certain no one could stay here now. He spent a few minutes quietly observing and listening to the sullen hatred of the captured men digging graves for their fallen comrades behind the house. He and Strickland were convinced that the escaped Tories would undoubtedly return to complete their mischief with a much larger force. The doctor understood readily. Mr. Phillips was horrified when he learned that he and his family would have to leave their home with nothing more than what could be carried on their backs and wherever a few items could be tied to the overloaded wagons.

Space was made for Silas and the other wounded men. Sergeant Duncan made it very clear that the military stores were vastly more important than any personal property belonging to Mr. and Mrs. Phillips. In the end, they were only able to collect a small portion of their most cherished possessions. Mr. Phillips showed Sergeant Duncan where his stored food supplies were, and great effort was made to divide most of these provisions between the militiamen to be carried on their backs along with their personal gear.

All three wagons were emptied and reloaded with their contents redistributed to allow room for the doctor's patients. Some of the least important objects were eventually discarded. Most of these small items belonged to farmer Phillips and his wife. Billy let Duncan argue with them about this. He didn't want to hear any more about it and there was nothing he could do to satisfy them anyway. Mr. and Mrs. Phillips were casualties of war. They were now refugees. He hoped they would find a new life elsewhere, but he could offer them nothing more than limited protection for the time being.

Everything was finally loaded and they were ready to move out again within two hours. The dead were buried. The seven prisoners were rounded up under guard. Duncan wanted to bring the prisoners along with them, but both Billy and Strickland adamantly refused. They didn't have the men to waste guarding these loyalist thugs. Billy suspected that Sergeant Strickland wanted to shoot the men and be done with it. He couldn't do that, but he realized that is just what these men would do to him if their roles were reversed.

An inspiration came to Billy just after he ordered his men to burn the house and anything the Tories might find useful. Even Strickland smiled wryly as he ordered the men to be stripped to their underwear and tied securely to what was left of the rail fence. Each man was gagged and blindfolded. Gagging them was Strickland's idea. He was tired of listening to them spew their seething hatred for their captors, and Billy had forbidden him from bashing their teeth out with his musket butt. The blindfolding was Billy's idea. He didn't want the captives to be able to tell someone else the direction his convoy took. He realized eventually that this was absurd. Any fool would be able to follow their trail. The prisoners were blindfolded anyway.

The Tories were tied closely together with their hands behind their backs and their feet lashed to the fence rail. Two of Mrs. Phillips good quilt blankets were thrown over them. Billy made the woman give up the two blankets with the most yellow and pink color patches sewn into them. He wanted to humiliate these men. He believed this would cheer his own men, and might discourage these loyalists. He would have done more to this end, but he didn't have time.

Billy reminded the captives that they could have been shot had he not decided to be lenient with them. He thought he heard muffled crying from a couple of them as he walked away. He felt a brief twinge of remorse before shrugging it off as he encountered more complaints from the farmer and his wife while their house began to burn. Billy ended up shouting down the arguments with a veiled threat to leave the family here to deal with their hostile neighbors. Mr. and Mrs. Phillips exchanged glances before hanging their heads in resignation. Billy started to say something further, but thought better of it and ended up ignoring the forlorn little family altogether as he ordered his now smaller convoy back into motion headed south.

The weather improved as they traveled the rest of that day. They were nearly ten miles away by nightfall. Billy was not happy with this distance, and neither was Sergeant Strickland. They both believed they were in greater danger now following the attack at the farm. John Red and their other guide, Private Spate, went ahead of the convoy and found a good defendable hill where they could spend the night. Billy and his men were almost totally exhausted by the time they reached this place. The wagons were brought into a small clearing at the top of the hill and the animals were unhitched and fed.

The wounded remained in the wagon under the studious care of the doctor and his assistant. The Phillips family managed to erect a make-shift tent using a tarpaulin and tree branches. The three civilian refugees disappeared unceremoniously into this shelter within moments after its completion and didn't reemerge that night. Billy and the two sergeants distributed their men into a loose perimeter around the hilltop and created a watch bill to ensure that one of every three men was awake and alert in shifts through the night. Sergeant Duncan took the first watch followed by Sergeant Strickland. Billy planned to take the last watch early in the morning. He was sound asleep in a pile of leaves under his own canvas tarpaulin within minutes.

To Billy's intense displeasure, he woke just before dawn to discover that Sergeant Strickland refused to wake him when the time for his watch started. He confronted the man a little more sharply than intended only to realize later what a tremendous compliment he was shown by this hardened veteran. A meal was quickly prepared and eaten. The camp was stricken and the draft animals were hitched to the wagons. Billy held a quick council with the two sergeants and the doctor to ensure they all understood the plan for this day's march. He learned during this meeting that one of the wounded men had experienced a turn for the worse during the night. His fever was raging and the doctor suspected blood poisoning from one of his leg wounds.

Billy took a few moments to talk with the now conscious Silas Whitaker before giving the order to move out. The earlier conversation with Dr. Bolt reminded him of the precarious condition of his friend and these other wounded soldiers. He resolved to make as much haste as possible between here and the promise of safety and help at their destination. The wagons were soon moving steadily southeast on the hidden farm road.

The militia company was becoming an effective unit made up of soldiers who were disciplined in the heated necessities of combat. They were well led but no longer required much instruction, as each man moved out to perform his own critical function. Strickland watched the first squad and the wagons pass before turning to Billy with a profound observation. "You know, Lieutenant, I believe this gaggle of bumpkins might actually turn into somethin' resembling soldiers yet!"

There was no smile. Billy understood and nodded. "I believe you may be right, Sergeant."

CHAPTER 22

Ira Fletcher came out of the mill to find the sun shining brightly through the clouds above the eastern tree line. It was still cold outside, but the wind was gone. It seemed that the day would grow warmer with each passing moment. He experienced new life and incredible cleansing through the awesome grace of God in the secret cavern under the mill. He walked down the road toward his house. He paused to cheerfully greet Captain Robertson and one of his sergeants as they strolled up the road deep in conversation. The change in his host's demeanor was not lost on the young captain. The pleasantry made the brightness of the new day a little warmer somehow.

Ira climbed the front steps of his house in a lighter mood than he had felt for quite some time. He couldn't help realizing the dramatic change in his emotions since he stomped down these same stairs hours ago while it was still dark. He now remembered meeting Mona on the stairs in his earlier fury. The realization that he may have offended or hurt her pricked his conscience deeply. He made a mental commitment to find her and offer his profound apology as soon as possible on this beautiful morning.

Ira opened the front door of the house to encounter his granddaughter, Elizabeth, dutifully cleaning the front parlor. Several scraps of colored cloth were still visible scattered all over the room. The girl smiled at him as he entered, but the smile seemed guarded as if it were the product of an inner grace rather than actual joy at his presence. Ira was struck momentarily with another pang of conscience and paused to give her his full attention. His uncomfortable memory regarding his behavior was immediately replaced with the striking realization that Elizabeth was growing up. She was indeed a beautiful young woman. Ira felt another stab of anguish as he realized that she bore a striking resemblance to her grandmother, Mary, at this same age. He forced the bitter longing for his dead wife back and stood staring at Beth from the entry foyer. She paused in her actions as well. They both remained motionless waiting for the other to speak. Ira finally broke into a deep smile. "Good morning, Beth! You're a beautiful sight this morning, my dear!"

Elizabeth straightened up fully and involuntarily reached down to adjust her apron. Her own smile turned quite genuine as she realized that her grandpa was indeed cheerful and glad to see her. She didn't know what had come over him lately. She knew that he was a very complex man. She loved him inexhaustibly, but she never fully understood him. She did not remember her father, her mother, or her grandmother. The only family she had ever known was Grandpa Ira, Ezekiel, and Mona Partridge.

This was her family plain and simple, whether they were all blood kin or not. She was afraid her grandpa would never fully realize or admit that he loved Mona far more than as a family friend. Elizabeth had always thought of Mona Partridge as her surrogate mother. She wouldn't describe the relationship that way, but she knew that more than mere friendship bound them together. She knew her grandpa loved Mona deeply, but he was too stubborn and thick-headed to acknowledge his feelings and do something about them. Elizabeth wanted her grandpa to be happy. She knew he loved her completely. Elizabeth knew him to be a jumble of conflicting emotions buried deeply under a tough and proud exterior that was very difficult to penetrate. She believed that during her lifetime, she, Ezekiel, and Mona were the only humans who had heard Ira Fletcher laugh or cry. She knew Mona loved her grandpa too. Elizabeth wished she could do something to make these two precious people reach out to each other.

Ira was as hungry as he was exhausted. He hung his hat on a peg by the door and asked, "Are you making breakfast today, Beth?"

Elizabeth responded with a faint smile, "Mona is in the kitchen now, Grandpa...." He never ate breakfast. What had come over him? His mood was so foul during the night that she actually became frightened when she considered what he might do. He seemed to have undergone some strangely cleansing emotional upheaval. He even looked younger at this moment than he had in several years.

Ira apparently noticed the cloth scraps again as he stepped from the foyer to the parlor. "Beth, you don't have to clean all of this up if you don't want to. You can sew your quilt in here. I don't mind. The thought of it reminds me of your grandmother." There was no sadness in this. There were no tears. He was smiling. She dropped what she was holding into her basket and stepped forward to hug him abruptly with a hearty kiss on the cheek. He reached up and grasped her wrists while looking straight in her eyes. Now there were tears, but the smile remained. "Elizabeth, I want you to be happy. I know you are growing up. A quilt for your hope chest is just the thing you should be making. It speaks of a future promise. The very term 'hope chest' suggests what your life should be about right now. Rather than the fear and rumor of war."

She said, "Thank you, Grandpa. I love you too. I would like to work in here. I'll keep the mess under control. Now you go see what Mona is doing in the kitchen." With that she gave him another peck on the cheek and turned back to her work.

The smell of bacon and fresh bread reached him with a faint blissful sweetness. He found Mona turning the bacon in a large iron pan over the kitchen hearth. Two marvelous loaves of sweet bread were cooling on the massive oak table next to a crock of churned butter and a small dish of honey. Coffee was steaming over the fire ready to pour, and he felt nearly weak-kneed as these wonderful aromas confronted him. This didn't compare with the sweet smile Mona greeted him with. Ira returned the smile with awkward timidity. Mona straightened up to survey him from head to foot as he stood staring at her from the doorway. Something was different about him. She knew it instantly. She loved this man. She would no longer hesitate to show him that love. Life was too short for that. The events of the past several days proved that if nothing else could. She had decided this morning on the front stairs. He treated her contemptuously, but she didn't care. She would love him through all of his turmoil. She and his late wife, Mary, were more like sisters than just friends. Mona's deep profound love for Ira grew after Mary's loss. She felt no guilt in this.

Ira needed her as much as Elizabeth did after Mary was killed. She hadn't intended to feel this way about her friend's widower. Mona repressed her feelings for years because it seemed wrong to love him. Ira was so changed by the events of that terrible night long ago. The old Ira was suddenly gone as if he had also been killed. He continued to preach. He continued to care for his granddaughter and his friends, but he developed a dark dangerous hardness that allowed him to say and do horrible things while apparently feeling justified. Mona told herself that she couldn't possibly love a man like that, but the more time she spent with him, the more she knew this was hopeless. She did love him. It was as simple as that. Years passed. Elizabeth was now fully grown.

Mona broke the silence. "Come on in here. You look starved, Ira. Have you slept at all?" Ira didn't answer, but he did come into the kitchen and sit down at the table. She quickly sat a china plate in front of him and filled it with bacon, scrambled eggs, and sliced fresh bread. The coffee was poured, and she sat down across the table to face him. He prayed quietly before launching into the food as if he hadn't eaten in weeks. She smiled broadly as he cleaned the plate in minutes. Mona picked up the plate and moved it to the sideboard before sitting back down and reaching across the table to grasp both of Ira's hands in hers. He looked up into her smiling eyes and couldn't keep tears from forming in his own.

Mona asked, "What is it? What has happened? You seem like a different person than the angry man I passed on the front steps this morning." He remained silent, but continued to gaze steadily into her eyes. He saw something there that he didn't notice before. She really did care about him. Could it be that this friend of many years actually loved him? The relief he felt deep in his soul this morning caused everything to seem brighter and more positive. He couldn't help himself now. He told Mona about the secret place. He told her about the money. He didn't fully explain where it was hidden, but she could guess. She didn't care about money anyway. In her world, the greatest treasure she knew other than Jesus Christ was the family in this house right now. Ira told Mona about the relief he finally felt after coming to the end of himself and fully, finally, surrendering everything to Jesus. She was crying now too.

Seventeen years had passed since Mary's death. Mona stepped in without hesitation or complaint to supervise the care and upbringing of the orphaned baby, Elizabeth. Neither Ira nor Ezekiel could have raised the precious girl on their own. The need was obvious, and Mona had filled it. Ira long believed this was done simply from Mona's sense of duty to Mary. Maybe it was only that at first. The years had passed. The girl grew to be the beautiful young lady of today. Mona was there through it all. She maintained her own home. Propriety demanded that, but she was always there for Beth. It finally dawned on Ira that she was there for him also. This magnificent woman had gracefully helped with every challenge his family faced during the darkest time of his life so far. It was now undeniable. The gratitude he felt began to change into something far more powerful. He involuntarily squeezed her hands lightly as these thoughts coursed through his mind. Mona felt this and her smile deepened.

CHAPTER 23

Crispin lay in miserable dejected silence. The storeroom was pitch-black save the sliver of light leaking in through the tiny gap along the top edge of the partition wall separating this room from the next. The other room must have a high window up at ground level which allowed daylight to enter. There was no heat in this dank empty place, but he hardly noticed the cold in his frustrated fury. He did his best earlier to write an acceptable report on paper supplied to him by the impudent young lieutenant who served as Willoughby's adjutant.

The lieutenant actually opened and read the document in Crispin's presence. He handed the paper back to the captain and asked, "Are you quite certain this is what you want to say, sir? You do realize this document will be used as evidence in your trial?" Crispin nearly screamed his response as he demanded the man take the report and get out. He stepped forward threateningly only to be brought up short by the lowered bayonets of the two armed guards standing in the store room at either side of the lieutenant. The smile that briefly flickered across the lieutenant's face was clear in its malevolence.

The adjutant clicked his heels together in an absurd show of mock respect and said, "As you wish, sir!" He picked up the oil lantern and stepped briskly out of the room. The door slammed shut behind the three armed men. Crispin heard the bolt shoot home and the padlock click into place. He had been in this damp, cold darkness ever since. He was given a single horse blanket, a jar of water, and a wooden bucket for his personal use. The storeroom had been cleared of other supplies to fulfill its current purpose. There was nothing else in the room but empty dark space.

Crispin wrapped himself in the blanket and slept fitfully before pride, anger, and fear brought him back to miserable consciousness. Of course, his mission was a failure. He refused to accept the idea that this was somehow his fault at first. He didn't care what Willoughby thought of him. How could the major possibly know what happened that day at Fletcher's Mill, or in the days since? He wasn't there. What did he mean when he said he didn't like officers like Crispin? Crispin was from a fine family. He was connected in parliament. Sir Thomas Willoughby ... who was he? How did he earn a knighthood? What had he ever done? Crispin had never heard of him. He would see the man broken for this!

Crispin lay coiled in the old horse blanket for hour after hour seething and scheming as he rationalized his involvement in all that occurred since he left Charlotte over a week ago. The passage of time began to seem almost meaningless. He feigned sleep when the bolt slid back and the door opened to emit the amazingly bright glare of another oil lantern. Two armed guards entered the room with another man who brought in a battered metal pot and fresh jar of water. The pot contained some unrecognizable smoked meat and two pieces of hardtack. The guards waited silently as the man took the personal bucket out, emptied it, and brought it back. The man paused briefly to see that the prisoner was still breathing before he nodded at the two guards. The three men left again, taking the lantern with them. The room once again plunged into deep darkness. Crispin was ravenously hungry. He found the pot with the food and devoured its contents swiftly. He drank some of the water from the jar, then returned to the foul-smelling blanket in the corner of his prison.

Time dragged on. Hours passed with the only punctuation supplied by the occasional brief return of light when his food and water were replaced. Crispin began to feel like an animal in a cage. He disgustedly realized that caged animals had an advantage that he did not share. They could at least see out. He could tell that a day ended when the light failed to come in through the gap at the top of the wall. He knew when a new day started when the light returned. He refused to acknowledge the presence of his guards when they came in. The silence was maddening. Crispin's rage grew, but there was no way to express it. He finally lost track of the passage of days and nights. He began to realize how utterly hopeless his circumstances were. He was responsible for the Fletcher's Mill incident and its aftermath. Those men trusted him and he failed them. He failed his family, his king, and himself.

The depression deepened as Crispin slowly faced his responsibility. He caused the deaths of those good men. He was certain they were better men than himself. Wasn't that what Major Willoughby thought? He should know. He was a professional soldier. Crispin was nothing more than the lying coward Willoughby thought him to be. He suddenly remembered the moment in that other storeroom when his pride and rage got the best of him. He murdered that young boy! He had crushed the life out of his victim's throat with his booted foot with total contempt while the boy struggled to survive. The realization of the filth polluting his dark soul overwhelmed Crispin in that moment. He lay weeping on the stone floor with the filthy blanket wrapped around his head.

Something heard somewhere earlier began to gnaw at him then. It was something about Fletcher's Mill. That old man, Ira Fletcher, was said to be incredibly rich. Fletcher didn't have noble blood, though. How would he have obtained wealth? He was said to be a personal friend of the estranged royal governor. That's one of the things Major Willoughby was so angry about. Somehow he, Crispin, managed to impugn the honorable name Fletcher. The major wasn't there though. Willoughby hadn't seen what happened. He just assumed that he knew the truth. Well, Crispin had heard even stranger things about Ira Fletcher and his precious mill.

That fool boy in the mill almost let it slip that night when he told Crispin and Sergeant Smythe about the rebel contraband stored under the mill in a secret cave. Crispin slowly came to realize that all of the rumors he heard about treasure hidden under Fletcher's Mill could be true.... They must be true! Why else would that old black man have dared try to interfere with him? Why would the villagers openly rise in revolt against him and his armed party of dragoons? Why would the place be violently protected by Reverend Fletcher himself and that large group of hidden militiamen? The more he thought about it, the more it made sense to Crispin. Ira Fletcher could afford to buy and pay for his own armed force ... that was it ... that must be it! Those men weren't just members of the "Provisional Militia of the sovereign State of South Carolina" as Fletcher arrogantly described them that day! They were Fletcher's own men! He was sure of it. He continued to mull these thoughts over hour after hour until he finally lapsed into a fitful sleep.

Crispin woke hours later still in abject despair. Sitting up, he removed the blanket from his head and neck. There was dim light leaking into the room from above the wall. He looked down at the blanket as if he were seeing it for the first time. Crispin suddenly knew what he must do. He wouldn't wait to be tried by people like Willoughby. Looking up at the dim rafters of the ceiling, he decided to throw the end of the blanket over and knot it so that the timber would support his weight. He could stand on the overturned bucket to make a noose out of the trailing corner. He stopped sobbing as he considered how to end his own misery in the most cowardly way of all.

Crispin was sitting there considering this option when he heard footsteps and voices from the outside hallway. He didn't try to feign sleep this time as the lock was removed and the bolt was withdrawn. The door opened, and he stared in curiosity as the adjutant entered the room with the same two guards. They were half dragging the still tied, gagged, and blindfolded form of a battered and filthy, but fully uniformed, Continental Army major. The major involuntarily fell to his knees on the floor as the bonds were cut from his wrists and the blindfold and gag were removed. He sat there staring around the room and blinking at Crispin sitting in his own filth in the corner.

The lieutenant smiled broadly. "Well, Captain Crispin, you have company now! I hope you two will enjoy the time here together as we decide what to do with you." The same man who had been bringing food and water to Crispin entered with another horse blanket and another water jar. It was clear without any explanation that both of the prisoners would be expected to use the same necessary bucket. The man left the storeroom as quickly and quietly as he appeared. The young officer and guards were also gone in seconds and the room was plunged back into darkness.

Awkward silence prevailed for what seemed like hours. Neither of the two prisoners wished to be the first to speak. It took quite some time for their eyes to adjust to the near blackness well enough to see each other. Crispin's curiosity finally got the best of him. He toughened his voice as much as possible as he rose to his feet and asked, "Who are you, sir?" He didn't really understand why he referred to the other man with the honorific "sir." Crispin remembered that he was contemplating suicide only minutes before this strange visitor was added to his prison cell. Perhaps visitor wasn't the correct term. The other man didn't respond at first. He was seated in the far corner vigorously trying to rub life back into his swollen and chafed wrists. Crispin became irritated and tried again with, "Did you hear me, sir? I asked who are you?"

The tattered continental officer finally spoke in a frightened voice, "My name is Major Theodore Throckmorton. I'm the deputy quartermaster of the Southern Continental Army." Throckmorton hadn't realized that Crispin was a British officer.

Crispin no longer wore a uniform coat, and his clothing now bore no resemblance to a uniform. Crispin was surprised more by the content of the information than the overly frank way it was delivered. He paused before saying, "My name is Captain Reginald Crispin. I too am, or was, a deputy quartermaster … of His Majesty's Southern Royal Army."

Throckmorton sat in shocked silence for some time before he finally mustered the courage to ask, "What on earth are you doing in this place?"

Crispin wasn't offended or surprised by the question. The terror and trauma of the last several days had unnerved him. He was beginning to believe he couldn't be shocked by anything he might experience in the future. He knew he had enemies in the army. His survival in a future court martial was not as assured as Major Willoughby believed it to be. He was glad to have someone, anyone, to talk with now. Crispin soon found himself telling this enemy officer about everything he had been through over the preceding week. Throckmorton listened in silence. He was amazed how much he had in common with this young British captain.

Throckmorton and Crispin both felt severely misused by their superiors and their subordinates. They had both faced their enemies with frighteningly disastrous results. Their personal economic interests made their duty positions potentially lucrative if they were willing to compromise what others would call integrity or character. Throckmorton and Crispin began to understand that they had a powerfully compelling mutual interest. This turn in the conversation brought them to open discussion of fabulous treasure rumored to be hidden inside or under Fletcher's Mill.

CHAPTER 24

They were moving very slowly, but they somehow managed another fifteen miles well before nightfall on the second day after leaving the Phillips farm. Billy was exasperated with the pace and so was Sergeant Strickland. Sergeant Duncan was more pragmatic about it. The doctor was concerned about his patients and started asking Billy to halt the march before night made his work too difficult in the moving wagon. He lost another patient and it was clearly weighing heavily on him. They desperately needed to avoid possible ambush on the trail during the march, but moving at night was out of the question.

Billy was acutely aware that they were in country crisscrossed with hostile bands of Tory militia, British regulars, and groups of rebel partisans. Few if any of the armed militia groups wore uniforms. It was impossible to tell which side of the conflict strangers might support. He knew none of the wounded men would survive a pitched battle in these circumstances. They thankfully encountered no one on the trail all day. Billy believed getting the wounded men and the supply wagons to safety quickly was the best way to protect them. Doctor Bolt would have to do the best he could for them while they were moving. He could perform any intense treatments by lantern light when they finally did come to a stop as night fell.

The map Billy received from General Morgan indicated they were less than five miles from Fletcher's Mill if Spate was correct about the town they just went around being Fish Dam. Nearing completion of his mission was somehow making Billy's anxiety increase rather than easing it. The map showed that they would have to cross the Broad River before they reached their destination. He didn't want to attempt a river crossing at night. He hadn't yet thought through crossing the river. He sent John Red and two other scouts forward to search for boats of any kind along the riverbank, but they hadn't returned.

The map showed a possible ford in the area, but it was further north on the main road. Private Spate advised him that the flooding of the river would render any ford useless now anyway. Billy called a brief halt while it was still light enough to bring the two sergeants and Spate into a quick council. The entire convoy showed immediate relief as the teamsters moved the wagons deeper into the trees. The escorting infantry automatically took up stations in a loose perimeter around them and went to ground.

Billy was questioning Spate about the river again when Dr. Bolt walked over to join the conversation. Billy's glance at the man was rewarded with a dismal frown of worry. The doctor didn't try to buffer his report. "Another of my patients has died." None of them needed to ask. They knew which one it was. The man was crying out in a loud feverish delirium an hour earlier before the doctor took drastic action to silence him. Billy asked him about the rest of the wounded. The doctor shook his head and looked down for a moment before answering, "We must get them somewhere out of the elements very quickly or they may all die. I have been doing what I can under these circumstances. I've prayed for each of them and I believe God Himself is the only reason more of them have not yet perished." This comment surprised Billy. He hadn't thought of the diminutive doctor as a religious man. He seemed to be more of a man of science. Letting these thoughts go, he turned back to Spate and asked him how the locals crossed the river in times like these.

Spate shifted from foot to foot nervously under the steady gaze of his lieutenant and the two sergeants. Finally, his face brightened noticeably. "Well now, sir, come to think of it, there is a ferry that's used to cross the river along the main road that runs from Fish Dam to Rocky Mount." He flinched when he noticed the flash of anger on the faces of Billy and Sergeant Strickland. "Now ... I didn't say anything about it earlier cause I didn't think it would serve for us.... With us bein' so secretive and all...."

Sergeant Duncan broke the ensuing silence with, "That's all right, Spate. How far are we from the ferry now? Is it still in operation? Who owns it? Who runs it?" These were obvious questions. Billy appreciated Duncan taking charge of the conversation.

Spate told them that as far as he knew, the ferry was still working. It was owned by an old man and his three sons. He thought the name was Simpson or Simons or something like that. He didn't know if the ferrymen were rebel or loyalist. He suspected that they were probably Tories because the Royal Army allowed them to remain in business. Billy unfolded his map again and had Spate point out the ferry's location. It wasn't shown on the map. He would have noticed it. This probably indicated that whoever drew the map either didn't know about it or considered it completely useless for rebel purposes. That was absurd though. Something as important as a functional ferry would certainly have been thought important enough to add to the hand-drawn map. Unless it wasn't there.

Billy looked up at Spate and asked, "Are you sure there is a ferry on the river there?"

Spate looked mildly offended and said, "Yes, sir. I've been across the river on it myself ... durin' happier times ... sir." Spate leaned over the map to look closer for several moments before pointing down and exclaiming, "Look here, sir! There's lots of stuff missin' from this here map!"

Billy looked over his shoulder and said, "What? I got this map from General Morgan himself."

Spate shook his head. "Beggin' your pardon, sir, but I don't rightly care who it come from.... There's stuff missin'. In fact, there's whole farms missin'. There's creeks missin'. The truest part of the map is toward the middle. The further out toward the sides of it, the less it shows what's really there...."

Billy looked up at Strickland and Duncan. He was angry with himself now. How could he be this stupid? Of course! This hand-drawn map was excellently done, but it was more concerned with the main supply routes, towns, and major terrain features. The high quality of the drawing made it seem more reliable than it actually was.

A cold chill coursed its way down Billy's spine. He had been pushing this critical convoy down this trail mile after mile with no real understanding of the area. He realized that they owed a tremendous debt to the knowledge of this old smuggler, Private Spate. Something the doctor said a few minutes ago also nagged at the back of his mind. The doctor said that he had been praying for those wounded men. He was even giving credit to God for protecting them. Billy couldn't help wondering if the doctor's prayers had somehow influenced God to help them pass through all these miles of hostile country in spite of Billy's own ignorance. He turned back to Private Spate.

"How far are we from the ferry crossing right now, Spate?"

The man looked around and rubbed his chin for a moment before responding. "I make it about two and a half miles ... maybe a little further. But we'll have to backtrack and then go around Fish Dam to the south. The ferry crosses the river a little more than two miles east of the village. There's no good road from here to there since we need to stay away from the village and not be seen."

Billy turned immediately to Strickland and Duncan. "We're going to stay right here tonight. We can't leave until our scouts return, and we don't have time to move all the way back north to the ferry crossing. I want to go myself and take a look at it now. Sergeant Duncan, you stay here and take charge 'til I get back. Get set in for the night, you know what's needed. Sergeant Strickland, you and Spate are coming with me. Pick out two good men to come with us. Be ready to move out in thirty minutes."

Strickland nodded and hurried off with Spate to find "volunteers." Duncan asked a few brief questions and moved away to start setting up camp. Billy and Dr. Bolt were left standing alone. The conversation immediately turned to the disposition of the man who died a couple of hours ago.

They agreed that he should be buried here. They would mark the grave carefully and make a notation on the map showing its location. It didn't take long to make the preparations. The doctor and Billy presided over a short makeshift ceremony for the man as he was buried in the presence of the Phillips family and a few of the militiamen who weren't needed right away by Sergeant Duncan. Billy thought a great deal about the event after it was finished. He hadn't known what to say over the man, but he knew some show of respect for the departed was needed.

The doctor surprised Billy with an offer to help. He nodded his consent, and Dr. Bolt stepped to the head of the grave. The old man removed his hat and handed it to farmer Phillips. Billy was even more surprised when the doctor produced a small worn Bible from his medical bag and turned to an apparently familiar passage in the book. The ensuing funeral ceremony was well and clearly spoken. It was solemn and beautiful in content. It somehow offered hope to those listening, while at the same time remaining brief. The fact that it didn't look like the doctor was actually reading from the book as he spoke the words seemed quite odd. It appeared that the doctor was speaking the words from memory in his broken accent. When Billy looked over at the open page, he found that the words were written in a foreign language. The old doctor did the whole ceremony, including several Bible passages, in his strange heavily accented English, purely from memory.

Sergeant Strickland had his small group of men ready to leave as soon as the ceremony was done. Billy spent several more minutes discussing his intentions with Sergeant Duncan in case something happened and he was unable to return from his reconnaissance of the ferry crossing. He paused briefly to speak with Silas and to offer his hearty thanks to the doctor for the respect he had shown the dead soldier. He and the four other men were moving swiftly through the woods a short time later in the direction of the ferry crossing on the Broad River.

Billy didn't know if the ferry was there or not. He wondered if he would be able to make use of it even if it did exist. He suspected that they would have to seize the ferry by force if it was there at all. He knew that he had to get the convoy across the river as soon as possible. He realized that he was terrified. He wasn't afraid of death. He was afraid of failure. More specifically, he was afraid he would fail these men, that he would fail the general, that he would fail in this important mission after he was entrusted with so much. Running quietly through the woods with this small group of men, Billy began to say a prayer of his own.

CHAPTER 25

Captain Robertson bound up the steps two at a time and knocked on the door of the Fletcher house a little harder than he intended. Elizabeth yanked the door open with a look of disdain that caused him to momentarily falter in his excitement. "Yes, Captain, what is it? Why are you pounding on this door? Don't you understand that we have a very feeble injured man upstairs?"

Robertson removed his hat and stilled his anxiety as he said, "Yes, miss. I do understand. It's just that I need to speak with Reverend Fletcher right away. Would you please let him know that I'm here?"

Elizabeth stepped back and pulled the door open. "Let him know yourself, sir. He's in the kitchen eating breakfast." Robertson nodded his thanks as he hurried through the parlor toward the kitchen at the back of the house. Elizabeth closed the door and wondered what could possibly be agitating the man so. His manner didn't suggest fear. What was it? Excitement? There must be some news from outside the village. Maybe their fears were unfounded and the crisis had passed. She heard Ezekiel quietly calling from upstairs in that moment. She left all thought of the militia captain behind her as she rushed back upstairs to Ezekiel's room.

Robertson heard quiet laughter from inside the kitchen. He tapped once on the door and pushed it open. He was immediately surprised to see Reverend Fletcher holding hands across the kitchen table with Mona Partridge. The captain stood momentarily speechless. The two turned and looked up to see who was interrupting the special moment they were enjoying in each other's company.

Ira broke the silence. "Yes, Captain?" He wasn't angry. He wore a peaceful, pleasant expression that surprised Robertson even more.

The captain nearly forgot what he came to say. Its importance brought it back suddenly. "We just received critical news, Reverend." Ira turned to face him directly, and Mona got up to finish straightening the kitchen. Robertson went on, "A rider just came in from Colonel Marion. He is headed this way from over east of Camden with a large body of men. It seems there was a fierce battle several days ago northwest of here at a place called the Cowpens."

Captain Robertson had Ira's full attention. Mona excused herself and brushed past the captain, moving quietly out through the parlor door. Robertson continued, "Francis Marion doesn't have any reason to come this far west unless he really believes it's crucial. He must know something we don't about British intentions. I wonder what could be so important?"

Ira thought a moment and asked, "You don't think the Continental Army is headed this direction from this 'Cowpens' place? Would the British follow them? Could a significant battle occur here?"

Robertson didn't know the answers to those questions, but he was wondering the same things.

Both men stared silently until Ira realized that his thoughts were fixed on the missing Captain Crispin. He wondered if the man had made it to a British garrison by now. This brought another train of thought. Crispin identified himself as a quartermaster. He was here trying to forage, or steal, provisions for the Royal Army. Could that oddly sinister fellow have persuaded the army to return here in force as Robertson expected? Was Colonel Marion reacting to something he had heard in this regard, or was this new information completely unrelated?

Captain Robertson was apparently thinking along the same lines when he said, "Whatever would influence the British to move on us here, has apparently been presented to Colonel Marion as reason enough to come to our aid. The message specifically refers to the results of the battle causing Colonel Marion to feel he needs to reinforce this place. The strange thing is that the message also says the battle was an overwhelming victory for our cause."

Another thought occurred to Ira. "Maybe there is something else involved in all of this." Robertson remained silent, but his thoughts began to settle on a likely theory. Ira went on, "Surely you have heard the rumors of treasure hidden somewhere in or near Fletcher's Mill, Captain?" Robertson was surprised to hear Ira mention the subject, and it must have shown on his face. Ira turned directly toward him. "Captain, we have been besieged by these rumors for years. You are well aware that I am a wealthy man. I make no pretense otherwise. God has blessed me profoundly. I have many friends in this colony on both sides of the current political debate. I also have many enemies. Some of my 'friends' are simply interested in my wealth. The interests of my enemies are more complicated. You see, I, like my father, abhor slavery. I believe it to be morally repugnant. The fact that I own no slaves and yet possess great wealth shows that riches are attainable without the sin of slavery. This threatens the interests of many in this and the other southern colonies."

Captain Robertson was beginning to better understand some of what he heard about Ira Fletcher from angry and jealous men all over the colony. Ira was warming to his topic as he went on, "Many of my neighbors find it morally wrong for me, a private subject of the Crown, to refuse to be complicit in this evil practice! They are even more alarmed and offended that my father and I would not only set these unfortunate people free, but we would actually employ one of them in a position of authority in our private business affairs!"

Robertson understood that Ira was referring to the position Ezekiel held here at the mill. He ventured the comment, "None of the villagers seem to be offended by Ezekiel, sir. Why is that?"

Ira began to pace again with his hands clasped behind his back. The kitchen was just large enough to allow him several steps back and forth between the hearth and the table. He shook his head without missing a step. "No. The villagers are personally loyal to my family. They are all good God-fearing Englishmen. They recognize injustice when they see it! They agree with me in any event. Ezekiel has done more to endear them during his long life than could ever be undone by the poison of pride, selfishness, and greed!"

Ira's thoughts shifted back to his earlier musings. "I believe the British may have more dubious motives for attacking us here than some strange retaliation for a battle lost elsewhere. I don't think their sole motive would be theft of the supplies in our storage rooms either. I believe there are two other things that will drive them here. You have already explained one of these. They simply can't allow what happened here with Crispin and his men to go unanswered for reasons of morale and politics. They will believe that they can't leave a hostile act unpunished. My friendship with the governor and others in the colonial government will not protect us if the authorities choose to believe what Captain Crispin tells them. Why wouldn't they believe him? I think the rumors of treasure may bring them here anyway."

Ira paused and looked at the captain with an expression full of frustration, fatigue, and sadness. Robertson noticed something else there also. Reverend Fletcher usually wore an almost expressionless mask. Not of indifference, but of authority. Whatever was going through Ira's mind was being displayed in an oddly animated way. A powerful conflicting emotion seemed to be struggling to gain control of Ira's thoughts and his demeanor. What was it? Irony? Fatalism? Hope? Ira's features slowly calmed and Robertson began to understand. He was watching this complex man work through a desperate struggle with an old enemy. Neither man spoke for almost a minute.

Robertson slowly sat down in one of the chairs while Ira resumed his pacing. Then, like beams of sunshine coming through parting rain clouds, a smile crept over Ira's face. He stopped and pulled his shoulders back while he straightened the front of his coat. Robertson noticed a brief twinkle in the older man's eyes. Ira took in a deep breath and exhaled slowly. He had come to grips with his emotions and was now obviously relieved by a peace that seemed to wash over him and bring everything under control.

Ira surprised Robertson by sitting back down across the table from him. He slowly reached over and removed the coffee pot from its iron hook above the fire. He poured himself a steaming cup of Mona's strong brew and offered a cup to Robertson, who gladly accepted. Ira put the pot back on the hook and sipped thoughtfully. Something occurred to him suddenly and he looked up to ask, "Captain, what if there is an altogether different reason for us to be visited by the armies of our friends and enemies alike?"

Robertson curiously asked, "What could that reason possibly be, sir?"

Ira said, "The messenger reported that there was a large battle and that the continentals were the victors. Did they give any further information about it? How large was the battle? How decisive was the victory?"

Robertson took a sip of coffee and shook his head. "I don't know, sir. There were no further details other than the names of the officers commanding the opposing sides, and that the battle was a great victory for the Continental Army."

Ira leaned back and said, "Well, sir, let's suppose this was a truly great victory and that many of the British soldiers were killed, captured, or driven from the field. What would happen to their weapons and supplies?"

Ira leaned forward on his elbows with the coffee cup between his hands. "Who were the opposing commanders?"

Robertson replied, "General Daniel Morgan commanded the continentals. That murderous scoundrel, Colonel Tarleton was in command of the British."

Ira said, "I've heard of both men. I can only imagine the carnage that must have resulted in a meeting between those two. You didn't answer my other question, though. What would have happened to the arms, ammunition, and other military supplies of the men vanquished in such a battle? I suppose the saying, 'To the victor go the spoils' would apply here."

Robertson shrugged and said, "Well, yes. Of course."

Ira sat back and said, "Is it possible that General Morgan would send some of those supplies here to be given to Colonel Marion and others like him ... to you, for that matter?"

Robertson suddenly understood. "Why, yes, sir! That would also explain why Colonel Marion is coming here so quickly and in force. We have no way of knowing how much, if anything, might be headed here as a result of the battle, but it could be a large quantity of critical supplies. A convoy carrying these things would be priceless to us here."

Ira sat his cup down and rubbed his chin before saying, "Captain, it really doesn't matter why Colonel Marion is coming to us. No, and it doesn't really matter why the British would choose to attack us. It seems that something profound is going to happen here. I know you think my mill is a fortress. I know you have made elaborate plans to defend us. It seems we will be significantly reinforced very soon. However, I also know what King Solomon said in a Psalm inspired by God's Holy Spirit thousands of years ago. "Except the LORD keepeth the city, the watchman waketh but in vain." We must have God's help here, or I fear the enemy will destroy us and those we love." Captain Robertson understood. He was mildly surprised, but didn't object when Ira began to pray.

CHAPTER 26

Lieutenant Robert Cloyde led the thirty exhausted members of his light dragoon troop into the dusty outskirts of Rocky Mount late in the afternoon. The picket guard stopped him briefly, then passed the small column on toward the center of town. He was met by an inquisitive young sergeant of the guard near the head of the main street. Cloyde explained who he was and asked directions to the officer in charge of the garrison. The sergeant explained that a large house near the village center was used as the headquarters building. Major Willoughby, the commander, could be found there. The house was easy to find. It was the largest structure in town, and was previously the property of a wealthy colonial who unfortunately chose the wrong side in the present conflict. Cloyde gave instructions to his sergeant regarding the immediate care of the men and horses. He then dismounted, gave the reins of his own horse to an orderly, and went to report to Major Willoughby.

Willoughby listened to Cloyde's report from a seated position behind his desk. He had already heard about the tragic events at Cowpens. His worst fears were verified when he interrogated the captured Major Throckmorton. He now listened aghast as Cloyde filled in the gruesome details and horrible nature of the defeat. Major Willoughby knew many of the officers lost in the battle. His stomach twisted as he learned more about their fate. Anger swelled in his chest. Intense professional resolve was required to maintain his stoic composure while Cloyde finished his report. Willoughby found that most of his fury was not even directed toward the rebel forces who inflicted this humiliating defeat. No, what galled him the most was the prideful stupidity of one of his superiors, Lieutenant Colonel Banastre Tarleton. He listened to the rest of the report while thinking there were odd similarities between that arrogant fool Tarleton and the cowardly charlatan, Crispin, who was locked up in a makeshift cell downstairs.

Cloyde stopped speaking but remained standing in front of Major Willoughby at rigid attention. The major missed the last several words spoken in his angry distraction. He was further frustrated by having to ask the lieutenant to repeat himself when he realized that the man was waiting for his response. "Will you provide me with reinforcements so that I can comb the countryside to the south and apprehend the rebel convoy, sir?"

Major Willoughby considered the request. His first instinct was to refuse. He wanted to order Cloyde and his men to return to Tarleton immediately. He wanted to let the colonel face the realization that this was a further blunder in his tragic series of mistakes. Tarleton had sent an inexperienced subaltern, with too little force, to seize the valuable convoy and deny the rebels use of its priceless cargo. Willoughby's own professional pride wouldn't allow him to do that. He would do the right thing here regardless of the glaring incompetence of those around him.

Willoughby sadly realized that Reverend Fletcher may have chosen rebellion rather than loyalty to the king. He thought he knew Fletcher. The disappointment was powerful. His heart wanted what he was hearing to be incorrect. He didn't want to believe it. How could this man, who owed so much to his sovereign, treacherously turn like this? Was he so corrupted by his wealth that he couldn't see the evil of his actions? Could he possibly believe that he would be allowed to keep the property he held? The more Willoughby thought about it, the angrier he became. He realized with a start that he was again ignoring the young lieutenant.

Willoughby stood slowly and leaned forward with his hands resting firmly on top of the table he was using as a desk. He stared at Cloyde while his expression changed to decisive resolve. He said, in a quietly controlled voice, "Please stand at ease, Lieutenant. I want you to meet someone. We are holding two very unusual prisoners. I believe you will find what one of them has to say interesting. The man I'm referring to is a rebel major. He claims to be the deputy quartermaster of the southern Continental Army. The other is also a quartermaster, a captain in fact. Unfortunately, he belongs to us. The major is obviously a prisoner of war. The British captain is under close arrest pending court martial for cowardice and gross negligence."

Major Willoughby moved from behind the desk and stepped past Lieutenant Cloyde to pull the door open. "Come with me," he said as he strode down the long hallway toward the front of the house. The sentry guarding the outside of the major's office door fell in step with him, leaving Cloyde feeling like he might trip over the man's trailing musket as he tried to keep up. They went down a flight of stairs to the first floor, then through a door near the kitchen that led down still more stairs. The bottom steps were lamp-lit even during broad daylight. They were now in a huge cellar divided into numerous storage rooms on either side of a long hallway leading away from the stairs. The corridor was well lit. The major and guard moved briskly down this hall without pausing. Cloyde could see another armed guard standing outside the last door at the far end. The guard snapped to rigid attention at the approach of the major. He barked a brief report. Willoughby ordered him to open the door.

The inside of the storeroom was pitch-black. The guard removed a lantern from its hook in the hallway and stepped inside with the light held at arm's length. Major Willoughby stepped into the room and motioned for Cloyde to follow. The other guard entered behind them with his musket held at port arms. Cloyde's eyes were adjusting to the darkness. He could barely see two men sitting near a bucket in the far corner. The guard with the lantern moved closer to the corner. Cloyde could see that one of the prisoners wore the tattered remains of what once was a well-made blue and buff continental officer's uniform. He thought the creature inside the clothing wouldn't look much like an officer, even in broad daylight when the uniform was new. The man peered up at the visitors with a peculiar look that combined the expression of fear and cunning of a cornered sewer rat. The other man was younger. He didn't seem to be wearing a uniform, but the trousers and shirt were clearly British military. His expression showed cold offended rage.

Major Willoughby startled everyone by shouting, "On your feet, Captain Crispin! How dare you remain seated when I enter this room?" The guard without the lantern was holding his musket at the ready. The bayonet was attached to the muzzle, even in this confined space.

The younger prisoner remained seated. The guard moved a step closer with the bayonet offered as incentive to respond rationally. The man slowly stood. "I am a captain in His Majesty's Royal Army. I've been falsely accused and treated with total contempt by you … sir."

It seemed he might have said more, but his speech was interrupted by Willoughby. "Shut your mouth! Let me remind you, Captain, you are under arrest. You are facing charges which could result in you being shot or hanged! I'll not listen to your self-righteous protests. You can save them for the court!" The captain stood with his mouth opening and closing in the lamplight.

Crispin's expression changed to a smirk. He straightened his posture very slowly into what might almost be considered the position of attention. "Yes, sir. At your service, sir. Is there anything I can do for you Major Willoughby, sir?"

Willoughby ignored him and turned to the continental officer. "Major Throckmorton, I would like to offer better 'accommodations' and better company if you are willing to give me your parole. Do you swear, as an officer and gentleman, that you will not attempt to escape or bear arms against the Royal Army during your imprisonment here?"

The question seemed absurd to Lieutenant Cloyde as he stared at the ugly and frightened little man. The effect of the words was actually surprising. Throckmorton seemed to swell perceptibly and grow a few inches taller as he considered Willoughby's offer. It seemed as if the remains of the uniform took over and molded Throckmorton into what an officer and gentleman must look like. Cloyde gasped as the man tried to click his heels while responding to Willoughby. "Yes, Major, I agree to your terms. You have my parole, sir!"

Willoughby nodded curtly. "Major Throckmorton, please allow me to introduce you to Lieutenant Cloyde. Mr. Cloyde arrived a short while ago with information that I believe holds great interest for both of us."

Throckmorton remained silent. Cloyde took the hint from Willoughby and said, "It is an honor to meet you, sir!" He feigned respect for the rebel prisoner. Willoughby continued to ignore Captain Crispin. Turning his back on the angry and confused young man, he waved his hand toward the door. "Major Throckmorton, it would give me great pleasure, in light of your parole, to ask you to come with us."

Throckmorton looked furtively around at the surrounding faces before nodding and walking toward the still open door. Captain Crispin started to shout something as the lantern light moved out of the room. Whatever he said was stifled by darkness and the slamming of the door. The Yankee major looked shabbier in the light of the hallway. Major Willoughby led the small party back to his office. A short time later, Major Throckmorton was seated in a comfortable chair near the fireplace. The three men shared brandy and laughter as if they were old and dear friends. They were joined by a young officer introduced by Willoughby as his adjutant. Cloyde was not surprised when this man sat on the other side of the room and began quietly taking notes. This was so subtle that the other two men didn't seem to notice.

Lieutenant Cloyde was amazed at the way Major Willoughby put this paroled enemy officer at ease. The lieutenant understood the major's purpose, or at least thought he did. Cloyde lacked Willoughby's masterful ability to judge character. He didn't see through the other man's speech and bearing as quickly as his superior. Willoughby interviewed this man earlier under more formal circumstances when he was brought in by the Tory militiamen.

Major Willoughby understood there was little difference between this man and Captain Crispin. He knew immediately that there was little useful military information to be gained from this conversation. However, he soon knew the size and composition of the small rebel convoy. He gained an astoundingly accurate knowledge of the weapons, ammunition, and military supplies in the wagons. He learned more of what really happened in the battle at Cowpens. He knew who was involved in the confrontation on both sides, and had a good idea of the casualty figures. Some of this information was gathered during the first interview. This second conversation allowed him to fill in some details, but he was really trying to learn about a more challenging subject. It seemed, unfortunately, that this colonial buffoon could tell him little he now desperately wanted to know.

Finally, after about two hours of insufferably tedious conversation, Major Willoughby stood and turned to his adjutant. He instructed the young man to take Major Throckmorton to an upstairs room in the house and provide him with food and clean clothing. He insisted that something be done to launder and repair the continental uniform, and offered his apologies to Throckmorton for the unfortunately abrupt end of their conversation. The adjutant stepped forward and guided the colonial officer out of the room with smiling grace. They quietly disappeared from view when the door closed behind them.

Willoughby stepped behind his desk and flopped down in the chair with a disgusted sigh. He motioned Cloyde to sit again in the chair on the other side of the desk. He stared silently at the notes the adjutant had deftly placed on the desktop in front of his chair before leaving the room. Willoughby looked up and said, "Now listen carefully, Lieutenant. You and Colonel Tarleton were both quite correct regarding the value of those captured stores. Except that the reason for their importance isn't about saving face after losing the battle at Cowpens.

"The real importance of that material is how it could be used in the hands of the rebel militia bands that terrorize our supply lines and the loyalists all over this colony. I have encountered another rather shocking bit of news through all of this."

Cloyde looked up and asked, "What news, sir?"

Willoughby leaned back in his chair and stared at the ceiling briefly before looking back down and saying, "News regarding the apparent treachery of a man I would never have suspected of disloyalty." Cloyde didn't know who the major was talking about, so he said nothing.

Willoughby read the adjutant's notes quickly and folded the paper without setting it aside. Looking back up at Cloyde he said, "Lieutenant, I'm going to join you in your mission with two full squadrons totaling two hundred of my best dragoons. I will add an additional company of about one hundred Tory militiamen. You will attach your depleted troop to me for the time being. Be prepared to leave tomorrow morning. We will go south from here to recover those military supplies. I believe I know exactly where they are headed. When we reach the place, we may or may not find a dangerous nest of hostile rebels. We may also find an even greater cache of rebel military supplies."

Major Willoughby was back on his feet again. He moved absently over toward the fireplace with the adjutant's notes in his hand. "We will seize anything that would be valuable to the cause of our king and the Royal Army. My intention is to eliminate what we cannot recover. I intend to destroy any rebels found there, ending once and for all their constant harassment of our supply routes." Willoughby stared into the fireplace for several seconds with a strange stillness hanging in the room. Then he slowly shook his head and cast the now crumpled paper into the fire. Looking back over his shoulder at the younger man, he quietly added, "Yes Lieutenant Cloyde, we will probably find your elusive quarry at Fletcher's Mill."

CHAPTER 27

It was almost dark. Fog moved along the river in eerie silence. Lieutenant Billy Morgan and Sergeant John Strickland slowly crept forward through the underbrush on the high embankment at the south side of the road. A faint cold breeze caused lanterns marking the ferry landing to cast moving beams of light as they swung on their tethers in the short distance. Two large men were cajoling a mule up the road toward them. It strained to pull the ferry cable dragging the large flat-bottomed boat across the river from the other side. Lantern light was spilled from the window of a small shack on the riverbank next to the point where the road on this side ended. A small older man came out of the shack and stood in the middle of the road. The old man glanced at the mule before looking back out at the blackened mass of the ferryboat coming slowly across the river.

The road was considerably wider here as it reached the riverbank. The ferry landing was situated to one side while the wider part of the road seemed to drop right down into the river itself. Private Spate had earlier offered a simple explanation for this. The river was low enough during the summer months to be easily forded here. Cherokees built a dam to make fishing easier here centuries earlier. This manmade feature was even the source of the nearby village, Fish Dam. Most people ignored the ferry and saved their money when they could walk or ride across the shallow ford created by the old fish dam. Business for the ferrymen was limited to people with money and cargo that could not or should not get wet at these times. The ferrymen made up for the lost revenue during times like this when the river was up so high it was impassable at the dam. Billy wondered vaguely why a bridge hadn't been constructed for this busy crossing place.

The boat finally arrived, and the old man stepped onto the wooden landing to grab the lines thrown to him by the boatman. Three dismounted British officers led their horses off the vessel and out onto the road before climbing into the saddles. A brief conversation took place between one of the officers and the old man. The toll was paid, and the officers rode off toward Fish Dam engaged in quiet small talk. One of the ferrymen led the mule back toward the shack and secured it in a small corral near the back of the building. The other man connected the cold waterlogged tow cable to a strange contraption with a single shaft joining two large spoked wheels a couple feet apart. Billy wondered what this could possibly be until he saw the cable coiling around the shaft as the man pushed the device back down the road toward the landing.

All four of the ferrymen soon went inside the shack and shut the door. They didn't post any kind of watch, and didn't seem to expect any kind of danger. Billy thought this was strange until he realized this road must be very heavily traveled by the Royal Army. It was fairly close to Fish Dam. He had posted Spate and the other two militiamen about a hundred yards back up the road toward the village to give him and Strickland warning of any threat from that direction. He turned now to Strickland and asked, "What would you suggest we do? Do we seize the ferry now, tonight?"

Strickland recoiled in shock at the suggestion. "No, sir!" He hissed. "It looks to me like the old man runs the ferry with his sons just like Spate said. I believe they live in the shack yonder. They probably don't get much business during the night. In fact, I'd wager that was the last crossing of the day. If we take them now, we'll have to hold 'em till we're ready for the wagons to cross."

Billy got the point. He thought a few seconds and whispered, "Here's what we'll do. I want to leave the two extra men here to watch the crossing overnight and report anything they observe when we get back. Me, you, and Spate will head back to the wagons. It'll be a long night, but I want to bring the wagons back here before first light. That should make it easier to get past Fish Dam without drawing attention to ourselves if we're careful. We'll keep the wagons up the road out of sight while we take the ferrymen. Then we'll bring them forward to make the crossing one wagon at a time." He paused and thought about this plan. A startling realization struck him and Strickland simultaneously. Both men stood and looked into the distance at the opposite bank of the river. There, like two tiny sparks floating in the murky darkness, were two lanterns marking the ferry landing on the other side. They could just make out the small dark shape of another shack on that side of the river not far from the landing.

They crouched quickly as the implications washed over them. Strickland whispered first. "Of course sir! They have another mule team on the other side of the river. How can we possibly get the crew on that side to haul us across so that we can control both landings?" Billy looked again at the dark river. He could hear the rushing water of the flooded watercourse. He knew it would be useless to try swimming across to take the other landing. The only solution suddenly presented itself with stark clarity. "We'll just have to get the old man to signal his partners on the other side to pull the boat across the first time. We'll put men on the boat who will seize the other landing quietly when they get there. We'll control the ferry after that until we get all of the wagons across."

Strickland looked at him and blinked in the near darkness. The idea was so ridiculously simple that it just might work. He finally nodded and said, "All right, Lieutenant. I can't think of any better way to get across. I'm for it. Now we better get back to the convoy and get it headed this way."

They got up and started back through the brush along the side of the road to find Private Spate and his companions. Billy personally took the two men back to the spot he and Strickland had used to watch the events at the landing. He gave the men careful instructions to keep watch in shifts so that the landing was observed constantly until he got back. He rejoined Strickland and Spate several minutes later, and they were soon running back through the dark woods toward the convoy encampment.

It took nearly an hour to get everyone in the convoy ready to move out. Dr. Bolt was very worried about his surviving patients. He understood the need for stealth and speed, but he also made it clear to Billy that he could not guarantee the welfare of the injured men unless they reached the right kind of shelter and warmth soon. Billy was well aware of this concern, and the reminder set him further on edge. He nearly offered a sharp retort to the diminutive old physician. He inhaled in frustrated anger, then suddenly remembered the kindness shown by the doctor in the earlier funeral. This helped him squelch the barb before it was uttered.

The Phillips family surprised Billy by not offering any resistance. The farmer was concerned about the time they were spending in the open country and wanted to get his family to safety as soon as possible. Mrs. Phillips seemed to have been cowed by the loss of her home and the death of a young soldier she had been helping the doctor with. The little Phillips girl was sound asleep and couldn't be roused easily without noisy complaint. She was eventually laid out in the back of the ambulance wagon, as it was now called, to sleep next to Silas. Billy couldn't help observing that there was sadly more room in the wagon now than there had been when they left the Phillips farm.

The convoy made the trip back down the trail and through the woods on the south side of the village without any significant difficulty. The night was far spent by the time they reached the east-west road and turned toward the river. Strickland insisted that they stop several hundred yards away from the landing so that the ferrymen wouldn't hear their approach. Billy agreed. The wagons were driven off the roadway into the woods. Sergeant Duncan brought all the militiamen close so that Billy could quickly explain his plan for seizing the ferry crossing. Sergeant Strickland added a stern warning for absolute silence when Billy finished speaking. The teamsters were left to guard the wagons and the Phillips family with the doctor, his assistant, and the wounded men. The rest of the small company soon moved quietly through the woods and brush near the road toward the river.

Billy and Strickland made contact with the two men left watching the landing and learned that no one had stirred in or around the shack since they left hours earlier. The lanterns were still burning on the landing stage, but the light had been extinguished inside the shack. Billy left Strickland on the high ground with half the men to provide covering fire if it was needed while he went quietly down the embankment with the rest of the men toward the shack. They quickly surrounded the small building. Billy felt decidedly inept as he realized that he didn't know what to do next. He expected to be challenged by one or all of the ferrymen by now. The silence was surprising. He found himself squatting next to Spate and Howard at the corner of the small building near the door.

Billy searched his imagination swiftly for ideas that would allow the shack to be seized noiselessly and came up empty. He finally shrugged and stepped over to the door. He motioned for the two privates to move to the sides of the doorway and be ready to rush inside while he prepared to kick the door in. A light was stuck inside the shack at that moment, and they heard a gruff Irish voice from inside shout, "Ere now ... who's out there...!?"

Billy was poised to kick with his leg in the air. The door was suddenly yanked open, and his eyes were startled by the seemingly brilliant light of a flaming candle in the grizzled hand of the old ferryman. Time seemed suspended as the occupants of the shack realized they had interrupted the forced entry of their home. One of the ferrymen fired a pistol in the direction of the blue coated apparition in the doorway. Billy felt the ball cut through the outside of his trouser leg and several skin layers along his lower right thigh. It was like being kicked in the thigh and sliced with a cleaver at the same time. He was flung back into the darkness as Howard and Spate rushed into the shack with their muskets leveled, forcing the ferrymen into immediate surrender.

Billy picked himself up slowly from the ground and heard the thundering footfalls of Strickland and his men as they ran down the embankment to lend assistance. His leg was bleeding profusely already. It felt like it had been seared with a hot knife. Spate herded the four ferrymen out of the shack near him, while Howard ripped the kerchief from his own neck and tied it tightly around Billy's leg.

Billy was more angry than frightened. Shrugging Howard away, he stepped forward and aimed the muzzle of his rifle at the wide-eyed face of the huge oafish young man who had fired the pistol. He might have shot him then if the oldest of the ferrymen hadn't spoken. It was the same voice he heard a few seconds earlier before the door opened. "Ere now.... Please, sur.... Don't harm the lad, sur.... E meant no arm, sur...." Billy turned toward the old man in growing rage and pain. He suddenly noticed that the kindly face was pleading for mercy not for himself but for his son. He looked back at the younger man and realized that he was some kind of simpleton. The still smoking pistol was lying on the floor of the shack and the young man's hands were raised in front of him as if to ward off Billy's anger more than the very real danger from the shaking rifle barrel.

CHAPTER 28

Major Throckmorton was exhausted. He slept fitfully through the short night although the room he was in could be considered quite comfortable. His mind held a mixture of greedy apprehension, worry, and indecisiveness. He supposed that he should feel some sort of shame for having been captured in the first place, and for sharing information with that pompous Major Willoughby. He didn't. His pragmatic selfishness allowed him to rationalize each of his decisions. He believed himself to be endowed with great cunning if not vast intelligence. The problem that plagued him through the night was not his lack of personal honor. The subject that tormented him right now was the apparently fleeting nature of what he perceived to be a once-in-a-lifetime opportunity to obtain untold riches with no risk to his personal reputation.

Throckmorton heard the sounds of troops mustering all around the house as dawn approached. He wasn't sure what was happening, but he could easily guess. Willoughby was pumping him for information in the presence of that cavalry lieutenant. Cloyde was different from the impudent young adjutant. Cloyde was apparently a recent acquaintance to Sir Thomas Willoughby. The condition of Cloyde's uniform and boots suggested that he had been in the field for several days rather than here in this comfortable garrison town.

Throckmorton listened to the growing sounds of preparation from outside the house with the realization that a large body of troops, probably most of the garrison, was preparing to depart. He briefly wondered whether this was some kind of escort preparing to move him and Captain Crispin to the main British headquarters. That was ridiculous, though. The sounds told him that this was a much larger force than the escort of two prisoners would require. He tried to see what was going on through the window, but the room was located at the back of the house. The area below was still shrouded in early morning darkness.

The major was peering out through the window in this way when he noticed a huge oak tree very near the house on this side. The window opened onto the roof. He stepped back and examined the window itself. This was a fine house, and the multipane windows were hinged on the sides with a center latch that allowed them to be swung open to allow fresh air to enter. He tried the latch and found that it opened easily. Closing the window quickly, he sat back down on the bed and considered his options. He gave his parole to Sir Thomas, but he hardly cared about that. He wouldn't go to a miserable British prison hulk if he could avoid it.

Throckmorton was sitting on the end of the bed when the door opened abruptly. The adjutant entered with an armed guard and a bright lantern. The lieutenant was carrying a folded pile of clothing which he dropped on the bed next to the major. Throckmorton realized that this was his uniform coat and a clean pair of trousers. The coat had been cleaned and mended. The lieutenant stepped back, and another man entered the room with a tray containing a covered dish and a steaming cup of what could only be coffee or tea. The tray was placed on the small table in the corner of the room. The man picked up the chamber pot from the side of the bed and left silently.

The adjutant said in a cheery voice, "Good morning, Major! I trust you slept well, sir! Major Willoughby wished me to offer his regret that he will not be having breakfast with you as his duties require him to be elsewhere." Throckmorton moved to the small chair at the side of the table. He was drawn involuntarily by the smell of what must be fried ham and eggs under the cover on the tray. He heard himself asking about the noises outside the house and got the blunt rebuff he should have expected. The lieutenant seemed to realize what he was thinking earlier and said, "Have no fear, Major. You will remain our guest here for some time. There is no plan afoot to spirit you away from here. Your partisan friends are far too active in the area now in any event. You will be moved from here along with the rest of the garrison should we find it necessary to abandon this place."

Throckmorton tried to seem pleasant with the young man, but ended up remaining silent. He sat in the chair staring at the tray of food. The lieutenant finally looked appraisingly around the room and walked out. The guard departed on the lieutenant's heels and locked the door behind him. Major Throckmorton devoured the food as if he hadn't eaten in a week. He wanted to slow down and savor the still scalding hot coffee. There was no time for that. He needed to act quickly and decisively or the opportunity before him would vanish.

Major Throckmorton got up from the table and quickly pulled on the clean trousers. He left his uniform coat folded and rolled it up in the blanket covering the bed. The air was cold outside, but he didn't want the blue coat to be seen and fired upon by sentries surrounding the house. He couldn't bring himself to abandon the cup of coffee, so he stepped back over to the table and gulped the still hot liquid down. The only eating utensil his jailers apparently trusted him with was a spoon. He picked this up from the tray and stepped over to open the window. He Looked around the room and decided to prop the single chair under the door handle to make the room more difficult to enter from the outer hallway.

Throckmorton then picked up the blanket bundle containing his uniform coat and climbed out through the window onto the roof. There was no immediate challenge to this strange apparition moving down the steep shingled surface to the place where a branch of the old oak tree came within a few feet of the roof edge. The light was increasing rapidly, but it was still fairly dark on this side of the house. He stopped at the edge and gazed down into the gloom. He saw no one. Fear was growing in his chest rapidly. He brought it under control and dropped the bundle to the ground below.

The major stood up straight now and peered out at the tree branch. It hadn't seemed so far away a few minutes ago from inside the window. Now it looked like a great gulf separated him from this perceived route to freedom. Breathing deeply, he railed silently at himself for his obstinate cowardice, and stepped a few paces back up the shingled roof. He didn't want to see what happened next, but didn't dare close his eyes either. With no further consideration, he lunged down the roof and flung his gangly old body out through the open space in the direction of the branch.

The gnarled old branch didn't give much as Throckmorton landed on it chest first. His legs continued to move forward under the branch. He felt the skin tearing under his shirt as his body twisted out horizontally. There was nothing to hold onto but bark and twigs. The rest of his descent was as absurd as it was inevitable. He landed flat on his back in the leaf-covered wet winter grass. He was still conscious, but the air was nocked completely out of his lungs. He thought this is what a fish must feel like when it is brought onto dry land.

The terror was even greater than the pain. Throckmorton knew someone must have heard him fall. He couldn't move. He lay there trying to breathe waiting for the inevitable challenge. He wondered what it would feel like when he was shot or impaled on a guard's bayonet. His breathing slowly returned, and he finally realized that his fall wasn't noticed. Slowly turning onto his side and then onto his stomach, Throckmorton found that he was now able to push himself up onto his hands and knees. It didn't seem like anything was broken. He may have lost consciousness briefly when he hit the ground, but he wasn't sure. Looking around again furtively, he rose to his feet and bent double as he ran over to retrieve his bundle, then turned to dart into the bushes behind the house.

Throckmorton made it to the edge of town before he realized that he was making a terrible mistake. He needed help. There was no way he could accomplish what he wished alone. One of his assistants deserted him in terror on the road and the other one was dead. The only person he believed he could trust now was as much an untrustworthy scoundrel as he was himself. Captain Reginald Crispin. Yes. He believed he could trust this man … somewhat. They wanted the same things. The brief conversation they shared in their mutual prison cell revealed similarities between them that didn't stop with their identical job titles. Both felt sorely used by their superiors, peers, and subordinates. Both believed they deserved better than they had in terms of wealth and position.

The prisoners had spoken at length about the situation they found themselves in. Both attributed their plight to the unfair circumstances of the present conflict. They also discussed what they had heard about the rumors of great treasure horded by an old man named Ira Fletcher. Crispin had been there. He managed to escape from captivity in the very mill supposedly concealing the treasure. Crispin was convinced that the armed men at the mill were present for a greater purpose than the rebellion. He convinced Throckmorton that he must be right. The major still wanted vengeance with the young militia lieutenant who claimed to be General Morgan's kin. Now, however, there was a larger consideration that demanded his attention. There was treasure to be obtained somehow.

Throckmorton made up his mind and doubled back toward the large house near the center of the small town. Daylight was almost upon him. He suddenly found himself huddling in bushes at the side of a smaller house and watching in frightened fascination as Major Willoughby and Lieutenant Cloyde rode by with over three hundred men. They were on their way out of town headed southwest. Throckmorton realized this must be nearly the full garrison. They must be headed toward Fletcher's Mill. The fools…. Let them go. Their absence might make his next task easier. He wasn't fool enough to believe the house would no longer be guarded. In fact, he was certain the young adjutant would have been left behind in charge of the remaining British troops.

Throckmorton wound his way through the trees and bushes near the edge of town retracing his steps. The journey somehow seemed longer on the way back. He knew Crispin was held in the cellar. They wouldn't have moved the captain. He remembered that there were no windows in the storeroom prison cell. There was a guard in the hallway, and the hallway was well lit. He had seen several doors along this corridor as he was brought upstairs by Major Willoughby yesterday. He finally reached the house and worked his way around looking for some kind of exterior cellar entry. There was a stone outcropping near the back door of the house leading to the privy. This held what appeared to be two large wooden doors that leaned inward toward the side of the building. The doors covered stairs leading downward. So, this was the entry. He couldn't use it. Searching further along the wall, he noticed two small shuttered windows at ground level on the same side of the house with his friend, the oak tree. It was strange that he didn't notice these earlier.

There was still enough shadow on this side of the house to offer some concealment as he moved to one of the windows. Crouching down, Throckmorton found that the shutter opened easily from the outside. Unfortunately, the window seemed to be latched from the inside and it wouldn't budge. Feeling the edge of the windowpanes, he found that one of them had a small separation near the top edge of the frame. He fished in his pocket and drew out the large pewter spoon he liberated from his breakfast tray. Breakfast ... that seemed like several hours ago. It couldn't have been more than an hour though. He was sure his jailers would soon discover his absence. Why hadn't this happened already?

Placing the spoon in the small space above the pane, Throckmorton was able to carefully pry upward. He almost laughed as the small glass pane popped silently out onto the ground. The wood of the frame was wet and rotten. It should have been painted more often to protect it. He silently thanked the carelessness of the original homeowner. Reaching in through the hole, he was able to feel around and find the simple bolt latch that secured the window. He pulled this sharply and the window opened. He managed to wriggle his scrawny frame through in moments and settled in the dark room among stacked barrels and boxes for several minutes before convincing himself that he wasn't heard. It was quite dark in the room, but he could see light coming from the corridor under the door. Moving there and feeling for the latch, he managed to pull the door open slightly and peer down the hallway. A single sentry was posted in front of the one important door just as he expected. Pulling his door shut again, he settled back to consider what to do next.

Major Throckmorton was not a brave man. Necessity demanded action, however. Leaving the door unlatched, he climbed up onto a barrel near the doorway and hoisted a small keg over his head. Pushing out with his foot, he knocked another keg over so that it fell with a resounding crash. The noise was rewarded with the swift approach of booted feet down the corridor. The light grew suddenly bright as the young soldier pushed the unlatched door open to investigate the noise. He never looked up, and didn't know what hit him as the small keg crashed down on his head.

Throckmorton relieved the now unconscious guard of his musket, cartridge belt, keys, and lantern before dragging the inert form into the room and moving quickly to Captain Crispin's cell to offer him freedom and opportunity. It didn't take much to convince Crispin. He had other motives, but he saw the possibilities presented to him by his strange new ally. The two desperate men were outside the building through the open cellar window within minutes. Crispin had further relieved the guard of his uniform coat and boots. A short while later they were headed southwest far behind Major Willoughby and his cavalry force toward Fletcher's Mill and the treasure they hoped to find there.

CHAPTER 29

They were surrounded by Strickland and his men who were looking on with leveled muskets. The old man identified himself as Lucas Hayden. These were his boys. Mr. Hayden's brother, Matthew, was on the other side of the river with his own son. Almost as if on cue when his name was mentioned, they heard the faint shout of Matthew Hayden from across the river, "Ho there? What's going on, Luke? We heard a shot! Who are those men?"

Old Mr. Hayden stepped around two of the militiamen and cupped his hands to shout back. "Tis all right, Matt! The pistol was discharged on accident by young Donald...! These ere men are friends, Matt. I expect we'll be needin' you to tug us across shortly!"

There was a short pause before another light showed itself dimly in front of the shack on the other side of the river. Matt Hayden's voice floated across. "Aye then ... we'll be gettin' ole Joe ready to pull...!"

Mr. Hayden turned back around and explained, unnecessarily, to the crowd in front of him. "Joe's our other mule."

Howard and Spate were helping Billy into the shack as Dr. Bolt came quickly out of the darkness with his assistant and Mrs. Phillips trailing close behind. The farmer's wife was ringing her hands and looked like she had been crying. Dr. Bolt inquired, "We heard a shot! What has happened?"

Sergeant Strickland said, "It's the lieutenant. He's inside here."

Strickland was headed back out through the door and stepped aside to let the doctor and his helpers enter. The contents of a large table were quickly cleared, and Billy was lifted onto the tabletop by the two privates. He was beginning to feel a little faint, and he found this extraordinarily embarrassing. The result was a curt thanks to Howard and Spate followed by a sharp order for them to get outside and be useful.

Dr. Bolt went silently to work with speed and dexterity that again surprised Billy. The doctor's helper quickly had Billy flat on the table with his equipment belt and coat off. Billy's rifle was propped in the corner. Mrs. Phillips took station at his head and the assistant stood near his feet. A folded leather strap was shoved between Billy's teeth without explanation. The doctor took a ragged blanket from a cot near the wall and threw it over him. The assistant yanked off his bloodstained trousers and rolled him onto his side so that the wound was clearly visible when the blanket was pulled back. The assistant continued to hold onto his legs with one arm while holding a lantern over the wound with his other hand. The doctor peered at the wound critically before reaching into his bag and producing a few metal instruments that he laid on the table between himself and the injured leg.

Dr. Bolt looked around the room and didn't immediately find what he wanted. Shouting for the owner of the shack, he returned to his new patient and did the best he could to clear the blood away without opening the wound further. Mr. Hayden came in and announced himself. The doctor spoke without looking up at the man, "I need spirits ... rum, whiskey, gin, anything! Do you have alcohol of any kind here?"

Mr. Hayden hung his head as if he were somehow embarrassed and said, "Well, yes. I do keep a drop or two for doctorin' ... I'd rather me boys didn't know of it, but aye ... there's a bottle close by...." The doctor looked at him so sternly that no words were needed to convey his meaning. Mr. Hayden nodded and disappeared back through the open door.

Dr. Bolt used a damp cloth to carefully swab the drying blood away from the long swollen wound. The area around the wound was deeply bruised. The ferryman returned shortly with a clay jug. Placing this on the table, he rummaged around in a small cabinet and produced a surprisingly clean-looking china cup. The doctor was preoccupied with his examination. He didn't notice when Mr. Hayden uncorked the jug, filled the cup halfway, and emptied the contents with one profound gulp. He refilled the cup and stood quietly waiting for instructions. Dr. Bolt seemed to notice him again, and nodded for Hayden to put the cup down on the table near him and then move out of the light. The doctor dipped the cloth in the alcohol and squeezed the contents into and around the wound.

Billy nearly screamed at the searing pain this brought. The wound hurt terribly before, but now it felt like the doctor had stuck a red-hot iron into it. He struggled against the restraint that was applied by Mrs. Phillips and the doctor's assistant. Dr. Bolt seemed unmoved by Billy's discomfort as he continued to probe the wound while pouring even more of the fiery liquid into the gash directly from the cup. The probing stopped momentarily. The doctor took the lantern from his assistant and leaned forward to peer more closely into the wound. The probing resumed for a few seconds more before the doctor finally leaned back. He declared that the wound was now free of cloth and debris, and that the pistol ball hadn't lodged in the leg. Billy was lightheaded with blood loss and relieved that the probing had stopped. He barely understood what the doctor said.

Dr. Bolt turned in the chair and pulled his leather satchel onto his lap. The wound was again bleeding freely. He gave his assistant curt foreign language instructions. The man leaned forward to cover the wound and apply pressure to it with a clean piece of folded cloth. The doctor dug through the satchel to find a smaller leather case containing what looked like large sewing needles and a spool of white silk thread. He threaded one of these needles with the silk and immersed both needle and thread in the teacup which was again filled with liquor. Billy saw all of this through lightheaded, pain-shrouded haze. His mind slowly realized what was coming next and he gasped deeply before passing into unconsciousness.

Dr. Bolt noticed this and nodded thanks to his Creator for easing the young man's pain. He leaned forward again and began to deftly sew the wound shut with forty-three neatly applied stitches. The leg was cleaned once again and two layers of bandages were tied securely in place. Mrs. Phillips and the assistant rolled Billy onto his back and covered him back up with the blanket. None of the three noticed when Lucas Hayden crept quietly back into the shack, recovered his clay jug, and carried it back outside to return it to its hiding place.

Almost an hour passed when Billy felt consciousness returning to him amid the searing pain in his thigh and the insistent shaking of his shoulder by a very distraught Sergeant Strickland.

"Please, sir, you've got to wake up! Can you move, sir? It is near dawn now, sir! We've got to make the river crossing now with the last wagon!" Billy managed to pull himself up to his elbows. He was still lying on the table. No one else was in the shack at the moment. He was covered with the blanket, but he was shivering with cold. Billy saw his blood-soaked trousers lying across the back of one of the few chairs in the room and motioned for Strickland to hand them over. The blood was mostly dry on them now, but nothing had been done about the long tear on the right thigh. He managed to struggle back into them with Strickland's help. He got off the table into a wobbly standing position.

Billy steadied himself for a moment before asking Strickland to help him get his equipment belt on and hand him his rifle from the corner. Using the rifle as a makeshift crutch was out of the question. This was the most valuable object Billy owned. Strickland saw the problem and hurried outside for a few minutes to find an alternative. He returned shortly with a long straight piece of tree branch that had a forked end. Strickland unceremoniously ripped a long strip from the blanket. It took a few precious seconds, but he soon had the blanket strip wound around the forked end of the branch. This provided enough padding for Billy to brace it under his armpit without causing him further injury. Using this crutch and holding his rifle in his left hand, Billy experimented with hobbling across the floor a few paces to make sure he could move on his own.

Billy stopped and turned to Strickland as he remembered what was said regarding the status of the river crossing. "Did you say 'the last wagon,' Sergeant?"

Strickland nodded as he picked up the rest of Billy's 'necessaries' and handed them over. "Yes, sir. We've got the other wagons across. The ferry's been hauled back over, and the boys are just now loadin' the last one. I wanted to give you as much time as possible, but we got to get across before the light gets any stronger and the town folk or soldiers start stirrin." Billy nodded, "Right! Let's go!" He hobbled toward the door. Strickland opened it, and Billy was surprised to see that it was indeed growing light outside. A momentary feeling of panic struck him. He desperately didn't want to be caught with his small force separated on either side of the swiftly moving river in broad daylight.

Strickland seemed to read his mind. "Yes, sir. We've got to cross right now! That's certain sure, but we'll be all right ... I've got most of our men across and coverin' us from the other bank. There's just you, me, Spate, Howard, and the ferrymen over here now, along with the last of the teamsters. Look yonder, they have the wagon loaded now." He nodded toward the landing stage, and Billy felt some relief as he saw that the old ferryman, Hayden, was motioning for him and Strickland to hurry aboard the boat with the wagon and the last of the militiamen. Minutes later, they were moving slowly across the powerful river current toward the relative safety of the convoy waiting in the woods near the opposite bank. Billy was in terrific pain. He was lightheaded from the ordeal at the shack and loss of blood. He wanted to express his thanks to Mr. Hayden, but he didn't trust himself to say the right thing.

They reached the east bank of the river, and Billy hobbled out of the boat onto the landing stage before the wagon was off-loaded. He hobbled toward the tree line and the rest of his convoy with Strickland at his side. Sergeant Duncan walked out of the trees at the side of the road and quietly pointed back across the river and up the road in the distance. Billy and Strickland turned quickly to peer into the far morning haze. They saw a small but unmistakably red over white form slowly descending the distant hillside. The tiny blob moved in rhythmic precision that clearly showed it could only be a small column of British infantry.

Billy shouted for the ferrymen and teamster to get the wagon unloaded immediately and get it into the trees with the others as soon as possible. He hurried back to the landing stage and quickly conferred with old Mr. Hayden as the wagon reached the ground and the mules were reattached to it. The teamster jumped aboard with the remaining militiamen and the mules were encouraged toward the trees with the end of the teamster's whip. Billy finally managed to offer a quick curt thank-you to Mr. Hayden. The latter nodded with a smile as he held out his hand apparently expecting payment. Billy was stunned. He started to say something and thought about laying the brazen man out with his make-shift crutch. Hayden leaned further forward to grasp Billy's right hand in his own and say, "No, sir…. It's I that must say thanks. Thank you for not killing my boy last night! Thank you for what you and your men are doing to win our freedom here! Now … don't you worry about this lot…."

He nodded toward the now closer infantry column. "They don't know nothin' about you, fellas. They're just comin' down to cross the river on their way to Rocky Mount. It ain't uncommon this time of the mornin'. Just get on out of sight. They're gonna find out that I had earlier customers and they're just gonna have to wait till we manage to get the ferry hauled back over before they can start to cross. I'll make sure you have plenty of time to get well away from here before they get one boot over on this side…." Hayden was smiling broadly now. Billy couldn't help himself. He was smiling too as he shook the man's hand again and turned to hob-ble back up the bank toward the convoy waiting in the trees.

The road to Rocky Mount turned northeast about a hundred yards from the ferry landing on top of the low bluff bordering the river. The southern road toward Fletcher's Mill intersected at the bend. They no lon-ger needed Private Spate to guide them. The road was good from here all the way to the mill according to the map. Speed now seemed more important to Billy than secrecy. He sent Spate and John Red ahead again to ensure that the convoy didn't blunder into an ambush. He then allowed

Sergeant Duncan and Private Howard to lift him up onto the front seat of the lead wagon. Billy paused to thank God silently before giving the order to drive on as quickly as possible toward the safety he desperately hoped waited for them at their destination.

CHAPTER 30

The preparations seemed as complete as they could be. Captain Robertson and Reverend Fletcher walked through and around the village countless times looking for weaknesses. They had done everything they could think of to prepare an adequate defense. The mill would be the final strong point. It was the stoutest structure for many miles. They would force the enemy to expend a great deal of energy and effort in the village and its surroundings, but the plan they worked out called for the defenders to fall back on the mill in the end. The other buildings could be rebuilt if they were destroyed.

They just didn't have enough men to protect the entire village and its numerous approaches. They expected an enemy force to be made up mainly of cavalry. Robertson knew he could take a powerful advantage away from the British if he could force them to dismount. Great effort was devoted to the construction of fascines, deadfalls, and other traps to this end. He and his men did what they could to enhance the advantage given to them through the long-range accuracy of their rifles. His sergeants continued to drill the recruited villagers. These men could reload weapons and carry ammunition if they could do nothing else.

Ezekiel was finally able to get up and walk around some. Mr. Griffin, the blacksmith, had taken a turn for the worse. The apothecary, Amos Reynolds, suspected that the amputated leg was "putrefying," as he put it. The leg was frightfully hot to the touch, and the man was in terrific pain when he was conscious. They were running low on laudanum, but there was a surprisingly ample supply of liquor available in the village. Ira had forbidden anyone from consuming it for any purpose other than medical, but there was already one incident where two of the village ner-do-wells took it upon themselves to "self-medicate." This resulted in both men spending a night and a day locked up in the mill storeroom formerly occupied by the two British prisoners.

All of the village women were now gone except Mrs. Reynolds, Mrs. Griffin, Mona Partridge, and Elizabeth Fletcher. These four brave souls worked tirelessly to clean and care for the wounded blacksmith and Ezekiel while cooking and baking to feed all of the men left defending their homes. Tobias and two of the other village men tried to help with these chores as much as possible. There were plenty of food stores, but cooking this much food was a daunting process. The baking went on almost constantly. Mona was also kept busy sewing and repairing clothing that was damaged during the hurried preparations. Elizabeth chose to work beside her wherever she was needed.

This particular morning found Mona and Elizabeth making and kneading dough for twenty loaves of bread. The bread would be baked in the large oven at the Fletcher house five loaves at a time. Twenty more loaves would be started as soon as the first twenty were done. Mona intended to bake and store enough bread to last through the next few days. Elizabeth was excited to help her, not because she loved the hard work, but because it allowed a quiet time for them to talk. Mona was intensely focused on the task at hand, but she too appreciated the time they spent together.

Elizabeth folded the huge loaf in front of her again and paused to look over at Mona. She wore a sly smile on her flour-dusted face as she said, "Mona, you know I love you. You know I love Grandpa."

Mona nodded without looking up from her work. "Yes, dear. I know you love us both."

Elizabeth paused again. "Everything is still a fresh memory to Grandpa. The things that happened here. The fire. All those things. He remembers all of it like it just happened. I don't think he understands that I don't remember any of it. I was only a baby. I don't remember my mother, father, or grandmother. Mona, you are the only mother I've ever known."

Mona stopped working and reached over to hug Elizabeth close. "I know, dear. You have always been a daughter to me as well."

Silence prevailed briefly as the two women went back to work on the bread dough. Elizabeth hadn't fully expressed herself yet, though, so she tried again. "Mona, I know that you love Grandpa, and I know he loves you too. I just want you to know that I understand and I want you two to be … together."

Mona blushed involuntarily and looked down as she said just above a whisper, "It's that obvious then, child?"

Elizabeth barely managed to restrain herself from giggling out loud as she exclaimed, "No! It isn't obvious! That is the problem! No one would notice anything at all between the two of you unless they knew you as well as Ezekiel and I do. That's just the trouble … I don't even know if the two of you are fully aware of your own feelings, and it is so perplexing to watch you waste all of the precious time you could be spending together."

Mona continued to work the dough in front of her as she considered Elizabeth's words before responding with, "It's true, Beth. I do love him more than life itself. I know he feels the same."

Elizabeth felt she would nearly burst with exasperation as she dropped the lump of dough in her hands on the table and turned to face Mona. "Why won't either of you do something about it then?"

Mona looked at the girl for a moment and averted her eyes downward again before responding, "It isn't as simple as that dear!"

Elizabeth was still staring with her hands on her hips. "What? Why isn't it that simple? You are the stubbornest hard-headed people! I won't have this anymore! If you won't let your feelings be known, I will!"

Mona wiped her hands on her apron and stepped back from the tabletop slightly as a gentle smile settled onto her still red face. "Elizabeth, dear, we have been letting each other know how we feel in special ways.

Your grandpa is a private man even if he is a preacher. That's one of the things I love about him. He has asked my permission to use my first name in private, and we have held hands more than once."

Elizabeth went back to work on the dough and said, "Well, that is something grand then.... Did he really? I believe he must finally be coming out of his hard shell.... You have been holding hands?"

Mona was back at work also. Her face was still bright red, and she continued to smile. The smile slowly tempered. "Yes, dear. Your grandpa has finally started to put the past behind him and reach out toward a future with something other than grief in it."

A little over three miles away to the north, on the Fish Dam road, Sergeant Strickland brought the convoy to a halt. He saw John Red approaching from over the next small rise to the south. They had just passed a most disturbing and inexplicable sight a few hundred yards back. The carcass of a partially saddled horse was sprawled near the middle of the forested lane. The animal was still outfitted with bridle and saddle, although it looked like the saddle blanket had been removed. It was difficult to tell because the animal was now bloated and it was partially eaten by scavengers of some kind. The stench was horrible. They had great difficulty getting the draft animals to move past the mess until it was dragged off the road.

Lieutenant Morgan passed out on the front seat of the lead wagon after Dr. Bolt gave him a large dose of laudanum for the pain in his leg. This happened as they turned south on this road. He was sleeping fitfully sitting up in the jerking wagon seat for some time now. Strickland had taken charge. He knew they were only a short distance way from Fletcher's Mill. He couldn't imagine what might have happened to the dead horse. There was no sign of the animal's rider. They saw no one since they left the ferry landing an hour or two earlier. The mystery turned to intrigue in his mind as Red ran quietly back to report what he found ahead of them.

Red told him that he smelled smoke near the riverbank to their front on the other side of another distant rise. He moved close enough through the brush to learn that the smoke came from a small fire in front of a low poorly fashioned lean-to shelter covered with leaves and small branches. A closer look revealed that the shelter was occupied by a disheveled man wearing the filthy remnants of a British dragoon sergeant's uniform. The man appeared to be sleeping, but Red couldn't be certain because the man's head and chest were not clearly visible. He considered moving in and cutting the man's throat, but decided they might need information from him. He was baffled by the presence of the man here in this condition. He might be a deserter. He might even be the one who rode that poor horse to death. In any event, Red wanted Strickland to see the man undisturbed as he found him.

Sergeant Strickland had to disturb the lieutenant now. Billy woke slowly and had difficulty clearing his mind enough to understand what Strickland was trying to tell him. He finally managed to climb down from the wagon and get the makeshift crutch under his armpit so that he could stand. His head swam. His thigh felt like it was on fire. Strickland repeated the report that they were only a few miles from the mill and they were stopped to check out something suspicious ahead. Billy nodded and tried to walk a few paces before stumbling back to the side of the wagon and leaning over to vomit. Strickland waited patiently for him to collect himself. Billy looked up and apologized before telling the sergeant to use his best judgement. Strickland nodded and turned to select several nearby militiamen to accompany him and Red as they went forward to investigate.

It only took a few minutes to reach the spot where Red had first smelled the smoke. Strickland smelled nothing, but he trusted Red completely. Red showed him signs and tracks in the mud that told him someone had fallen near the side of the roadbed. The person was then apparently dragged off or had crawled away toward the river. He led them off the road in this direction after motioning for complete silence. They reached a small rise near the riverbank, and Red took it on himself to place the extra men in hidden positions from which they could provide cover. He then motioned for Strickland to follow him and started carefully over the embankment toward the sound of the flowing water.

Sergeant Strickland saw the makeshift shelter and a small wisp of smoke coming from a tiny pile of embers in front of it. The uniformed legs and booted feet of a man protruded from under the pile of branches next to the fire. A cavalry carbine lay across the man's legs. There was no obvious movement or sign of life. Red paused until he was certain Strickland had seen everything. Then he dropped back down behind the embankment followed by the sergeant. Red whispered quick instructions to his superior. Strickland had no thought of overriding Red's judgement in this situation.

They rolled quietly over the embankment toward the back of the shelter a few seconds later. Strickland took position at the back of the brush pile with his musket ready to fire through it. Red moved in a silent crouch around the shelter until he was within a few feet of the opening but still invisible to the occupant. He paused there and looked back at the sergeant. Strickland nodded curtly. Red sprang forward with an animallike yelp and grabbed the carbine from the man's legs before grasping one of the protruding ankles and physically yanking the man out into the open. The man gave no resistance. His hands were held pitifully upward in a show of weak abject surrender. Strickland bound around the shelter to Red's side. The latter was now staring openmouthed at a terribly wretched sight.

The prostrate man was wearing the uniform coat of a British dragoon sergeant. There was no dragoon helmet. There was no hat of any kind save a brown crusted semblance of some kind of bandage. The man's head seemed to be swollen to nearly half again it's normal size. Both eyes were swollen shut and the skin of the face was a patchwork mixture of blue-black bruises and oozing abrasions. Most of the damage appeared to be concentrated near what could be seen of the right cheek. The man's nose and mouth seemed to be swollen nearly shut and it looked like he was barely breathing. There was no speech. The only indication that the man recognized the presence of another human was his pitiful waving hands.

Red unsheathed his knife and moved forward to put the man out of his misery. Strickland grabbed his arm and stopped him. He couldn't allow the man to be executed this way after he had clearly done so much in an effort to survive. He pulled Red around and quietly said, "Go back to the road and find the doctor. Tell him what we have found and bring him back here on the run." Red just stared at him. "Don't look at me like that, John Red! Go back and get the doctor … now!" Red shook his head and left swiftly as the other militiamen made their way down the embankment to offer muted comments regarding their new "prisoner."

Dr. Bolt wasted no time reaching the ghastly site. He took decisive control of the situation as soon as he arrived. The doctor did a quick examination after carefully removing the filthy bandage from the man's head. He used some of the ice-cold river water to rinse most of the caked blood and dirt from the face and scalp. The poor man barely seemed to notice what was happening. There was no resistance. He did finally begin to utter a low groaning noise from deep in his throat. This somehow seemed encouraging, as it showed some indication that the man might actually be aware of the treatment he was receiving.

Dr. Bolt was especially concerned with trying to open the airway as much as possible and keep it open. He searched in his leather satchel until he found a peculiar-looking wooden mouthpiece with a hole in the center. Prying the man's mouth open, he inserted this device and let the jaws tighten involuntarily around it. He then carefully wrapped the man's head loosely in a large linen cloth while being careful to leave the limited airway uncovered. He enlisted the help of some of the ogling bystanders and had the man moved onto a makeshift stretcher to be carried up the embankment. Dr. Bolt accepted no input from Sergeant Strickland on the matter. He had the man placed in the back of the ambulance wagon along with the remaining wounded continentals.

Elizabeth and Mona were still baking bread two hours later in the kitchen at the Fletcher house. Ira was upstairs in Ezekiel's room talking with the old man as he sorted out his surprising, but not uncomfortable, feelings for Mona. Captain Robertson walked out to inspect the furthest northern picket position he established outside the village. He was there now talking with his men when one of them noticed the furtive motion of a man moving quietly through the trees and brush near the roadway in their direction. They froze and waited for him to come much closer before one of them shouted a challenge.

The man seemed to realize that he was in the open with no hope of cover or concealment. He stopped moving forward and stood upright with his left hand held high and his rifle raised over his head in his right. He wore no uniform. He looked a lot like one of the indigenous frontier savages although he was clearly a white man. The picket guards were concealed behind a huge fallen tree near the side of the road. Captain Robertson ordered them to cover him and stepped out onto the lane where he was clearly visible to the new arrival.

Robertson called out, "Who are you? What's your purpose here?"

The stranger remained motionless as he replied, "I could ask you the same ... sir!"

Robertson subdued the growing frustration and said, "I'm Captain Robertson of the South Carolina Provisional Militia! You are covered by several well-aimed rifles at this moment! You will identify yourself and state your purpose sir!"

John Red smiled broadly as he identified himself and let the good captain know that he was followed by a small but important convoy carrying military supplies and wounded men from the battle at Cowpens to their destination at Fletcher's Mill. Robertson matched the other man's grin as he strode forward to shake his hand. He then sent one of his own militiamen forward with Red to intercept the approaching wagons and dismounted infantry so they could be escorted into the mill's defenses without further incident.

A strangely animated atmosphere of celebration entered the village a short while later with the arrival of these heavily loaded wagons and the extra military strength of the escorting militiamen. Ira shook hands vigorously with Dr. Bolt when they were introduced. They made all of the necessary arrangements to move the wounded men into his house. It was the most likely building to use for a hospital in the village, and it was close enough to the mill so that the wounded could be moved there if needed.

The military supplies were removed from the wagons and secured in the mill.

Elizabeth and Mona came out of the house and started working with the doctor's assistant and Mrs. Phillips as soon as they understood the circumstances. The wounded men were carried directly into the parlor and the upstairs bedrooms that were still available. Elizabeth Fletcher found the still sleeping form of Lieutenant William Morgan perched in the seat at the front of the wagon. She first noticed that the handsome young man was dressed differently from the others. He groaned deeply and slumped further over on the seat. This uncovered the still ripped thigh of his right trouser leg and she saw the blood-soaked bandage underneath. Wasting no time, she climbed up into the seat next to him and demanded that someone help her get him into the house.

They laid him on the parlor sofa after covering it with a huge hand-sewn quilt. One of the other men was laid on the floor padded with numerous blankets. The doctor and his assistant were busily working on this man who seemed to have serious injuries involving his face and ribs. She looked back at the young man on the sofa in the dark-blue uniform coat with yellow facings. There was nothing for it. She would care for this one herself.

CHAPTER 31

Captain Jonathan Watson was sent west in great haste by Colonel Francis Marion. Colonel Marion knew the critical importance of the captured supplies headed to Fletcher's Mill. He intended to go himself, but he and "Light-Horse Harry" Lee were ordered to attack the port of Georgetown by General Greene without delay. Captain Watson was a trusted subordinate, a good leader, and a ferocious soldier. Watson was once a color sergeant in the Royal Army. He and his British officer defected from the king's service upon meeting Francis Marion late one night to discuss a prisoner exchange over a dinner of boiled sweet potatoes deep in a heavily overgrown swamp. They were greatly impressed with Marion, his men, and their ironlike resolve to be free.

The truth was that they also longed for freedom. Neither of them had family or loved ones waiting for their return to England. Both were awed by the enormity of the land and the apparent wealth it held. They recognized a rare opportunity in the small but amazingly effective fighting force of Francis Marion. They were treated with respect that night and honor by men who were the subject of both ridicule and terror throughout the British army in the south. A short conversation brought both men to a quick decision, and they never looked back with regret. Colonel Marion welcomed their services immediately. It took some months and several small but vicious battles to earn the wholehearted trust of all their new comrades.

Jonathan Watson followed and fought with Francis Marion through many hair-raising fights all over the southeastern half of the colony since joining him that night. His knowledge of the British army and its methods made him invaluable on several occasions. Watson was a quick study in his own right, and he swiftly learned to master the application of Marion's favored guerilla tactics. Colonel Marion promoted him to his present rank as a reward and further sign of his trusted acceptance. Watson's new men grew to trust him with the same fierce loyalty they once reserved for Marion alone.

Captain Watson was now moving swiftly through the forest with eighty-seven of Marion's most effective guerilla fighters. Colonel Marion would rarely concentrate this many of his men in one place. The purpose of this mission demanded mass, though. Marion needed the precious supplies headed to Fletcher's Mill as soon as possible. He was intensely aware that if he knew about the small convoy, the British must also know about it. Watson was the best man to lead the effort, and Colonel Marion sent the most effective fighters he could spare to ensure Watson's success.

Watson's men had been running and speed-marching over a day and a half now with only brief halts to rest. There were no complaints. They all knew how desperately important their mission was to the cause. Colonel Marion retained less than half of their number with himself to support Colonel Lee in the attempt on Georgetown. Unlike their counterparts in the Royal Army, all these men were fully informed regarding the nature and importance of their objective. They were not blindly following the orders of their superiors. Each one of them knew enough about the situation to continue the mission even if they were separated from the rest of their company.

They were accustomed to attacking large objectives as a unit, then escaping in groups of two or three to reform and attack again in another place at another time. This was what made them so effective. Now, every one of them ran through the woods toward Fletcher's Mill with a single-minded intent to succeed, and a clear understanding of what success might require.

They saw no signs of movement from the garrison at Camden when they skirted furtively around it a few hours earlier. Watson's gut told him that the most likely British force to attack the convoy or the mill itself would come from Winnsborough or the small garrison at Rocky Mount. Whatever force the British could muster might be joined by troops from Camden or even from the small garrison further west at Number 96. Word of the battle at Cowpens might not have arrived at any of the more distant garrisons. The British might not yet suspect that the materials were even headed to Fletcher's Mill.

Watson thought through all of this hundreds of times as he hurried relentlessly onward. He intended to ambush any enemy force headed south toward Fletcher's Mill. This was the most effective use of his men. He knew his company might be greatly outnumbered. He also knew the incredible advantage of surprise when confronting a larger force. Watson meant to use this advantage wisely. He called a halt at midmorning with this in mind.

They were moving in a loose column with pickets in front and on both flanks. Watson stopped them in a small grove on the western slope of a ridge overlooking a substantial river valley running north and south. He knew this area. He had been to Fletcher's Mill on several occasions, but these visits were always made at night. Watson usually camped a short distance east of the mill village and waited for darkness to conceal movement in and out of the mill. They were further north now, but the landscape was very familiar. He was certain that the forested valley visible a couple miles away held the bed of the Broad River. That meant that the road from Fish Dam and Rocky Mount was very close.

Captain Watson called his sergeants together and held a brief council of war. He sent his best scouts to locate the road and search carefully northward for the approach of British forces. He designated the place they currently occupied as a rallying point in case his men became separated during possible enemy contact. Watson was prepared to wait at least a day along this north-south route in an effort to gain tactical advantage over any approaching British force before going on south to Fletcher's

Mill. Marion had dispatched a messenger to the mill when he learned about Cowpens. Watson felt honored that the colonel trusted him enough to lead this endeavor in his place. The company was moving again shortly after the scouts departed. They reached the road less than half an hour later.

Watson found a likely spot where the east side of the road was over-shadowed by a steep embankment. The west side of the road was bordered by heavy bramble thickets and dropped off gradually to where the river flowed quietly in the distance. The ground above the embankment was heavily wooded, but held far less undergrowth and brush than the western side. These features extended over a hundred yards, from a shallow creek bed on the north end, to a place where the road turned sharply west at the south end to avoid a substantial rock outcropping. The men knew what to do without instruction. They participated in many ambushes. Most of them were under cover along the high side of the road within minutes. Ten of the best riflemen took position above the rock pile at the turn in the road from which they would have clear shots straight north all the way to the creek bed.

A few men collected canteens from their companions and slipped off to fill them at the river. There were no fires. No one slept. The men were so quiet once they were in position that the birds and forest creatures resumed their calls and movements as if no one was there. Two of the scouts appeared less than three hours later. They were winded from running and soaked with sweat. They had located a large British cavalry force moving south in column just north of the Fish Dam Ferry. The column had stopped to close up and apparently send riders across the river to Fish Dam for information. One of the scouts reported that he saw the British resume their movement south as he began his run back with the information. The column couldn't be more than a half mile distant now. Watson felt no surge of pride in being right about the British and their methods. He knew them so well that he would have been shocked if no column was found.

Captain Watson personally took a position at the southern end on the rock outcropping above the bend in the road. He had a clear view of everything from this place with his ten picked riflemen. His men knew not to fire until he did. The British would have mounted pickets moving well out in front of the main body. They would try to keep pickets moving through the woods to their flanks to prevent the very thing Watson planned for them. The terrain here wouldn't allow flankers to keep up with a swiftly moving column. The enemy would sacrifice security for speed with the arrogant belief that they could overwhelm any hostile force and just keep moving. This was a perfect ambush site.

An inexperienced commander might be tempted to drop a tree across the road to stop the column at the point of contact. The site of a barricade crossing the road would force the British to deploy and ruin the shocking effect of surprise. Watson wouldn't give up such an important advantage. He would allow the pickets to pass under his position and move around the bend. A smart British sergeant would probably keep one man stationed at the bend to maintain visual contact with the main column until they reached that point. One of Watson's men would dispatch any such unfortunate observer.

Minutes passed slowly. They finally saw a group of seven dragoons in loose formation ride up out of the creek bed and continue swiftly down the road in their direction. These were the leading pickets. They were alert as they quickly searched the roadsides for any sign of a rebel presence. Watson and his men were frozen in camouflaged anticipation. A burly old sergeant was in charge of these horsemen. He paused at the bend in the road just under Captain Watson's position and sent the other men on around the bend. It mildly surprised Watson when the sergeant jumped down from his horse and scrambled quickly up the large pile of rocks, leaving the horse's reins wrapped loosely around a small sapling. The sergeant clearly intended to gain a better view from the top of the rocks before returning to the horse with the approach of the column.

It wouldn't matter. Captain Watson was concealed well. He now watched the main body of the British column moving up out of the creek bed and continuing toward him down the road. There were hundreds of them. He waited until they were all clearly visible on the roadbed, then directed his attention to the officers at the head of the column. Watson was startled to recognize Major Sir Thomas Willoughby, one of the few officers in the Royal Army that he actually respected. Willoughby was riding next to a ramrod-straight lieutenant in the hated uniform of Tarleton's legion. Two dragoon captains rode further back in the column leading their own men.

The head of the column was now less than twenty yards away. It was time to act. Watson couldn't shoot Sir Thomas like this. He had too much respect for the man. The column was getting much closer. It would soon be too late. Watson could feel the expectant stares of the militiamen all around him. It was now or never. Taking another breath and letting it out, he shifted his aim to the lieutenant from Tarleton's Legion and squeezed the trigger.

Chapter 32

Billy swam slowly upward toward the faint light. A warm cloying darkness seemed to envelop him on every side. A cool sweet fragrance emanated from the light in the upper distance. He strove to reach it with all his might, but his arms wouldn't cooperate. The light grew clearer while moving toward him as if in response to his desire. Suddenly, it was accompanied by the musical beauty of an angel's voice. He couldn't understand the words at first. He realized then that he was not hearing the voice of an angel, but that of a young woman. The words were common, but still beautiful. He heard, "Aunt Mona, Doctor, it looks like he is waking up."

Billy forced his eyes open, and his head swam. The room was dark except for the light of a few candles. He was on his left side on a grand sofa in a well-furnished parlor. His uniform coat, shirt, and trousers were gone. His boots were on the floor at the end of the sofa. He was now wearing a long silken night shirt and was wrapped in a huge hand-sewn quilt. Billy's eyes slowly focused on the beautiful young woman leaning over him with a bright candle in her left hand. Her right hand held a damp cloth. She had apparently been swabbing his forehead with this object. His mouth felt dry as dust. Billy's thigh seemed to be on fire. He was trapped and becoming increasingly anxious in the cloying quilt. He struggled to sit up.

The young woman sat the candle and cloth on a side table. She then placed her hands on his shoulders and gently pushed him back down while uttering soothing words of careful restraint. "Now, now, Lieutenant Morgan, please lie back. You are safe and in good hands here."

Her voice sounded like the angel from his dream. He realized that the sweet fragrance came from her hair as she leaned over him. Two other faces appeared over her shoulder. One of these belonged to Doctor Bolt. The other was an older, but strikingly beautiful dark-haired woman who said, "Move back, Elizabeth, and let the doctor see to him."

The angel responded with, "Yes, Mona dear." There was a ruffle of skirts as the beautiful fragrance moved away to be replaced with the serious probing visage of the elderly doctor.

Billy was awake now. He realized that the angel's name must be Elizabeth. Doctor Bolt felt his forehead and pulled back his eyelids one at a time to peer at the pupils below them. The doctor leaned forward to sniff Billy's breath and sat back to make notes on a small tablet with the stub of a pencil. He then stood up and pulled the quilt away from Billy's legs and raised the nightshirt so that he could examine the wound on his thigh. Billy saw Elizabeth's face flash crimson before she looked away from his heavily bandaged thigh. Mona told the girl to leave the room in a quiet but stern whisper.

Dr. Bolt undid the bandage slowly and carefully. He examined the stitches and sniffed at the now dried blood and fluid around the wound before standing back up and making more notes on his pad. He and Mona replaced the bandage and covered Billy again with the quilt. Billy ignored the doctor's protests and sat up on the sofa. Mona moved to pick up the soiled bandages and called Elizabeth to come back in. Billy cleared his parched throat and croaked a question to the doctor about his burning thigh.

Dr. Bolt sat down in a straight-backed dining chair that was strangely out of place in this room. He thought for a moment. "Young man, I was afraid that your wound was poisoned ... infected.... It seemed that I might not have gotten it completely cleaned before I sewed it shut that night." He now had Billy's full attention. "You see, if it was poisoned, I couldn't remove it... The wound.... It is too high on your leg.... If it turned to gangrene ... you would have died."

Billy silently absorbed that statement. He finally looked up. "Is it ... poisoned?" The doctor sat back a little further and showed what could almost be mistaken for a smile. He gestured toward the ladies in the room. "We have been praying for you! No! I don't think it is infected! I believe you will be quite well in two or three weeks. You will probably have pain in the leg for some time, especially during cold weather. You should be able to return to normal duties within a couple of days if the wound is kept clean and the bandage is changed regularly."

Billy's head swam again briefly. He asked why he felt so sick. Dr. Bolt told him that he believed there was some infection which his body and God's grace had overcome. The dizziness he now felt was probably caused by the lingering effects of shock and the laudanum he was given for the pain.

Billy was very thirsty. He was pondering this realization when Elizabeth reentered the room carrying a silver tray with a steaming tea-pot and several silver cups. He was amazed at her timing. She sat the tray down and poured hot tea into one of the cups before handing it to him with a gracious smile. Billy nodded his gratitude and sipped at the tea too quickly, burning his lips and spilling some of it. He felt a strange embarrassment in front of Elizabeth and looked down as he tried to wipe his chin with his forearm. She leaned forward and gently caressed his cheek as she cleaned his chin with the damp cloth she used on his forehead earlier.

The effect on Billy was as overwhelming as it was immediate. He somehow stammered a weak "Thank you" and again tried to sip the hot tea. Honey was mixed with it. He felt like he was in paradise in the presence of this beautiful girl sipping hot sweet tea. The events of the past weeks seemed very distant right now. So many dramatic changes had occurred in his life. So many things had happened. It all seemed distant, fantastic, surreal when considered from this beautiful place.

Reality came shrieking back to Billy with the tormented cry of another wounded man at the other side of the parlor. The man seemed semiconscious as he struggled to find the missing portion of his lower left leg. The doctor called for his assistant and moved quickly to restrain and quiet the man. Billy saw that there were several other wounded men lying on the floor in the room. One of them was his friend Silas who lay awake staring at Billy from several feet away.

Silas was positioned flat on the floor with his head propped slightly, allowing him to observe Billy on the sofa. When he realized that Billy saw him, he smiled broadly and tried to speak. This brought a low cough and a look of deep agony to his face. Billy sat the teacup down while attempting to move off the sofa to his friend's side. His head spun again and he nearly fell forward before Elizabeth caught him and eased him back down. He finally managed to say, "Easy, Silas. Don't try to talk!" Billy took several quick breaths as he settled back onto his side.

Elizabeth noted the looks exchanged between them and perceived that Lieutenant Morgan and the other injured man were close friends. Mona had left the room to tend to Ezekiel and to help Mrs. Phillips with the wounded men who were taken upstairs. Elizabeth stayed in the parlor and listened a moment longer before going upstairs to find Mona. Dr. Bolt and his assistant managed to quiet the crying soldier and moved on to other patients in this makeshift hospital. The room returned to deep quiet.

Silas took a careful labored breath and managed to whisper, "Well, Billy ... I understand that I should be thanking you ... sir."

The smile was painfully strained but very genuine. Billy smiled back sheepishly and said, "You must have heard something about what happened since the battle then...."

Silas whispered, "Yes. I've learned some fantastic things about a young man I know from Sergeant Duncan and some of the others." Billy said nothing. "Seems you really are kin to Daniel Morgan...?"

Billy hung his head in refreshed shame. "I'm so sorry about all that, Silas! I don't know what comes over me sometimes...."

Silas gasped and coughed before sternly whispering, "Hush that talk now, Billy ... I mean Lieutenant. I understand the others finally saw you for who and what you are!"

Billy gasped, "You mean a low-down lyin' bumpkin?"

Silas nearly sat up at this. The result was an angry fit of coughing that brought immediate panic and regret to his young friend. He finally managed to whisper, "No. That's not what I mean, Billy! The general and all those other men saw the courage and character of the real you that day! I don't care what you think. I understand General Morgan promoted you on the spot for what you done that day. You know he wouldn't a done that if he hadn't seen more in you than what you see in yourself!"

Billy remained silent. Silas paused for several minutes before he went on. "Seems you proved him right after all, Lieutenant ... I mean we're here, ain't we? This is the place you was supposed to get us to, right?"

Billy looked up to see Silas smiling again. He nodded slowly. "Well, yes. I guess this is apparently Fletcher's Mill, although I haven't seen anything other than the inside of this room."

Silas leaned his head back and whispered again, "I been talkin' with Duncan and that other sergeant, Strickland, this afternoon. They was both in here to check on you a couple hours ago. Seems like you succeeded on your mission better than even they expected. They're both really impressed with you, Billy. Turns out that the owner of this place, Reverend Fletcher, and a militia captain named Robertson have been pushing all the men here to get ready for some kind of British attack. They think we've been followed or something. Anyway, they expect that the lobsters know this place has been used for storing contraband and weapons and they'll come here to take it or destroy it."

Billy took this in with growing alarm. Silas stopped talking and seemed to have drifted off into fitful sleep. Time seemed to stand still for Billy as he thought about what Silas said. He struggled to sit back up. He wanted to know where his uniform was, but there was no one to ask. He thought about calling out, but he didn't want to wake Silas or the other men in the room. Pulling the quilt around himself, he rolled back up into a seated position. The dizziness had mostly abated. He found that he was able to sit up straight. He waited several seconds before leaning forward and forcing himself to stand.

The front door of the house opened at that moment. Billy heard a couple of men with booted feet enter. He was still lightheaded, and he didn't know whether to try and remain standing or fall back onto the sofa. He desperately wanted to recover his clothing and go look for Strickland or Duncan to learn what was happening. As it was, he just stood there wavering. The new visitors came into the parlor a few seconds later and stood staring at the quilt-wrapped apparition in front of the sofa. One of these was Captain Robertson of the South Carolina Provisional Militia. The other was Reverend Ira Fletcher.

CHAPTER 33

It was night again. Throckmorton and Crispin remained hidden through the daylight hours. They were terrified of recapture for different reasons. Crispin knew that a hangman's noose or firing squad awaited him if the British found him. Throckmorton was still stinging from the vicious treatment of his earlier Tory militia captors. He couldn't bear the thought of a British prison hulk in Charleston harbor. Both understood that their problems could be overcome with the wealth they believed existed at Fletcher's Mill. Neither had any clear idea how to seize that wealth from its current owner. They both saw an opportunity and they intended to pursue it.

The air turned bitterly cold again with nightfall. They scurried along the edge of the road in the darkness hoping to reach shelter in a house or barn. They were afraid they would blunder into the rear guard or the night camp perimeter pickets of Willoughby's cavalry force from Rocky Mount. Neither man really trusted the other. They were learning more about each other as they talked and argued in whispered tones along the road. Their lives were incredibly similar, yet dynamically different. They were stuck together in this questionable partnership through immediate need and bizarre circumstance.

Major Throckmorton suddenly grabbed Crispin by the sleeve and pulled him to a halt. He smelled wood smoke. It required no genius to understand that smoke meant fire. Smoke indicated the presence of either a campfire or a chimney. A campfire meant a military presence. The armed forces of either side in this conflict must be avoided of course. The possibility of a chimney as the source sent both men moving carefully forward again in the quiet darkness. Less than a hundred yards further on, they stumbled onto a low stone bridge over a gurgling creek bed. They found a trail cutting away from the road through the trees just on the other side of the bridge.

A quick desperate reconnaissance revealed the existence of a wealthy-looking farm on the side of the hill above the road. There were no visible lights. It was very late. The smoke was curling from two brick chimneys at either end of the large farmhouse. Their first instinct was to go seek shelter for a while in the barn. Both men wanted to keep moving, though. What they really needed was food and warmer clothing that could only be found inside the house. One look at either of them would cause any intelligent farmer to refuse them entry.

A sharp whispered argument ensued. Throckmorton wanted to keep moving south without coming in contact with anyone. Crispin maintained the illogical attitude that any colonial property rightfully belonged to the Crown. He somehow managed to rationalize his current circumstances to the point where he felt like a victim of treachery. He argued they should force entry to the house and take what they needed. To reinforce his argument, he brandished the stolen musket he was carrying. Throckmorton finally gave in.

More sharp conversation followed, and a plan of sorts developed. The two scoundrels moved furtively toward the house a few minutes later. Crispin took a position behind a tree near the front porch from which he could easily cover the door with the loaded musket. Throckmorton stepped gingerly onto the porch and sidled up to the door. He paused and looked back at Crispin. Crispin nodded once, and Throckmorton banged on the door with his fist several times.

Silence prevailed for nearly a full minute. Throckmorton banged on the door again. Nothing happened. He was about to suggest they should kick the door in when he saw the dim glow of approaching light through the small square windowpane in the center of the door. He heard a vaguely familiar male voice from inside the house. "All right, all right! I'm coming! Stop pounding on my door!" He knew he had heard the voice before, but he couldn't place it. He stood back a little further and held his tongue.

Crispin came from behind the tree in exasperation and shouted, "Open that door at once in the name of the king!"

Throckmorton couldn't believe he heard the absurd words and was about to laugh at Crispin in nervous surprise when the door bolt was drawn from the inside. The door jerked open a moment later. Throckmorton found himself staring in slack-jawed shock at the young man standing in the opening. The person was holding a lowered pistol in one hand and a guttering candle in the other. He was clad in a long flowing nightshirt and a wool coat that he apparently threw on before opening the door. This wasn't what surprised Throckmorton. The man standing in the doorway was the same Tory militia officer who captured and tormented Throckmorton less than three days earlier.

Crispin surged onto the porch with the cocked musket aimed at the man's face before the other two could voice their mutual recognition. "Drop that weapon, sir!" The man glanced away from Throckmorton toward Crispin and saw the looming barrel of the musket only inches from his nose. He dropped the pistol without ceremony. It was the last mistake he made this side of eternity. Throckmorton lunged forward and kicked the man in the stomach with all his strength. He then scooped up the pistol and began beating the fallen man mercilessly with it. Crispin pulled him away finally, as the man slumped unconscious onto the porch floor in the doorway. Throckmorton shrugged Crispin away and cocked the pistol before he could be stopped. He then aimed the pistol at the man's chest and fired.

Crispin shoved Throckmorton back and bent over the man as if to verify what he had just seen happen. People were stirring now inside and outside the house. Crispin made sure the musket was primed and cocked before anyone arrived. Throckmorton was on his feet again now and wanted to run. Crispin shouted for him to stay. They came this far now.

They had to see this disaster all the way through. He remembered in a flash of dubious cunning that he was wearing most of a dragoon private's uniform. Throckmorton was still dressed as a Continental Army major. Crispin would use their appearance to the best advantage he could make of it.

Light was approaching from further inside the house. He could hear footfalls as several people approached from what he thought must be the slave quarters near the barn. Three large black men climbed onto the porch. A young woman and a little boy in nightclothes came into the entry foyer from the back of the house. The woman saw the man, apparently her husband, on the floor surrounded by a spreading pool of blood. Her hand went to her mouth and she screamed. The little boy pulled away from her and surged forward yelling, "Father!?"

Crispin snatched up the pistol and shoved it into his belt while aiming the musket at Throckmorton and yelling, "Down on your face, you rebel scum!" Throckmorton obeyed like some kind of automaton.

The oldest of the apparent slaves asked, "What is going on here? What has happened? What have you done to Master Richard?" The woman was now on her knees sobbing. The little boy was crying wildly and shaking the dead man by the shoulders begging him to wake up. One of the slaves stepped through the doorway and picked the boy up to carry him back inside. An elderly black woman appeared on the porch and moved inside to take charge of the deceased farmer's weeping wife.

Crispin turned to the elderly black man who was still standing his ground waiting for an answer. "I'm Private Reynolds of the 5th Dragoon Guards," he lied forcefully. "My sergeant and I were escorting this prisoner to Rocky Mount when we were ambushed on the road. My sergeant and two of the horses were killed in the fight. The other horse ran off. I marched the prisoner as far as the bridge down below and decided to see if I could obtain fresh mounts from this farm when I realized it was here. This filthy scum somehow managed to get loose from the rope his hands were tied with and I didn't realize it. Your master opened the door with a pistol in his hand. Before I could stop him, the prisoner grabbed the pistol and struck your master down with it. The pistol discharged during the struggle and your master was shot."

Throckmorton listened to all of this in shock. He hardly realized what he had done only minutes earlier. It was as if the rage possessed him and took over his faculties. He still struggled to regain his reason. Now Crispin was telling the most outlandish story he had heard yet. Somehow, though, the story made perfect sense. The farmer's wife and child could be heard crying inconsolably from a room deep in the house. The slaves moved the body from the doorway, and a woman was already on her hands and knees scrubbing away the pool of blood.

Crispin took charge of the slaves gathering on the porch. He was clearly a man of authority, and they were accustomed to obeying the orders they were given. He told them to move the body to the barn and get two fresh horses saddled. He demanded extra wool overcoats from inside the house along with enough provisions to last him and his prisoner all the way to Rocky Mount. He demanded powder and extra shot for the pistol he had confiscated. Throckmorton was tied roughly with his hands behind his back and his feet lashed together. Crispin had the slaves throw him face down over the saddle when the horses were brought to the front of the house.

Crispin promised to have the proper authorities return to the farm and make amends for this disaster when he reached Rocky Mount. He then swung into the saddle and took the reins of the horse carrying Throckmorton's miserable form. Minutes later, he was cantering down the drive. Crispin turned south when he reached the road, rather than north toward Rocky Mount. He pulled to a halt after a mile or two and dragged Throckmorton down to the ground. He untied the major and stared him in the face for a long moment before both men remounted and rode silently through the darkness toward Fletcher's Mill.

CHAPTER 34

The report of the rifle was heard at the same time the bullet struck home. Lieutenant Cloyde was hit in the chest just above his right lung and below his collar bone. This first shot was followed within a half second by over seventy more shots from above the embankment on the left side of the road. More fire came from a large rock pile directly in front of the column. All the shots were well aimed and fired at close range. Nearly forty saddles were suddenly empty. Several others held desperately wounded men who simply failed to fall.

Most of Cloyde's men, the green-coated members of Tarleton's Legion, were hit in this first volley. Some of these men were stuck more than once. Two pistol shots from the top of the rock pile dispatched the sergeant standing there. The dragoons of the advanced picket were dropped in the road with rifle shots as they tried to return to the column. The air was torn with the screams of men and horses. Pandemonium reigned as the middle of the column continued to surge forward into the collapsing lead elements for several seconds. Many of the survivors from the front of the column did exactly what their hidden attackers wanted and expected them to do. They turned their mounts in the road and attempted to flee.

Confusion added fuel to the panic like lamp oil cast on open flame. The trailing elements of the column were made up mostly of Tory militia. These units were strung out as much as a quarter of a mile back along the road. The sound of battle and the smell of powder smoke mixed with fear had a dramatic effect on these inexperienced soldier farmers. Their officers tried to hold them together on the road. Some of them even tried to drive their men forward toward the sound of the guns. The effort was useless. The frightened men began to break and run as soon as they saw the first terrified wounded dragoons galloping back along the road toward them. Every member of the proud and loud-mouthed Tory militia vanished into the trees and scrub within seconds. Many of them didn't stop running until they were miles away to the north as they scurried in panic toward their homes and farms.

Major Willoughby couldn't understand why he was not hit in the initial volley of the ambush. He had to do something immediately before more of his men were lost. Seconds seemed like minutes now. He twisted violently around to assess the situation and began shouting orders. Willoughby knew the only way to survive a well-prepared ambush was to charge into the enemy fire and break it with overwhelming force. The enemy was well concealed on higher ground here. The rebels chose this site well, and he foolishly rode his column right into it. Fear and rage intermingled to send his pulse rate surging and force adrenaline to animate his already decisive instincts.

Willoughby knew that to stay frozen on the road or to order a retreat would mean many more of his men would die. He began shouting for the next two troops in the column, about seventy men, to charge the left flank embankment. He ordered the now mostly dismounted survivors around him to seek cover and open fire with anything they could bring to bear. He knew that his survival demanded he and his men overwhelm their enemy with a higher volume of fire. He could tell from the sound of the enemy weapons that they were firing rifles. The British carbines and muskets could be reloaded and fired at a much higher rate than rifles no matter who was using them. The roadbed was covered with smoke. The riflemen in the trees above couldn't see his men as well now to effectively use their more accurate weapons.

Willoughby pulled both of his horse pistols from the holsters on his saddle and discharged them toward the rock pile in front of him. He then drew his sword and forced his horse off the road into the trees and thick underbrush on the left side. He would personally lead his still mounted surviving dragoons in a direct charge up the embankment. The captains commanding the trailing cavalry troops knew what to do. They were well-trained British professionals. They would force their way up through the woods to the left from the rear of the column to drive the rebels from their concealed positions by turning their flank. Willoughby thought a moment about Lieutenant Cloyde, but there was no time for that now. Another volley rang out from the wooded embankment just as his dragoons were starting to force their mounts upward in the attack. More saddles were suddenly empty.

Captain Watson ordered his men to begin their withdrawal from the ambush site before he saw Willoughby begin his charge onto the embankment through the smoke followed by many furious dragoons. He knew these would be reinforced by more cavalry from the rear of the column. They would quickly turn his flank if he tried to stay and fight. He had no intention of doing that. He fired both of his pistols at the British sergeant a few yards below him on the rock pile after firing the rifle shot that started the battle. He reloaded his rifle without conscious thought as he yelled instructions to the men around him during the next few harried and blinding minutes. Many of his men reloaded very quickly. They saw the threat coming up the embankment and fired without command. Most of these shots slammed mercilessly into the closely packed troops of charging cavalry.

Watson was still on the rock pile. His vantage point allowed him to see Major Willoughby rallying his men to push them further up the embankment. He still couldn't bring himself to shoot his old comrade. Instead, he took careful aim and shot Willoughby's horse. The major felt the animal collapsing and kicked himself clear before it slid and rolled back down the embankment. The counterattack lost momentum when the major went down. It proceeded up the embankment more slowly. The musket fire from the roadbed didn't slacken, but it was poorly aimed. The dragoons forcing their way up the slope realized that they were as likely to be shot by their comrades on the road as the enemy above them. Several of them came to a stop in the absence of the major's leadership.

The momentary delay gave Watson's men enough time to disengage and move deeper into the surrounding woods from their concealed positions. Suddenly, there were no shots at all from the embankment. The shots slowly died away on the roadbed as well. The smoke began to clear in the faint breeze. The rebels separated into groups of two or three men each within seconds and swiftly spread out through the deep woods, moving away from the ambush site. None of the continental militiamen were lost. They would travel furtively through the trees and undergrowth for hours, if need be, to avoid further contact and return to the rally point designated earlier in the day by Captain Watson.

Major Willoughby's surviving cavalry moved on up the embankment and through the trees and brush searching for any sign of their rebel attackers. They found none. It was as if no one had ever been there. The only real evidence that the ambush had happened was in the bullet-riddled bodies of their dead and wounded comrades. Willoughby was himself shocked by the astounding violence of the attack. His mind continued to seethe with fiery rage. He struggled to gain control of himself before trying to take charge of his now depleted force. Subordinate commanders began reporting the damage that had been done. He listened with a sullen countenance that made some of them think he didn't hear them. He finally forced himself to acknowledge the reports with nods and terse comments if only to keep the annoying young officers from repeating themselves.

Major Willoughby lost nearly half the men he brought out of Rocky Mount in a battle that lasted less than five minutes. Seventy-one of his men were now dead. Another thirty-nine were wounded. Many of these would probably die of their wounds. The ratio of killed and wounded was inexplicably opposite anything he had ever seen in battle. The range was so close. It seemed that few, if any, of the rebel shots missed their marks. He lost all the cowardly Tory militia. The furious growl he uttered as he thought of those useless farmers escaped him before he could contain it.

Lieutenant Cloyde was still alive. Willoughby's personal surgeon was working on him before the lingering powder smoke completely cleared the road bed. The major obtained another horse. There were plenty of spare mounts now. He ordered his men to discontinue the search for the rebels in the surrounding countryside. It was pointless. They would not be found. Any further search would only risk more casualties to his already decimated command. He decided that they would regroup right here on the high ground above the road. His men needed to bury their dead and tend to their wounded.

Major Willoughby realized that it was also pointless to push on toward Fletcher's Mill with the force he had left. He believed the rebels must surely have a far greater force at the mill than he anticipated. Whatever they held at the mill must be very valuable indeed. He would need reinforcements. Only a much larger force would do. He must report this horrific incident as soon as possible. His colonel would be furious. He should not have come on this fool's errand without a much larger force in the first place. He certainly shouldn't have risked his command on this sunken road surrounded by deep forest. He realized that his career was now in deep jeopardy. He hardly cared about that. He had lost these good men, and this was inexcusable.

Not one rebel was taken. None of them were visible save the telling puffs of smoke from their weapons. They could have been a band of ruthless savages for all he knew. He saw no uniforms. He saw none of these men at all. Was this what modern warfare had come to? His heart screamed that this was nothing more than a cowardly attack waged by unscrupulous villains. His emotions told him that his men were the victims of senseless massacre. His military mind knew better. This was a well-planned and masterfully executed ambush by a relatively small group of dismounted infantry against a larger mounted force. His temper cooled as he began asserting control over the battle's aftermath. He even began to have a grudging respect for the rebel commander, whoever he was.

This tragedy would not be repeated. He would get his reinforcements.

His attack on Fletcher's Mill would be overwhelming. It took several hours to reorganize his depleted units and bury the dead. The wounded were loaded onto the supply wagons and the column was turned around headed away from their original objective. They wouldn't return to Rocky Mount. Willoughby now had them headed toward Camden. The wounded would get the best treatment there. His men would rest, resupply, and be reinforced. Willoughby knew what force was needed and how many men were available at Camden.

His superiors would see the need as he had. There would be no Tory militia involved next time. He would move on the rebels again within days. There would be no half measures this time. He would bring all his surviving cavalry and any reinforcements he could obtain from among the hundreds of regular infantry troops located at Camden. He looked around at his exhausted men as they finished the burials and mounted for the next leg of their journey. A price would be paid for what happened today. It would be collected at Fletcher's Mill.

CHAPTER 35

Ira looked around the room in deep concern for a moment before his gaze returned to the quilt-wrapped lieutenant wavering on his feet in front of the sofa. He quietly stepped forward and gently grasped the young man's upper arm to help him sit down. Billy resisted and whispered, "Please, sir, I need to find my trousers and uniform coat. I need to see about my men. I need to talk with someone in authority here. My mission.... The wagons...."

Ira leaned his cane against the wall and slowly removed his gloves as he introduced himself. "My name is Ira Fletcher, son. I own this house and most of the buildings and land surrounding it. Fletcher's Mill belongs to me. I have only recently begun to learn of its military importance. I understand that the mission you were given by General Morgan was to deliver your convoy of supplies and wounded men to my mill."

Billy was surprised to realize that Reverend Fletcher was offering his hand in friendship and what appeared to be ... respect. Ira glanced to his side and introduced the other man as Captain Robertson. Robertson stepped forward and reached out to shake Billy's hand. Robertson said, "You have done a fine job getting these men and supplies here, Lieutenant Morgan. We received a detailed oral report from Sergeants Strickland and Duncan. Duncan also told us the most amazing tale of your participation in the battle at Cowpens. You seem to have made a dramatic impression on those two! I must say, we were not expecting the great number of weapons and the vast store of ammunition your wagons contained, not to mention all the other supplies. I assure you they will be put to good use. My men and yours are now transferring the material from the wagons to a fortified cave behind the stone mill building."

Billy heard all of this while still standing uncertainly before the two men wrapped in the quilt he so desperately wanted to trade for his uniform coat and trousers. Elizabeth and Mona reentered the room from the door behind Reverend Fletcher. The older woman quietly moved from one patient to another in the parlor, carefully checking on them in the candlelight. Elizabeth gracefully moved through the room picking up colorful cloth scraps that were scattered about on the floor. Reverend Fletcher was talking again. Billy suddenly realized that he didn't know what his host had said to him. Elizabeth glanced up and their eyes momentarily met. Her cheeks seemed to brighten, and she smiled before looking back down to her task.

Reverend Fletcher didn't seem to notice, and Mona was busy with the restless amputee near Silas. Billy turned his attention back to Ira and tried to remember what he asked. It was useless. Ira waited patiently for another moment and then said, "Well, no matter. I see that you are still recovering from your wounds." He looked appraisingly at Billy. "Did I hear you right, young man? You are searching for your trousers and your uniform coat? Whatever happened to them?"

Mona stood and intervened when she recognized the growing concern in Ira's voice. "The lieutenant's clothing was filthy, Ira. The trousers also needed mending. They were removed while he was sleeping so that he could be bathed before the doctor worked on his wounded thigh.

"He is wearing one of your nightshirts, along with one of my best quilts." She smiled as she nodded toward Billy's humiliated form.

Reverend Fletcher stared at him with a strained expression on his face, then seemed to notice Elizabeth in the room for the first time. Ira turned toward his granddaughter and said, "What on earth are you doing here, Beth?"

She said, "I've been helping Aunt Mona and the doctor care for these poor men, Grandpa."

Ira looked at Mona quizzically. Mona silently answered him with a return gaze that implored him to treat Elizabeth with greater understanding. "These injured men…? Mona, I don't want Elizabeth exposed to this!" He glanced around the room as he said it to emphasize his point.

Elizabeth spoke up immediately with far more passion than she intended to convey, "Exposed to what, Grandpa? To the suffering of these poor souls? To the torn bodies of other women's fathers, husbands, and sons? What would you have me do, Grandpa? Do you want me to hide from this? Is that what the 'Good Samaritan' did in Jesus' parable…?" The girl's outburst seemed to hang in the air for several seconds. The room remained silent but for the labored breathing of the wounded soldiers.

Ira looked from Elizabeth to Mona and then back again. Billy broke the silence by clearing his throat as he carefully sat back down on the sofa. When Ira turned back toward him, his expression had changed. He now seemed overwhelmingly sad. It was as if he aged several years in those few moments. Ira spoke softly to Mona while looking into Billy's eyes. "I simply want to protect her as long as I can from the horrors occurring around us." He didn't break the eye contact with Billy as he said to Elizabeth, "No Beth, I don't want you to run and hide. You are growing up in very troubled times, and these men need our help. That is why they are here in our home. I love you so much though … I just want to protect you…."

Ira slowly turned toward the parlor door and said, "Please return Lieutenant Morgan's uniform to him as soon as possible, Mona. He clearly yearns to return to his duties." He made no further attempt to force Elizabeth from the room. This surprised the girl and somehow saddened her. She felt, in that moment, that her guarded childhood had suddenly ended in her grandfather's eyes. There was a fleeting regret, but she brushed it away as she resumed her earlier task. Ira paused briefly in front of Mona near the doorway. She reached up and touched his cheek with a look in her eyes that said *Thank you* much more clearly than words could convey. Captain Robertson followed Ira out. Mona left the room to go and get the lieutenant's clothing. A few seconds later, Elizabeth and Billy were the only conscious people in the parlor. The silence slowly became palpable.

Curiosity finally overcame Billy and he asked, "What are all those cloth scraps, miss?"

Elizabeth smiled and blushed slightly again. "I was working on a quilt for my hope chest sir ... before ... before so many things started happening at once. I meant to clean up the mess I had made, but there just didn't seem to be time to spare for it ... until now...." Her efforts slowly brought her across the room near the sofa.

Billy said, "I've watched my mother and sister quilting ... I don't think I could ever have patience enough for such an endeavor."

Elizabeth replied, "Where is your family, Lieutenant?"

Billy felt a pang of homesickness as he said, "Pa's dead, but Mom and Sis still live up in the mountains of western Virginia." Elizabeth said that she had never been there, and expressed that it must be a beautiful place. Billy couldn't imagine why she thought it must be beautiful, but didn't reply. He thought any place would be beautiful if someone like Elizabeth were there.

Their conversation went on quietly for several minutes. Neither of them seemed to realize that Elizabeth was now seated at the other end of the sofa. Nor did they notice when Mona came back into the parlor carrying Billy's now clean, mended, and carefully folded uniform. Mona was not a prude, but she recognized that it was totally inappropriate for these two young people to be seated together on the parlor sofa like this. She could only imagine what people would say if they heard about it. The thought of Ira coming back in right now sent her into a state near panic. She placed the folded uniform on the end table and said, "Elizabeth Fletcher, I need you to help me out in the kitchen." Elizabeth seemed startled as she looked up and realized where she sat. She stood quickly and excused herself before picking up her scrap bag and following Mona out of the room.

Billy leaned back while thinking along lines that he had never investigated to any great extent in the past. He couldn't shake the strange emotion he felt since first seeing the face of this angel a short time ago. He slowly leaned forward and stood to carefully dress himself while keeping the quilt draped over his body in case the ladies returned suddenly. The uniform was clean and dry. The trousers had been expertly mended with a perfectly matched piece of patch material replacing the area damaged by the bullet several nights ago. The process of dressing took much longer than it might have at any other time. He was still very weak, and the pain in his thigh was overwhelming. Billy finally sat back down fully dressed. He carefully folded the quilt and placed it on the sofa next to him. He remained deep in thought as he tried to regain his strength. It took several more minutes of pained struggle to put his boots on.

Silas quietly but suddenly spoke again from the shadows across the room. "That is a very beautiful young woman, Billy! Yes, a very beautiful girl indeed, sir...."

Billy replied, "Yes, she certainly is!"

Doctor Bolt came back into the parlor with his assistant and Mrs. Phillips trailing him. The three were very purposeful in their movements, but they all seemed nearly exhausted. The doctor noticed that Billy was fully dressed now and sitting up on the sofa. He said, "Just what is it that you are about, young man? You shouldn't be up like this. The stitches in your leg.... This is dangerous for you. I insist that you lie down and rest!"

Billy wasn't persuaded. "I'm fine, Doctor. You've done an excellent job treating my wound, but I need to go and see to my own responsibilities. I must check on my men. I must learn more about this place and what needs to be done here before we leave to rejoin our army."

Doctor Bolt shook his head vigorously and said, "No! This is foolishness! You might reopen the wound! There still might be infection!"

Billy assured him that he would be very careful, but he wouldn't change his mind. He was now standing. He looked about the room for the crutch he used earlier on the road near the river. It was not there. Doctor Bolt seemed to realize what he needed and whispered something to his assistant who silently departed. Billy heard the front door open and close as the man left the house. He remained standing with the best look of silent resolve he could muster. The doctor shrugged and turned away. He and Mrs. Phillips continued with their ministrations to the other patients in the room.

Billy was about to give up and collapse in frustrated resignation a few minutes later when he heard the front door open and close again. The doctor's assistant had returned. This time, he was accompanied by a frustrated Sergeant Duncan who was carrying a pair of makeshift crutches hastily devised from two tree branches padded with long strips of cloth.

Duncan said, "Now what's this, Lieutenant? You mean to get out and about, do you? Sergeant Strickland and I have everything well in hand, sir! There's no need for you to get about yet!"

Billy silenced him with a raised hand. "I can't bear being in here. Let me have those sticks. Now let's go see what is happening while you tell me everything that I've missed during the last several hours."

Duncan stared at him for a second longer than was prudent, then grudgingly handed over the crutches. Billy tested them by moving carefully up and down the parlor floor, then headed for the doorway into the hall. He paused to get his bearings and turned toward the front door of the house. Duncan reached up to steady him when he stopped moving. Billy shrugged the help away stubbornly and resumed his movement. They were out on the porch before he stopped again to look around outside. Duncan again stepped dutifully up next to his hard-headed young officer. He realized that he had little idea what was going on in the young man's brain. On the other hand, he had come to like and respect William "Billy" Morgan with a reverence that most men might think odd. If Billy was strong enough to carry on with his duty, Duncan wouldn't offer further argument.

The sergeant explained the layout of the village and the mill. He gave a detailed report regarding the preparations being made here to defend the place against British attack. Billy listened quietly. He had a good understanding of the whole situation at Fletcher's Mill within a short time. His mind busily worked through what his new responsibilities must be. His earlier mission was accomplished. The lingering memory of Miss Elizabeth Fletcher began to compete with his thoughts of military duty. Billy nodded to Sergeant Duncan and they started off to search for Sergeant Strickland and the rest of his men.

CHAPTER 36

Major Sir Thomas Willoughby tried to regain his normally martial posture on the borrowed horse as they rode into Camden. It took a long time to reach this place from the ambush site along the river road south of Fish Dam. His men were moving like beaten animals. Willoughby understood their dejection, but knew it was not caused solely by the attack along the road. These men were tired. They were tired of this seemingly endless war. The pride in their unit, the love of the king, the will to win, all of it was wearing thin. The horrific losses in the ambush accentuated the growing sense of purposelessness.

Lieutenant Cloyde only lasted a few hours after the battle. His death was particularly grievous to Major Willoughby. Cloyde was a promising young officer. It was too bad that he was part of Tarleton's legion. Tarleton. What a fool. The man had so incensed the rebels with his refusal to accept quarter. Now they would fight to the death in any encounter. Tarleton would somehow survive the debacle at Cowpens though....

Willoughby was lost in thought. He suddenly realized that the column was stopped. They had passed through town and were in the military encampment on the other side. He gave instructions to his subordinate commanders, and they were quickly engaged in the actions required to bring the exhausted men into military order. Billet areas were assigned and the troops were soon involved in the tedious effort required to make camp. The wounded were transferred to the hospital in an old warehouse on the edge of town. The mounts had to be cared for, weapons had to be cleaned, units had to be reorganized after their heavy losses.

Junior officers and sergeants would manage most of these things. Major Willoughby took the few minutes required to ensure that his instructions were understood, then remounted to ride back into town to report to the garrison commander. A large house was appropriated here as a headquarters just as had been done in Rocky Mount. Camden was a larger town, but finding the correct house was simple in any event. The bustle of military activity around it made it obvious.

The town was garrisoned by a mixture of light infantry units which combined to comprise a full battalion of Royal Infantry and two batteries of regular artillery. The commander was an Irish aristocrat, thirty-two-year-old Lieutenant Colonel Lord Francis Rawdon. Rawdon had taken part in many significant battles during this long war, from Lexington and Concord to Bunker Hill, and Long Island. He initially commanded the Royal Army forces, including Willoughby and his dragoons, here at Camden in the decisive defeat of Horatio Gates five months earlier. Now that General Cornwallis had moved further north, Lord Rawdon remained in essential command of His Majesty's forces in South Carolina. The younger man was Major Willoughby's immediate commander.

Lord Rawdon was well known to Willoughby. They were not friends, but they had been together in difficult battlefield circumstances in the past. Some thought Lord Rawdon to be a foppish martinet. Willoughby knew different. He watched Rawdon storm the redoubt on Breeds Hill in Boston. He had seen the young man in action since then as well. They shared a mutual respect for each other as soldiers. Major Willoughby believed that Rawdon would immediately see the need for an attack on Fletcher's Mill.

Willoughby was led upstairs in the headquarters building to a large bedroom. He found Lord Rawdon receiving the attention of a dubious-looking physician as he lay under a mass of blankets in a huge bed. The window drapes were closed and the light in the room came from a small dim lamp on a nightstand and a fire roaring in the grate. The room was overly warm and smelled of illness. Willoughby made his presence known. The physician turned with a startled and annoyed look on his face. His right hand held a lancet and his left held a small metal bowl.

Major Willoughby got a clear look at the colonel lying in the bed as the physician moved away. The man barely resembled the dashing young Irishman he last saw on horseback several months earlier. Rawdon's eyes were sunken. The skin on his face had a strange yellow-gray pallor. He was breathing roughly and appeared to be covered with sweat. Willoughby recognized the signs of a man suffering from malaria. He overcame a powerful urge to grab the fool doctor and throw him out before he could further injure the brave young man lying here in this stifling stinking room.

Lord Rawdon's eyes opened slowly and he recognized his new visitor. He shuddered as he struggled to sit up against the insistence of the doctor. Shrugging off the constraint, he croaked, "What on earth are you doing here, Sir Thomas?"

Willoughby briefly turned his gaze on the doctor with an expression that sent the man scuttling from the room in haste. He stood at attention near the foot of the bed as he began to explain his presence to his superior. Rawdon was sitting up now. He interrupted the major long enough to put him at ease and offer him the use of a large leather chair near the end table at the right side of the bed. Willoughby gratefully sat down before continuing with his verbal report.

He began with information about the battle at Cowpens. It didn't take long to explain the actions he had taken since Lieutenant Cloyde arrived at Rocky Mount with information about the captured military supplies and their apparent destination at Fletcher's Mill. Rawdon listened silently through all of it, even the horrific recounting of the ambush on the Broad River Road. He nodded his head in acknowledgement of Willoughby's decision to divert to Camden for reinforcements after the losses he had taken. Both men sat in silence for almost a minute after the major finished speaking. The only sound came from the crackling flames in the fireplace and the labored breathing of the very sick man who had just listened to an alarming report regarding two military disasters.

Willoughby could only imagine what Rawdon was thinking. Major Ferguson allowed his Tory force to be annihilated, and lost his own life, at King's Mountain in October. Tarleton's fool pride cost nearly a thousand good men at Cowpens, and now this. The successes enjoyed by His Majesty's forces in the south were beginning to seem almost irrelevant to both of these professional soldiers. The rebels seemed to be gaining momentum. British forces were stretched very thin even when the entire southern army was together in South Carolina. Now General Cornwallis had moved into North Carolina trying to force a decisive confrontation with the main body of rebels there. It seemed he didn't comprehend that the rebel partisans here were still a very dangerous threat.

The rebels would be even more troublesome now if they received more weapons and ammunition carried away from Cowpens. Lord Rawdon knew instinctively that Willoughby was right to move with great haste to recover or destroy these supplies before they were distributed among the rebels. Both Rawdon and Willoughby knew Reverend Ira Fletcher, though. It was still almost impossible for either man to grasp the idea that Fletcher could possibly be involved in rebellion against the king.

Lord Rawdon broke the silence as he threw the blankets off his legs and turned to face Major Willoughby in the dim light. "Bad business, Willoughby, the way those rascals mistreated you and your men! How many did you lose again?" The colonel's face was beginning to regain a more natural color. It seemed that the challenge of military events at hand were forcing life back into him. Willoughby recited his losses again as he looked directly into the other man's eyes. He felt the fury growing again in his chest.

Rawdon's eyes were now sharply focused, but his expression remained inscrutable. He nodded when Willoughby finished and struggled to stand up. Willoughby helped steady him. Rawdon was soon pacing back and forth in front of the fireplace. Several minutes passed as he continued to absorb the shocking news. He paused to lean and rest with his hand on the fireplace mantle more than once. He finally collapsed into a chair near the fire and looked over at Willoughby with a sad but determined expression. Beads of perspiration were forming on his brow, and he shuddered visibly before speaking.

"Major Willoughby, you will reform your men with the added strength of half my infantry. Let's see, that will be most of what's left of the 33rd Fusiliers. You will make sure the men are rested through tonight, tomorrow, and the next day as you reorganize your force and issue orders to your subordinates. You will advance on Fletcher's Mill three days hence. It should take you no more than four days to complete the march. You will seize the mill and any military contraband found there. I sincerely hope nothing is there, and the people who ambushed you are not connected with the place. If you do find military contraband, you will detain any colonials present including Reverend Fletcher, his family, and the other village leaders. They are to be brought here for disposition, unharmed, unless you encounter resistance. In that case you will destroy the mill and any rebel force present. Do you understand?"

Major Willoughby listened carefully. He hesitated a moment as he considered the political implications of arresting Ira Fletcher and his family. Lord Rawdon seemed to understand his thoughts and said, "Don't worry, I will put these orders in writing so that the sole responsibility will fall on my shoulders."

Willoughby was startled by that. He responded a little too forcefully with, "No, my lord, that was not my hesitation. I'm just concerned about how it will be received in court if we arrest this man. It seems that his property could have been misused by others without his knowledge. He is well loved by the locals, but hated by many surrounding Tory leaders. They have not kept their feelings secret from the Crown, and yet Ira Fletcher has been given royal grace and protection in the past."

Lord Rawdon nodded and seemed to deflate slightly. "Yes, yes, you are absolutely right. That is why you will use the least amount of force possible, unless you encounter actual armed resistance. Reverend Fletcher will be brought here and safely protected from those who would do him harm. He will be treated with the utmost respect and deference as he is allowed to show evidence that he is not personally involved with the rebel activities we suspect in and around his home. However, if you do encounter armed resistance, you will destroy the threat with overwhelming force and an example will be made of the place."

Willoughby was standing now. He found himself bowing slightly. "Yes, my lord. I understand, sir." He excused himself from Lord Rawdon and went downstairs to await his written orders. They were delivered by a very tall captain of the 33rd Fusiliers about a half hour later. The officer identified himself as Captain Jones, and explained that he was the regimental adjutant for the 33rd Fusiliers. He would help Major Willoughby organize the combined force over the next couple of days. When they were ready to advance, he would be at the major's service. There was a great deal of work to do in a very short time. The two men were completely immersed in deep conversation within minutes. They were professional officers in His Majesty's Royal Army. They would take their time to organize their force with care. Major Sir Thomas Willoughby would not be surprised a second time when he led his men toward Fletcher's Mill.

CHAPTER 37

Throckmorton and Crispin left their horses tied in a thicket. They moved as quietly as they could through the forest underbrush as they approached the mill village. It was so dark under the trees that it was all they could do to avoid being torn to pieces in the thick growth. Crispin was beginning to doubt the sense of returning to this hated place. Throckmorton felt no such hesitation. Something else was slowly beginning to develop in Crispin's thoughts. He was afraid of his companion. He questioned the other man's sanity. He still couldn't wrap his mind around what happened at the Tory farm the night before.

Throckmorton was also shocked by what he had done. It had happened so quickly. He felt no deep remorse, though. The Tory deserved what he got as far as he was concerned. He knew Crispin was afraid of him. Let him be. Crispin had his own murderous history. The similarities between them struck him again as odd. He entered this dubious partnership to pursue his own interests. He would remain loyal to his newfound "friend" as long as loyalty served his purposes. He knew with razor-sharp certainty that Crispin's virtue was no deeper than his own. Besides, they were on opposite sides in this fool war in the first place.

Crispin tripped on an exposed tree root and fell headlong. He was pushing a low hanging pine branch out of his way when he fell. The branch snapped back and slapped Throckmorton in the face, knocking him down. The brief ensuing conversation effectively displayed the darkness in each man's soul. No apologies were offered. Silence reasserted itself as they resumed their tortured movement through the woods. They were trying to find the edge of the north road. They didn't want to be on it, they just wanted to follow it to the edge of town.

Crispin came to a stop. Throckmorton didn't notice, and the resultant collision brought more sharp discussion. Crispin turned completely around now. He reached out unnecessarily to make sure he knew where his companion was before announcing that he had an idea. Throckmorton paused in the darkness and tried to brush some of the filth from the back of his clothing. "Pray tell, what scheme have you developed while we struggle blindly through this frigid wet jungle?"

"Well, see here now. I've no great desire to be discovered again by the locals here. The last time they had their hands on me, I was locked in a mill storeroom as I've already told you. In our escape, we were forced to kill a young man who unwittingly entered our cell and offered us opportunity. My sergeant was lost later on the road north of here." He didn't bother to give further details. He wasn't proud of killing the boy or abandoning Sergeant Smythe on the road. Crispin was beginning to feel growing remorse for the poor choices he had made over the past few weeks. Major Willoughby openly accused him of both incompetence and cowardice. He was starting to understand that the flaws in his character were much deeper than professional failure and uncontrolled fear. He knew himself to be a liar, a coward, and a thief. Now he was a fugitive murderer. Crispin suddenly realized that the two most despicable people he had ever met were standing here tonight in this cold wet underbrush.

Throckmorton asked, "All right, you don't want to be discovered at the mill—then what do you propose?" Crispin brushed past him and started walking back the way they came. He saw no point in continuing toward the village now. They had made a trail of sorts that he was just able to follow. Throckmorton hesitated a moment, then started following his companion. He realized in frustration that he had no choice if he didn't want to be left in the woods all alone.

Crispin spoke over his shoulder while he struggled back through the brush. "Let's get back to the horses and find a place to make camp for tonight. I think we're going about this all wrong. The rebels with the stolen weapons know who you are, Major. Isn't that correct? That's what you told me."

Throckmorton responded, "Well, yes. They do. They have shown absolutely no respect for my rank or position, but yes, they do know who I am. Why?"

Crispin paused and looked back toward the other man in the darkness. "Because, sir, you can simply ride into the village in the open uniformed as you are. They may not like you. They clearly don't respect you. But you are 'one of them' after all. They won't arrest you or shoot you on sight!"

Throckmorton immediately understood. Yes. It was simple. He could gain access. He could then find a way to bring Crispin in to help him. He thought about it as they stumbled through the darkness toward their horses. He knew he would meet the same resistance from Lieutenant Morgan and his men. He admitted to himself that there was no legitimate way he could gain control of the captured military stores now. He no longer cared about that. He saw that he could use the previous altercation with the inexperienced young Morgan to his advantage. His interest now was the rumor of hidden gold.

Major Throckmorton would ride in alone. He would apologize to Morgan. He would explain his presence and the condition of his uniform by using part of the truth. He tried to follow the convoy. He lost his men and was captured by Tories. He was taken to Rocky Mount and escaped, but not before learning that a large British force was headed this way. They would believe him when he expressed his concern for the captured material and the Continental Army interests here. The most effective lie always included a kernel of truth.

Dawn was approaching by the time they found their horses again. They mounted quickly and headed north trying to move back from the village before full daylight. They were not on the river road, but they were on a trail of sorts. It seemed to run northeast away from the village. It didn't appear to be used much, but neither man wanted to chance being discovered here. They rightly assumed that anyone else they encountered would naturally be their enemy. The two scoundrels finally moved away from the trail through an area where the trees were thinner and found a good spot to make camp. They would rest here and prepare to carry out their new plan. They did their best to clean Throckmorton's tattered uniform and straighten up the tack of his stolen horse. They even made a small fire. Both men were ravenously hungry. Crispin remembered the food they confiscated from the Tory farm.

The frightened slave at the farmhouse threw several items into the bag when he filled it with provisions. He was terrified of the British soldier who was shouting at him. The slave paid little attention to the items he threw into the bag demanded minutes after the rebel major overpowered and shot his master on the front porch of the house. Crispin now riffled through the bag and found several welcome food items including bread, cheese, and part of a cured ham. He also discovered an old metal teapot. The vessel contained a small bag of tea leaves. This was an unexpected treasure. All they needed now was a little water. The only bottle they possessed was empty and needed to be refilled.

Crispin showed the discovery to Throckmorton and asked him to find some way to hang the teapot over the fire while he went to get water from a nearby creek bed. Throckmorton shrugged and nodded, then moved away to find a few stout sticks. Crispin started out of the small clearing and moved cautiously back through the thick trees to the trail they were on earlier. It was now broad daylight. He was thirsty and he remembered the fresh gurgling water they rode through in the early morning light. He couldn't remember how far back the creek was, but the further he ran along the path, the more he questioned his judgement. Finally, he came so far that he could no longer smell the smoke from the small campfire. There was still no creek.

Crispin pushed ahead a little further telling himself that he would only go another hundred paces before he gave up the search and returned to camp. He walked a little over half this distance when he heard the welcome sound of running water. A few minutes later, he was on his chest at the edge of a beautiful fresh water brook drinking deeply from the cold water in complete abandon. He would drink 'til he was satisfied, then fill the water bottle before heading back to Throckmorton at their small campsite. He didn't hear or see the approach of the two scouts from Captain Watson's swift-moving company of militia.

The scouts could scarcely believe what they saw at the edge of the small creek right next to where the trail crossed the creek bed. The man was clearly a British dragoon, although his uniform looked ragged and incomplete. Both men decided this must be a Royal Army deserter. They had the man on his feet at knife point within seconds. They gagged Crispin with a leather strap and tied his hands mercilessly tight behind his back. One of the men moved off to search the immediate area for more "deserters."

The other militiaman grabbed the leather strap gag at the side of Crispin's right cheek with his left hand. His long rifle was in his right hand. He was headed back up the trail a few seconds later to meet Captain Watson who was headed south a few hundred yards behind his scouts. The tight leather gag brought excruciating pain to Crispin's mouth and jaws. The only way to ease the pain was to keep up with the merciless woodsman who silently dragged him along the path. The militiaman didn't speak, but Crispin was making enough noise for both of them as he whimpered and gasped while being dragged at a dead run with his hands lashed behind him.

Captain Watson signaled a halt for the main body when they heard the two men approaching. Crispin was dragged in front of him and thrown unceremoniously to the ground. He lay gasping and trying to spit out the blood that was being drawn from the corners of his mouth by the rough leather of the strap. The scout quickly explained the circumstances surrounding the capture of the bedraggled Englishman. He told his captain what he and his partner thought about the man being a British deserter. Watson agreed and ordered the leather strap removed from Crispin's mouth.

Crispin was pulled to his feet facing Watson by two other militiamen.

They held him up because he looked like he would quickly pass out. Watson asked him who he was. Crispin said nothing. Watson was about to become more insistent when another of his scouts ran up and reported that they smelled faint wood smoke coming from the area east of the trail. Watson made up his mind that further questioning of the prisoner could wait. They were very close to Fletcher's Mill now. They would move on without further delay. There was no point investigating the source of the smoke. It would be a waste of time. He gave the order to replace the gag in Crispin's mouth and add a blindfold. They were swiftly moving south moments later.

Throckmorton became increasingly concerned when Crispin failed to return to the camp. Exhaustion finally asserted itself, however. He fell noisily asleep shortly after devouring more than his half of the food without water to wash it down. He woke early in the morning. That fool Crispin still hadn't come back. Throckmorton was very thirsty. This was made more intense when he remembered Crispin had gone to fetch water.

Major Throckmorton decided to proceed with his part of the plan with or without Crispin. He would find some way to gain access to the treasure he knew must be hidden at his destination. His uniform was as neatly organized as he could make it. He climbed onto the best of the two horses and towed the other animal as he rode purposely through the woods headed west. He continued past the trail he and Crispin used earlier. Throckmorton was surprised when he realized how far away the river road was when he finally reached it. Moving out of the brush onto the roadbed, he paused to check his appearance as best he could, before turning south and heading on toward Fletcher's Mill.

CHAPTER 38

Captain Robertson was a quarter mile north of the village checking on the picket outpost stationed there a few days earlier. His company's senior sergeant was managing the rotation of the militiamen in and out of these key positions. Robertson had complete faith in his sergeant, but he knew it was very important to regularly interact with his men often. He knew them all well. He knew their families. He knew their strengths and weaknesses. Robertson was a good leader. He had been elected by the men to fill the position of captain and company commander. His leadership and instincts kept the company together through some very difficult circumstances.

They were all from the same collection of small villages on the western frontier. Several of the men were related. There was even a pair of identical twins, the Johnston boys, among them. They were in many small skirmishes and a few larger battles during this long guerilla war. The worst they saw so far was King's Mountain. They didn't spend as much time in towns and villages as their eastern counterparts fighting with Frances Marion and the like. None of them had been home in nearly two years. They foraged and lived off the land. The most valuable piece of personal property any of them owned was his long rifle. They would share everything from their last morsel of food or ammunition to their last drop of water. Friendship between these men was almost more important than kinship, and some of them shared both relationships.

Robertson would never think to question their loyalty to him or to each other. They instinctively distrusted and resented the high-handed members of British aristocracy. It seemed to Captain Robertson that this impression should fit Reverend Fletcher in their minds, but somehow it didn't. Most of the men seemed to hold the old man in an attitude of respect that bordered on awe. None of them had ever been near someone as rich as the Fletchers. They had difficulty understanding that one man, or one family for that matter, could own so much land and other forms of material wealth. The fact that Ira Fletcher and Miss Elizabeth conducted themselves in such a humble unassuming manner around them was shocking. Reverend Fletcher went out of his way to be generous with them. Miss Elizabeth was even helping treat the wounded along with Miss Mona.

Robertson realized with a start that even the land he was standing on now belonged to Ira Fletcher. This made him look around at the well-tended fields on both sides of the well-kept road leading out of the village toward the main river road in the direction of Fish Dam. He saw the furtive movement at the same time one of his pickets noticed it. He and the other two men went silently to the ground without hesitation. A moment later, they spread out instinctively and their rifles were trained in the direction of the movement. All of their attention was not locked on this spot in the distance. The private in the center strained to search for more movement there, while Robertson and the other private scanned the flanks to the left and right. Silence prevailed. Each of them felt they could hear their own hearts beating.

Captain Robertson nearly fired when a man suddenly stepped out from behind a tree to his left less than twenty yards away. The man was aiming his own rifle directly at Robertson's head. Another twitch of movement, lower this time, and he saw another rifle aiming at him from just over the exposed roots of the same tree. He knew that if he moved he would die. The clothing worn by these men was very similar to his own. It wasn't martial. It wasn't a uniform of any kind really. It was ... practical.

Robertson didn't have a chance to speak before the other did. "Now yall don't move! Don't even twitch! We been listenin' to yall for the last five minutes. What are ya supposed to be … some kinda picket? We know yas friendly militia … we just don't cotton to getting shot while we try tellin' ya who we are, so just don't move while our capn comes up to meet ya." With that said, the man turned his head to the left and gave a sharp whistle.

Robertson was shocked again when he saw a large number of militiamen move out onto the road a short distance to his front. One of these men moved to the fore. This must be the captain. Robertson was slowly rising to his feet alongside his two bewildered privates. He still couldn't believe these men had gotten the drop on him. They must have slowly and silently been crawling for some distance to get this close without discovery. The realization caused his features to betray a conflict between humiliation and outright respect.

The rifle of the militiaman to his left slowly lowered, and Robertson stepped forward to introduce himself to the approaching officer. He was further amazed at the huge number of soldiers quietly moving out of the trees and brush to surround him and his two privates on the road. He was no fool. He knew that several other men, invisible to him right now, were forming a protective cordon around this large group to allow the meeting to take place in relative safety. With a wry smile and an outstretched hand, he greeted the other captain with the words, "Hello there! Welcome to Fletcher's Mill. I'm Captain Robertson. My detached militia company is here to defend this place."

The other man shook his hand without smiling and said, "My name is Watson. I'm the captain in command of this force sent from Colonel Marion for the same purpose. I must say, Robertson, I'm surprised your boys didn't challenge us as we came through that heavy brush like a gaggle of elephants."

Robertson didn't offer a reply immediately. He wasn't sure whether Watson was serious. Finally, Watson broke the silence again with a grin as he slapped Robertson on the shoulder and said, "You should see the look on your face! I thought you might cry or something! Don't fret, sir!

I'd a really been surprised if you or your men had heard us!" Robertson relaxed immediately sensing that Watson was actually quite friendly. He and Captain Watson spent the next few minutes talking quietly about the events that happened after the battle at Cowpens and the shipment of captured material that was sent to this now important place. He couldn't avoid showing his surprise when Watson described his ambush of a large British force along the Broad River road not many miles north of where he was now standing. It turned out, however, that this would not be the greatest shock he would experience during this meeting.

A member of Watson's force moved to his commander's side and mumbled something so quietly that Robertson didn't hear all of it. What he did catch had something to do with a strange prisoner. He couldn't imagine that Watson would have taken a prisoner in the ambush. This must be someone captured either before or after that event. The mystery didn't last long. Watson nodded his head, and the other man moved swiftly back into the brush behind them.

Robertson thought he must be seeing things a few seconds later. He recognized the wretched prisoner dragged out of the brush and roughly deposited in front of the two captains. The man was wearing most of a British dragoon private's uniform. There was a leather strap gag stuffed in his mouth and a blindfold tied tightly around his head so that he couldn't see. He looked as though he had been through horrible wear since the last time Robertson saw him. However, even with the blindfold and the change in his clothing, Robertson immediately knew Captain Reginald Crispin.

The blindfold was ripped from the man's head, but the gag was left in place. Crispin's eyes darted about like those of a wild animal until they rested on Captain Robertson. The rage in them turned to terror as realization asserted itself. Robertson heard himself saying, "Well now! Welcome back, Captain! What on earth are you doing here? What is that you're wearing? Did your people finally realize your true worth and promote you to the lofty rank of private?"

Crispin offered no explanation for his appearance or his presence.

Robertson explained Crispin's true identity to Watson who now viewed the strangely-clad British captain with even greater interest. Robertson briefly toyed with the idea of having Crispin hung right here and now, but better judgement took control of his emotions. He offered to relieve Watson of his responsibility for the prisoner. Watson agreed immediately after hearing what events surrounded Crispin's original capture and escape from Fletcher's Mill.

Robertson was concerned about the remnants of the force Watson ambushed further north. Captain Watson told him that he recognized the British major commanding the column. He and his men had inflicted terrific damage on the larger force, and his scouts reported seeing the surviving British troops moving away toward Camden. He believed they would probably seek reinforcements there. In his opinion, they could be expected to once again move toward Fletcher's Mill within a week or maybe sooner. The British wouldn't easily be ambushed again.

Robertson was delighted to learn that Watson had over eighty experienced troops with him. The two captains decided to move immediately to the mill village and strengthen the defenses there to resist whatever force the Royal Army sent. Captain Robertson turned and gave fresh instructions to his two privates. He would have them reinforced with a few extra men to guard this approach. He asked Watson to pull his men into a column on the road so they could be seen marching into the village together. He believed the appearance of these men would encourage and strengthen his own company and the remaining villagers.

Bringing all the men together like this seemed silly to Captain Watson, but he was willing to concede to Robertson's wishes. He and Robertson marched into the village a short time later at the head of a large body of heavily armed men. The result was better than even Robertson expected. They were received with great celebration. Captain Watson was introduced to Reverend Fletcher for the first time. Although Watson and some of his men had been to the mill before, their earlier activities were always conducted in great secrecy.

Watson was greatly impressed with young Lieutenant Billy Morgan who brought the captured military stores all the way here from the bat-tlefield at Cowpens. Robertson took his time explaining the plan he had developed for the defense of the village and the mill. Watson was again impressed. He immediately realized why he and his men were so welcome here. Defending this place would not be easy against a professional enemy force. He didn't say anything, but he quickly surmised that the best plan would be to burn everything and move the military stores somewhere else before the enemy arrived. Exposure to Ira Fletcher soon made him realize this was not politically possible. This place had to be defended. Robertson made the same conclusion earlier. This was also the basis of Watson's orders from Colonel Marion.

Captain Robertson chose to keep his prisoner on the edge of town temporarily while he was showing Watson the local situation. The two captains worked well together as they incorporated Watson's men into the overall plan developed by Robertson. Watson was older and more expe-rienced than Robertson. The two decided quickly that Watson should take overall command of the militia troops here. Robertson would act as his second. Billy Morgan would act as third. Once this was decided, they quickly reorganized all of their troops into small companies with a sergeant in charge of each unit.

The air of celebration in and around the mill village continued until Captain Robertson decided to bring his prisoner into town so that his disposition could be decided by the lawful civil authority. The celebration abruptly ended when Reverend Ira Fletcher laid eyes on the totally unex-pected form of Captain Reginald Crispin.

CHAPTER 39

A cold damp mist hung low over the encampment in the predawn darkness. Hundreds of cooking fires were being stoked into life to feed over five hundred men. Major Sir Thomas Willoughby finally had his reinforced battalion ready to move out in the direction of Fletcher's Mill. He would not be surprised on the road again. The column would be preceded along the route of march with a large picket screen. They would move slowly. Every possible choke point and ambush site would be carefully scouted and occupied until the column passed. Additional scouts were sent ahead of the pickets to ensure they were not surprised and compromised.

Lord Rawdon insisted that he bring along two small three-pounder field guns. The colonel understood that the mill building itself was made of stone. These guns were not large enough to reduce a stone structure, but they could be employed at great range to cause the defenders to seek cover. This would allow a methodical approach of infantry in an assault. Willoughby appreciated the input of his superior and gladly accepted the artillery along with the attendant caissons and gun crews.

Major Willoughby was a determined man. He knew that his professional reputation was at stake, though Lord Rawdon didn't display any sign of adverse judgement. Rawdon was too professional for that. He was also too much of a gentleman to be petty. Willoughby's actions before during and after the ambush on the river road were in compliance with current British tactical doctrine. The only thing he could be blamed for was the failure to maintain an effective picket screen on the flanks of his moving column. Rawdon seemed to understand when Willoughby explained that the terrain and the column's speed of movement wouldn't allow it. Besides, Willoughby had known no reason to expect the type and size of rebel force that conducted the ambush so far south and west.

Lord Rawdon's opinion of him, whether good or bad, was not what was bothering Major Willoughby. It was his own self-incrimination that tormented him at this moment. He walked among his men as they prepared to move out and listened carefully to both their laughter and their complaints. He was trying to gauge their readiness and morale. Spirits seemed to have recovered since they rode into Camden a broken and bleeding group of defeated men. Plentiful food and sleep over the last two days had done wonders, but it was more than that. He began to realize that these men didn't blame him as he did himself.

His men seemed to have pushed past the dreadful defeat on the road. They seemed to be pulling together with a mutual intent now motivating their preparations. What was it? Anger? Yes. That was it. These men were not only mauled on the road by the rebels. They were humiliated. Willoughby continued to listen carefully as he moved among them. Yes. These men were eager to reclaim their pride. That was fine with their commander. Willoughby shared the sentiment. He would not let them down this time. He paused for a moment and turned slowly around as he took in the deliberate actions of his subordinates. No. He would not fail them this time. Nodding his head absently, he turned and walked back toward the headquarters to complete his own final preparations.

He and Captain Jones of the 33rd Fusiliers Regiment worked feverishly to incorporate the extra Royal Infantry units with the survivors of Willoughby's original force. During this process, they also worked out a simple plan to seize or neutralize their objective. They both knew that the best tactical plans were always very simple. Complex plans never survived the first hint of powder smoke and crash of gunfire. Only an inexperienced fool failed to realize that the best plan in battle was a simple plan that was violently carried out with overwhelming force.

They intended to move this larger and better organized column with a clear intent focused on a singular objective while doing everything necessary to avoid another ambush. They would proceed directly to Fletcher's Mill from here, a distance of almost fifty miles. The trip would take four days due to the needed security and the slower pace of the walking infantry. Willoughby would carefully reconnoiter the mill and village to verify the suspected rebel activity there. Seeing nothing, he would make discreet contact with Reverend Fletcher to further investigate and dispel the rumors involving him and his property. On the other hand, he intended to attack suddenly with great force if the rumors appeared to be substantiated by observed rebel activity. The good Reverend Fletcher would be allowed to defend himself in a court of law once he was apprehended if the rebels were using his property.

The darkness was giving way to the steel gray of daylight as the column finally began to move out along the road through Camden toward the deeply forested and broken terrain of western South Carolina. The fog still hung like a cold damp blanket over everything so that the marching men looked like phantoms moving in a dense formation through the center of town. Willoughby noticed that Lord Rawdon was standing on the front porch of the headquarters mansion wrapped in a heavy cloak and blanket. One of his aides held a lantern aloft so that the colonel could see and be seen. Willoughby saluted his commander stiffly as he rode past. Rawdon nodded and returned the salute before turning and moving back inside the house.

Major Willoughby knew he was on his own now. He must resolve the problem of Fletcher's Mill to recover his reputation. He knew that. He also needed to find and destroy the rebel force that ambushed his column on the river road if at all possible. The thought that the rebels had managed to increase their presence this far west in the colony would be an annoying source of worry for Lord Rawdon, Willoughby, and the other senior British commanders until it was confronted and eliminated.

The Tory militias had proven to be unreliable at best after they showed such promise during the early months of the southern campaign last year. The Crown could not allow the rebel forces in the south to gain momentum furnished by battlefield successes like King's Mountain and Cowpens. A rebel force large enough and experienced enough to conduct an ambush like the one he suffered was a terrible threat to British interests. They would be more dangerous if they were further supplied with ammunition and materials captured at Cowpens.

Willoughby's thoughts were interrupted abruptly as Captain Jones rode up next to him. The column was now well out of town and making slow steady progress. He noticed with annoyance that a light rain was falling once again. The fog was lifting, and the air seemed somehow colder in the daylight. Willoughby pulled the collar of his greatcoat tighter around his neck as he turned his head toward Jones to hear what the man had to say. He didn't want to talk right now. Jones could not possibly know that, though. Willoughby, ever the gentleman, would not signal his frustration with this interruption to a professional officer like Jones.

Captain Jones seemed to be quite animated in his assessment of the column's present movement. It surprised Willoughby to realize that the man must have been speaking even before he reached the Major's side. Jones was now saying something about the artillerymen lagging far behind the slowly plodding infantry. Jones responded to Willoughby's quizzical look by explaining that the draft animals couldn't keep the guns consistently moving. The young lieutenant in charge of the cannons explained to Jones that the gun trucks and caissons kept bogging down in the deep mud. He didn't know how to remedy the situation and asked that Willoughby either slow the column significantly or dispatch infantrymen to help pull the guns along the trail.

This infuriated Major Willoughby without good reason. He didn't want to slow down, and he certainly wouldn't send good foot soldiers to act as draft animals. He immediately resented his own anger. He struggled to control both his words and his countenance. He reminded himself that he was a professional officer in His Majesty's Royal Army. He understood the importance of the guns and knew that they would be potentially valuable at his objective. He rode on next to Jones for a moment before turning his horse on the trail and trotting it briskly back toward the rear of the column through the splashing water and mud.

Willoughby silenced the artillery officer with a glare as he reached the half-buried gun trucks. The mules were struggling and blowing great puffs of steam as they were whipped to a frenzy trying to pull the guns forward. Willoughby knew instantly what he must do. He would leave the lieutenant and his guns behind. The trucks and caissons were indeed submerged to the axles. It looked like they sank deeper with every inch gained forward. The animals were clearly exhausted. The column would be easy to follow if the artillerymen managed to get them onto more solid ground. The infantrymen were leaving a trail that was unmistakable. The artillery would catch up when it could. Besides, the guns might not even be needed at Fletcher's Mill.

CHAPTER 40

Lieutenant Billy Morgan slowly limped up the muddy hillside alone after touring the town's defenses with Sergeant Duncan. The pain in his thigh was once again excruciating. He neared the front of the Fletcher house to find Elizabeth vigorously sweeping the front porch. The angry expression on her face was nothing like the angelic look he witnessed earlier. Her actions seemed to indicate that she was working out her frustrations on the defenseless broom. This changed abruptly when she noticed him struggling up the steps with his makeshift crutches. The broom disappeared and she was at his side in moments.

Billy could have made it up the steps without help, but he appreciated the assistance from Elizabeth. He felt a strange lightheaded moment as she wrapped her arm around his waist and pushed her shoulder under his arm to offer support. They made it up the steps too quickly in his opinion. They paused for a moment in this strange embrace before Elizabeth helped him over to one of the porch chairs. The smell of her hair forced a smile from him as she helped him sit down.

The porch was protected and the chairs were dry, but it was still cold and damp outside. Billy didn't want to go into the warm house. It smelled like a hospital now despite the intense effort to keep it clean applied by Mona, Mrs. Phillips, and Elizabeth. He was mildly surprised when Elizabeth sat down in the chair next to his. He asked her, "Miss Fletcher, you seemed quite upset when I walked up just now. Is something wrong?"

Elizabeth sat with her hands folded on her lap for a moment before glancing at him sidelong. "No. Nothing is wrong. I was upset … a little, but it isn't your concern, Lieutenant."

Billy smiled. "Well, I'm glad to hear that! I was afraid for a moment you were either angry with me, the porch, or the broom!"

Elizabeth looked up and rewarded him with a brief dazzling smile before looking back down again. "I was a little upset with my aunt Mona. Well, she isn't really my aunt…. She was my grandma's best friend. She knew my mother and father. They all died when I was a baby. Grandpa Ira and Ezekiel raised me with Aunt Mona's help. I love all three of them dearly. I never knew any folks other than them. They just make me so mad sometimes…." She trailed off and Billy waited. She finally continued, "Aunt Mona just gave me a harsh tongue lashing over sitting in the parlor with you earlier." Her head was lowered, but Billy saw a single tear appear on her cheek and roll down to her chin.

Billy found himself growing angry at the very idea that someone could do anything to cause this beautiful girl to cry. She looked up in time to see the sentiment cross his face. She blurted, "No, please, don't be upset about me and Aunt Mona. She loves me and wants the best for me. So does Grandpa. Mona is the only one who really understands me. I mean … I'm no longer a child. Aunt Mona understands that. Sometimes Ezekiel does too. Most of the time Grandpa still sees me as a little girl." Billy was shocked. How could anyone think of this beautiful young woman as a little girl? He sat back in the chair to gaze out across the yard toward the mill village. Neither of them spoke. It seemed best to silently enjoy one another's presence until the cold finally became undeniable and they both stood.

They heard distant shouts then and saw several men moving up the hill toward them. Billy stepped away from the chair on his crutches when he recognized Reverend Fletcher striding up the road in front of a small group of soldiers. These men looked like they were half dragging someone wearing what appeared to be a British cavalry uniform. Elizabeth fled into the house when she saw the look on her grandpa's face. Ira Fletcher stomped up the steps at the front of his home and pushed past Billy to stand in the center of his porch facing the other approaching men. More soldiers were moving toward the house from both the mill and the village.

Billy saw Captain Robertson and another apparent militia officer walking at the head of a larger group coming up the road now from the village. This column halted on the road in front of the house and faced to the left toward the front porch three ranks deep. He counted about eighty men. All of them were strangers to him, but he could see immediately that they were veteran militia. They all carried long rifles and wore cartridge belts and powder horns. Several of them had long knives and tomahawks shoved into their belts. However, it wasn't the military equipment that impressed Billy. It was the look in the men's eyes.

The smaller group dragged the man in the British uniform up onto the yard in front of the porch and shoved him face first onto the ground. The man's wrists were tied behind his back, and he lay nearly motionless for several seconds. No one said anything as he lay there panting. Captain Robertson and the other officer moved quietly forward toward the porch and were now standing immediately behind the prostrate prisoner looking up at Reverend Fletcher expectantly. Billy found himself involuntarily backing away from the top of the steps as if he wasn't worthy to occupy the same space with Mr. Fletcher right now. There was something about the old man that held him in awe.

Billy didn't know if it was Fletcher's ramrod straight stature, the fiery anger displayed on his face, or the awful silence of the moment. He knew something profound was happening, but had no idea what it was all about. The cold damp breeze continued to whip the loose clothing of the men standing in the yard, but no one seemed to notice. Finally, the silence was broken by Reverend Fletcher's resounding voice as he shouted, "Stand him up!" Two militiamen stepped forward to grasp the prisoner at his elbows and yank him to his feet.

Through the mud and grime on the British soldier's face, Billy saw something that he didn't expect. It wasn't the defiant look of a captured enemy. No. It was stark, unabated terror. This man recognized Reverend

Fletcher. It was now clear that Reverend Fletcher also recognized him. The Englishman's eyes darted about furtively as if they were searching for any kind of hope in his surroundings or the men standing near him. He found nothing to reassure himself, and his gaze was drawn inexorably back to Reverend Fletcher towering above him in the center of the porch.

Fletcher stared silently down at the man. He then moved a half step forward and began to speak in a strangely quiet but unmistakably authoritative voice. "Captain Crispin. I cannot imagine what must have influenced you to return this place." Billy was confused. The man was dressed in what still appeared to be most of a cavalry private's uniform. The Englishman opened his mouth but said nothing. Reverend Fletcher raised his voice as he continued, "Whatever brought you back here, sir, I thank my God that you have returned to face justice for what you have done!" The man seemed to flinch backward slightly as he heard these words. Fletcher continued remorselessly, "You will answer for the murder of Peter Johansen, sir! Yes! That was the name of the innocent young man you brutally killed!" Fletcher was shouting as he spoke these last words. His voice carried into the house. Billy noticed when Elizabeth and Mona came quietly out onto the porch to stand behind Ira.

Reverend Fletcher now shouted to the militiamen approaching the yard from the front of the mill. "You there! Go to the mill and fetch a stout rope!" The men stopped walking and looked expectantly at Ira, then toward Captain Robertson. The latter stepped forward and raised both hands toward Ira as he began to speak in a firm but consoling voice. "Reverend Fletcher, I will remind you that this man is my prisoner. Yes, he escaped, but he has been recaptured. No matter what happened during his escape, our actions here must be subject to the rules we abide by as civilized men. The murder of young Mr. Johansen should be answered for, but I will not countenance your execution of my prisoner without a trial!"

Reverend Fletcher appeared to have been physically struck. Billy hobbled forward as Fletcher turned his fiery gaze toward Robertson. Fletcher gasped and pounded his silver headed cane resoundingly on the porch floor as he shouted, "How dare you interrupt me, sir?" He started to move down the first steps toward the captain as he spoke. Two of the militiamen stepped in front of their officer and raised their rifles in a menacing fashion. Mona now bounded forward and grasped Ira by the arm from behind, uttering quiet words into his ear. Billy grasped the old man by the other arm.

Billy felt the tension slowly ease as he and Mona turned Ira around and started back up the steps with him. Captain Robertson and the other officer followed them up onto the porch. Ira stood silently between Billy and Mona as Robertson introduced the other man to him as Captain Watson. Ira nodded but didn't speak. The militiamen remained in the yard before the porch waiting silently for whatever would happen next. Elizabeth opened the front door of the house, apparently expecting her grandfather and the others to move their conversation inside. No one else moved.

Finally, Captain Robertson spoke. "Reverend Fletcher, I understand your anger. I understand the need for swift justice. But justice isn't true or real if a man can be executed without being allowed to defend himself." When there was no response, he continued, "We think we know what happened to the Johansen boy, but we don't really know...." Ira was looking down at his feet now. The rage had dissipated. He felt completely deflated, old, and useless. He realized in this moment that he had been acting like a fool when these people needed him to display the wisdom seven decades should have earned. He couldn't fight back the moisture welling in his eyes when he looked back up at Robertson.

"Yes. You are quite correct, young man. We all deserve the right to defend ourselves. I believe that is one of the things you are fighting for in this outlandish war of rebellion. It would seem that hanging this person...." He nodded his head toward Crispin. "Executing a man without a proper trial would indeed be evil.... After all, we can't behave as his kind do when the boot is on the other foot so to speak...." Robertson nodded and smiled as he realized the danger had passed. He and Captain Watson stepped away and conferred quietly for several seconds before Watson walked briskly down the steps, past the bewildered Crispin, and rejoined his men on the road.

Captain Robertson walked back over to Ira who was still standing between Billy and Mona. "Reverend Fletcher," he said, "we intend to secure the prisoner again in your storeroom. With your permission, we will convene a trial tomorrow at noon. We ask you to act as judge, since you are the logical civil authority here. I will prosecute the case against the prisoner, and Captain Watson will attempt to defend him. We will have Lieutenant Morgan and all of our sergeants sit as a jury. If the evidence shows that he is indeed guilty of murder, we will carry out whatever sentence you deem fitting."

Ira nodded without speaking. Captain Robertson spun on his heel and strode down the steps to escort Captain Crispin back to the same storeroom he had occupied so many days ago. Ira went on into the house. He was followed by Mona and Elizabeth. Sergeants Strickland and Duncan joined Billy on the porch with inquisitive looks regarding the events of the past several minutes. Most of the troops in front of the house moved on to other duties a few minutes later. Billy and his two sergeants sat down on the porch chairs in quiet conversation.

Sergeant Strickland suddenly leapt to his feet gasping in startled awe as he said, "My eyes see it, but it can't be so...."

Billy asked, "What has come over you, Strickland?" Duncan was standing now too. He gasped as he pointed toward the village road. Billy stood up to look in the direction Duncan was pointing. His mind initially failed to grasp what he could clearly see. When it did, he struggled to marshal his own growing fury. There, coming up from the village on a horse that looked too good for him, was the filthy but fully uniformed Major Theodore Throckmorton.

CHAPTER 41

Major Willoughby consolidated his troops on the east flank of a heavily wooded hillside. They were off the Camden Road several hundred paces. He posted pickets near the road with instructions to quietly apprehend any travelers in either direction and bring them into the camp for interrogation. Willoughby and his men were exhausted. The weather was brutally wet and cold, but he knew their fatigue was more about the constant state of alert vigilance along the way than the rigors of the march itself.

The artillery finally caught up with the main body after a harrowing struggle through the mud and broken terrain between here and Camden. The young artillery lieutenant reported that one of the gun carriages was damaged. Two spokes had cracked on one of the heavy wheels as the troops manhandled it through a place where it was buried axle-deep. It was a miracle that they managed to drag it this far at all. It would not be useable until the wheel was repaired or replaced. The lieutenant explained that they had no replacement wheel, and there was no way to adequately repair the damaged spokes.

The lieutenant then displayed great initiative as he suggested that the wheels of the gun caissons were the same diameter, and the caisson axles were the same size as those of the guns. The caisson wheels where marginally lighter than those of the gun carriages, but still, they were designed to carry very heavy loads of powder and shot to feed the guns. He believed that they could transfer enough powder and shot onto the other caisson to be able to supply the guns adequately for a full day's engagement if needed.

The artillerymen could unload the contents of the useable caisson when they established their firing point near the objective. They could then send it back to retrieve the supplies they had left behind. He wanted Willoughby's permission to replace both wheels on the damaged gun carriage with these caisson wheels. Major Willoughby wanted both guns brought forward if he was going to use them at all. He was encouraged by the young man's confidence and a little curious regarding the ingenuity of the artillery crews. He consented immediately, and the lieutenant moved quickly away to begin shouting orders to his men.

Major Willoughby thought through this mission several times during the difficult journey from Camden. The anger and self-recrimination eased with time regarding the river road ambush. He was now intently focused on resolving the issue of Fletcher's Mill peacefully if possible. He would use overwhelming force if necessary, and the artillery seemed even more important to that end. He hoped force wouldn't be needed, though. Willoughby still couldn't imagine that Reverend Fletcher would betray his king and native country. The old man was not a noble by birth, but his astounding personal wealth made that circumstance largely irrelevant. Fletcher was also a man of the cloth. Shouldn't that effect his sense of loyalty? Willoughby couldn't imagine anyone risking such a vast estate on this ridiculous rebellion.

Major Willoughby and Captain Jones decided to remain encamped in this place for at least a full day so that their men could rest and prepare themselves for whatever awaited them at their objective. Willoughby, on the other hand, would not remain idle. He realized that he might be able to complete the mission in a totally satisfactory manner without bringing this large force close to the mill. He would send a small group of infantry scouts forward to look for any signs of hostility. He would follow them with a small group of cavalry escorts and carefully reconnoiter the mill surroundings. They would quietly and carefully observe the mill and village looking for signs of rebel activity.

Willoughby was an experienced professional soldier. He would have done a careful personal reconnaissance of this type objective anyway, even if his sole purpose was to attack and destroy it. He remained hopeful that he would see nothing untoward in the vicinity. He was increasingly optimistic that he would be able to ride into Fletcher's Mill with a small escort to question the Fletchers and put this whole thing to rest without bloodshed. He was still painfully aware that his professional reputation was at stake.

The three infantry scouts, led by an older sergeant, listened carefully to his instructions and asked some sensible questions. This didn't anger Major Willoughby as it would many other officers. The effect on him was quite the opposite and gave him heightened confidence in the men's professional ability. The questions were answered, and final quick preparations were made. The scouts quietly left the encampment perimeter and spread out through the woods as they silently headed toward Fletcher's Mill.

Major Willoughby put Captain Jones in charge during his absence with carefully worded instructions. He and his escort rode out of camp an hour later. He arranged a rally point with the scout sergeant before the man left. Willoughby would move along the side of the road so that the horses could avoid the thick underbrush of the forest. They would halt within a mile of the mill and wait for the sergeant to report to him there. He would have a much clearer picture from the scouting report. He then intended to move carefully closer so that he could make a personal observation to confirm the hoped-for tranquility of the place, before riding down the road and into the village.

Willoughby and his escorts travelled the two miles carefully. They saw no one on the road and reached what he thought to be the agreed-upon rally point without incident. Everything was very quiet. The weather improved, and the sun seemed like it was trying to break through the clouds. The wind died to a slight whispering breeze, and he realized with almost a start that the rain had completely ceased. His clothing was feeling dryer than it had in days. Willoughby dismounted to wait for the sergeant's report. The six escorting dragoons remained in their saddles at nervous alert. They waited an hour. Nothing happened. They waited two more hours. Still nothing happened.

Major Willoughby grew increasingly impatient. The impatience turned first to anger, then to apprehension. He needed to know what was going on. They had seen and heard nothing but the birds fluttering through the trees alongside the road for the past three hours. He finally decided that he would have to go forward himself if he was going to learn anything. Shrugging in frustrated resignation, he ordered his escort to dismount and secure the horses deeper in the tree line. They crossed the road into the trees on the other side and moved as quietly as possible in the direction of the mill village.

Willoughby and his escorts were soon soaked from the underbrush. This did nothing to ease his frustration. They found themselves making several detours to avoid open clearings and impassible obstacles. Willoughby never knew what a miracle it was that they were not captured by the same intense patrols who had surprised and silently killed all three of his infantry scouts. They finally neared the outskirts of the village after the long wet struggle through the trees and brush.

Major Willoughby found a relatively high point on the edge of the woods from which he could use his glass to make careful observation of both the village and the mill. He settled himself and cleaned the lenses on the glass before slowly starting to scan the area. He could not contain a sudden intake of breath. What he saw was shocking. He was not looking at a placid village scene. No. He found himself fixated for several minutes on the intense preparation of heavily fortified defensive works occupied by what appeared to be a great many well-armed hostile militiamen.

Willoughby finally saw enough to understand what happened to his scouts. He knew that he and his men were in very grave danger here. He was amazed that the rebels knew nothing yet of the large British force preparing to attack them from only three miles away. He considered waiting for darkness to escape, but even then, he doubted they could avoid capture. It seemed like hours were passing slowly, but only minutes elapsed since they arrived at this spot. They would go back the way they came. He and his men held their breath at one point, and narrowly avoided observation when a party of these rough mountain men passed very close to their hiding place. The militiamen were not carrying muskets captured from the Royal Army. They were clearly armed with long wilderness rifles. All of them had long knives and tomahawks in their belts.

Major Willoughby carefully observed all of this and more. He knew with a sick feeling in the pit of his stomach that he was facing a confrontation far more dangerous than he earlier expected. The rebel preparations put him deeply on edge. He saw his enemy at close quarters now. What concerned him most was the look in the enemy militiamen's eyes. There he recognized the intense animallike gaze of savage wilderness fighting men. He suddenly knew instinctively that he had encountered these men before ... on the river road between Fish Dam and this place, Fletcher's Mill.

CHAPTER 42

Lieutenant Billy Morgan and his two sergeants stood breathless for a few seconds as Major Throckmorton neared the house on the back of a horse that seemed too large for him. Billy snapped out of the shock when he heard Sergeant Strickland utter a quiet oath. He turned to Sergeant Duncan and said, "Go in the house and bring Reverend Fletcher back out here." He then turned to Strickland and said, "You come with me." He was moving across the porch toward the steps before Strickland could say anything else. Billy didn't see Strickland roll his eyes in disgust before gritting his teeth and moving out sharply to catch up with his lieutenant. Several other soldiers saw the approaching major and were returning to the front of the house as Billy and Strickland came down the steps.

Billy noticed Captain Watson approaching from the direction of the village as he and Strickland came to a stop on the wide stone landing just above the roadway waiting for the major to dismount. Throckmorton remained on the horse as he slowly looked around with a peculiar air of superiority. He and his uniform were filthy. A sudden shift in the slight breeze caused Billy and Strickland to recoil at the surprising stench emanating from this strange little man. Throckmorton's gaze finally settled on Billy waiting quietly with his arms crossed on the landing.

Major Throckmorton sniffed and leaned slightly forward while continuing to peer sidelong into Billy's eyes with a malevolent gaze that reminded the young lieutenant of snakes he had killed in the past. The major finally broke the uneasy silence as Captain Watson moved up onto the landing and stopped next to Strickland.

"Well, I've finally caught up with you and your band of filthy cut-throats, you impudent young thief!" Billy opened his mouth in anger as he unfolded his arms, but didn't have time to speak before Watson stepped in front of him.

Throckmorton made what could have been a fatal error at that moment. Sitting up abruptly, he snarled, "And who might you be? Another member of this young whelp's treasonous thieving band of cowards maybe?" A moment of stunned silence prevailed before Captain Watson calmly stepped off the landing to grasp the bridle strap at the side of the horse's mouth and gently pull the animal forward so that he was standing with his chest against Throckmorton's left knee. The major recoiled slightly at this invasion of his proximity. Watson suddenly moved with a speed that shocked everyone. He reached up, grabbed Throckmorton by the front of his coat, and yanked the smaller man out of the saddle. The fact that he calmly intoned, "Let me help you down, sir" during this event did nothing to disguise Captain Watson's clear intent.

Major Throckmorton found himself looking up into the angry smiling eyes of a very powerful and furious man. Watson spoke so softly that Billy and Sergeant Strickland could barely make out what he said. Even Throckmorton found himself leaning forward slightly to listen. "My name, sir, is Captain Jonathan Watson of Marion's Division, South Carolina Militia. I would like to know who you are before I demand satisfaction for the unfortunate way you addressed me and my fellow officer just now…."

Throckmorton realized that he was in great danger. His knees shook. He was lightheaded. He knew he was showing his terror to these men, as the blood drained from his face. Silence reigned several seconds as Watson waited patiently for an answer.

Throckmorton slowly mastered himself. He shrugged and drew his diminutive body up in sullen, terror-tempered pride. "By all means, Captain, I apologize for my words. I didn't recognize you in your civilian clothing. My name is Major Throckmorton. I'm a quartermaster with the Southern Continental Army. I'm afraid I mistook you for one of the thieving ruffian cohorts of that young man standing behind you."

Captain Watson's smile widened as he reached out to brush Major Throckmorton's lapels into place and spoke in a louder voice. "I heartily accept your apology Major, no harm done. You must be mistaken, though, about my young friend here. This is Lieutenant William Morgan, who I know to be a brave and upright young officer. He is also the nephew of General Daniel Morgan as I understand. I've never personally met the general, but any nephew of his comes from good stock." Realization washed over and through Throckmorton. He would not be able to use his rank and bluster to advantage here. He found himself nodding slightly as he murmured, "My mistake Captain, I would have sworn the young man was the young scoundrel I've been chasing many long miles over the past several days." He looked sideways at Billy in seething hatred as he said this. Captain Watson pretended not to notice.

Ira Fletcher pushed through the slowly growing crowd of onlookers at the side of the road in front of his house. Introductions were made. Captain Watson told one of his men to care for the major's horse, as Reverend Fletcher graciously invited Major Throckmorton into his home. Ira gave no visible sign of revulsion as he observed Throckmorton's filthy appearance. He wondered if the awful smell he was assaulted with could possibly be coming from this ugly, unkempt Continental Army officer.

Throckmorton accepted the invitation with a strange, out-of-place aura of entitlement. The crowd parted, and they began moving up toward the house. Ira leaned down toward the shorter man as they walked and quietly said, "Major, I realize you have been traveling through rough country for several days. I will have a bath arranged for you while the ladies of my home launder your uniform." Ira looked around then and realized that the major apparently had no baggage of any kind in his possession. He thought this strange, but dismissed it as he said, "I will have my granddaughter find you a suitable change of clothing to wear in the meantime." Throckmorton offered his profound thanks.

Billy and his sergeants were left on the landing with Captain Watson. Captain Robertson walked up after the small crowd dispersed. Watson asked Billy if he could explain what the major was talking about. All five men walked slowly away toward the mill as Billy started from the beginning and recounted his brief and odd history with Major Throckmorton. Both captains listened intently and only asked questions when the story was finished. Sergeants Duncan and Strickland corroborated Billy's account.

Captains Watson and Robertson looked at each other for a few moments in stern deliberation, as they stood outside the lower entry to the mill. Billy began to worry that he might actually be in some kind of trouble for assaulting a superior officer. He candidly told the whole strange story to these two men, leaving out none of the details. Captain Watson suddenly broke into peals of laughter as he shook his head and slapped his right knee. He was joined immediately by Robertson and the two sergeants. Watson finally mastered himself and gasped, "That was the funniest thing I've heard in months. If I hadn't personally met that old persimmon just now, I might a thought you made the whole thing up!"

The next few hours passed quickly. Billy found himself seated that evening at the dining table with Reverend Fletcher, the two militia captains, two other militia lieutenants, and Major Throckmorton. There were three empty chairs at the table. One of them was directly across from him, and another was next to Ira Fletcher. Mona and Elizabeth entered the room from the kitchen carrying platters piled high with steaming roast beef, potatoes, carrots, and fresh bread. The food was placed on the table, and the men stood quietly while the ladies were seated by Ira and Captain Robertson. Mona took the place next to Reverend Fletcher. Billy observed with a glance that Major Throckmorton was now dressed in clean but ill-fitting civilian garb at the opposite end of the table from Reverend Fletcher. The man had apparently bathed. Thankfully, at least his earlier noxious odor was gone.

Reverend Fletcher stood to pray over the meal and offer a cordial welcome to his dinner guests. There was something about Ira that made it seem perfectly natural for him to be standing at the head of the table as he did this. The prayer was not memorized or stilted. Ira Fletcher sounded like he was speaking with a close superior friend. He thanked God for the food. He asked God to bless those at the table and protect the men outside struggling for their freedom and safety. The prayer ended, and a few of the people seated around the table said "Amen." Billy couldn't help notice the silent sullen form of Major Throckmorton throughout the process. Ira seated himself gracefully, and the meal began with the passing of food dishes and moderate conversation.

It wasn't long before the discussion moved to the defense of the village and mill. They were soon talking about the future of the captive now securely guarded in the same storeroom he escaped from so many days ago. Throckmorton listened to the conversation quietly before suddenly speaking up with words directed more to Reverend Fletcher than to the militia officers seated at the table. "I will gladly serve as presiding judge in this man's trial as the highest ranking military member here. This is obviously a military matter, since the man is a captured British officer accused of committing a crime while trying to escape."

Billy noticed that there was a firelike glint in Ira Fletcher's eye belying the calm smile on his face. Ira laid both hands on the table in front of him before responding. "That won't be necessary, Major. I am the head of civil authority here. The crime this man is accused of was perpetrated against one of the civilians in this village. I will preside over his trial. You are welcome to give evidence in the proceedings, simply watch, or try to defend the man if you must. Thank you for your offer, but we will handle this." A subdued silence reigned over the table for several seconds before Throckmorton shrugged, raised his hands in mock surrender, and offered a wane smile in reply.

The meal was nearly concluded when Mona looked up with a startled smile. Elizabeth also looked up, then stood abruptly. Everyone at the table turned to see the bandaged elderly black man standing in the doorway leading to the parlor.

Ezekiel wore a weak smile. "Excuse me, Ira, Mona, and you other gentlemen … I didn't mean to intrude on your dinner … I just heard talk, and was curious … maybe even a little hungry…. I'll just find something in the kitchen pantry…." Mona was now standing. Elizabeth hurried around the table to put her arm around Ezekiel's waist and steady him. Mona looked sternly at Ira. He also stood and pointed to the remaining empty chair at the table near Throckmorton. "No Zeke, my old friend. You will sit here with us while we prepare a plate for you. There is plenty of food here. There is always plenty at my table for you."

Billy didn't know what to think about the old man. It seemed somehow odd when a few of the dinner guests made excuses for leaving to see to their duties shortly after Ezekiel sat down. Throckmorton was the first to depart. Captain Watson was introduced to Ezekiel by Captain Robertson. Both of these men stayed with their host through the rest of the meal enjoying the now lighter conversation. Billy couldn't remember a more enjoyable dinner. He couldn't, for that matter, remember the last time he actually sat at a table in a house to eat. Ezekiel finished his meal with a tired smile and said, "I pray that God will continue to bless this wonderful family with grace and loving kindness. I'm goin' to wander up to the mill now and check on things there if I can get some help from these young'uns." He nodded toward Elizabeth and Billy as he said this.

Billy and Elizabeth soon found themselves walking slowly toward the mill with Ezekiel between them. Billy didn't mind. There were other things to do, but any excuse to spend time with Elizabeth was a gift of growing importance to him. Ezekiel asked questions about what happened since he was knocked out days ago. Elizabeth answered those. Billy tried to explain his own presence and the obvious military preparations going on around them. They reached the mill, and Ezekiel did a cursory inspection of the premises before noticing the two armed guards standing outside the closed storeroom door. Billy was looking for a way to speak quietly with Elizabeth when he saw Ezekiel moving toward the storeroom and being confronted by one of the guards. He stepped away from the young lady to intervene with the guard on the old man's behalf.

The guard was one of his own men, none other than John Red. The other man was Private Plunkett. He knew instantly that Strickland or Duncan were involved in assigning these two men to this duty. He knew they would be relieved by other trusted members of Billy's company. The sergeants sensed that their young lieutenant had other important matters to tend to. Elizabeth was standing patiently near the mill entry. Billy looked at her now with a slightly guilty feeling regarding his military duties. That passed immediately. He found himself introducing Ezekiel to Red and Plunkett. Red helped the old man open the door while Plunkett fetched a lantern down from its wall hanger.

Billy knew Ezekiel was curious about the condition of the stores in the room, but he didn't realize that Ezekiel knew so much about the prisoner. Billy was earlier told that this was the British officer responsible for the injuries suffered by Ezekiel and other members of the village. He was aware that the prisoner was accused of killing one of the mill workers when he escaped days ago. Plunkett led the way into the storeroom with the lantern followed by Ezekiel and Billy. Red stayed out in the corridor. Elizabeth curiously walked over to the storeroom door to hear what was said inside. Billy expected Ezekiel to harshly lash out at the cowering man they found huddled in the corner of the room. The old man took the lantern from Private Plunkett and told him he could leave. Plunkett gave a quick curious look to his lieutenant, and Billy nodded.

Billy was shocked when Ezekiel sat the lantern on a shelf at the side of the storeroom and stepped over to gently help the prisoner, Captain Crispin, up from the floor with quiet soothing words. Crispin, though clearly frightened, allowed himself to be moved to where he was seated on a crate near the middle of the room. Billy stepped a little closer as Ezekiel seated himself on another crate directly in front of the prisoner. Billy was even more shocked when he heard this injured old man tell his former assailant that it didn't matter where he had been or what he had done, God loved him. Ezekiel explained that Jesus died to pay the penalty for our sin, and rose again three days later to rule as the Rightful King. He explained that even Crispin could live forever if he surrendered what was left of his life to Jesus and trusted him for redemption. Billy,

Elizabeth, and the two guards were more astounded than simply shocked. They heard Crispin agree and begin to pray with Ezekiel.

Ezekiel leaned closer to the weeping form of Captain Reginald Crispin and said, "Welcome to the family of God, brother. If they hang you tomorrow, which seems likely, you will be with King Jesus the moment you leave this life." Ezekiel hugged Crispin closely until he stopped sobbing. When Crispin raised his head, he wore a bright smile. Billy wondered that a man could smile when he believed this was his last night on earth.

Two distant explosions sounded outside at that moment. These were followed by two loud crashes against the stone wall of the mill above them. Sudden frantic commotion and a growing chorus of shouts could be heard from outside the mill. Billy swallowed deeply. He ordered Plunket to stay here with Elizabeth, Ezekiel, and the prisoner. He motioned Red to follow him outside. The expected British assault on Fletcher's Mill had apparently started.

CHAPTER 43

Major Sir Thomas Willoughby was no fool. He had seen his enemy, and he was deeply concerned. He understood that his scouts must have been captured. It wouldn't be long before the rebels knew he was here with a large force. It was perfectly clear that the place was a rebel stronghold, whether Reverend Fletcher was an agreeable participant or an unfortunate captive. Willoughby had no choice. He must attack. He must do it very soon with a good plan to overwhelm and capture or destroy everything here. He would not repeat the mistakes made by that pompous buffoon Tarleton. There was no way he would feed his men into this attack piecemeal as Tarleton did at Cowpens.

Willoughby and his escort somehow made it back through the rebel patrols to regain their horses and return to his command in great haste. He began bellowing orders as soon as they entered the encampment. He had Captain Jones summon all the officers for a quick council so that he could effectively issue his instructions. This was not a council of war in the traditional sense. Major Willoughby was not seeking the advice or opinions of others. He formulated his entire plan of attack on his way back out of the rebel perimeter. He expected his orders to be obeyed without hesitation or question. Success depended on surprise and overwhelming force in this situation.

Major Willoughby would bring the infantry and artillery forward behind a screen of light skirmishers and cavalry. This was a classic

273

textbook approach to an attack on a fixed fortified position of this sort. He knew this was the only tactic that would work. He was pleased to learn that the disabled gun carriage was effectively repaired by replacing both wheels with those from one of the caissons. Glancing at the gun actually reassured him further. He would have his dragoons each carry an extra powder charge and ball in bags tied to their saddles as they moved forward. The surviving caisson could be double loaded as well for this short distance. He would attempt to place the guns at the high spot he occupied a short while ago.

The attack would wait until all of Willoughby's units were on line and ready. It would commence with an artillery bombardment of the mill and the solid Fletcher house nearby. Part of his infantry would occupy the village quickly while a small cavalry contingent demonstrated to the front. The majority of the cavalry would swing to the left and attack the fortifications from the woods on that flank. When he heard that attack start, he would push forward in a concentrated rush through the village and up to the mill itself. He would consolidate his forces on this objective and secure it with overwhelming force.

Willoughby didn't know if the rebel militia would stand and fight a defensive battle. His instinct told him that this kind of warfare didn't suit them. He would not give them time to sort their opinions out on the subject. Major Willoughby laid out his instructions to his subordinates within minutes. There were no questions. All these officers knew what was expected of them and knew not to question their commander from the tone in his voice and the look on his face. The entire force was in motion less than an hour later. Willoughby desired silence to maintain the element of surprise, but his instinctive need for speed in closing on this objective was very powerful. The wind was blowing toward them from the direction of Fletcher's Mill anyway. This effectively muted the noise of their approach.

The large infantry screen he sent ahead was carrying unloaded muskets. They were strictly forbidden from loading until they were specifically ordered to do so, or the artillery opened fire. They were to advance quietly with the bayonet and overwhelm the rebel patrols in the woods north of the village in silence if possible. Willoughby doubted this would happen. Surely the rebel patrols would fire when confronted by his men. As it turned out, few shots were fired while many vicious horrific struggles for life and death played out in the shadows and undergrowth. The vastly superior number of British troops made it impossible for the light rebel patrols to stop them. Many men died quietly in this violent portion of the battle.

Major Willoughby and the artillery lieutenant had the guns in place quickly and without compromise. The extra ammunition was stacked on and under tarpaulins within minutes. The light infantry moved into the village carefully before the first artillery round was fired. He waited until two troops of dragoons moved to his front and slightly to the right while remaining concealed in the trees. The rest of the cavalry began their movement forward and to the left around the village.

Willoughby knew the time had come. Amazingly, not one sign of recognition or alarm came from the rebel fortifications on the other side of the village. He was very pleased that they somehow managed to get this far undetected, but didn't pause to think about it. The guns were loaded and aimed. The gun sergeants were standing to the side of their gun carriages. Both held aloft long linstocks with glowing slow matches fastened to them ready to be dropped onto the touchholes. Willoughby took a deep breath and nodded curtly to the lieutenant. The man spun immediately and shouted. "Number one, FIRE! Number two, FIRE!"

The sound was earsplitting in the quiet darkness of the overhanging trees as the guns fired and were thrown back in recoil. Willoughby had no time to watch as the crews jumped to sponge out and reload before dragging the heavy weapons back into firing position. He willed the smoke to clear and strained to see the impact of both rounds on the outside of the mill building at the upper floor. The shots were surprisingly accurate. The range was relatively short, and the guns had been loaded and aimed carefully.

The demonstrating dragoons moved out of the tree line to begin a feint charge toward the mill across the relatively open ground to the right of the village. The guns were reloaded and fired again. He didn't notice where the shots went this time, as he saw some of the cavalry horses stumble or fall, apparently tripped by unseen objects in the underbrush. He saw a huge volley of smoke plumes erupt all along the nearest rebel trenches. Many of the saddles in the two troops were suddenly empty. Willoughby remembered the effect of the incredibly accurate rifles from his encounter with them on the road from Fish Dam.

There was scattered musket fire now in and around the village. Willoughby saw two men exit the mill building from the front door and run toward the house. One of the cannons had shifted fire toward the house after the second round was fired. The artillery lieutenant was applying regular fire on both buildings now as fast as his guns could reload. Willoughby knew he must wait here long enough for the main cavalry contingent to get into position on the rebel flank before he led his infantry into the main assault. He ordered his men to prepare to advance but continued to wait. A sudden plume of dark gray smoke appeared above the Fletcher house followed immediately by tongues of flame. One of the artillery rounds must have upset a light inside the upper floor of the house.

Seconds later, Willoughby heard the distant report of many dragoon carbines coming from the place where he ordered Captain Jones to commence the main cavalry attack. Near the house, he saw small figures of men struggling to get themselves and others out of the burning building. He raised his sword and the drummers started their steady roll. Major Willoughby dropped the sword to the horizontal and shouted, "Advance!" Kicking the horse into motion, he foolishly allowed his stress to propel him far ahead of the surging infantry that followed him. Realizing his mistake before it was too late, he reined in and allowed the lines of infantry to pass around him. They were moving at the quick step. The men in this main assault were loaded, ready to halt and fire on command. The advance was urgent.

More volleys of rifle smoke appeared along the rebel trenches. Men began to fall in the British lines. The sergeants kept the gaps filled by closing the lines as more men fell. The range was too great for the muskets to answer. They had to close the distance quickly. Willoughby ordered the charge in that moment. It was like releasing a pent-up thoroughbred. The lines surged forward while somehow maintaining their dress. He knew that many years of disciplined training was all that made this possible. A second later, he heard the gratifying roar of the dragoon charge to his front left on the rebel right flank. Many of his men fell, but the rest made it into the nearest rebel trenches now.

Major Willoughby was mildly surprised when he saw that the rebels had apparently begun to withdraw. He realized that he was right about them. They were not prepared to maintain a fixed defense in the face of a well-organized assault by a superior force. This simply wasn't their way of fighting. These guerilla partisans would clearly prefer to escape and fight another day. He noticed that people were dragging what appeared to be stretchers out of the house and up past the mill into the hills on the other side of the creek. He wondered vaguely if one of these might be the Reverend Fletcher.

CHAPTER 44

Lieutenant Billy Morgan and John Red left the mill by the lower front door. They found themselves moving into a world of exploding chaos. Billy wasn't sure what to do at first. He knew he needed to reach his men in the forward trench on the other side of the road. He saw British cavalry advancing across the open area next to the village, and initially thought the greatest threat must be coming from there. Another cannon ball slammed into the front of the mill and they were both thrown to the ground. He heard another round strike the front of the Fletcher house in the near distance to his right. Bits of stone and debris were cascading on them as he and Red realized they needed to get to the house and get the wounded men out.

A huge volley of rifle fire erupted from the trench to their front as they pulled themselves up from the ground and started toward the house. Billy glanced toward the advancing dragoons in time to notice several British saddles were now empty. The sight reminded him of that awful day at Cowpens. This brought his friend Silas to mind. He felt a surge of panic as he heard another ball strike the house. Now he saw smoke at the roof of the house followed instantly by licking flame. A lamp or something must have been knocked over by one of those British cannon rounds. He and Red were moving toward the house as if running in a nightmare. They didn't appear to be getting any closer as time seemed to slow perceptibly.

Billy heard a roar of musketry coming from the southeast side of the village now. He also heard the unmistakable sound of rolling drums from the woods beyond the village to the north. He and Red saw people struggling out of the house from the back doors carrying wounded men away from the building. They neared quickly now. Billy saw that Dr. Bolt, Mr. and Mrs. Phillips, Reverend Fletcher, Mona, and a few of the village men were carrying the wounded on anything that would suffice as a stretcher. He saw most of the remaining wounded survivors from Cowpens. He even saw an injured dragoon sergeant carried out on a broken door. He didn't see Silas though. Billy screamed at John Red to help these people move back to the mill or to the woods around the mill pond. He then rushed into the house. The building was almost totally ablaze, and it continued to be struck by cannon rounds.

Billy bent double and pushed his way through the kitchen to the parlor where he last saw his friend the night before. Silas wasn't there. Billy realized that he hadn't seen any of the wounded men here during dinner earlier today. He began to shout. The only response was the roar of flame and the crashing of timbers as the house began to collapse. He was nearly blind in the smoke and his own tears. There was no way Silas could be alive in this inferno. He must leave now or die right here for no good purpose. A battle was raging outside. He was still needed. His men needed him. Elizabeth needed him. He had to get out now. With those thoughts overcoming his grief and terror, he surged out through the smoke toward some faintly visible daylight at the back of the house.

Billy cleared the doorway into the small wash-yard at the back of the house just as the center of the building collapsed into itself with a horrific crash. To his gasping smoke-blinded amazement, he nearly tripped over the prostrate form of his best friend, Silas Whitaker. Billy fell at his friend's side in a coughing spasm. He felt Silas trying to slap him on the back and looked up to see his friend blinking in the swirling smoke. Billy stifled an absurd laugh as he realized this was the second time this month he had found Silas still alive on a smoking battlefield while thinking him dead.

Billy struggled to his feet. He knew that his friend's injuries wouldn't allow him to be carried over the shoulder. His own thigh wound was throbbing fiercely. He looked around and found a partially scorched plank near the back of the heap of ruins. He quickly pulled Silas onto the plank and started dragging him away from the building. Billy noticed that the gunfire had increased and was drawing nearer from two directions. The cannons both shifted fire back to the mill itself. A sudden realization again stunned him. Elizabeth was in the mill with Ezekiel and the others.

Elizabeth and the others were huddled in the makeshift prison of Captain Crispin wondering what to do next. The mill was a very sturdy building. Several militiamen were firing fiercely from the upper floors and roof under the command of Captain Robertson. The noise of gunfire, crashing glass, and collapsing stonework was horrendous. They didn't hear the sound of the mill door opening and slamming shut. Seconds later, they looked up to see the strange form of a heavily armed though physically diminutive Major Throckmorton framed in the storeroom doorway. Throckmorton was carrying a musket in his left hand and a pistol in his right. Three more pistols were shoved into his waistband. There was a crazed look in his eyes which was all too familiar to Reginald Crispin.

The major pushed into the room, and was met by a willing Private Plunket who was glad to see an officer show up in the middle of current events. Crispin and Ezekiel were still seated on the crates in the middle of the room. Elizabeth was standing next to Ezekiel with her hand to her mouth in terror. Throckmorton gave curt orders to Plunket about securing the prisoner and paused as the man turned to face Crispin. The major then shocked the other three in the room as he used his pistol butt on the back of Plunket's head to render him unconscious. Plunkett fell at the feet of Captain Crispin, who was now standing.

Throckmorton ignored the captain and turned his now fully cocked pistol on Elizabeth and Ezekiel. More cannon rounds struck the outside of the building and dust sifted through the ceiling above them to fill the air in the room. The major stood very still and said, "Miss Fletcher, it's my understanding that a great deal of gold and silver is stored somewhere in the hillside at the back of this mill house. I...." He looked sideways at Crispin. "We ... intend to relieve you and your family of it."

Elizabeth was confused as she replied, "I don't know what you're talking about, Major. My grandfather is quite wealthy, but I know of no gold or silver kept here."

Throckmorton turned to Ezekiel and said, "Old man, I believe I understand you to be a longtime family 'friend' of the Fletchers and the miller who oversees this facility. You must know what we are interested in. I will give you one minute to show me where it is or I will shoot you." Elizabeth gasped and stepped in front of Ezekiel. Throckmorton pushed her roughly out of the way and again addressed Ezekiel. "Before I shoot you, I will shoot Miss Fletcher. You must decide to help us or not now. You only have seconds left."

Major Throckmorton had turned his back on his erstwhile ally Crispin. The emotion and resolve exploding through Reginald Crispin's mind in this instant could only be empowered by God and the feeling of complete freedom from the guilt of his miserable past. He reached down and snatched up Plunket's rifle. Aiming it at Throckmorton's back, he yelled, "You will do nothing of the kind, sir!" Throckmorton whirled around to face him.

Crispin drew the hammer on the rifle to full cock. In that instant, he noticed to his horror that the weapon was not primed. The major must have seen the look in his eyes. Before another word could be uttered, he raised the pistol and shot the captain in the chest. Crispin's spirit was with Jesus before his body hit the floor. Throckmorton turned back around while dropping the pistol and cocking the musket. Elizabeth and Ezekiel were staring in stunned shock. Ezekiel finally broke the silence. "I'll show you where to find what you want, Major. I don't care what you do to me, but please don't harm Miss Elizabeth."

The massed gunfire was growing closer. Billy saw Captain Watson start to withdraw the militiamen from the trenches to the hills above the mill. He noted that Sergeant Strickland was pulling some of his men back toward the higher ground as well. John Red was nowhere to be seen. Billy sensed that the man had either helped with the wounded as ordered or joined in the fighting near the house. He didn't know where Sergeant Duncan was with the rest of his men. Billy dragged Silas across the grass toward the trees as fast as he could until he saw Ira coming to help him with one of the villagers. Ira told the other man to take Silas on up the hill as Billy stopped breathless in front of him. They both ducked very low while Billy shouted that Elizabeth and Ezekiel were still inside the mill. Ira became frantic as two more cannonballs crashed into the mill and continued rather than bouncing off. The outside wall had been breached on the upper floor. They both began to run toward an upper side entry.

Ezekiel slowly led Elizabeth and Major Throckmorton to the back of the lower milling station and opened the door that led to the huge storage cavern behind the building. Throckmorton took down a burning lantern hanging from a hook near the mill wheel while keeping the musket aimed at Ezekiel. Setting the lantern on the floor, he backed away and told Elizabeth to pick it up. When she did so, he transferred the musket to his left hand and drew another of the pistols from his belt. Flicking open the priming pan on the musket with his thumb, he turned the weapon over and emptied the primer onto the floor. He threw the musket behind a stack of flour bags near the front wall and moved back to his two captives. He hadn't taken his eyes off either of them. He now used his left hand to fully cock the pistol in his right and pulled another of the pistols from his waistband.

Throckmorton abruptly ordered Ezekiel and Elizabeth into the cavern. He was right behind them as they went through the doorway. They couldn't help noticing that a large number of powder barrels were stacked in the center of the cavern alongside stacks of British muskets and other clearly military items. Throckmorton saw that someone had broken open one of the powder casks at the bottom of the stack and piled loose black powder all around it. There were three trails of powder leading away from this pile toward the door. Someone had prepared a way to fire one or all of these obvious fuses and explode the powder to blow up the mill if the British forced entry to this place. He suspected this was the work of one or both of the two militia captains he ate dinner with earlier. He had to physically overcome a wave of loathing for the man who removed him from his horse earlier in front of the house.

Throckmorton ordered Elizabeth to come closer. When she hesitated, he aimed his pistol at Ezekiel's head. She was sobbing quietly, but she finally stepped nearer. She was still holding the lantern. Throckmorton put the extra pistol back in his waistband and forced Elizabeth to turn around before wrapping his arm around her and aiming the still cocked pistol in his right hand at the side of her head. The girl was slightly taller than he was. He pulled her to the left in order to stare at Ezekiel. There was nothing the old man and the girl could do. They had seen this man kill. They both understood that they were unlikely to survive this. Ezekiel said, "I've told you that I will show you where the Fletcher gold is hidden. Please don't harm the girl."

Throckmorton nodded and spat, "Get to it then. Your time is very short." Ezekiel moved over to the shelving at the side of the cavern with the major and the girl shuffling to follow. In moments, Ezekiel activated the hidden latches and moved the shelf to uncover the stone slab over the vertical tunnel mouth. It took all of his feeble strength to move the slab so that the black opening was visible. Throckmorton tried to think what to do next. He had no intention of climbing into this hole alone to possibly be entombed under the slab by these two. He didn't want to release the girl, and he didn't trust the old man to climb down without him. They heard voices from the front of the mill then over the din of battle above them.

Ira and Billy entered the mill through the upper side door and moved quickly downstairs. A few more steps took them up the corridor to the storeroom. They found Plunket still unconscious and Crispin dead from a gunshot wound. Billy picked up Plunket's rifle. He couldn't tell if it was loaded, but it clearly wasn't primed. Ira picked up the burning lantern from the shelf where it was placed earlier. Billy was trying to rouse Plunket when they heard a muffled female scream from deep in the back of the mill. The name "Elizabeth!" escaped from Ira's throat before he ran out of the storeroom toward the lower milling station with Billy at his heels. The lantern was missing from the middle of the room. The cavern door was standing open. They could see a dim light from within. They entered the cavern expecting almost anything. Ira was shocked, nevertheless, to see Major Throckmorton standing behind his granddaughter with a pistol to her head. Ezekiel was standing over the open entry to the secret family treasure vault.

Billy didn't know what was happening, but he knew Elizabeth was in great danger. He lunged forward only to be restrained by Ira. Throckmorton's tense voice squeaked, "How convenient it is to see you two. I will kill the girl and this old man before you can interfere, if you do not do exactly what I ask. Drop that weapon, Morgan!" Billy dropped the rifle. "Now, both of you slowly come over here." They moved to within a few feet of Elizabeth and the major. Throckmorton asked, "Where is your vaunted treasure, Reverend?"

Ira paused only for a moment before he looked at Ezekiel knowingly and said, "There is a strongbox containing a great deal of money in the small cavern at the bottom of that shaft."

Throckmorton ordered Billy to take the lantern from Ira and climb down into the lower cavern. Billy immediately found the strongbox, but saw no other exit from the small chamber than the one through which he entered. He sat the lantern down and hefted the box. It was quite heavy for its size. Throckmorton screamed at him to bring the box up quickly. Billy shoved it up over his head and somehow managed to get it to the floor above him. The major ordered Ira to open the box and marveled with a strange glint in his eyes when he saw what it contained. Ira slid the box over to him with a look of pity mixed with contempt.

Throckmorton forced Elizabeth to kneel with him in front of the open chest. Keeping the pistol aimed at her head and his eyes fixed on Ira and Ezekiel, he used his free hand to scrape the contents out of the box and fill his pockets. He was on his feet with the girl again in moments and the box lay empty in front of him. He began backing toward the door with his arm around Elizabeth's waist. Ira followed them closely. She was still holding the lantern aloft, but her exhausted arm was shaking uncontrollably in her terror. At the doorway, the major shoved the girl toward Ira before leaping through the opening and slamming the door shut. He had it bolted and locked before Ira could reach it. The British were making entry to the lower part of the mill building as Throckmorton fled up the stairs to the upper mill station and made it out to the platform overlooking the mill pond. He quickly joined the retreating militiamen as they scrambled around the pond to the safety of the woods beyond, and disappeared in the confusion of the retreat.

Ira quickly made his decision. His family was immeasurably more important than this place. He told Ezekiel to help Elizabeth down the shaft with Billy and show them how to access the hidden tunnel at the back of the cavern. He took the lantern from Elizabeth and stepped over to one of the fuse trails leading to the pile of powder kegs. He had to think. He needed time. Finally, he pulled a box over and sat the lantern on top of it. He found a spool of line and tied it to the top of the lantern. He unrolled the line and dropped the spool into the shaft. Climbing down to the lower chamber, he saw that the tunnel was open and the others were already gone. He continued to unroll the line from the spool and made it nearly to the other end of the tunnel. He then tugged on the line so that the lantern fell over onto the powder trail. Ira reached the far tunnel opening seconds later when a huge explosion erupted behind him. Fletcher's Mill had ceased to be a military concern to either the rebels or the British.

EPILOGUE

Two weeks passed following the battle at Fletcher's Mill. Major Throckmorton had managed to escape among the retreating continentals. He hadn't been seen since. Captain Watson and Captain Robertson both survived. Tobias Griffin and the apothecary managed to carry the very ill Robert Griffin several miles south through rugged country to the remote farm now shared by the survivors of Fletcher's Mill. It was also now used by Dr. Bolt as a hospital. The doctor was able to save the blacksmith's life. Many wounded men including Silas and the other few remaining injured survivors of Cowpens soon owed their lives to God's grace and the medical skill of the wise old surgeon. Tobias said goodbye to his father and joined Billy's militia company.

The former prisoner, Sergeant Smythe, was on the way to complete recovery. Spending time in the care of Dr. Bolt had an amazing effect on this professional British soldier. Using Sergeant Duncan as a mediator, he informed Captain Robertson that he wished to join the rebel cause. He had been abandoned to die by Captain Crispin. This treatment mirrored the experience he endured in the British army for decades. He was tired of it. He saw hope for a bright future in this new world.

Watson and his company departed to make the return trek to Francis Marion's command on the east side of the colony. Billy and his men were sent by Captain Robertson to reconnoiter the mill and surrounding area to learn what the British had done following the battle. The Royal Army troops were on their way back to Camden. They marshalled the prisoners who were able to walk and herded them like animals back to an uncertain future of captivity. Severely wounded rebels were left behind to fend for themselves. The British looted all the barns and outbuildings before torching them along with the remaining village houses.

Billy and his men shadowed the British column for several miles. They even managed to take a couple of prisoners. He learned from these men that the commander of the British force, a Major Sir Thomas Willoughby, died in the mill explosion as he led his men into the building in the final assault. The British suffered extremely high casualties in this ill-fated attack on an obvious rebel stronghold. Nothing significant was gained, though. It was doubtful that the incident would receive any notoriety.

Billy reported all of this to Captain Robertson who thanked him profusely before telling him to follow through with his original orders and rejoin the Southern Continental Army as soon as possible in North Carolina. Robertson and his men were planning to move out toward Camden in an attempt to liberate some or all of the rebel prisoners held in the stockade there. Robertson said he would like to take the young lieutenant and his company along on the raid, but Billy's orders from General Morgan took precedence. Billy understood. He would obey the orders, but he didn't have to like them. He excused himself from the captain as soon as possible and went to find the Fletchers. He gave instructions to Sergeant Strickland and Sergeant Duncan while walking toward the house. The company would rest here for a couple of days before they headed north.

It occurred to Billy that he didn't want to leave here at all. Not in two days. Not ever. He didn't want to leave Elizabeth. He knew she felt the same way about him. Could this be love, or was he just a fool? He found Ira Fletcher sitting on the front porch of the house with Mona Partridge. They both stood as he climbed the steps. Billy learned that Elizabeth was inside the house helping Dr. Bolt and the Phillips couple with Silas and the other wounded men. Silas would receive the care he needed here until he was completely well and able to travel. Mona excused herself and went inside to find Elizabeth.

Ira reached out to shake Billy's hand while saying, "Thank you for all that you have done to protect my granddaughter, young man. I know she is very fond of you."

Billy felt his face turning red as he nodded in return and muttered, "That feeling is quite mutual, sir."

Ira released Billy's hand and cleared his throat abruptly while looking down at the toes of his shoes. He looked back up and said, "Well, in any event, I wanted to let you know that I have asked Miss Partridge to be my wife and she has accepted."

Billy was not at all surprised. He had watched the two together. He felt a momentary pang of remorse before speaking. "Reverend Fletcher, I'm sorry to have to tell you that the village, the mill, your house … all of it has been destroyed. There is nothing left."

Ira smiled dryly and patted his right coat pocket. Billy heard a faint clink of coin. Ira said, "No, son, it isn't all destroyed. Yes, the mill and the other buildings are gone, but they can be rebuilt. The people, the family, young man. They are the real treasure. Our love for God and each other as creatures made in His image. This is what really matters…." Billy nodded understanding. Ira patted him on the shoulder and said, "Besides, I own all of the prime land for as far as you can see, Lieutenant. Technically, I even own this farm. Furthermore, Zeke and I happen to know where even more gold is buried."

Elizabeth came out on the porch at that moment and greeted Billy with a bright welcoming smile. They stood staring at each other for several seconds before Ira shook his head and coughed discreetly. Moments later, the two young people were walking hand in hand down the path away from the house. Ira smiled deeply as he went inside to search for his friend and fiancé.

LT Billy Morgan's Trek to Fletcher's Mill

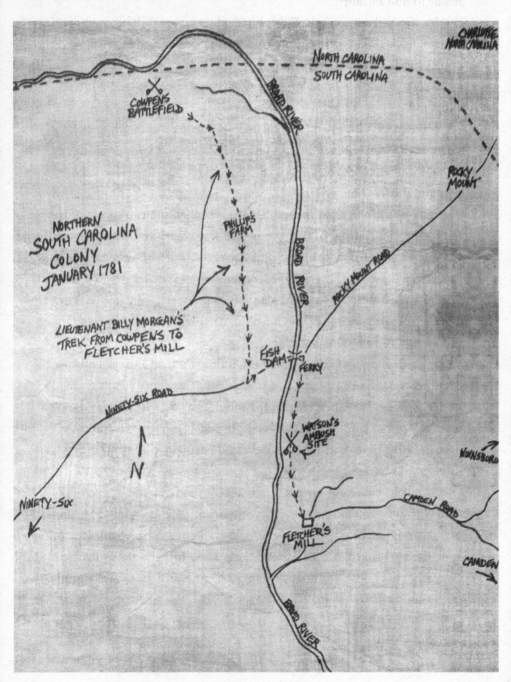